ROB ROGERS

WIZARDS OF THE COAST
DISCOVERIES.

DEVIL'S CAPE

©2008 by Rob Rogers
Cover Art and Design ©2008
Wizards of the Coast

Published by Wizards of the Coast, Inc.

WIZARDS OF THE COAST, WIZARDS OF THE COAST DISCOVERIES, and their respective logos are trademarks of Wizards of the Coast, Inc., in the U.S.A. and other countries.

Printed in the U.S.A.

Cover art by Chris McGrath
Book designed by Matt Adelsperger
Map by Rob Lazzaretti

First Printing: April 2008

9 8 7 6 5 4 3 2 1

ISBN: 978-0-7869-4901-4
620-21727740-001-EN

Library of Congress Cataloging-in-Publication Data

Rogers, Rob, 1970-
  Devil's Cape / Rob Rogers.
    p. cm.
  ISBN 978-0-7869-4901-4
  1. Louisiana--Fiction. I. Title.
PS3618.O466D48 2008
813'.6--dc22

2007021311

U.S., CANADA,
ASIA, PACIFIC, & LATIN AMERICA
Wizards of the Coast, Inc.
P.O. Box 707
Renton, WA 98057-0707
+1-800-324-6496

EUROPEAN HEADQUARTERS
Hasbro UK Ltd
Caswell Way
Newport, Gwent NP9 0YH
GREAT BRITAIN
Save this address for your records.

Visit our web site at www.wizards.com

DEDICATION

For Dina, Alex, and Zack.

ACKNOWLEDGMENTS

This book would not have been possible without the support of many people. I can't name everyone who ever encouraged me to write or fired my imagination, but I'd like to recognize a few people for their efforts in helping me with Devil's Cape.

First, I'd like to thank the handful of early readers of this book who reviewed various drafts and gave me candid feedback. These include Kevin Caperton, Michael Cunningham, Charmaine Cooper Hussain, James Kunke, Chris Lockheardt, Troy Marsh, Carol and Bob Rogers (Mom and Dad), and Dina Rogers (my lovely wife).

Thank you to Shawna McCarthy, my agent.

Thanks also to Kirill Gill for his Russian translation.

And thank you to the great folks at Wizards of the Coast for this opportunity. I know that many hands touched this book. I'd particularly like to thank Peter Archer, for liking the book first; Phil Athans, for rescuing it from a box and liking it, too; Mark Sehestedt, for his terrific support and shrewd suggestions; Jeanne Bretschneider, for shepherding my contract through; Matt Adelsperger, for art direction; Elena Johnston, for leading the marketing effort; Carmen Cheung, for typesetting; Randall Crews, Josh Fischer, and Kris Walker, for production; Robert Lazzaretti for the great map of Devil's Cape; and Chris McGrath for the eye-catching cover.

Finally, thanks to Dina and our terrific sons Alex and Zack for their patience and support during the long hours that the book pulled me away from them. I love you all.

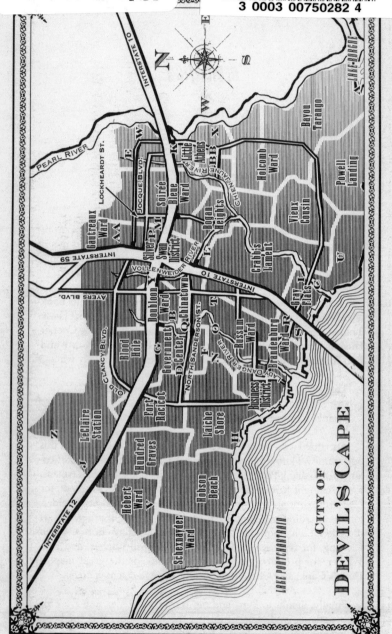

CITY OF
DEVIL'S CAPE

CITY OF
DEVIL'S CAPE

Sites of Interest

A. *The Bloody Dirk*
B. Bullocq Park
C. Butler's Billiards
D. Castelo Branco City Courthouse
E. Chien Jaune River Bridge
F. *Devil's Cape Daily Courier* Building
G. Devil's Cape Public Library
H. Devil's Cape Lakeside Airport
I. Elizabeth Colan Junior High
J. Fyke General Aviation Airport
K. Holingbroke Psychological Institute
L. Jazz's House
M. Julian's Penthouse
N. Kate's House

O. Lady Danger River Commons
P. Lehane University
Q. Lo Center
R. The Naked Eye
S. Palm Lake
T. Pepe's Athletic Center
U. Pier 42
V. Sebastian Hebert International Airport
W. Smith's Roadhouse
X. St. Tammany Parish Juvenile Detention Center
Y. Vollenweider River Bridge
Z. Worldwide Papyrus's Fyke Paper Mill
AA. WTDC
BB. Zorba's

If New Orleans has earned its "Sin City" nickname for its debauchery, then its nearby sister Devil's Cape has earned its "Pirate Town" moniker for the violence and blatant corruption that have marred the city since its founding. Yet Devil's Cape draws us, like a glittering treasure dangling from a skeleton's beckoning hand.

— Excerpted from
A Devil's Cape Traveler's Guide

ONE

Pericles Kalodimos wiped his forehead with the back of his sun-darkened hand. Scars from spattered grease pockmarked his arm, and the pale scar tissue glistened in the fluorescent light of his restaurant like chips of mica on brown earth. He'd turned up the heat in order to keep his newborn children warm, but he'd turned it up too far and the room was stifling even to a man used to standing over hot stoves.

He watched the sleeping babies, who looked to him like a single child beside a mirror. Often, they even moved in sync. Desma had snorted and rolled her eyes when he'd suggested tattooing each on the foot to tell them apart, but he still wondered every time they bathed the twins if he hadn't somehow mixed them up.

It had taken some quick talking to convince Desma to leave him alone with his sons for these brief two hours before their baptism, but he had a baptism of his own in mind for the boys before the family arrived. His family. He sighed. Whatever he could do to keep his sons out of the Kalodimos "family business," he would do.

Pericles walked over to his restaurant's front window, his bad leg forcing him to take five halting steps instead of the three he might have taken in his younger days. He'd named the restaurant Zorba's after *Zorba the Greek*, had plastered red velvet on the walls, then hung neon

1

signs, bottles of olive oil and ouzo, and framed posters of the Parthenon and the Aegean Sea. It was everything that someone who knew nothing of Greece would expect a Greek restaurant to be. The air hung thick with the scents of spiced meat, feta cheese, and strong coffee. At the window, he flicked off the OPEN sign and the overhead lights, shut the window's thick Venetian blinds, and reached over to lock the door. It left the room dark and quiet. The only light in the room—the red light of the EXIT sign—flickered across his sons' faces.

Stepping into the kitchen, he filled a small basin with warm water then carried it back and set it beside his sons. He reached over to one of the tables and lifted up a small, sealed urn, its face decorated with the black-etched figures of Greek heroes wielding spears and swords. The urn was dusty and smooth in his palm. He held it in front of his sons' faces. As one, both boys woke and reached for it, their newborn attention gaining new focus. He smiled and pulled it back.

"Not quite yet," he said. He ran a knife-scarred finger along the urn's surface. "It is entirely possible, my boys, that your father has been sold a bill of goods. If so, I'd appreciate it if you kept it secret, yes?"

His broad smile revealed cracked, coffee-stained teeth and a flash of gold. Then, with a sudden squeeze, he crushed the urn in his hands. It made a popping sound like an old balloon. The odor of stale air filled the room. He let the clay dust and shards flow between his fingers, then fall to the deep blue tablecloth. Two long, gold hairs remained in his hand, glistening like wounds in the red EXIT light.

"These strands," he said to the boys, who looked in his direction in mute fascination, "are from the Golden Fleece itself. I was told they can pass on the strengths of the mighty Argonauts." He shrugged self-deprecatingly. "It is foolishness, of course, but it is all I have."

The boys reached out their arms toward each other. Their fingers entwined. Slowly and carefully, he pulled one of them away. They both began to wail. Moving quickly now, he dropped one of the golden hairs into the basin of water. It sank below the surface, curling and uncurling, and he imagined that he saw steam rising from the water, though it wasn't hot. He pulled off the infant's diaper, then lifted him into the air.

"This is Julian," he said.

He dipped the boy below the water's surface, and it seemed to shimmer with gold. When he pulled Julian out, the boy had stopped crying and stared around as if in sudden wonder. The strand of golden hair—or fleece—was gone.

He repeated the process for the boy's brother, this time saying, "This is Jason." As he lifted Jason from the water, the boy peed on him and Pericles laughed heartily. He cradled the boys to him then, both dripping wet from the basin, one clutched in each arm. "I love you, my sons," he said. "I hope I have done you good this day."

Then he carefully dressed the boys and prepared the restaurant for his family's arrival.

The hooded crime lord called the Hangman rose to power shortly after the Second World War and quickly became the most feared man in Devil's Cape. His hold on the city lasted until thirty years ago in December when he . . .

— Excerpted from *The Masks of Devil's Cape*, special documentary airing on WTDC News, Jason Kale reporting

Cap de Creus Street, the main artery of Devil's Cape's business district, was named for the farthest eastern point of the Iberian Peninsula, where the winds could carry a fisherman's cap out of sight between two heartbeats or send the beam of a sail whipping around with murderous speed. The sailors of the Pyrenees called Cap de Creus "Devil's Cape," and when the masked pirate St. Diable founded a city of his own in Louisiana in 1727, he chose to honor not just himself—for his name, of course, meant "Saint Devil," and he was notorious for the flowing black cape he wore—but also the deadly winds of Cap de Creus. "I slit my first throat in the waters off that Devil's Cape," St. Diable was reported to have said, "and Devil's Cape is as good a name as any for the place I make my mark."

Perhaps by coincidence or perhaps by the pirate's own design, Cap de Creus Street was angled in such a way that the breezes from off of Lake Pontchartrain seemed to mingle and breed there, and the tightly packed buildings formed a wind tunnel that whipped and howled for most of the year. "You can walk up Cap de Creus Street in ten minutes with the wind behind you," the locals were fond of saying, "but it will take you twenty to get back again."

Even on its best days, Cap de Creus Street didn't

5

have the hustle and bustle of Wall Street or Michigan Avenue. On warm days, which were most of them, men would walk slowly down the street in sweat-dampened seersucker suits, calling out to each other, conducting more business over three-hour lunches of freshly shucked oysters and iced bourbon than they ever did in their own offices. And when the weather was bad, the street became so empty that no one walked the sidewalks except ghosts.

On this day, the weather was especially bad—and cold, as well. An arctic front had made it all the way down to the delta, and the wind roaring up Cap de Creus Street had an icy sharpness. Costas Kalodimos, a thin, dark-green overcoat wrapped around him, stood shivering against the side of a Masonic lodge. Hatless, he hunched his shoulders forward, staring through the wind, a tooth-pick clenched in his teeth. Mint-flavored. He'd picked the toothpick up after an early dinner at his brother's restaurant. Maybe he'd ask Pericles why he'd switched to mint-flavored. Conversation with his brother, who didn't approve of Costas, was always strained. Costas realized that it was a sign of the chasm between them that he would struggle to make a conversation about toothpick flavoring just to ease the time.

He snapped the toothpick in half with his chattering teeth and spat it on the sidewalk. His ride was late. One hand reached under the overcoat to the pistol he had stowed in a pocket, a Luger his Uncle Ilias had brought back from the Second World War. He traced his fingers along the handle, then pulled them away. The weapon was cold.

His Uncle Ilias.

Uncle Ilias had told their grandmother he'd won the pistol in a poker game he'd played with a German soldier during a Christmas Eve détente, but Costas and Pericles had always known that that was a lie. Uncle Ilias had killed for it. Something in the way he held it, the way he talked about it, told them that much. He'd given it to Costas many years before, something else Pericles had disapproved of, although Costas's brother didn't know what Costas had done to earn it.

Uncle Ilias wouldn't be pleased to know of the meeting Costas had agreed to on this cold day. He wouldn't be pleased at all.

Finally, Costas spotted the car. It was long and quiet, a dark blue Lincoln Continental with a golden roof and trim. The windows were tinted dark, shrouding the driver in shadows. The car braked to a stop beside Costas and the passenger door opened. Warm air and the scent of tobacco drifted out. He stepped inside and lowered himself into the golden leather seat, pulling his coat around him and slamming the door shut, shivering despite himself even as the car's heaters began to take the edge off the cold.

"I apologize for the inconvenience," the driver said, quickly starting the car rolling down Cap de Creus Street. Once away from the curb, he didn't accelerate much, and Costas understood that he was in no particular hurry to be anyplace—he just hadn't wanted anyone to pay undo attention to the sight of Costas Kalodimos, feared second in command of the Kalodimos crime family, climbing into his car.

Costas didn't answer at first. He just rubbed his fingers against the cold. The skin on his calloused knuckles was dry and cracking. The gold of his wedding ring barely glistened in the shaded car. He waited a few seconds, then turned slowly and deliberately to look for the first time at the man driving the car.

He'd been told to expect the mask, so it didn't come as a surprise, but still it drew his immediate attention. It was a bandit mask like Zorro might have worn, but blood-red, tied at the back of his head, the ends dangling down from the knot. His skin was tan and smooth, his nose aquiline. His beard and moustache were neatly trimmed and might even have been waxed. His hair was jet-black. He wore a loose-fitting red shirt that matched the mask, and black pants, vest, and gloves. His eyes crinkled in amusement as Costas took him in.

"So you're the Robber Baron," Costas said.

The driver gave the barest hint of a nod. "Do you like music?" he asked. "I have a nice Verdi." He gestured vaguely at the glove compartment.

Costas shook his head. "I don't have much use for dagos," he said.

The Robber Baron clicked his tongue against his teeth then shrugged dismissively. "You might need to learn to get over that," he said. There was steel in his voice.

Costas turned and looked out the window. They had turned onto Old Clancy Boulevard, a curving four-lane road that made a meandering loop around the entire city of Devil's Cape. This particular stretch was flooded with flashing neon from a dense pocket of strip joints, massage parlors, and adult bookstores. Costas had been in most of them. "So it's true about you and the Ferazzolis, then?"

"I am not certain what you've heard." The Robber Baron's voice was cultured, reserved. But again there was that touch of steel. He was treating Costas respectfully, but there was no question that he intended to be in charge of the conversation. "But yes, we have an understanding." He brought the car to a stop at a red light. A police car sat at the opposite side of the intersection, waiting for the light to turn, but the Robber Baron gave it barely a glance. "Arturo Ferazzoli was not particularly interested in an alliance, but Lorenzo has proven much more . . . pliant."

Costas swallowed, his eyes drawn first to the police car, then to the Robber Baron again. There was no hint of hidden meaning in the man's blue-gray eyes, but still . . . Arturo Ferazzoli had been found in an alley behind one of his dry cleaning joints three weeks before, his belly split open with a boning knife, his two bodyguards in the wind. His brother Lorenzo had stepped into his role as head of the family. Costas opened his mouth to ask the obvious question, then shut it again. The car rolled through the intersection and past more neon lights. The police car moved down a side street.

Costas turned back to the masked man beside him. "What is it you want?" he asked.

The Robber Baron smiled, reached down to the console to turn the heater down. "You know," he said.

Costas stared at him, unblinking.

The car accelerated. They crossed a bridge over the Lady Danger River, and the Robber Baron frowned slightly as a gust of wind hit the Continental broadside and the car shimmied. After they were over the bridge, he turned back toward Costas, any hint of humor gone from his face. "The Hangman," he said. "It's time for the Hangman to die."

The Hangman. Costas sighed, wished he had a cigarette, wished he still had that damned mint-flavored toothpick to chew on. Anything to busy himself. Uncle Ilias might run half the numbers rackets, extortion schemes, and money-laundering operations in Devil's Cape, but the Hangman ran Uncle Ilias.

Costas had met the Hangman, the most feared criminal in the city, a handful of times. An aging bull of a man, he wore a mask, too, but there the similarities to the Robber Baron ended. The Hangman's mask was a hood—more or less a burlap sack with eyeholes cut into it—that covered his entire head. He wore rugged clothes—often a gray flannel shirt and workman's jeans—and heavy, well-worn leather gloves and boots. He never wore a belt. Instead, he wore a length of rope, perhaps as much as ten yards of it, wrapped several times around his waist. They said he'd used that rope for the first time in the early '60s to lynch a black civil rights activist. They said that the Hangman had carried the man up to the roof of his own church, tossed one end of the rope around the top of the steeple, and nearly pulled the man's head off while stringing him up. He'd killed dozens of people over the years with that rope, which always looked streaked and spattered by the residual blood and gore.

And he stank. He rarely changed his clothes and never seemed to clean that heavy, soiled hood or the gloves or boots. He smelled of old sweat and blood, of tobacco and spoiled food, of whiskey and death.

Uncle Ilias sided with the coarse Hangman in part because he had to. The Hangman was simply too powerful a force in the city to be overthrown. But they also shared many hatreds. For blacks. For Italians in general and the Ferazzolis in particular. For the police. Those hatreds united them.

Costas Kalodimos shook his head. "You should be patient," he said. "The Hangman won't live forever. When he dies, maybe then you and I can talk about an alliance." He looked over at the Robber Baron, whose eyes were flat and expressionless behind his mask. "Uncle Ilias has sworn an oath to the Hangman and I've sworn an oath to Uncle Ilias."

He tapped his fingers nervously on the car window. They were driving through the edge of the city's Brandenburg Ward. He spotted the diamond store where he'd bought Agatha her engagement ring.

His mind flashed from his wife to the Hangman. The last time he'd seen the Hangman had been in a dive of a strip club called the Naked Eye. Between sets, the hooded man had leaned close to him, patted him on the leg with a heavy gloved hand. There was nothing sexual in the pat, but it was territorial. Exerting his dominance. "You be good for your uncle like he is to me and you'll be rewarded," the Hangman said in his thick Cajun accent. His breath stank of cigarettes, beer, garlic, and decay. "Be a good soldier," he said.

"I hate him," Costas said suddenly. "I hate him." He swallowed. "But I can't help you without betraying my family."

Of course, he was betraying Uncle Ilias just by meeting with the Robber Baron without the old man's knowledge. And he was in danger, he knew. If the Robber Baron decided that Costas was of no use to him, then the Luger in his pocket might not be protection enough.

"I will keep this meeting confidential," he said. "It goes no further. But I can't help you kill the Hangman."

The Robber Baron said nothing for a minute. He hit the turn signal and moved the Continental onto a side street. They turned into a parking garage. Half of the old, graying building's lights were burned out and most of the rest of them sputtered. They ascended a low ramp past oil-stained parking spaces, the Continental finally emerging on an empty rooftop. Costas could make out several brightly lit buildings in the panorama below them. Here it comes, he thought. The Robber Baron would murder him and leave his body on the roof of the decrepit garage. Costas slowly moved his hand under his coat toward the pistol.

But the Robber Baron made no aggressive move. He put the car into park, then casually drummed his fingers on the steering wheel. "You misunderstand me," he said.

Costas hugged himself, shivering from the cold. The motion allowed his fingers to close around the handle of the gun. "What do you mean?" he asked.

"I don't expect you to help me kill the Hangman," the Robber Baron said. "I don't expect you to betray your uncle. They are of no consequence." He reached down to a vest pocket. When he saw Costas tensing, he smiled. One tip of his waxed moustache twitched. "You don't need to shoot me, Costas," he said. "I'm only reaching for my tobacco."

Costas's face hardened. He put his finger onto the trigger. If he needed to fire, he could do it right through the pocket and the coat. "Go ahead," he said.

If the fact that a gun was being held on him made the Robber Baron nervous, he didn't show it. He unhurriedly pulled a velvet pouch out of one pocket and an antique meerschaum pipe from the other. The head of the pipe, carefully and exquisitely carved into the face of a man with a plumed hat, had been stained a rich golden brown by years of use. "What I want from you, Costas, is the same type of loyalty you have shown to your uncle." The Robber Baron carefully tapped some tobacco from the pouch into the pipe. He packed it down with a gloved thumb.

"In exchange for what?" Costas asked.

"My loyalty in return, of course," the Robber Baron said. He poured in more tobacco, then began packing that in as well. "I can strengthen your position." He twisted his thumb in the pipe. "When your uncle passes on, an alliance with me will cement your own role of authority within your family. You'll keep your family in line with my agendas, and all of us will benefit as a result."

"My grandfather lived to be ninety-six," Costas said. "I expect Uncle Ilias to be around a very long time."

"Hmm." The Robber Baron half-chuckled. His pipe fully packed, he tied the drawstrings of the velvet pouch and replaced it in his pocket. "Nevertheless," he said. "When the Hangman's time has passed, when your uncle's time has passed, you will become my ally, yes?" He pulled a white handkerchief from the pocket that held the pouch and carefully began cleaning the tobacco off the thumb of his glove. He still hadn't lit the pipe.

Costas turned away from the other man and stared out the window over the walls of the parking garage. Darkness was falling quickly. The city below was streaked with the dull red of the dying sun. "I'll have no part in anything that harms my uncle—"

The Robber Baron waved it off. "Of course, of course," he said. "Nevertheless."

Costas's mouth was dry. He tasted bile. The Robber Baron was moving into Devil's Cape. He already controlled the Ferazzolis. Costas had heard rumors of other alliances. The drug runners. Some of the politicos. If anything happened to Uncle Ilias, if the Hangman's organization fell apart, the Kalodimos machine would either need to join with the Robber Baron or be crushed under his polished heel. "Yeah," he said. "Yeah, okay."

The Robber Baron nodded gravely, as though *yeah, okay* were a solemn oath. And perhaps it was. He replaced the handkerchief and pulled out a book of matches. He tore one free, then struck it, placing it against the tobacco. He leaned into the pipe and puffed slowly, drawing the flame in.

"When and if that time comes," Costas said.

The Robber Baron nodded again. When the match had nearly burned itself down to the fingers of his glove, he shook it out briskly, tossing the spent match into the car's ashtray. Orange embers glimmered from the pipe. He folded the matchbook back and Costas noticed the insignia now. The Naked Eye. The Hangman's favorite strip club. The Robber Baron followed his gaze and smiled, nodding and sliding the matchbook back into his vest. He inclined his head toward one of the buildings below them. Purple and blue neon lights flashed across its concrete walls. The Naked Eye. The Robber Baron had chosen this spot very deliberately. "The time has come," he said.

And then Costas saw the smoke. Not the gently scented smoke of the pipe, slowly swirling in the Continental. Thick, gray, roiling smoke breaking out of the Naked Eye, billowing out into the setting sun. The purple and blue lights on the walls of the strip joint undulated as the smoke poured out of the building. After a long few seconds, Costas heard sirens in the distance, but they were far, far away.

"A fire," Costas said, for lack of anything better to say. "And the Hangman and Uncle Ilias are inside."

The Robber Baron said nothing. He just took a long draw from his pipe.

"They could get out," Costas said. The pipe smoke was cloying now. He felt like it was choking him, though he knew that that was just a reaction to what he was watching below. "It's just a fire. They could get out."

The Robber Baron shook his head. "No one's getting out," he said.

Costas shoved the door open, the cold air sudden and cutting. He rushed out of the car toward the edge of the rooftop wall. He could see flames now. The club didn't have many windows, of course, and the ones it had were shaded, but he could see the blaze inside, flames creeping across the roof. And then he saw that the doors were blocked. A van was parked against one door, a trash

13

dumpster shoved against another. A car had driven right up against the front door of the club, its bumper holding everything shut. He wondered how many people were trapped inside the club. Maybe a dozen strippers. Another dozen staff. Twenty or thirty patrons. And not just Uncle Ilias and the Hangman, but their bodyguards. His cousin Nick. He imagined he could hear screams, but it might just have been the howling of the wind.

He felt the Robber Baron's hand on his shoulder. "The time has come," the masked man said.

The sirens were still a long way away. "Yeah," Costas Kalodimos said with a sigh. "Yeah, okay."

In August twenty-three years ago, the Devil's Cape press corps was surprised to be summoned to an impromptu press conference by the Omega, a Chicago-based superhero who held the conference on the steps of City Hall, in the shadow of the bronze statue of the pirate St. Diable.

A former Navy SEAL named Lieutenant Dale Thorp, the Omega gained his powers, which included astonishing strength and speed, during the course of a mission that has yet to be declassified. Upon retiring from the Navy, Thorp took on the Omega identity and earned a reputation as one of America's greatest heroes, revered for his bravery, self-effacement, and calm in the face of adversity.

So if the reporters gathered there on that hot day were surprised to see the Omega in Devil's Cape, they were even more surprised at his demeanor . . .

— Excerpted from *The Masks of Devil's Cape*,
special documentary airing on WTDC News,
Jason Kale reporting

ROB ROGERS

THREE

*T*he Omega stood at the top of the City Hall steps looking down at a throng of men and women armed with cameras and notebooks. Tall, muscular, and ruggedly handsome, he had a pale complexion and shortly cropped black hair that flickered in the faint, humid breeze. His uniform was navy blue at the chest and shoulders and the center of his stomach, the boots a matching shade. The rest was crisp and gray, with the exception of a red belt and a red omega symbol with white borders in the center of his chest. The Omega had never worn a mask or gloves. He wasn't sweating like the crowd below him. The sunlight in his eyes didn't make him squint. But his face was flushed and angry.

"I have come to Devil's Cape today," he said, "to clean up a mess that the citizens of this cesspool should have cleaned up themselves." He turned and pointed at the statue of St. Diable. "This is your city's beloved founder. A pirate. A brigand. A criminal. You *venerate* your pirate origins." He turned back, sweeping his hands wide. "You *tolerate* your criminal reputation." He shook a fist. "And you *assassinate* the people who try to pull you up to something better."

He stomped his foot on the concrete, which shook and cracked from the loud blow, dust rising and curling around his boot.

"I lost a friend yesterday," the Omega said. He lowered his head, and the cameras zoomed in to capture the tears in his eyes. "Navy Lieutenant Victor Garavello joined the Devil's Cape police force to try to clean up some of your corruption for you." He pointed at the reporters. "He told me that in particular, he was trying to find enough evidence against the man you call the Robber Baron to force even your crooked judicial system to put the man behind bars."

The Omega lowered his hand and the anger leached out of his face. He looked tired, sad, and a little confused.

"Victor was found murdered yesterday," the Omega said. "Shot in the back of the head with a shotgun. His fellow police officers, the ones who should be moving heaven and earth to uncover the truth of his murder, have already labeled the evidence inconclusive and told me they have no real leads." He shook his head. "I'm amazed that people still come to this city. People come here to live. Tourists come in by the busloads to see the pirate artifacts and live on the wild side. You even have crime tours that celebrate some of the worst tragedies this city has inflicted." He shook his head again, lowering his voice to barely above a whisper. "I wonder if Victor's death will stack up."

The reporters looked at each other. They hadn't even had time to ask him a question yet.

"I've had enough," the Omega said. "If you won't address your problems, I will address them for you. I am going to find out who is responsible for murdering my friend. And heaven help anyone who stands in my god-damn way."

With that, he turned his back on the gathered reporters and walked away from them, making his way into Devil's Cape's Government Center district.

That was the last time anyone ever saw the Omega, at least anyone who would admit to it. It was as though he had disappeared off the face of the earth, or as though Devil's Cape had swallowed him whole.

The site of his last speech is a regular stop on the city's popular crime tours.

— Excerpted from *The Masks of Devil's Cape*, special documentary airing on WTDC News, Jason Kale reporting

Ma's Spectacular Amusements offers Action, Adventure, Sensation, and More Fun.

— From the side of a carnival truck

FOUR

Although they were coated with dust and spattered with mud and muck, the three trucks stood out against the green and gray expanse of the Louisiana swamp like flaming cinders in the ashes of a dying fire. The thick haze of dusk and the coating of debris weren't enough to dim the bright red and orange and cerulean paint that decorated the trucks carrying the sideshow performers from Ma's Spectacular Amusements traveling carnival.

The driver of the front truck was immensely tall and muscular, bald, and covered from throat to toes with tattoos. His body was big—he topped seven feet—and his head was disproportionably larger, like a barrel placed on his neck. That humid summer night, he wore a sleeveless black shirt and cut-off jeans with no shoes. He was called the Behemoth by others in the carnival. He'd abandoned his real name—Zechariah Woods—long ago, and though he was billed as "the Bayou Barbarian Behemoth" and carnival owner Justin Ma had taken to calling him "Triple B" in a failed attempt at bonhomie, it was "the Behemoth" that stuck.

The bullshit back story that Ma had come up with for him involved him being discovered living alone in the bayou as a child, already covered with tattoos, with no family but a nest of alligators. The spiel continued with the heroic Ma rescuing him, taking him in as his own son, and trying in vain to civilize him. Onlookers would gawk as the Behemoth scurried around hunched over in a cage, knuckles dragging the ground, howling and snapping his jaws like a gator. Sometimes he'd end the bit by catching a chicken that had "accidentally" made its way into his reach, biting its head off and drinking its blood. Other times he'd climb a wall, unscrew a light bulb, casting dark shadows into the cage, and then proceed to eat the bulb, crunching the glass in his teeth like peanut brittle. And then the lights would go out, the audience would be shuffled on to the next attraction, and if the Behemoth were lucky, he'd have five or ten minutes to relax with a cigarette and a Flannery O'Connor or Faulkner paperback before the next set.

Frank Horodenski, the carnival electrician or "juice man," shifted restlessly in the seat next to the Behemoth, holding up a copy of the *Devil's Cape Daily Courier* and tilting it this way and that, trying to catch the last few rays of fading sunlight so that he could finish his story. Lean and young, with mud-brown hair, Horodenski sported a perpetual sunburn. The Behemoth wished he'd stayed with the generator truck and the other carnival trucks, already on their way to Jackson, Mississippi, but Horodenski was one of those who liked hanging out with the freaks, and it hadn't seemed worth the effort of dislodging him.

One of the trucks behind them had something fouled in its engine, and it popped and wheezed and smoked as they drove along. As the dirt and gravel road made a lazy curve, following the edge of an old creek bed, they could hear that truck's engine stuttering and coughing, like someone was banging rocks together underneath the hood.

"Fouled carburetor, probably," Horodenski said, looking up from the paper. "Sounds like it to me."

The Behemoth grunted noncommittally.

Horodenski squinted at the paper one last time, then set it down beside him with a sigh. "Did you hear about the Omega?" he asked.

The Behemoth reached forward and turned the truck's headlights on. He thought about turning the interior light on so that the juice man could finish his paper, but he decided he didn't want to.

Horodenski rolled on as though the Behemoth's silence were an invitation to continue. "Comes in two days ago and makes a big stink," he said. "Planning to take on the Robber Baron, clean up the crime in Pirate Town. Yells at a lot of people. Then nothing. Nobody knows where he is."

"Probably found himself a whore," the Behemoth said.

"You think so?" Horodenski poked at his own forearm, testing to see how bad his sunburn was. He shrugged, fishing around in his pockets for a cigarette. "I wonder if the Robber Baron chased him off."

The Behemoth slowed the truck without warning, swinging it over to the side of the road. The brakes of the truck behind them squealed in protest. "Just stay here," he said to Horodenski. "We'll be back on the road in five."

He cut the engine, shoved the door open with a clank, reached one hand over to the handrail on the side of the cab and lowered himself to the ground, the entire weight of his body suspended in transit by one tightly flexed arm. As he lowered himself, the tattoo of a skeleton in a sombrero danced on his forearm.

"I think this is far enough," he called out to Hector Nelson Poteete, the driver of the second truck, who waved back in acknowledgment and cut his own engine.

The Behemoth peered back down the dirt road, then out into the bubbling swamp, and finally up into the darkening sky. They were a good fifteen minutes outside of Langdon Fork, a tiny hamlet that was itself a good thirty miles from the edge of Devil's Cape. Aside from the three sideshow trucks, he saw no sign of other people.

The third truck was the one whose engine was stuttering. The Behemoth pointed at the driver, then drew his finger across his throat, just over the black spider-web

tattoo there. The third driver turned his engine off, too, and the sudden reduction in noise almost rocked the Behemoth back. He cupped a hand to his ear and listened. He heard crickets and fish, the bubbling of swamp gases, the rustling of something large—probably an alligator—moving through the muck. But no other cars, no approaching boats. He nodded his oversized head in satisfaction.

"What the hell are we doing way out here in the swamp?" The driver of the third truck trotted forward, his steps long and awkward. He was walking with the outer edges of his feet on the ground, the soles of his feet pointing toward each other. Clayton Xavier Stecker was the carnival's "Indian" rubber man, and he was so used to twisting his double-jointed limbs that normal locomotion seemed to be beyond him. "Did you hear that sound my rig was making?"

The Behemoth sighed. It was just one damned thing after another. "Go back to your truck, Stecker," the Behemoth said. His brown eyes were flat.

Although he was over six feet tall when standing straight, Stecker—"the Karnivorous Kraken of Kiribati"—was a thin, blond stick of a man. That night, he was wearing an old orange Florida Gators T-shirt and red running pants, and his tanned limbs jutted out of his clothes like broken broomsticks. He tilted his head over to one side, peering up at the Behemoth. If the Behemoth had seen someone else with a neck tilted like that, he'd figure the person was dead. But he knew it wasn't unusual for the contortionist.

Stecker reached up to poke the Behemoth in the chest. "You get a promotion I don't know about, makes it so I can't ask you questions?"

The Behemoth looked past Stecker toward the second truck and the driver inside, Hector Poteete, the fire swallower. After all, this unscheduled detour was Hector's gig. He should be the one dealing with Stecker and his questions. Poteete looked back at the Behemoth, nodding to acknowledge the situation, but then he busied himself gathering together some items in the cab. Passing the buck.

Stecker scratched at the collar of his shirt. "Did you get us lost? You show me a map, I can point you back in the right direction." He shrugged philosophically. "Ain't no shame you can't read a map, big old blockhead like yours."

The Behemoth dropped a heavy hand onto the rubber man's shoulder, the thumb pressing into the hollow of the other man's collarbone. Stecker gasped in pain. The Behemoth dug in harder. "They call it macrocephaly," he said. "The big head. It doesn't mean I'm slow. It doesn't mean I'm crazy. All it means is I've got a big damn head." He leaned toward Stecker, smelled onions on the other man's breath. "Albert Einstein was macrocephalic," he said.

Stecker nodded, tears in his eyes as the Behemoth's fingers grated harder into his collarbone. He quivered.

"You going to go back to your truck now, Stecker?" The Behemoth leaned closer so that their foreheads were nearly touching. There was something stuck in Stecker's teeth, a piece of chicken, maybe. He thought about breaking Stecker's collarbone. The skinny little shit just pissed him off. Rumor was he'd come to Ma's Spectacular Amusements because the police were looking at him for a string of rapes—something like half a dozen coeds from across the Florida panhandle during spring break. The Behemoth didn't care much about the rapes except for what they said they said about Stecker—that he was a petty, stupid little shitweasel who could bring trouble on all of them if they weren't careful. And that he had good reason to be looking for anything he could trade to the cops if he ended up getting caught.

He heard footsteps brushing through the dirt behind them. Hector Poteete—billed as "Hector Hell, the Foremost Fire-Eater of His Generation"—had finally climbed out of the second truck and was making his way over, dragging his leather sandals through the dirt. Short and paunchy, Poteete had thinning red hair and was the only

fire-eater who the Behemoth had ever heard of who wore a beard. The beard was a point of pride for the man, and the Behemoth had to admit that it was impressive that he'd managed to avoid burning the thing off before now—especially since Poteete never seemed to shy away from an open flame. That level of skill put him a cut above the other working acts, at least in the Behemoth's eyes.

"Let's settle down, fellas," Poteete said in his gentle Southern accent. He laid his hand on the Behemoth's arm, just above the tattoo of the screaming eagle.

The Behemoth let go of Stecker, who gasped at the release.

Poteete smiled at Stecker. "Clayton," he said, "we're just taking a piss break. Why don't you head back to the truck? We'll all be back on the road in a few minutes."

Stecker rubbed at his chest, fingers splayed wide. "Maybe I have to take a piss break, too," he said petulantly.

The Behemoth gnashed his teeth. All they needed was about a minute of peace and quiet to do what they needed to do. One goddamn minute without Horodenski asking a bunch of questions or Stecker acting like a spoiled child or some other damned thing cropping up. And they weren't getting their minute. It was enough to make him sick. In his mind's eye, he could see the tarp he and Poteete had stowed in the luggage compartment of the truck he was driving, the tarp and the contents rolled inside. He wanted it gone. It was weighing on him. They just needed one minute.

Poteete stepped closer to Stecker. He looked up at the tall rubber man and his smile faltered, his eyes empty. "I have a shy bladder," he said. "Head back to the truck and wait your turn."

Stecker's fingers dropped away from his chest and he put his hands on his hips, spreading his legs out wide. A standing strut. He smiled back. "I don't know what you two are up to, Hector, but I'm not skedaddling on your say-so." He jerked his head at the Behemoth. "Or his."

He puffed his narrow chest out. "You've got some kind of scam running and I want a cut. You dragged us out to this godforsaken stretch of swamp, off of Ma's route, and you must have had an awfully good reason."

The tarp and its contents were a pretty damned good reason, the Behemoth thought. He wondered what it would take to break Stecker's neck, if the fact that he was double-jointed meant he'd need to break the neck twice.

The remains of Poteete's smile dropped from his face. He raised a hand and pulled at his beard. In his other hand, he held one of the torches he used in his act. It was shaped like a tree branch, but in truth it was made of cast iron, the top wrapped in fire-proof rope. A brackish, moist breeze rolled in from the swamp. "Get back into the truck right now, Chester," he said softly.

"Chester" wasn't Stecker's name. "Chester" was carnival slang for child molester. Whether Poteete was using it because he knew something that the Behemoth didn't or because he was threatening Stecker with a reputation that could spread easily, it was effective. The thin man seemed to wilt, his shoulders slumping. He turned quietly and began to slump away.

Poteete grinned at the Behemoth, who grinned back. They waited until Stecker had climbed back into the cab of his truck. Then Poteete nodded. He slid the metal torch through a belt loop at his side. "Let's get this done before some other damn thing happens," he said.

The Behemoth walked back to his truck and popped open the luggage compartment, wincing at the squeak of the metal door as it opened. Then he reached inside and scooped up the tarp with both hands. It was wet.

The Behemoth grunted, holding the tarp away from his body. "He's leaking," he said. He could smell blood. It wasn't very different than what he smelled when he ripped chickens' throats out with his teeth. But there weren't any chickens in that tarp.

"Hell," Poteete said, stepping forward for a look. "He shouldn't be. The bleeding had stopped a long time

before I helped them wrap it up." He ran a finger along the bottom of the tarp, then held it up into the beam of one of the truck headlights. His finger was red and slick with blood. "Hell," he said again, pulling out a rag he used to clean his torches and wiping his hand off on it. "He shouldn't be leaking blood anymore," he said. "There's no reason to, unless—" he broke off.

"Unless his heart was still beating," the Behemoth said.

They were standing there looking at each other, drops of blood falling off of the tarp and landing in the dirt road, when they heard the door of the rear truck crash open. Stecker came sprinting out, legs splayed, feet turned sideways, and two smaller figures jumped out of the cab and ran after him—Errando the Wolf-Boy and Sasha Crozier, the youngest of a family of aerialists.

The Behemoth was sucking in a lungful of air to bellow at the three of them to get the hell back in the truck when Stecker shouted, "Hey, Rube!"

Any anger at Stecker dropped away as the Behemoth spun around, peering into the darkness beyond the blinding beams of the trucks' headlights, trying to see what Stecker had seen. In a carnival or circus, "Hey, Rube" was a warning that outsiders were present. It was a rallying cry that a fight was imminent and that the carnival family had to work together. It was a call to war.

The Behemoth managed to blind himself by looking right into a headlight, so he heard the intruders before he saw them. And the sound he heard first—penetrating over the noise of the running feet on the gravel and dirt, over the sound of Frank Horodenski opening his own door to see what was going on, over Sasha Crozier's soft cries of "What is it? What is it?"—was the distinct chu-chuck sound of a round being chambered in a shotgun.

Everyone stopped then. Stecker and the kids behind him ground to a halt. Horodenski stopped halfway out of the truck. Poteete started wheezing. And the Behemoth slowly turned, the tarp in his arms, to see who was holding a shotgun on him.

His eyes focused on two figures, a man and a woman. They wore khaki pants and lighter tan shirts, with patches on the sleeves. The man was holding the shotgun. The woman had her arms crossed in front of her. She was the one in charge.

"We're from U.S. Fish and Wildlife," she said. "I'm going to need you to bend down real slowly and put that parcel on the ground." She had a Yankee accent. Maine, maybe. "Parcel" came out "pah-sell."

U.S. Fish and Wildlife. Mother of God. Where the hell had they come from? He looked past them. No sign of a car. A boat, maybe? He looked over at Poteete. What were they supposed to do now? But Poteete was just standing there looking like he'd eaten something that didn't agree with him.

"Don't look at him," she said. "You look at me. Or you can look at Agent Mathews and his weapon if you prefer." She was tall and muscular, with mid-length black hair tied back and weathered skin. Her gaze was steady on the Behemoth's face. If his size or tattoos intimidated her, she gave no sign of it. "Put that parcel on the ground," she repeated.

The Behemoth shrugged. "It's just some of our gear," he said. He knelt and gently placed the tarp on the road. He kept his voice casual, like he was really curious, like he was really doing nothing wrong at all. "What difference does it make to you?"

Agent Mathews, a broad-chested man with long sideburns and a bald patch at the crown of his head, gestured with the shotgun for the Behemoth to step away from the tarp, which he did. The Behemoth wondered just when U.S. Fish and Wildlife had started packing heat. Had they always done that? Or was the shotgun really there to use on gators and water moccasins? The agent's eyes were darting from one member of the sideshow to the next. He blinked when he got to Errando the Wolf-Boy, the kid's face covered with long black fur. Blinked again at Stecker, who was doubtless twisted into some uncomfortable-looking position. But most of his attention was on the Behemoth. It wasn't time to make a move. Not yet.

The female agent moved one hand to her belt, and the Behemoth wondered if she had a gun there, in the small of her back. "A lot of people have been poaching alligators in this region," she said. "Now we come across you with that parcel, it makes us curious."

The Behemoth almost laughed. They thought he was poaching alligators. But what could he say? You've got it all wrong, ma'am. We're not taking anything out of the swamp. We're just disposing of a body, that's all. Not your department at all. Have a nice day.

What he said was, "No, ma'am. This isn't any gator. This is some of our gear, like I said. I just took it out of my truck." He looked at the tarp. The bottom of it was obviously stained dark and dripping. "I think some paint spilled," he said. "I was just going to clean it up." Off to one side, he could see Poteete nodding confidently. But the Behemoth knew they were screwed.

"What's going on out there?" a voice shouted from the second truck. Bernice Hutchins, billed as "Fat Bertha, the Biggest Woman in the World," was lowering the ramp at the rear of her trailer so that she could walk down and see what all the commotion was about.

"Federal agents, ma'am," answered Agent Mathews loudly. "Please stay inside your trailer."

"My word," Hutchins said, continuing to lower her ramp. "It sure is getting hot in here." The other freaks and carnival workers began to move forward, too. Frank Horodenski finally finished stepped all the way out of the truck. Errando stepped up quietly, scratching at his furry face. Sasha Crozier came up beside him, the shiny sequins of her acrobat uniform glistening in the headlights, and the Behemoth wondered fleetingly just what she and Errando had been doing in the cab of the third truck with Stecker. Stecker walked forward on the sides of his feet, head rocking back and forth. The Behemoth could hear Bitzie the Pinhead and Lorana the Mule-Faced Girl coming out of their part of the third truck. None of them

were advancing fast and none of them were acting in a threatening way, but it was becoming clearer and clearer just how badly the agents were outnumbered.

"Federal agents!" Agent Mathews barked again, raising his shotgun in the air. "No one step any closer." The air was hot and muggy. Sweat was dripping into Mathews's eyes, but he was blinking it away instead of raising a hand to his face and letting down his guard.

"Everything's all right, y'all," Hector Poteete drawled. He raised a hand to the others, who for the most part stopped their advance. "Nothing but a misunderstanding. Nothing to see here." He made eye contact with the Behemoth.

The Behemoth nodded. He knew what Poteete was thinking. One way or the other, the Fish and Wildlife agents had to go. If too many people got close, it was going to be that much worse. Chaos.

The shotgun was the problem. The agent was too on his guard and too far away.

Poteete turned toward Mathews. "You don't need to look at that tarp," he said. "Like my friend said, it's just some gear and some leaking paint."

For a second, the Behemoth ground his teeth in anger. Telling them not to look in the tarp was just sealing the deal. There was no way they wouldn't look now. But then he realized what Poteete was doing. The agents were going to look in the tarp anyway, that was a given. Poteete was making a subtle push. By telling Mathews not to look, he was choosing which agent he wanted to be the one to lift the tarp.

It worked. Mathews glanced at the female agent, who nodded back. "I apologize if that's the case," she said to Poteete, without a hint of apology in her voice. "But we need to see for ourselves."

Mathews dropped to one knee beside the tarp. He kept the shotgun in his right hand, but rested the butt against the ground, taking his finger off of the trigger and closing his hand around the stock. Then he reached over with his left hand to roll back the tarp.

He would be expecting an alligator. He wouldn't get one. The Behemoth breathed in, tensing his muscles, waiting for the moment of greatest surprise in which to strike.

Mathews swept back the tarp with a clean jerk of his arm, the cloth rustling and snapping. It took him a second to process what he was seeing, and the Behemoth couldn't help but look, too.

Instead of an alligator, the agent was confronted by the broken body of the Omega, the superhero from Chicago who had come to Devil's Cape, made threats against the establishment and the Robber Baron, and then gone missing. The Omega's blue, red, and gray uniform was soaked with blood. His face, once movie star handsome, was a swollen, pulpy mass, and a shadowy hole gaped where his left eye had been. His black hair was matted with dried blood and there were flakes of white there that might have been bits of plaster or might have been shards of bone or teeth. There was another hole just under his jaw, and that was where most of the blood seemed to have come from, as a thick wash of it descended onto the navy blue on his shoulders and chest, over the red omega symbol, and down onto the gray on his belly and below. His left arm was bent backward at the elbow and again at the wrist.

Neither the Behemoth nor Poteete had seen the Omega's assassination. Poteete had just been hired to dispose of the corpse—a test, perhaps, for future assignments. But Poteete had heard a little about the death and had passed the story on to the Behemoth. The Omega had been shot from absolute surprise with a high-caliber rifle. He'd then been attacked by half a dozen well-trained men armed with sledgehammers. He'd knocked three of them unconscious before another shot from the rifle stunned him long enough for the sledgehammers to finish the job.

Agent Mathews turned away from the body with a gasp. He looked at his partner, gesturing her over. "K.L.," he said, "you have to—"

The Behemoth didn't give him a chance to finish his sentence. He sprang forward, tearing the shotgun away from the agent with one hand while closing the other around the man's throat. They both fell across the Omega's body, but the Behemoth was able to put the bulk of his weight on the agent's midsection. He dropped the shotgun to the ground and proceeded to strangle him with both hands.

If the female agent—"K.L."—had a gun at the small of her back as the Behemoth had suspected, she never got a chance to draw it. While she moved forward to try to pull the Behemoth off of her partner, Poteete stepped up, pulled the iron flame-eater torch out of his belt loop, and swung it in a wide arc into her temple. She collapsed, legs twitching, and the Behemoth heard Poteete hit her again.

Even being strangled, Mathews was a fighter. He kicked at the Behemoth, then clawed at the backs of the huge man's hands. The Behemoth swore at the pain and at the damage the scratches were probably doing to his tattoos. He shifted his weight and his grip, took hold of the agent's head, and turned it fast, breaking it just like a chicken's. Mathews sighed, then collapsed lifeless on top of the Omega's body.

The world grew quieter for a few seconds. Rolling off of the Omega, but still on his knees, the Behemoth closed his eyes, panting with stress and exertion. He could hear Poteete wheezing, and the chirps of the crickets, and something splashing nearby in the swamp.

Then Stecker said, "You sure kicked up a shitstorm here." He chuckled to himself.

Someone—maybe Sasha Crozier—began to sob.

The Behemoth opened his eyes to look at Stecker. His hands ached. The Omega's blood smelled sharp and ripe. It made his nose itch.

Stecker held Agent Mathews's shotgun in both hands. "I bet you've got a good story to share with us," he said to the Behemoth. "And a good take to cut us in on."

The Behemoth sighed. He wouldn't have minded

killing Stecker, but there were too many other people there. They'd have to make some kind of arrangement. He nodded his head and prepared to get up. Then he stopped. Something groaned on the ground beside him, a low, guttural noise that chilled his gut. Agent Mathews, head tilted over to one side at a god-awful angle, rolled over on one side. But Mathews was dead, eyes vacant. He wasn't moving on his own—he was being pushed.

The Omega sat up.

"Jesus," Stecker said.

Blood oozed from the hole in the Omega's throat. Something oozed from his eye socket. He bent, began to push himself up with his broken arm, started to topple, righted himself, and pushed himself up with the good arm.

Stecker started to raise the shotgun. "Hey," he said. "Hey!"

The Omega backhanded him with his bad arm. There was a popping noise, and the Behemoth couldn't tell whether it was one of Stecker's bones snapping or the Omega's arm breaking even worse. The shotgun flew one way and Stecker tumbled the other, rolling end over end like a tumbleweed half a dozen times before he crashed into the side of the truck he'd been driving. Bitzie the Pinhead and Lorana the Mule-Faced Girl knelt over him, the excitable Bitzie beginning to hop up and down and sob at the same time.

Poteete had the iron torch in his hand again, but was backing away, mouth open.

Errando had reached a hairy arm up to shield Sasha Crozier, but she had stopped sobbing and was staring at the Omega, eyes intent and bright. The shotgun had fallen next to Frank Horodenski, who stared at it like it was a water moccasin.

"Kill you," the Omega said, his voice low and ragged. His remaining eye was so swollen and coated with gore that the Behemoth wondered if he could see at all.

"He's dead," Poteete said. "He was already dead."

"Kill you all," the Omega said.

The Behemoth stood. He looked past the Omega at Horodenski. "Pick up the shotgun, Frank," he said.

Horodenski looked startled, but bent and picked up the weapon. "He's bulletproof," he said. "I read it in the paper."

"Yeah," the Behemoth said. "Don't shoot him just yet."

Errando the Wolf-Boy trotted forward, his hairy bare feet clomping through dirt wet with the Omega's blood. He put his hand on the Behemoth's arm. "He's a super-hero," he said. "You can't just kill him."

The Omega grunted, moving toward the conversation he heard. He lashed out again with the broken arm, missing Errando by only a few inches.

The Behemoth could feel the air coming off of the blow, like a hot wind. "Didn't you hear what Hector said?" he asked Errando. "He's already dead." He leaped behind the Omega then. "Get ready, Frank," he said. He whipped his massive arms up and around the Omega's arms, grabbing Omega behind the neck in a full nelson. "Under his chin," he said. "In the hole. Quick."

The Omega struggled against him then, and the Behemoth could feel one of his own arms jerk out of the socket. He screamed. The Behemoth had never been hurt like that, never met anyone stronger than he was. The pain was incredible. He held on.

Horodenski didn't hesitate then. He rushed forward, jammed the muzzle of the shotgun into the hole in the Omega's throat and pulled the trigger.

There was a deafening roar as the shot split the barrel of the gun. Horodenski cried out as bits of shot bounced back and burned their way into his arm and chest and throat.

The Omega stood stock still for a second, seemingly unmoved by the blast. Then he slumped in the Behemoth's grip. "Oh, God," he said. Then the Behemoth could see little cracks appearing all around the Omega's body, like he was turning into a jigsaw puzzle. The cracks began to glow with a harsh white light. "Oh, God," the Omega said again.

And then he exploded.

The Omega had once been a normal man, the Behemoth had read. A Navy SEAL He'd been exposed to . . . something—the government never let anyone find out what—and he'd become . . . something more. And now that something, that energy, exploded out of him as he burst into a mess of blood, tissue, and liquid light. It sprayed over the area and showered the assembled freaks of Ma's Spectacular Amusements traveling carnival.

The Behemoth, who'd been holding the man, caught the brunt of the blast. It knocked him backward fifteen yards, and lights pulsed in front of his eyes. His whole body burned. But the pain ebbed quickly, even the pain from the dislocated shoulder, and he pulled himself back to his feet to the sound of screams of terror and agony.

Frank Horodenski writhed on the ground, his breath coming in little panting sounds as though he didn't even have the strength to scream. He'd been standing in front of the Omega and had probably been hit with nearly as much of the explosion as the Behemoth had. He looked liked he'd been flayed. His clothes and hair had burned right off. His skin was blackened. It bubbled and popped like the surface of boiling water.

Hector Poteete was on fire. He sat in the middle of the road, flames skittering up and down his arms, sparking out of his hair. It didn't seem to bother him. He stared at the orange-red flames in mute fascination, a mesmerized smile on his face.

Errando the Wolf-Boy lay on his side, his body warping. One moment, he looked like himself, then his body stretched and writhed, and a wolf lay there, howling. Then he shifted again into some hybrid of wolf and man, with long fangs and claws. Then he looked for all the world like a normal boy, not a freak at all, hairless except for his head and his eyebrows, his face smooth. The cycle kept repeating over and over while Errando whimpered.

36

Sasha Crozier was on her hands and knees crying in huge, ragged sobs, rocking back and forth. As the Behemoth watched her, her back arched. She shook, and it seemed for a moment that she was jutting her shoulder blades out. But then the sequined leotard ripped open and something crawled out of her back like a worm writhing free. Two somethings, because a second one popped out almost immediately. They looked liked roots at first, jutting out of her back, twisting this way and that as she tried to scream. But then the Behemoth saw flat gray feathers growing out of the roots. Wings. She was growing wings.

The explosion had knocked the two rear trucks on their sides. The Behemoth walked toward the middle truck in long strides, looking for Bernice, but the fat woman had been crushed under her own handicap ramp. Her dead eyes stared at the stars above and blood trickled from her mouth.

The truck in the back, the one Stecker had been driving, was just as bad. Bitzie the Pinhead and Lorana the Mule-Faced Girl lay dead in each other's arms, jagged pieces of glass and metal from the truck peppered throughout their bodies. Stecker sat next to them, screaming in numb horror, his arms and legs flopping and stretching to more than twice their normal length. His hair had fallen out and his skin had turned green and scaly. Wide-eyed, he reached out to the Behemoth, but his aim was off and his hand stretched a good ten feet past the tattooed man. The Behemoth shook his head unsympathetically and walked away.

He passed the winged Sasha and the shifting wolf-boy, stepping around Frank Horodenski, who was still panting and writhing. He walked to the truck he had been driving and then, sighing with trepidation, bent down to turn the side mirror so that he could examine himself. The first thing he noticed wasn't his reflection, but the fact that his fingers now ended in huge claws at least six inches long. He had grown taller, too. He could tell that just by comparing his height to the truck. He was

about ten feet tall now, stronger and more muscular. In the reflection he could see that he'd grown more monstrous than ever. His face was harsher, the nose flatter. His bottom canine teeth jutted out of his lower jaw like upside-down walrus tusks. He grunted, then crushed the mirror in his huge hands. Nuggets of silvered glass fell to the road like stardust.

The Behemoth turned and stepped over Horodenski, who just didn't seem to know when to die. He walked over to Poteete, who blinked up at him, the flames that had been covering his body suddenly sluicing away. The Behemoth made a sweeping gesture with his arm, taking in all of the carnage. "So what do you think?" he said. "Will we still get paid for disposing of the body?"

Sonic-Burst Doctor Camelot
Team Leader and Heroic Armored Warrior
10" action figure

- Three sound effects and flashing light simulate sonic-burst action!
- Twist figure for piston-backed punch!
- Glow-in-the-dark chest emblem, faceplate, and jet pack!

Re-create the greatest battles of the Storm Raiders with Sonic-Burst Doctor Camelot and other Storm Raiders action figures, sold separately. A portion of all proceeds from Officially Licensed Storm Raiders products are donated to the Vanguard City Children's Hospital.

— Excerpted from
a Storm Raiders action figure box

FIVE

Vanguard City, Connecticut
Early April, twenty-two years ago

In a month known for showers, the day dawned crisp and clear, the sky a vibrant blue. A nest of robins was chirping in the front yard and someone was mowing a yard nearby, the scent of fresh-cut grass floating through the neighborhood. Twelve-year-old Katie Brauer hated it all. Her father was dead. The skies should be weeping. The color should have leached out of the world. The air should reek of ozone and tears.

The black-haired girl sat on the kitchen window ledge, staring at the linoleum floor but not really seeing it. Friends and family had gathered. They'd brought food. Lots of it. There were chocolate chip cookies, slices of ham, and a tuna casserole with those little potato sticks on top. Uncle Rinji had even brought a plate of something called sushi. There was more than Katie and her mother could ever possibly eat, assuming they ever discovered their appetites again. She wished they'd take the food away. She wished they'd leave.

She wished her mother would turn the damned television off.

Some superhero had died. Doctor Camelot. So what? Her father had died, too, but the television stations didn't care about a design engineer who'd had a brain aneurism while working late at his office one night. They didn't care about his lopsided smile and the hint of Old Spice

41

in the air around him. They cared about the superhero who'd flown through the air in his shiny high-tech armor and who had fallen in battle against some sort of super-powered criminal team of monsters and freaks.

The television droned on . . .

"Vanguard City, of course, was named after the first known superhero," said a professor being interviewed by a blonde newswoman in a navy power suit. "The American patriot Roscoe Clay, who was said to have the strength of three men, donned a black mask and fought against the British during the Revolutionary War. He was christened 'Vanguard' by General Washington himself."

Katie knew all about Vanguard. She and her class-mates had toured his historic home back in October. She'd been surprised at how short his bed was, how low the ceilings of those old buildings had been. Clay had been a goldsmith by trade, and there were two huge anvils on display in his garden. The docent giving the tour had told them that Vanguard could lift both anvils over his head without straining. He'd hidden his face not so much to keep his incredible strength a secret, but to hide the depth of his hatred for the British. His father-in-law was a British colonel, and by feigning sympathy for the redcoats' point of view, he gained important information that he was able to exploit as Vanguard. No one knew exactly how Roscoe Clay had come to be so strong, but after America gained its independence, a few other people with extraordinary abilities had gravitated to the town—rechristened Vanguard City in 1784 by Governor Jonathan Trumbull—and it became a sort of crucible for free thought, artistic expression, and scientific development.

"How you doing, kid?" Katie's Uncle Samuel sat next to her on the ledge, then tentatively took her hand. He wasn't really her uncle, no more than Uncle Rinji was. Several close friends of Katie's parents were aunts and uncles to her. Uncle Samuel wore a charcoal gray suit and a dark blue tie. His eyes were red, and Katie realized with

some surprise that they were level with hers—he was just about her height of five feet.

She gave him a shy smile and shrugged. "I guess not very well."

He nodded, unsurprised. She thought for a moment that he was going to say something, but he merely patted her hand and remained sitting there, his feet with their shiny black shoes dangling near the floor like a little boy's. They made a soft clump-clump sound when they tapped against the ledge wall.

The newswoman was narrating now as a montage of images rolled past on the screen.

"This Doctor Camelot was believed to be the third person to bear that name. The first became active in Vanguard City in 1940, a—quote—mystery man who sported a flowing cape, a signature metallic shield, a British accent, and a sword reported to have been able to slice through steel. That Doctor Camelot, whose real name was never revealed, retired publicly in 1953, shortly after his long-time adversary, the Red Plague, fell to his death during a battle atop Caperton Tower."

Katie glared at the television. "Why won't she turn the TV off?" she whispered. "I don't care about Doctor Camelot. I care about Dad."

Uncle Samuel smiled thinly at her. "It's helping her, Katie. It's helping distract her and it's—it's helping her see that good people are respected."

She sniffed and wiped back a tear. "Doctor Camelot wasn't any better than my dad, you know."

Uncle Samuel nodded slowly. "You're right. He wasn't." He patted his pockets as if looking for a hand-kerchief to give her, came up empty, stood and fetched her a napkin from the kitchen table. Sitting beside her again, he said, "Your father was a brave and amazingly intelligent man. I was proud to—" He broke off. "Proud to call him my friend."

He had been about to say something different, Katie realized. "How did you meet Dad?" she asked.

He blinked. He looked around the room for a moment,

then turned back to her. "We were friends from college," he said vaguely.

"You went to MIT, too?" Katie wanted to go to MIT when she was old enough.

He blinked again. "Um, no. No, I went to Iowa. We just met back then, is all." He turned uncomfortably toward the television and Katie found herself doing the same.

The newswoman had moved past the career of the second Doctor Camelot and was starting in on the most recent one. While the first and second Doctor Camelots had carried various equipment in their wars against villainy, the third wore a high-tech armored suit—powered armor, they called it—that allowed him to fly, carried a variety of nonlethal weapons, and protected him from harm. That was until he fought the freaks calling themselves the *Cirque d'Obscurité*, or the Circus of Darkness, and a giant tattooed monster man calling himself the Behemoth had broken his neck.

The television showed footage of Doctor Camelot with Vanguard City's own Storm Raiders, one of America's most popular and effective superhero teams. His armor glistened in the sunlight like chrome, a violet cape—presumably pure decoration—fluttering out behind him in a gust of wind. He didn't carry a sword and shield like his predecessors, but he had a coat of arms emblazoned on his chest that bore tribute to them.

At the time of his death, he was the leader of the Storm Raiders, an impressive group of talented and powerful superheroes. The roster included the dashing acrobat Swashbuckler; Raiden, flying wielder of electricity; Sam Small, the six-inch man; Patriot, a strikingly tall woman who was reportedly bulletproof; Velociraptor, the saurian man, and Miss Chance, who claimed to wield "luck magic" to help her allies and bedevil her enemies. Other members joined and left from time to time, but those were the seven who had been captured on film that day in front of the gold-tinted windows of the Kunke Exchange Bank Building, smiling happily after having won a fierce battle

with Deadlock. On the television, they gathered around Doctor Camelot, one by one reaching out to touch him or pat his armor in some way, their faces filled with obvious pride and affection for their daring leader. During that battle, the newswoman related, Doctor Camelot had dived between Deadlock—a half-mad genius cyborg said to be able to bend titanium in his bare hands—and a suddenly trapped Swashbuckler and Sam Small, saving their lives at the risk of his own.

When Katie looked at Uncle Samuel again, she saw that his eyes were glistening with tears. "It will be all right," she said impulsively, drawn now somehow to comfort the man. Her stomach clenched with a pain that she felt would probably never go away. Her father was gone. "It will be all right," she said again. The air around them was empty.

The privileged of Devil's Cape see its beauty. The graceful replica pirate ships that circle each other in Mississippi Sound during the springtime, loaded with bejeweled partygoers, rum, and maybe a little fine Columbian blow. The tall, pillared mansions surrounding Bullocq Park, their eaves corded with wisteria. The dark, smoky opera house, which to this day contains an entire floor where the sight of a black man is as rare as an eclipse. They feel a sense of entitlement. But the children of the disenfranchised and working poor, the ones growing up in forgotten holes in the city like Crabb's Lament, those kids don't see the beauty. They spend days staring at gray. Gray dust. Gray concrete. Gray futures.

— From "Cemented by Strife:
The Rise of the Concrete Executioners,"
by Russell Hakes, *Devil's Cape Advocate Monthly*

Devil's Cape, Louisiana
Mid-August, twenty-two years ago

*T*he sun made the pavement almost unbearably hot, but Cain Ducett sat barefoot anyway, his dark feet almost as black as the asphalt of the street. He had a sloppy oyster po'boy in one hand, the mayonnaise and relish and paprika dripping onto the sidewalk and steaming. He'd take a bite of the po'boy, then lower it, raise his other hand, take a hit from the joint he had cradled there, and then return to the sandwich. He had an open thermos filled with ice, RC Cola, and Jim Beam cradled between his legs, but he wasn't touching it just then, just letting the cool air waft up out of it.

5-D Binoe crouched behind him, squatting on a jam box that was pulsing with music, leaning forward every time Cain exhaled after popping the joint, trying to suck up what he could from the surrounding air. 5-D was fat and stank, with sweat hung up in pouches of his dark skin, a little bit oozing free whenever he moved. Six fat inches of paunch protruded at the bottom of his shirt, revealing a round, pink, puckered scar where Cain had gut-shot him the summer before for taking a handful of quarters out of Cain's money jar. 5-D had worn a colostomy bag for nine months, but he was proud of the scar and had followed Cain around like a damn puppy dog ever since. He had a 9 mm stuck in his oversized jeans, and every time he leaned forward to suck the smoke near

Cain, he stroked the gun and made a high-pitched "Ooh, ooh" sound in a little girl's voice. Cain was damned if he was going to share a thing with him—not his sandwich, not his joint, not his drink.

Cain glanced up to see Jessica "Jazz" Rydland sidling down the street, a newspaper under one pale arm that never seemed to tan no matter how much sun she got. Her blonde hair damp with sweat and muggy Louisiana air, she bent down in front of Cain, making a show as her white T-top opened a little bit in front, and slowly pulled the cold thermos out from between his legs. She drank languidly, and let half a mouthful of the sweet, sticky drink dribble down her chin.

5-D said, "Ooh, ooh" again and lifted a fat arm to swipe his forehead.

Stamping out his joint, Cain reached forward and took the thermos back from her, plucking out an ice cube and drawing it across each cheek like he was applying war paint. He popped the cube in his mouth and crunched hard. "What you doing here, Jazz?" he asked. He stuck the thermos back between his legs.

Smiling, she pulled the thermos back out again, even more slowly, her eyes on his. She had ice-blue eyes, very pale skin, and very white teeth. "Just reading the paper," she said. She flicked it open for him, leaning close and holding it open. It was a supermarket tabloid and the lead story was about the "Devil Baby of Dubai."

"Why do you read that garbage?" he asked.

"There's half a world you know nothing about, Cain Ducett." Jazz liked to claim that she was a voodoo priestess. Cain would mock her about it, talking about her "white voodoo" and calling her a sham.

He stared at the photo of the devil baby, an obvious fake with horns and a pointed tail. "I know enough," he said.

She sat the thermos back down in his lap, dropped the paper on top of it, and leaned further toward him, staring in interest at his face and massaging his dark shoulders. "Do you, now?" she asked. "You know the street, Cain.

You know pain and drugs and violence." Her hair was almost in his face. "You don't know much else."

When he remembered it later, what would surprise him the most wasn't the abrupt violence of his reaction, but the complete apathy he felt while committing it. What he did to Jazz wasn't out of anger. It was more of an automatic reaction, like reaching out his hands to catch a fall or slapping down a dog that was trying to bite him.

Cain placed his hands on her chest and shoved her as hard as he could. She flew backward, her legs rising into the air so that he saw one brown sandal and one bare foot, toenails glistening with pale pink polish. Her hair surrounded her face like a shroud as she fell, and then he heard a crack as her back hit the curb, followed by a hollow thump as her skull hit the asphalt of the road. By the time she landed, he was on top of her, one knee smashing into her gut, a switchblade at her throat. Behind him, 5-D was saying, "Oh, man," over and over again.

Jazz didn't move. A puddle of blood was growing beneath her head.

Another voice boomed off to one side. "Back away from her, Ducett!"

Cain turned to see a man about a quarter block down the street. Dustin Bilbray was a hulking cop with thinning brown hair combed over a ragged bald patch. He was nearly as overweight as 5-D and looked like a stuffed sausage in his police uniform.

"Paid you last week, Bilbray," Cain said. "Don't you try to squeeze me again."

Bilbray wiped a sweaty face with one hand and let the other slip to the holster of his gun. "Ain't gonna let you hurt a white girl, boy."

Cain glanced contemptuously down at Jazz's unmoving form, then pulled the switchblade up until the point was poking her cheekbone. He looked up at the police officer. "You know why I didn't know you were coming down that street, Dusty?"

Bilbray's hand slipped more firmly onto his gun. He flipped off the snap of the holster with his thumb. "Guess you were too busy to pay attention," he said.

Cain shook his head slowly. "Nope," he said. "My boys watch this street. Anyone comes up or down it, they let me know. Now why do you suppose they didn't let me know about you?"

Bilbray smiled. "Maybe they aren't as loyal as you think."

Cain stared at him, no expression on his face. For a few seconds, the only indication that Cain was even breathing was that his nostrils fluttered in and out. Then he dug the switchblade into Jazz's cheek. A drop of blood ran down her face like a tear. "They didn't let me know because they know you don't matter," he said to Bilbray. "I own you."

Dustin Bilbray's hand clutched his gun again and his face grew pale, but he looked sick rather than angry. "Nobody'd ever—" he started, then stopped as he saw the frost of Cain's eyes.

"I've got pictures, man," Cain said. "Tapes, videos, iron-clad witnesses. I don't even need to pay you anymore, except what I have to pay you is so little it ain't worth mentioning." He twisted the knife, making the tiny cut on Jazz's face into a small, moon-shaped wound. "Now get," he said.

The fat police officer stared at Cain, his eyes taking in Jazz's still form and 5-D's large one, snickering behind Cain's shoulder. For a moment, Cain even thought the man would vomit. Then he turned without a word and walked away, his steps slow at first, but speeding with a frantic intensity until he was out of sight.

"I believe he soiled himself," 5-D said. "You see that? His legs were pressed together like he was trying to hold it in."

Cain grinned at him, then cut his eyes back to Jazz, not sure what to do with her. A thin line of blood trickled down her cheek, and as his eyes followed it down, he saw it joining the larger pool at the base of her head. Leaning down for a better look at the blood, he wondered if he'd killed her.

Then her eyes opened. They seemed to be filled with dark blood, like those of the blind ten-year-old in Cain's building whose mother had shaken him for crying when he was just a baby, detaching his retinas and creating hemorrhages in his eyeballs. But unlike the kid, Jazz seemed to see just fine. She stared at Cain with hateful eyes and rose to a sitting position, her jaw tense, the bleeding on her face now looking like a single crimson teardrop. He'd later discount it, but at the time, Cain could have sworn he saw smoke rising from the corners of her eyes. "You'll pay for that," she said.

Any other time, cold, cool Cain Ducett would have had a hundred retorts or just gone for his knife or a gun. But instead, he stared at her, eyes wide. Behind him, he could hear 5-D whimpering, could hear the slow leak as 5-D's bladder let go. But neither of them moved.

Jazz reached forward and took the newspaper back into her hands. She crumpled it, then bent and dipped it into her own blood, which was pooling in the street. The Devil Baby of Dubai was painted bright red with it. She spat on the paper, then wiped her bleeding face on it, smearing even more blood across her pale features. Then she threw the wad into Cain's face.

Cain didn't even think to block the paper, didn't raise his arm, didn't move out of the way. It hit him like a fist, harder than he'd ever been punched before, harder than his father had ever struck him as a child before Cain had broken the man's kneecaps in his sleep, harder than the bullet that had once torn its way along Cain's ribcage. He flew backward through the air, thinking of nothing except that he wished 5-D would stop his screaming— only to realize the screaming was coming from his own throat. He saw a flash of red for a second, and beyond it the Devil Baby of Dubai screaming back. And then he slipped into unconsciousness.

It was dark when he woke up, still lying in the street, his head cradled in 5-D's lap, the fat boy's tears dripping onto Cain's forehead and the stench of his urine strong. Cain sat up, groaning with the pain of it, wiping dried blood and mucus from his face, peering around, staring blankly at 5-D.

They'd let him lie there for hours, no one coming to help him but 5-D, no one doing a thing except probably hoping he died.

"She gone," 5-D said. "She just gone. Don't hurt her none, Cain. I'm scared if you do."

Cain shook his head, patting 5-D on the head like a dog. He didn't know what to make of Jazz, wondered if her eyes were still filled with blood, wondered if his own were. He didn't know what to make of her or what had happened to him. He was tired and empty, and for the first time in a long while, he could feel that emptiness inside him. He shook his head again. "I'm going home, 5-D," he said.

But when the Argonauts, as these fifty brave adventurers were called, had prepared everything for the voyage, an unforeseen difficulty threatened to end it before it was begun.

— Excerpted from *Tanglewood Tales*,
by Nathaniel Hawthorne

You've got to help me, Jules." Jason Kalodimos's face glistened with sweat. His breath came in short gasps and his eyes darted from side to side, as though a monster were stalking him through the book stacks at the Devil's Cape Public Library. A tall, thin man in an Air Supply T-shirt walked by, nearly brushing Jason, and Jason, all of five foot six, stared him down, saying, "Beat it."

The man rushed off toward the periodicals.

"Don't call me that," Julian Kalodimos said, his voice an intense whisper. While Jason was dressed in a black T-shirt, torn jeans, and sneakers with no socks, Julian wore a white button-down shirt, khaki pants, and penny loafers. A maroon Members Only jacket was laid carefully on top of his backpack, and a copy of *Lord of the Flies* was propped open in front of him. "Whatever it is, it should keep."

When Jason leaned in toward his brother, Julian smelled body odor and cigarette smoke. "It won't keep," Jason said, and spittle flew from his lip with the last word.

Julian shrugged. "I warned you," he said quietly.

Jason spread his hands. "It's not like I have a lot of choices here, Jules. Uncle Costas asks someone to do a favor, that someone had better do the favor, you know?"

Julian looked around to make sure that no one else was near, then leaned in close enough to his brother to kiss him if he'd wanted to. "We have choices," he said. "You know what we can do. No one can make us do anything we don't want to." He pressed a finger against Jason's collarbone. "And don't start in about Dad. You didn't do this for him. You did it for you. You liked the money and the thrill, and you liked being near Uncle Costas and knowing something he doesn't know." Then his face whitened. He pulled back, a lock of black hair falling across his face. "Jesus, he doesn't know, does he? You didn't tell him?"

Jason shook his head slowly. His throat rose and fell for a moment with no sound coming, like there was a sparrow trapped in there, trying to push its way out. "No, he doesn't know. But someone does. A cop named David Dees. I thought he was in Uncle Costas's pocket, but it turns out he's in Lorenzo Ferazzoli's pocket, too."

———

Detective Second Grade David Dees was in an alley near the wharves when they found him. He was smoking a Camel Light less out of addiction or habit and more to hold back the odors of salt, rotting fish, and diesel that filled the air. The breezes off of Lake Pontchartrain didn't seem to make their way into the alley where he sat hunched, waiting to meet with one of Ferazzoli's boys, sweating in his seersucker suit.

First Jason crossed into him, moving faster than Dees could have believed, rushing into the alley and then slamming the detective hard against a brick wall tagged with graffiti. Then both brothers were there, not touching him again, but actually floating in the air, dodging and weaving around him, hovering first to one side of him and then the other.

"Jesus, you can fly, too?" Dees said. He caught an angry glance from the uptight brother in the red jacket to the wilder one in the jeans. "And two of you, too. I figured maybe it was both of you, but I wasn't sure." He

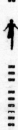

grinned and stubbed his cigarette out on the asphalt. "A lot of people would pay a lot of money to learn about you boys."

Still hovering, Jason leaped forward and punched him in the gut. Dees could take a hit, but this hurt like hell. He tasted bile in his throat and his stomach burned like he'd swallowed a handful of broken glass. "You're not telling anyone," the boy said.

Dees fought to keep from vomiting. He raised his head, though, looking from one brother to the other. "Yeah, sure. You make it worth my while and we can talk." He straightened up. "Look, kid. It's like this. You can give me the beating of my life. Fine. But we both know you're not actually going to kill me. Your cousins, maybe, but not you. I've met your father, you know." He raised his eyebrows. "Does he know, by the way?"

Julian had just started to shake his head "no," when Jason held up a hand to stop him. Dees caught it, though. Dees caught a lot.

"Our father isn't part of this discussion," Jason said.

Dees wiped a hand against his mouth. "Whatever," he said. "Point is, we all know you're not going to kill me. So that leaves us with a quandary. I'm either going to get paid to tell someone this information, or you're going to make it worth my while, you understand? Me, I'd rather have you both at my side, as it were."

To Dees's satisfaction, both boys looked pale and shaken. An artery pulsed in Julian's neck. Jason tried to say something, but the words didn't come, like he'd had the breath knocked out of him. Then he tried again: "Under your thumb, you mean," he said. His head slumped in defeat.

Dees focused on Jason, a smile on his face. Jason, after all, was the formidable one. He knew the other kid would cave. And Jason had gone under more easily than he'd ever thought. "Whatever you want to call it," he said. He smirked.

That smirk was still on his face when Julian Kalodimos hurled a loose brick at Dees's chest at something over five hundred miles an hour. The blow knocked him back ten feet against a wall, and he looked around in startled confusion for just a moment, even opened his mouth as if to speak, before he crumpled to the ground, his heart crushed, two of his vertebrae lying on the ground at his feet.

Jason stared open-mouthed at his brother, feeling a wave of nausea go over him. He moved toward Dees.

"Don't," said Julian, his voice like a razor blade drawn across glass, drawing Jason up short. "No more contact. You don't want his blood on you." The color was coming back into his cheeks. His backpack filled with library books was slung over his shoulder. He looked like he'd just stopped by on the way to class. "He would have held that over us for the rest of our lives," he said. "It would have only gotten worse."

"But you—" Jason was having trouble getting air.

"I what? I'm the fragile one, the peaceful one, the one who stays home with Dad while you run errands for Uncle Costas and the other hoods?" Julian shrugged, his face expressionless. "Maybe I just see what has to be done," he said. Abruptly, he stepped away from Jason, away from the wide-eyed corpse of David Dees. He headed out of the alleyway, toward the streets beyond. Without turning around, he said, "You coming?"

Devil's Cape's been accused, maybe with some justification, of having the most corrupt police force in America. Okay, fine. We're giving Tijuana and Bangkok and Kampala a run for their money. But you've got to keep in mind that most of the men in blue are on the up and up, making the best of a bad situation and trying to keep you and me and my Aunt Harriet alive with a couple bucks left in our wallets.

— Excerpted from "Devil's Cape blues," by Ed Clugston, *Devil's Cape Daily Courier*, editorial section

EIGHT

As he had for several nights now, Cain Ducett dreamed of blood and fire.

He pulled his bed sheets over himself, despite the heat of his room. He felt nauseated, his skin itched, and sweat soaked his pillowcase. It stank of fear.

He swore, throwing the sheets aside and sitting up. His body felt strangely light as he padded his way to the bathroom.

He turned on the light.

Cain was not given to fear. If anything, he displayed a complete lack of self-preservation when encountering danger.

But this was different.

The reflection he faced in the mirror was not his own. Or worse, there were elements of Cain Ducett in the image he confronted, but horribly, horribly different. His irises were blood red. His skin, even on his face, was covered with fine, short fur, a dusky scarlet. His ears and teeth were elongated and pointed, and two needle-sharp canines protruded from his lower jaw all the way past his top lip. Flaps of skin like bats' wings stretched from his arms to his sides.

He screamed.

61

Detective Second Grade Salazar Lorca didn't have much training in hostage negotiation. He'd attended a one-day seminar once in L.A. and had blown off the afternoon session after a rather successful negotiation of a different kind over lunch had netted him the attentions of an attractive waitress who said she had once guest-starred on *The Fall Guy*.

On this hot August night, he'd been about to come off a ten-hour shift in which he'd been searching fruitlessly for any leads in the Dees case. Lorca didn't smoke, and the recent development of a minor ulcer was keeping him off coffee and colas. The only thing with caffeine he'd found that didn't hurt his stomach was Mountain Dew, and he could barely stand the taste. When the call came in, he blinked, rubbed his eyes, looked at his watch, sighed, and downed a can of the stuff as quickly as he could, then cracked open another and hit the siren and the accelerator at the same time.

"What's the word?" he asked the officer at the scene when he pulled up. They were in Crabb's Lament, named after one of the ship captains murdered by St. Diable, the masked pirate who had founded Devil's Cape. It was one of the roughest neighborhoods in the city. Drugs, gangs, lots of tension between the blacks and the Hispanics. There were about ten officers scattered around the block, and the building seemed to have been more or less evacuated already, people milling around and pointing and trying their best to stay under the cops' radar.

The patrolman nodded in acknowledgment, looking past Lorca to see where the detective's partner was.

Lorca shrugged. "We were about to get off our shift. He left me to write up the fives, and then the call came in." His face twitched. Why the hell was he explaining this to a patrolman? "What's the word?" he asked again, this time slow and deliberate.

The patrolman shrugged back, taking his time with it. "Perp's a juvenile black male, fifteen, runs with the CEs." The CEs were the Concrete Executioners, a black gang suspected of running half the drugs in that ward. Two weeks before, the CEs had caught a nine-year-old Hispanic boy spray-painting—tagging—his name on a neighborhood McDonald's. They'd broken both his arms and one leg and stuffed so many french fries in his mouth that he'd nearly suffocated. "Name's Cain Ducett," the officer continued. "Word is he might have taken over the CEs after we busted Jimmy Smith back in November."

"And?"

"And he's up in his mother's crib, 304-C, waving around a 9 mm and God knows what else, has his mother and the next-door neighbor tied to the living room couch with an extension cord. Says he's the devil and he wants to hear some jazz before he blows his own brains out. Or something like that."

"Or something like that," Lorca said dryly.

The officer stepped back from Lorca's car, gesturing at the building. "It's a hostage situation, so we called it in." He rubbed his hands together in a "washing my hands of it" gesture and smiled smugly at Lorca.

There was another hostage situation across the city. Some superhuman who could move things around with just his brain. And half the force looking for clues about Dees. So Lorca and his one-day seminar were it. He drank the rest of his Mountain Dew, crushed the can in his fists, and handed it to the patrolman, who looked back at him with distaste. Lorca flashed him a grin. "Take care of that for me, will you?" he asked. He didn't wait for an answer, but moved on into the building.

This was a crock, he thought to himself. He shouldn't be going up alone. There should be snipers set up outside of the building, and there should be a trained negotiator on hand. But there wasn't and he'd have to hope for the best.

The carpeted steps smelled of mildew and cat piss. He could hear Ducett screaming from two stories down. No wonder the building had evacuated so easily.

There were two officers stationed outside Ducett's

door. They looked tired and nervous, and glanced at each other gratefully when Lorca appeared. He introduced himself, then motioned for them to stand back.

———————

Cain was considering slitting Mr. Marcus's throat with his mother's steak knife when he heard the cop walk up close to the door.

"Stand back!" Cain shouted even before the man had a chance to pull his hand back to knock.

Cain had long ago flipped off or broken every light in the apartment, but his hearing was incredibly acute. He could hear his mother's heartbeat, hear the ticking of Mr. Marcus's watch, hear the pigeons cooing to each other on the rooftop three stories above. He could hear the uniformed cops outside the door and could tell that they were uniformed by the way their heavy belts rasped as they moved. He could tell that the new man was wearing different clothes, different shoes. He was breathing hard from the walk up the stairs.

"I'm just here to talk," the man said. "My name's Salazar."

What, he didn't even rate a nice, soft-spoken black cop, ready to talk about how he understood what it's like to grow up in the ghetto? Cain spat on his mother's weathered avocado throw rug. "No use talking," he said. "I'm going to do what I'm going to do and no talking is going to change that." He licked his lips. "You should have sent old Bilbray up here. I could have put a bullet in his brain pan and done us all a favor."

The man outside the door whispered, "Huh," softly to himself, the sound coming across like he was biting back a chuckle.

"What, you don't like Bilbray, either?"

Mr. Marcus started crying again, but even above that rasping noise, Cain could hear the cop—Salazar—jump just a little in surprise. Cain wondered if even the other two cops had heard Salazar's little amused sound. He pressed the muzzle of his gun into Mr. Marcus's ear, driving it in so that the sight dug into the skin. He could smell the blood. "Now I told you to stop blubbering and be a man, Mr. Marcus," he whispered. "You're embarrassing me now." He wasn't really sure what to do about Mr. Marcus. He wasn't such a bad guy, really.

"Cain," the cop said outside, "We've got two snipers with night vision scopes aimed at you right now. We're only keeping you alive to be neighborly."

"You're lying," Cain said. There were no snipers. He could *feel* that there were no snipers.

Salazar sighed. He muttered something that sounded like, "a one-day seminar." And then, without warning, he kicked the apartment door open.

Cain was almost startled enough to jerk his finger on the trigger and splatter Mr. Marcus's brains all over his mother's living room couch. But instead, he pulled back his arm to cover himself. For some reason, he didn't want this cop to see the red fur, the elongated features, the teeth, the wings, the tail that he'd felt but been afraid to examine more closely. He made a sound like a hiss, then pulled the gun back and stuck it into his own mouth.

And then Salazar was standing over him, a pockmarked Hispanic man with thinning hair and a slight paunch, his gun pointed at Cain's forehead.

Despite the guns, despite the electric tension, what struck Cain first and hardest was the fact that the man didn't seem surprised to find himself in the room with the devil. Quietly, almost timidly, Cain cut his eyes downward to look at his own arm. It was dark, nearly hairless, normal. He breathed a choked sigh of relief into the barrel of the gun. Whatever had been affecting him was over. Had he really changed? He shook his head a little, shaking it off. The muzzle of his 9 mm tasted like pennies in his mouth. It didn't matter. Whatever it was—metamorphosis, hallucination, or bad trip—it was time to end things. He knew that. It was comical, really, that he was preparing to blow out his own brains and the cop still stood there pointing that gun at him.

Beside them, one of the two uniformed police officers was also pointing his gun at Cain, while the other was untying Cain's mother and Mr. Marcus.

Cain wanted to swear at the cops, but knew it would come out ridiculous with the gun in his mouth.

The gun still clenched in his right hand, Salazar wiped sweat off his forehead with his left. "I've heard about you, Ducett," he said. "And about the CEs." He shrugged. "If you do it, there's not going to be anyone who cares. Not your friends." He nodded his head at the apartment door, where Cain's mother was being led into the hallway, quietly avoiding looking back at him. "Not her. Not after what you did today. Certainly not me. Oh, I'll have to do some more paperwork, but it will be time well spent. A public service."

Cain narrowed his eyes at the man. What the hell kind of negotiator had they sent him?

"No," Salazar continued, "you should definitely do it. There's only one person in the world who would care in the least if you pulled that trigger, and that's the one you're holding a gun on right now." He wiped at his forehead again. "Damn, it's hot in here," he said. "I think that there's a tiny part of you that wants to live, Ducett. Maybe there's even a tiny, microscopic part of you that deserves to live. But you're the only one who cares about it. So go right ahead."

———

Salazar Lorca's arm was getting tired. He'd been talking to the boy for nearly twenty minutes now, and that was a long time to hold up a gun. He had a feeling that the instructor for his one-day course would be somewhat displeased with him for encouraging the kid to kill himself. But Ducett hadn't done it yet. He'd narrowed his eyes, given Lorca murderous looks, closed his own eyes for a few seconds at a time as if summoning something up, but he hadn't pulled the trigger.

Finally, the boy pulled the muzzle out. Lorca started to draw back, wondering if he was going to turn the gun

and shoot, but instead the gun stayed resting against Ducett's chin. The boy licked his lips and swallowed, then said, "If I put this gun down, will you please shut the hell up for a few minutes?"

It was a start.

The eccentric businessman known only as the Robber Baron is coming to the aid of the Juvenile Detention Center Fund. The Robber Baron said that he was moved by an article that appeared in this paper about the plight of teenagers convicted of criminal offenses who often have been detained long distances away from their families. "Family is a vital support system for youngsters in trouble," the Baron said at a press conference stating his intentions. "If these misguided youths must be incarcerated, it should be close to home so that they aren't denied the help of mother and father, sister, brother, aunt, uncle, and cousin."

The Robber Baron has established a grant that matches every dollar, up to $1 million, donated to the fund. This is expected to accelerate the facility's opening date . . .

— Excerpted from "Robber Baron matches donations to juvenile detention center fund," by Paulette Ragle, *Devil's Cape Daily Courier*

When it opened, the St. Tammany Parish Juvenile Detention Center had a planned capacity of fifty juveniles, but the needs of the city, and especially the rise in drug crimes and gang violence, ensured that the medium-security facility usually held close to twice that number. Now, less than three years after the first teenagers were moved in, it had already developed a tarnished reputation as a place where antisocial kids convicted of petty crimes went to learn how to become real criminals.

The walls of Cain Ducett's room—they didn't call it a cell, although the only way to unlock the door was from the outside—were painted white and baby blue, broken by a narrow window of reinforced glass that let the sunlight in and gave him a view of the parking lot. There was a slab with a plastic-covered mattress pad for him to sleep on, and a white cylinder that served as a stool. The room was two paces long and one pace wide and smelled of antiseptic so strong it sometimes gave him headaches.

Breakfast that morning had been some pasty scrambled eggs, toast, and a plastic cup of orange juice. Some of the other juvies were "studying" in the facility's small library or doing laps outside, but today the guards had let him stay in his room. It was safer there.

He'd been doing push-ups. He seemed to be able to do them now almost endlessly without tiring. Sometimes

he'd break them up by pushing off from the ground and clapping between repetitions, or doing them one-handed or on his fingertips. But mostly he just did straight push-ups, sometimes a couple hundred at a time. He was doing them fast that morning, burning off the weight in his belly from the breakfast, trying to make his arms strain, staring straight forward, his face only a few inches from a baby-blue wall. He was sweating a little. It trickled around his eyes and he could smell the salt in it, as well as the pasty odor of the deodorant they gave him.

"Ducett?" Marsh, one of the guards, knocked lightly on his door.

Cain sprang up to his bare feet, stepped backward so that Marsh could see him clearly through the narrow window in the heavy metal door. "Yeah?" he said. It wasn't time for a bathroom break yet. Not time for lunch.

Marsh tilted his head, looking at him, the fluorescent lights of the hallway making his bald head shine. "You all right?" he asked. He kept his voice loud, to be heard through the door.

"Yeah," Cain said, his voice loud, too. It echoed in the small room. "Yes, sir." The guards, even the gentler ones like Marsh, expected to be called "sir." He wiped the sweat off his forehead with the back of his arm. His arm was sweaty, too, so it didn't make much of a difference. "What is it?"

Marsh slipped a key into the lock of Cain's door and opened it. He dropped his voice lower. "Man here to see you," he said. He opened the door and stepped backward, keeping himself out of Cain's reach. He stowed the keys away. "SDPD," he said. "Detective Second Grade Salazar Lorca."

"The hell does he want?" Cain said. It slipped out that way. Not angry. Just surprised.

Marsh's hand slipped down to the nightstick he wore on his belt, but his eyes were soft. "He can come up here," he said. "Or meet you in the basketball court." He shrugged. "Up to you, he said."

Cain looked around his room. He could stretch his arms out and touch the walls on either side with his fingertips. The stench of his sweat smelled stronger. He picked up the thin navy blanket they gave him for his bed and wiped away the worst of it. He felt nervous and didn't know why. "Lot of people at the court," he said.

Marsh shook his head. "Just you and him," he said, "if you want to go there. He arranged it."

Cain looked out the window at the parking lot, spotting the unmarked car right away. Flat gray, no detailing.

"Don't have all day, Ducett," Marsh said. But his voice was soft, unperturbed.

Cain nodded. He tossed the blanket onto the mattress in a heap and bent down to put on his socks and shoes.

———————

It was hot, the kind of day where thin gray and white clouds diffused the light across the sky, so no matter where you looked, you found yourself squinting. They'd cleared the others off the basketball court, and when Cain came out of the building, Marsh behind him, he saw Salazar Lorca standing in the middle of the asphalt, a button-down shirt unbuttoned halfway to his chest over a graying undershirt, the cuffs of his khaki pants covering just the tops of his black cop shoes. He bounced a basketball down on the pavement, caught it, and then repeated the action. Each thump of the ball hitting the court echoed like a gunshot.

Marsh stopped near the gate while Cain walked onto the court. Lorca nodded at him. He'd grown a moustache since Cain had seen him last. It drooped around the corners of his mouth.

"Yo," Cain said.

Lorca bounced the ball again and caught it. "Yo," he said. He held up the ball. "You play?"

Cain patted down his shirt, which was bunched up from the push-ups. It bothered him that he looked messy and it bothered him that that bothered him. "Better than you," he said, forcing himself to meet Lorca's eyes.

Lorca smiled. One of his teeth was chipped. He bounced the ball toward Cain. "I don't doubt it," he said.

Cain caught the ball, holding it with his fingertips. "You come here just to get schooled in basketball?" he said.

Lorca shuffled his feet, squinting at a pelican that flew overhead. "Maybe a game of horse," he said. "You know horse?"

Cain wiped at his forehead. He dribbled the ball once then threw it at the hoop from midcourt in an easy arc. He had turned to watch Lorca again before the ball even reached the basket, but it swished through the net softly, no rim, then thudded to the ground and rolled off with Lorca chasing it. "When you miss," Cain said, "that'll be H."

Lorca chuckled. He walked to the midcourt point, beside Cain, and threw the ball. It hit the rim and bounced out.

Cain trotted forward and grabbed it. "H," he said.

Lorca nodded. "So do you get the next shot or do I?"

Cain shrugged. "You picked the game, Mr. Police Officer," he said. "You make the rules." He passed the ball to Lorca. He could hear shouting from inside the center. A game, maybe, or a fight. Probably didn't amount to much.

Hearing the noise, too, Lorca eyed the detention center, but when Marsh made no move to go inside to investigate, he shrugged and stepped just in back of the basketball goal. As he moved, Cain could see that he was wearing a gun in a shoulder holster under the button-down shirt. He remembered having that gun trained on him, the steadiness in the detective's eyes as he held it. "This is tricky," Lorca said. He threw the ball upward in a tall, narrow arc. It went over the backboard, then down through the hoop. It bounced once, then Lorca stepped forward nimbly and caught it. He passed it to Cain. "When *you* miss," he said, "that will be H for you."

Cain walked behind the goal, measuring his shot. Devil's Cape was so damn hot. Barely into March, not even lunchtime, and he was already wishing he could take another shower. "I won't miss," he said. He pulled his arms back to make the shot, then lowered the ball. "You going to tell me why you're here, Mr. Police Officer?" he asked.

Lorca clucked his tongue. He looked up into the clouds as if he were looking for an answer to Cain's question. "That 'Mr. Police Officer' stuff is going to get old," he said. "You can call me Salazar."

Cain lowered the ball some more and just looked at the detective.

Lorca shrugged. "I've been to your apartment," he said. "I almost shot you once. I almost saw you shoot yourself. Hell, we're practically family."

Cain realized his mouth was open. He shut it, forced the expression out of his face. He threw the ball and listened to it swish through the hoop. Lorca caught it before it landed. "You want me to snitch for you," Cain said, "you'll be disappointed. I got nothing. I been here like nine months. That's about half of forever. Anything I knew is old now."

Lorca tossed the ball up in the air, caught it, and then tossed it to Cain. "I'm not looking for you to snitch," he said. "I know you wouldn't."

Cain dribbled the ball over to the free-throw line. "I'll make an easy one for you," he said. He sank the shot, hopped forward, snatched up the ball, and handed it to Lorca. He realized how close he was to Lorca's gun, but blinked the thought away. The shouting inside the detention center seemed to have died down.

Lorca spun the ball in his hands as he walked to the free-throw line. He didn't line up for the shot. Instead, he looked at Cain. There were dark circles under his eyes. "Word is someone tried to shank you yesterday afternoon," he said.

Cain smiled at him. "No big deal," he said. He remembered the shiv coming up at his throat. It was shiny and green, the handle of a toothbrush that had been meticulously sharpened down to a point as thin and sharp as a needle.

"Jimmy Smith's brother Tyrell," Lorca said. He threw the basketball. It hit the backboard, then bounced over the hoop and down to the ground. "We're at H-O, I guess," he said. He trotted forward to get the ball. "Jimmy ran the Concrete Executioners before you," he said. "You think Tyrell resents you?"

As Tyrell had passed him in the hallway, Cain had heard a sudden breath from him as Tyrell was getting ready to strike. He turned just in time to see that green shiv arcing up, Tyrell's big muscles corded. By all rights, Tyrell should have punched a hole in Cain's throat with the thing. But Cain had heard it coming, had gotten his hand up in time to catch Tyrell's wrist. The shiv was maybe six inches away from Cain's throat when he grabbed Tyrell and it didn't move a single inch closer. Tyrell moaned with the sudden pain and fell to his knees. He dropped the shiv and Cain stood staring at it for a few seconds. It glistened there on the pale gray floor of the hallway.

"The guards weren't close by when it happened," Lorca said. "They said you had plenty of time to take Tyrell out with his own shiv and you didn't do it." He stood near the basket, threw the ball up and through, an easy shot.

He handed Cain the ball. An anemic breeze passed through the courtyard. Cain smelled car exhaust. He moved to where Lorca had thrown the ball. "Why would I want that much trouble?" he asked. He lined himself up and missed the net entirely.

"Air ball," Lorca said. "H to H-O." He held out the ball.

Cain took it and dribbled it a couple of times. Each time it hit the asphalt, the sound echoed around them. He jerked his head at the basketball goal. "Two dribbles, then a jump shot," he said. He dribbled the ball forward, then jumped up toward the hoop, throwing the ball. It slid through.

Lorca took the ball. "That's it?" he asked. "You just didn't want the trouble?"

Cain turned and looked at him. "You here about Tyrell?" he asked.

Lorca dribbled the ball up and jumped. He didn't get as high as Cain had, but the ball went right where it was supposed to. He smiled in satisfaction. "Nope," he said.

The ball rolled to the edge of the court, where Cain snatched it up. The grass lawn next to the asphalt was filled with weeds. There was an ant pile the size of a hubcap off to one side and Cain stood there for a few seconds, watching ants climbing in and out of the dirt. He turned back to Lorca. "Do you even know why you're here?" he asked.

Lorca frowned and pushed his thinning hair back. "No real reason," he said. "Someone told me about the attack and I thought I'd check on you."

"Why?"

Lorca looked annoyed. "You going to give me the ball?" he said.

Cain bounced it to him.

The detective turned the ball over in his hands, looking from it to the hoop and back again. He avoided looking at Cain.

"If you were like a lot of cops," Cain said, "you just would have shot me that night."

Lorca shrugged. "Off the backboard," he said. He threw the ball, which bounced off of the backboard, circled the rim twice, and dropped through the net. He snatched it up on the bounce.

"If I'd killed Tyrell yesterday after you left me alive," Cain said, "that might have been your fault, you want to look at it that way."

Lorca threw the ball to Cain, harder than he needed to. "I don't," he said.

Cain stepped forward. "You're here because you want to make sure you did the right thing in talking me out of shooting myself," he said. "You want to make sure that wasn't a mistake. You want me to—" He broke off, suddenly unsure of himself. He threw the ball. It arced gracefully through the net. "You want me to be good," he said quietly. The words felt odd to him.

Lorca stood watching the ball bounce away. "I said off the backboard," he said. "That's H-O to H-O."

A ray of sunlight broke through the clouds. Cain squinted. The ball had rolled into the grass, but neither of them moved to get it. They looked at the ball, not each other. "I made you mad," Cain said. His skin felt hot. His heart was pounding. He didn't want Lorca mad at him, but he didn't know why it mattered.

Lorca looked up at him then. He sighed. "Don't worry about it," he said. He walked over to get the ball, his cop shoes crunching the dry grass. "I've had a long, long week," he said. "I saw a lot of bad things this week." He bent down and picked up the basketball. "Then I heard someone—" He looked at Cain. "It was Dustin Bilbray, actually. I bumped into him at this gas station last night and he was laughing about how you almost got killed yesterday." He put the ball under one arm and just stood there, watching Cain. "I didn't know why I came here. I just did."

At another time, the thought of Bilbray laughing at him would have enraged Cain. But now he barely found himself picturing the man. Instead, he thought of Jazz flying backward. He could see her blood pooling on the street. He could hear 5-D sobbing. He could almost taste RC and Jim Beam, like bile in his throat. He felt sad. "I'm not any good, Salazar," he said. "Not killing Tyrell doesn't make me good."

Lorca didn't move. "Maybe not," he said.

Cain swallowed. "If you came here looking for me to be a better man than I was, you're going to be disappointed," he said.

"Maybe so," Lorca said.

Cain looked away.

"When I met you," Lorca said, "you didn't notice anyone but Cain Ducett." He bounced the ball to Cain, who caught it. "Back then, you would have killed Tyrell Smith without thinking about it. You might have wondered what I was doing here, but you would have been looking for angles to work."

Cain looked back at him now.

"Instead," Lorca continued, "you put yourself in my head. You thought of someone other than yourself long enough to pick my brain apart. I've had to meet with police shrinks half a dozen times after one incident or another and they've never gotten me to understand a damn thing about myself I didn't already know. You did it in less than five minutes. That's empathy." He nodded. "That's progress. That's something."

Cain felt like he might cry. He blinked and turned his head toward the sunlight. "It's H-O to H-O, isn't it?" he said. "We're never going to finish the game if you keep talking." He dribbled the ball and set up his next shot. The wind was picking up a little more now. He thought he could smell the ocean.

When the first Doctor Camelot retired, a second took his place immediately. That Doctor Camelot, in turn, was succeeded by a third, perhaps the most impressive and heroic of them all. When he died, Vanguard City waited with bated breath for a new Doctor Camelot to pick up his standard, to carry on his good works, to pull the sword from the stone, so to speak. But he never came.

— Excerpted from
"Whence Camelot: Five years later,"
by Leslie Flannigan, *Vanguard City Crier*

TEN

It was just a stupid accident that Kate Brauer ever stumbled on the picture. Her mother, Angela Brauer, usually kept it hidden away with everything else she kept hidden away. But the week before Kate came back from Cambridge for summer vacation, Angela had gotten word that Kate's "Uncle" Charles had been diagnosed with leukemia, and she'd retrieved the photo and wept over it a bit, then stuffed it in a bureau drawer under a stack of clothes and forgotten about it.

If Kate hadn't brought home so much dirty laundry, if she hadn't found herself desperately needing a clean T-shirt her first afternoon back while her mother was off at work, if she hadn't gone looking for something to wear in her mother's bureau, if she'd settled for the first, the second, or even the fifth T-shirt that she came across, Kate might have lived out her life blithely unaware of the truth about her father.

Kate tossed aside a solid blue shirt in disgust when she realized that it had a pale bleach stain marring one sleeve, then reached back into the drawer, intent on pulling out the whole stack of shirts she saw. Her fingernail caught against something hard and she felt it tear. She swore, pulled the drawer the rest of the way out, and reached inside more carefully to see what was responsible for her broken nail.

79

It was a simple wooden picture frame, holding a group portrait of her father with several of his friends, her "aunts" and "uncles." She blinked. At first, she thought it had to be from a Halloween party. But it didn't make any sense. Her father had kept his friends more or less separate. They didn't really even know each other. Uncle Rinji he'd met through work, Uncle Samuel through . . . well, college, wasn't it? Aunt Vikki through the Citizen's Action Committee. She'd had to introduce several of them to each other at her father's funeral. But here they were, together, their arms around each other and her father, glomming for the camera.

And their costumes . . .

Uncle Rinji was dressed as Raiden. He was wearing his glasses, of course—he couldn't see without them—while Raiden wore none, and his hair was looser and more flowing than Raiden's ever was, but still . . . Aunt Vikki wore a Miss Chance costume, the low-cut one the hero had worn back in the mid-eighties until that silly fight with the Mastermime, when the villain had yanked her top down and taken a picture. Her Miss Chance mask was hanging loosely around her neck. Uncle Samuel was dressed as Sam Small, just with no mask in sight. Uncle Charles wore a maskless Swashbuckler costume, Aunt Tanja looked like Patriot, and Uncle Jose was half-covered in some kind of latex makeup job that made him resemble Velociraptor. And her father . . .

Her father, smiling at the camera, his eyes twinkling, wore the armor of Doctor Camelot, the helmet in the crook of one arm.

Kate sat staring at the photo for perhaps twenty minutes, her quest for a T-shirt abandoned and her torn fingernail forgotten. Then she set the frame down on top of the bureau and left the room, her mother's shirts still scattered across the carpet.

Once she'd figured it out, once she put her mind to it, it took her only fifteen minutes to find her father's hidden lab. She knew it had to be in the basement—she'd found him coming out of there any number of times in her childhood, smelling faintly of Old Spice and motor oil. Once or twice, she'd even walked down there looking for him—it was forbidden territory, of course—only to come up empty, yet with him later emerging, a smile on his face, as if the room hadn't been completely vacant a scant few minutes before.

She was a more sophisticated searcher now. She tapped walls and bookshelves, the ceiling and the floor, comparing the sounds, until she had a good idea where the door had to be. And the hidden switch was obvious once she knew what to look for. It was disguised under a small knothole in the wooden book cabinet, right behind Sir Thomas Malory's *Le Morte D'Arthur*. He must have grinned to himself about that one, she thought.

She'd deduced that the hidden entrance was in the wall decorated with the framed album covers he'd treasured. "Ella and Duke at The Côte D'Azur," Bing Crosby's "White Christmas," "Tito Puente and his Concert Orchestra," and a dozen others, including, she realized with another touch of warmth for her father's humor, the soundtrack of *Camelot*. As she explored the walls, she noticed that each frame was attached to the wall at all four corners. It might just have been meticulous care, but she calculated that it was actually insurance that they wouldn't become tilted or dislodged when the wall itself moved.

She stared at the album covers for a full minute, her finger poised by the knothole, heart beating fast. Then she pulled the switch.

The wall silently slid backward six inches, then glided sideways until it was gone. She was amazed at how quiet it was, even after all this time. Her own breathing was louder than that moving wall. She closed her eyes for a second as a soft rush of cool, clean, ionized air swept out of the opening and over her. Then she opened her eyes and walked inside.

She'd been expecting a small room, but instead, she found herself at the top of a tall, broad staircase leading down into a chamber as large as a gymnasium, if not quite as tall. As she walked down the cut stone steps, squinting her eyes at the incandescent lights and the bright white paint of the walls, she thought first not of her father, but of Uncle Samuel, who'd sat so patiently next to her and lied so badly, though she hadn't realized it at time.

Her father, ever organized, ever methodical, had divided the room into sections.

The first, glittering with chrome, held equipment he must have used in designing and developing the Doctor Camelot armor and its systems. There was a large lathe, a series of diamond-headed drills, an air compressor, welding equipment, a pair of injection molding machines, a durometer for measuring the hardness of rubbers and polymers, and more she couldn't identify. She walked along his worktables there, her fingers tracing the blueprints and diagrams. There were dozens of note cards in his precise handwriting, some of them in small stacks and others clipped or stapled above different pieces he'd been working on. At the center of it all was a single comfortable office chair on well-worn casters, and she could imagine him rolling himself from one spot to another in an excited fury of work and experimentation, a pencil clasped in his teeth. She sat in it for a minute, the wheels squeaking a little in protest. His presence was strong there as she rolled herself gently from one station to another with her feet. It felt to her almost like she was a young girl again, sitting in his lap.

She stood. The next section contrasted starkly with the metal and tools. It was a small workout area with a punching bag, a jump rope, and a series of weights. A hooded New England Patriots sweatshirt she'd given him the Christmas before he died hung on a peg on the wall. She leaned down and held it against her face and imagined that she could smell Old Spice.

Beside the punching bag extended a long, narrow reinforced tunnel that served as a firing range. Colorful paper targets decorated the far wall, which was nicked and singed by whatever armaments her father had tested there. Another tunnel opened right out of the ceiling at the end of the range. It had no handrails—the only way anyone could travel through it was to fly. An alternate exit, she guessed.

There was a trophy area. Notes that had been sent to Doctor Camelot. Crayon pictures from kids. A headless robot with a plaque reading, DEADLOCK'S COMBAT DRONE X7-J. The signature metallic shield and sword of the first Doctor Camelot. A chest plate from an earlier version of the Doctor Camelot powered armor, the metal ripped; a plaque beside that one read TORN BY LIONMAN'S CLAWS. There was a clown car and a tusk from a woolly mammoth and a Polish 37 mm anti-tank gun.

The final section seemed to be devoted to research. There were several microscopes, an infrared spectrometer, a gas chromatograph/mass spectrometer, a centrifuge, an X-ray machine, photographic equipment, and other pieces. There was also a large computer with several monitors. Everything still seemed to be running, or had turned on when she opened the door. Lights blinked on the equipment and she was just barely conscious of a quiet electronic hum. There were stacks of note cards here, too, and some posted to corkboards. All were placed evenly, neatly squared, except for a single card near the computer, set at an angle, as though perhaps it was the last one he had been working on. She bent over it, reading her father's words, and her breath caught in her throat:

> Mercenaries.
> Circus or carnival sideshow acts?
> <u>Cirque d'Obscurité.</u>
> Roscoe Clay Bridge, planned attack, 8:32 a.m.
> matching Judge McBain's commute.

On a Friday in early April, six years earlier, just before 8:30 in the morning, the Storm Raiders had confronted a group of superhuman sideshow freaks who were making preparations to collapse the Roscoe Clay Bridge. The

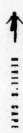

bridge, which crossed the Connecticut River, was the sprawling, gleaming symbol of Vanguard City, an architectural wonder of steel designed with the cubic forms and zigzag lines of art deco so typical of the city. The saboteurs had all previously worked for a small traveling carnival called Ma's Spectacular Amusements, but had split off from the main act a few months before to form their own troupe, which they called the *Cirque d'Obscurité*, or the Circus of Darkness. In the months following the attack on the bridge, the troupe would be linked to a variety of crimes across the United States and beyond, but at that time, they were known only as an interesting group of performers making their way from one suburban performance to another. The Storm Raiders had approached them expecting a fight, but had badly underestimated the abilities of the *Cirque d'Obscurité*. The heroes prevented the destruction of the bridge, but Doctor Camelot, the team's leader, was killed by the carnival strongman called the Behemoth, and in the chaos that followed, the carnival troupe escaped. They were still at large.

Kate stood bent over that note, picturing her father. She'd been told he'd died working late at the office on a Thursday, the night before Doctor Camelot had died, but that had been a lie. He'd spent that night here in his secret room, piecing together information, deducing the threat to the bridge and presumably rushing off to stop it. And that deduction might have saved hundreds of lives, but it had doomed him.

The death of Doctor Camelot had always seemed abstract to her, overshadowed as it was by the reality of her father's death. But now she was re-imagining things, seeing her father in that armor, associating her father with the hero and his death, seeing the other Storm Raiders not as distant icons, but as her parents' closest friends.

"Now I know why she wouldn't turn off the damn TV," she said to the empty room. And then she began to cry.

For Palm-Reading, Tarot Reading, Voodoo Cursing,
and All That Jazz, call or visit . . .

— A business card left by public telephones and
park benches across Devil's Cape

ELEVEN

*J*essica Rydland didn't go by any name but Jazz anymore. It suited her. Like the music she took her name from, Jazz was a mass of contradictions, varying rhythms, and improvisations. She was at times criminal, patriot, anarchist, philanthropist, coward, atavist, miser, and dreamer. She digested voodoo, tarot, phrenology, Mayan spirituality, crystal theory, SETI, astral travel, parapsychology, Kabbalah, and marijuana in roughly equal measure. Most of the time, she realized, she was stumbling through the edges of the vast, unknowable world, touching on truths that she could barely understand, much less communicate to others.

But sometimes, every once in a while, she channeled something greater than herself. She found herself bristling, electrified with power and certainty that defied explanation. It had been that way for her that hot day on the sidewalk when Cain Ducett had quite nearly murdered her. Filled with rage and a strange vision of things to come, she'd focused every bit of her will on laying a curse on Cain. She'd envisioned him changing, his beautiful face and body warping into a form as hideous and hateful as his soul. And she'd made it happen.

Jazz ran an anemic fortune-telling business out of her home at the edge of the tourist-friendly Silver Swan

district, just where the district began to run into the crime-ridden neighborhood of Crabb's Lament. Years ago, she had purchased a run-down shotgun house. Common in nineteenth century Devil's Cape and New Orleans, shotgun houses were narrow, rectangular buildings constructed on top of brick piers. They were built without hallways; each room simply ran into the next one all the way to the back of the house. Hers was actually a double shotgun home, with two sets of rooms running side by side to the back, with a camelback, or shortened second story, toward the rear.

The house had been infested with rats, crickets, and roaches when she bought it. One of the interior walls had hidden a perpetual leak from the roof, the water trickling inside and helping to brew a near-toxic mass of mildew, black mold, and roach eggs until the wood and plaster had begun to bulge out with the vile stuff, and roaches had scurried in and out of the faded wallpaper. It had taken her weeks and more than half of her savings just to have the wall replaced. The house had reeked of decay, stale cigarette smoke, and cat urine. A man had been murdered there in 1943, and the house was rumored to be haunted by his ghost; his blood still stained the front room's hardwood floor.

But her house's basic foundation and most of its walls were strong, and the antebellum fixtures and crown molding had held up well over the decades. Room by room, in the years since she'd purchased it, she'd added Victorian lace, painted walls in dark earth tones, and installed new fixtures. She filled the front rooms with decorations and sales items for her customers—shaded lamps, incense, tribal masks and drums, gris-gris, voodoo dolls, crystals, pyramids, dream catchers, tarot cards, and jars of chamomile, willow bark, ginseng, peppermint, mandrake root, catnip, hibiscus, lucky hand root, and St. John's wort. A bookshelf held copies of books with names like *Eshu-Eleggua Elegbara, Voodoo and Hoodoo,* and *The Cross of Baron Semedi.* The back rooms were less cluttered and more to her own liking.

Black predominated there—black walls, black ceilings, black light.

She was sitting in her foyer, patiently polishing a crystal ball with Windex, a bar of Nag Champa incense filling the room with a sweet, earthy haze, Gregorian chants playing softly from her stereo, when the Robber Baron walked inside, leaning on a brass cane that glittered in the dim light.

"Oh my God," she whispered to herself, pulling back from the crystal ball, sliding her bare feet to the floor and slowly standing, trembling.

The Robber Baron didn't make many public appearances, and when he did, he played the role of the eccentric Devil's Cape millionaire. His mask, he said, was an affectation, a tribute to old St. Diable the pirate, who had founded the city and worn a similar mask—and of course to the spirit of Mardi Gras. The name Robber Baron, he said, was a nickname attached to him in the early years of his business career by admiring enemies and jealous friends, and he kept it, he claimed, to protect his privacy. "If superheroes can enjoy the anonymity of masks and pseudonyms," he had famously quipped in a rare interview published in the *Devil's Cape Daily Courier,* "why not an aging philanthropist and businessman? The IRS knows my real name and so does one of my ex-wives, and that's plenty for anyone!" Everyone knew he was a criminal, the type of criminal who frightened other criminals, but he'd rarely even been charged with any crimes, and never convicted. He was too insulated by stooges, graft, and a wealth of secret leverage over highly placed officials in local, state, and even federal government. And except in those circumstances when he utterly controlled the environment, such as the popular soirees on his luxurious riverboat, he kept to the shadows, a recluse to rival Howard Hughes, emperor of a city that rarely saw him and never saw his face.

Yet there he stood in Jazz's small house, a black gaucho hat shading his face, his famous scarlet bandit mask

stretched over his eyes, its silk ties dangling down one side and barely touching his shoulder. He had a rakish gray beard, trimmed and waxed to a fine point, the moustache curving upward ever so slightly at the edges. His skin was smooth, his jaw strong. He was dressed in a black, crushed velvet topcoat with a matching cravat around his neck, over a blousy scarlet shirt that matched his mask. His black pants were crisply ironed, his black ostrich boots recently shined. Soft black gloves covered his hands. The half-inch or so of bare skin between his gloves and the ruffled cuffs of his scarlet shirt was tan and bristled with fine gray hairs.

Two people quickly stepped into Jazz's house behind the Robber Baron, flanking him. The first was a horrifically damaged man, every visible inch of his skin puckered and red with thick keloid scars from horrible burning. His nose was more or less missing; only a thin hump with two gaping nostrils remained. His lips were stretched tight against his teeth, twisting up on one side. What little hair remained grew in short, twisted, dark tufts patched in odd spaces on his scalp. His eyebrows and eyelashes were gone, though he still had eyelids. The scar tissue around his eyes was smoother than the rest, though that smooth patch ended in roughly scalloped edges on one side, like fingertips, and Jazz realized that, whatever had damaged him, he had thrown a hand over his eyes to protect himself, with limited success. He wore a crisp, bleached white T-shirt over stone-washed blue jeans and a worn leather belt decorated with a large, burnished silver belt buckle engraved with a flaming skull. The smile he directed at Jazz was mean and tight. When he hooked his scarred thumbs in the loops of his jeans, the muscles of his huge, veined forearms bulged with tension. He reeked of decay. She recognized him from the news. He was a member of a group of criminal carnival freaks who had been on the run for years and who were rumored to have come to Devil's Cape. She'd seen a report on WTDC. The *Cirque d'Obscurité*. They called him Gork.

The other person with the Robber Baron was a tall, slender woman with smooth café au lait skin, probably Creole, her ethnicity some mix of white, black, and Native American, with some Asian thrown in for good measure, judging by the slight curve of her dark-green eyes. She kept her curly rust-brown hair cut very close to the scalp and shaved at the sides. She wore a brown and black caftan, cut low in front, its fabric shimmering and stitched with feathers. As the woman turned and closed the door behind the Robber Baron, Jazz could see that the back of her dress hung out loosely, covering some large bulge back there as though she were concealing a backpack. Or wings. A pair of dark brown gloves hung loosely from a belt at the woman's waist, the fingertips ending in burnished metal claws. Another member of the *Cirque d'Obscurité*, Jazz recognized. Osprey, the bird of prey.

Jazz realized that she was still holding a rag damp with cleanser. She dropped it to the table beside her crystal ball, turned, and switched off the Gregorian chanting. The monks' voices echoed for just a second in her foyer before dying out.

The *Cirque d'Obscurité* was widely rumored to be in Devil's Cape and had been connected to the Robber Baron, though he had flatly denied it. The fact that he was appearing here with two of the team's members meant that he was very, very confident that he wouldn't be caught in a lie. Which didn't bode well for Jazz.

The Robber Baron's eyes flicked around the room, glancing first at a decidedly inauthentic tribal mask hanging from one wall, then at a small stone fountain bubbling in her entryway. He tapped her hardwood floor gently with his cane, its tip resting square in the middle of the old bloodstain of the man who had been murdered in the room in the forties.

Everyone stood there for a moment without speaking. When Osprey turned away from the door to gaze coolly at Jazz, the metal claws on her gloves clinked against each other. Gork's breathing was raspy and ragged, though the tight, mean smile didn't waver from his face.

Jazz's mouth felt dry. She wondered if they were there to murder her, though she couldn't imagine why. "Would you like—?" her voice broke. She stopped and swallowed. "Would you like to have your fortunes told?" she asked.

The Robber Baron smiled at her then, though the shade of his hat kept her from seeing if the smile reached his eyes. "Can you really see the future then, young lady?" he asked. He stepped forward toward her, leaning close in the small room. His breath smelled of peppermint and tobacco.

"Not really," she said, heart hammering.

Gork laughed, his voice thick with phlegm. "If she could see the future," he said, "she sure as hell wouldn't have been sitting here when we walked in."

The Robber Baron didn't really turn his head then. He just tilted it a few degrees toward Gork. That was enough. The man stopped speaking, his tight smile fading a notch.

"Sometimes I catch a glimpse of something," Jazz said. "Not the future. Just . . . an insight that I can't explain." She never spoke of this to her customers. With them, it was a running patter of her connections to the loas, her reading of the cards, her knowledge of the lines of their hands and the shapes of their fingers, and what they meant. But this wasn't an ordinary visitor. And if her insights were telling her anything, it was that she needed to answer him with utter frankness.

He tapped his brass cane lightly on the floor again, reached out with his gloved hand and wiped a smudge off her crystal ball. "Last week, you read the fortune of Tony Ferazzoli," he said.

"Oh my God," she whispered again.

"You remember this?" he asked. His voice was strong, old-fashioned, the accent difficult to place. Not Cajun, exactly. Not Southern, exactly. It managed to hint simultaneously at rich culture and just a hint of coarseness somewhere in his background.

"I didn't know his name," she said. The room felt humid and hot.

"But you know who I mean?"

She nodded, taking a half-step back from him. "I didn't have many customers last week," she said. She remembered a fat, balding man in a seersucker suit and a wide tie. He'd walked in, apparently on impulse, and asked for her to read his fortune. His palms had been so sweaty she'd made him dry them off with a towel. She hadn't recognized him as the notorious mafia figure Tony Ferazzoli, who controlled half the cocaine trafficking in Devil's Cape, not to mention a hefty percentage of other criminal enterprises, including prostitution, pornography, protection rackets, fencing of stolen goods, and gambling.

"And with him, you had one of your . . . insights," the Robber Baron said.

"Yeah," she said. "Yes." A lock of hair fell in front of her face, and when she reached up to brush it back, she could see her hand trembling.

"You told him that his boss was going to murder him," the Robber Baron said simply. There was no anger in his voice. He sounded calm and curious, patient.

She shook her head. "I didn't know that was you," she said. Her own palms felt sweaty now, and she wondered what had become of poor, frightened, corrupt, fat Tony Ferazzoli.

His smile showed white teeth, and she stood there half-expecting him to deny it, telling her that of course he wasn't Ferazzoli's boss, that he didn't consort with known crime figures, that he was a philanthropist who would never dream of hurting anyone. Instead, he said simply, "Of course you didn't." He turned to Gork. "Check the back rooms," he said.

Her whole body was trembling now as the scarred man brushed past her as he moved into the back of her house. His lumpy skin felt smooth and hot as his shoulder brushed against hers, and she realized that he'd bumped into her on purpose. She recoiled. "There's no one else here," she said. "I'm really sorry for what I said to him. I didn't mean anything. I'd never tell anyone."

The Robber Baron lowered himself into one of the ornate wooden chairs she kept for her clients. She'd selected them because the burnished oak looked sophisticated and the carvings exotic, but also because the chairs were uncomfortable enough that no one was tempted to sit in them for too long. He rested his brass cane next to the crystal ball on the small table. "Of course you wouldn't," he said. She could hear Gork climbing the stairs up to her house's camelback loft.

Jazz felt ill. She breathed deeply, concentrating on the scent of the incense and trying to make herself calm. "Are you going to kill me?" she asked simply.

Now Osprey laughed, a low, seductive chuckle. "You tell us," she said.

If the Robber Baron was annoyed with Osprey's interruption as he had been with Gork's, he gave no sign of it. "I was intrigued," he said, "when Tony told me about what you'd said to him."

She swallowed. "I didn't mean any harm," she said. "And I didn't see much. He was afraid. He was terrified." There had been half-moons of sweat under Ferazzoli's arms that had soaked all the way through his jacket. "My insight was just that he was scared, that he probably had very good reason to be scared, and that the threat came from someone in authority over him." She shrugged, ticking off the next facts with her fingers for him. "I had no idea who that person was. He didn't name any names. And no one would believe a fortuneteller as a witness anyway."

Gork walked back into the room. She began to step aside, but he brushed past her again anyway, his elbow rubbing across her chest. As he turned and stood beside Osprey, who rolled her eyes at him, he shook his head. "No one," he said.

The Robber Baron nodded once, then stared at Jazz, considering. "That's not really my concern," he said.

"Did the man—?" She couldn't stop herself. "Did Mr. Ferazzoli . . . die?" she asked.

The Robber Baron smiled and stroked his waxed beard with a silky glove. "I don't imagine you'll be seeing him again," he said. He tapped on the crystal ball. "Does this give you insight?" he asked. He gestured at the jars and general décor of the room. "Does this?"

She shook her head. "No," she said. "It's just me." With him sitting down, looking up at her, she could see his eyes. They were a washed-out blue, nearly gray, like storm clouds. "What do you want from me?" she asked. "What can I do to reassure you that I'm no threat to you?"

And then he surprised her. "Oh, I'm not worried that you're a threat," he said, his voice amused. "Tony's story of you—he was distracted when he told it to me, but he was nonetheless very detailed, very discerning— intrigued me. Tony Ferazzoli had many people to fear for many reasons and yet he focused that fear on me, on your word. Because of your insight. He shouldn't have been afraid of me—I'd been careful to allay any fears—and yet you persuaded him. He tried to run away and he very nearly succeeded. On your word."

"I'm sorry—" she began.

"Oh, no. I am most curious about your insights," he said. "You see, someone is betraying me. And I'd like you to tell me who that is."

———————

Jazz ultimately, with great difficulty, convinced the Robber Baron and his trained killers to leave her home.

She tried desperately at first to find some way to appease him, to get a flash of whoever was betraying him and to give him what he wanted. She would have little compunction about exposing someone in that way, if it could save her from the Robber Baron's attentions. When she felt nothing—nothing—that gave her any idea of who was betraying the man and why, she pressed him for more details. Why did he think he was being betrayed? What led to his suspicions? He shook his head and said, "It shouldn't work that way, Jessica." Her real name sounded, somehow, terrifying to her. "You need to tell me *your* insights, not vice versa."

She briefly considered making something up. She knew enough from the papers to blurt out the names of a few people who worked for him. She could even have named Gork or Osprey, though both looked ready to leap forward and murder her at any moment. But she ultimately decided against lying. Too much could go wrong.

And so she finally convinced him that, though her insight hadn't come yet, she would persist. Soon, she told him. She would have his answer soon. And he nodded at her, the genteel manner gone from his face, his expression empty and pitiless. "Soon," he echoed. "It will have to be soon." He didn't bother to elaborate on the threat implicit in the words.

After they left, Gork's lashless eyes running up and down her body as he slowly closed the door, she stamped out the rest of her incense, staggered to the bathroom, and, weeping, lowered her face to the sink. She turned the faucet on cold and let the water run onto her scalp and the back of her neck. She stared at the mirror, then, thinking, calculating.

Sometimes Jazz was filled with a mystical certainty about the future. Tonight certainty filled her again, though of a less supernatural sort. She knew that she was going to die, horribly and very soon, unless she could find some means of protection against the Robber Baron.

And she thought of Cain Ducett.

Clean up the Cape. Elect Warren Sims D.A.
— A campaign bumper sticker

TWELVE

On paper or in person, Warren Sims, district attorney of Devil's Cape, didn't seem like the type of man to get a group of heroes murdered. But he did.

A handsome black man in his mid-thirties, a quarter Puerto Rican, lean and muscular from an intense tennis regimen—he could have gone professional, the commercials said, if he hadn't been so focused on putting bad people into jail—Sims had come to Devil's Cape from Miami and taken a position as an assistant district attorney, earning one of the highest conviction records Pirate Town had ever seen. He'd subsequently been elected D.A. off of a "clean up the corruption" campaign that had made pointed references to the Robber Baron and the Ferazzoli and Kalodimos machines. During the election and beyond, he grabbed the city's attention and respect.

When Sims was A.D.A., the Robber Baron tested the waters through proxies and found the prosecutor essentially incorruptible. He had no close family and was a bachelor. He was vice-free and fearless. When he wasn't working cases or playing tennis, he was sponsoring school fundraisers or taking up a hammer to help build houses for the homeless. So although the crime lord himself lost little sleep when Sims was elected D.A., the criminals who worked for him worried. It was hopeless to try to intimidate or bribe him, the Robber Baron's men told him.

"I could have him whacked," Tony Ferazzoli said.

"The school fundraisers," Costas Kalodimos said, "I could put him in a room with a young boy, make it look bad, run him out of town."

The Robber Baron had smiled at their enthusiasm and shaken his head. Instead, he had looked deeper into the background of D.A. Warren Sims and found a college sweetheart, the one who got away. Her name was Hope. She was still single, a human resources manager in Charlotte, North Carolina, who had reached a plateau at her company and had begun sending out résumés. And so the Robber Baron found her a job in Devil's Cape—a good one, but not so good as to be unbelievable. He'd never tried to corrupt her. He never even met her. All he did was reach out from the shadows, get her a job that she was well-qualified for, and make sure that she was invited to one of the same parties as Warren Sims. That was all it took.

Six months after the party, Sims married his old sweetheart, marveling at the good fortune that had brought her back into his life. Three months after that, they were expecting their first child. And then the Robber Baron had his lever.

July, three years ago

The Robber Baron laid it out for Warren Sims one warm July evening. Sims was walking out of the courthouse to his car. The air outside Government Center was thick with humidity, and the district attorney's shirt, crisp and white that morning, was now wrinkled. His gray blazer was tossed over one shoulder, his tie was loose, and perspiration showed under his arms. He was walking briskly, probably intent on getting home to his pregnant wife.

He took note of the limousine parked next to his own car, a dark-blue Chrysler, but brushed past it, concentrating on pulling his keys out a pants pocket and no doubt

looking forward to getting the air conditioner running.

The Robber Baron rolled down the tinted window beside his seat and Sims turned with a start. His eyes narrowed when he recognized the other man's scarlet mask, but if he felt any fear, he didn't show it. "Baron," he said, turning to face the other car fully and dropping his keys back into his pocket, "why don't you take that mask off and face me like a grown-up?"

The Robber Baron smiled. He reached a gloved hand up as though to pull off the mask, but instead simply scratched at the corner of his eye. "I prefer my air of mystery," he said. He dropped his hand back down, then opened the car door and stepped out, pulling a shiny brass cane with him. He swept his cape across his back and stood, leaning slightly on the cane, shutting the door firmly. Behind him, the window he had rolled down raised back up as the chauffer thumbed the button. "You don't have much tolerance for mystery, do you, Mr. Sims?"

Sims shrugged, his neck muscles tense. "I don't have much tolerance for crime," he said. "What is it you want?"

The Robber Baron feigned surprise. "Why, it's a lovely evening," he said. "The grackles are darting to and fro, the sunset is fusing streaks of rose and orange and purple into a collage, and I believe I can smell someone grilling peppers and pork sausages nearby." He inhaled deeply. "I thought we could take a walk together."

Sims was obviously in no mood for a stroll, but he'd had few opportunities to meet the Robber Baron face to face. He sighed, then nodded once. He unlocked his car door, tossed the blazer inside, and swung the door shut.

A tall Hispanic woman in a floral dress, a briefcase in her hand, stopped short when she spotted them. Her heels clicked on the sidewalk.

The Robber Baron swept off his hat and bowed to her. "Good evening," he said.

She smiled and waved back, blushing. "Good evening, Mr. Baron," she said. She stepped quickly out of the way and headed down the street. They soon heard her on her cell phone. "Guess who I just saw," she said. "No! Guess . . ."

Sims snorted.

At first, the two men didn't speak as they walked down North Sanderson Street toward the heart of Government Center. The buildings on North Sanderson Street dated nearly to the city's founding. Granite slabs fronted the buildings, which were decorated here and there with different colors of marble. Many of the materials used to decorate the city, particularly in the first few decades after its founding, were stolen from Spanish, French, Dutch, and British merchant ships. The results sometimes seemed haphazard since the pirates founding the city made do with what fortune and theft brought them. For example, half of the old mercantile building was decorated with pink marble, the other half with white. And the rooftop of the Devil's Cape Public Library featured half a dozen angel statues flanked by a pair of gargoyles. But the older streets carried a certain charm.

Devil's Cape's Castelo Branco City Courthouse featured a spectacular stained glass window depicting the Great Flood. It had been commissioned for a cathedral in St. John's, Antigua, but the masked pirate St. Diable had taken it as part of the plunder seized from a British ship he raided in 1733. There had been talk over the years of returning it to Antigua, but nothing ever came of it, and the finely detailed design was featured on many postcards of the city. That evening, the window glimmered with the orange light of the sunset that the Robber Baron had praised.

"What do you want, Baron?" Sims asked again. The sidewalk was crowded with office workers heading home for the night or moving toward one of the dozens of bars at the edge of Government Center. The prosecutor and the crime lord were going against the flow.

The Robber Baron took a few more steps, leaning slightly on his brass cane as he walked. People turned and gaped at him as they drew near. Several made a point of giving him a wide berth, yet others nodded to him in respect. A police officer walking by tipped his hat, then noticed Sims and turned quickly in the other direction. "Most people seem to like me better than you do," the Robber Baron said, coming to a stop.

Sims shook his head, reaching up and wiping sweat away from his eyes. "They're afraid of you," he said. "You and your mask."

The Robber Baron smiled. He squinted toward the sunset and raised the head of his cane until it sparkled in the dying sunlight. "You have a thing against masks," he said.

Sims started walking again. "No one has any business hiding his identity," he said.

The Robber Baron began walking again, his cane clicking against the sidewalk. "The courts disagree, don't they?" he asked. "Take the precedent set in *City of Miami v. Trainwreck*." He stopped talking for a moment as though surprised, touching the tip of his beard with his knuckles. "Why, that was your case, wasn't it? And you lost?"

The district attorney snorted. "So you've read up on me," he said. "That's fine. I've done the same on you. You've been much subtler than the Hangman was. The details of your life and your crimes are much better hidden. But I'll get you anyway." They walked under a series of buildings decorated with gargoyles, their claws and wings outstretched, their mouths gaping. "I'll send you to jail, mask or no mask."

The Robber Baron nodded as though in agreement. "As I said, you do not like me much."

"No."

"And this walk is not going to make you like me any more."

"Probably not."

"But we will come to an agreement tonight," the Robber Baron said.

Sims stopped. The shadow of a gargoyle stretched across him, the edge of one of its wings striping his face.

"I doubt that," he said. "Are you going to threaten me now?" he asked. "Is that what this is about? If I don't back off, you'll have me killed?"

"No," the Robber Baron said simply. He reached his hand into a velvet pocket in his waistcoat. He brought up a small device not much larger than his palm. It had a video screen—the image of the glowing gadget incongruous against his silk glove and the rest of his antique finery. "I'm not here to threaten you," he continued. He held up the device, tilting the screen so that Sims could see it. "I'm here to threaten her."

Sims exhaled softly then, almost a sigh, and his shoulders slumped. He reached lethargically for the object and stared at the screen. He could see his wife in their house. She was in the room they were preparing for the baby, standing on one of their dining room chairs, patiently spreading a wallpaper border with little ducks on it across the top edge of the wall. As he watched her spread glue across the back of the border with a plastic spatula, he noticed a tiny red dot on the screen. It began on her temple, then slowly made its way down her chest, finally settling on her belly, right about where their child was growing. At first he thought it was something being displayed on the screen, something there to intimidate him further, as though he needed that. But then he saw her bend down and brush at her belly as though swatting a bug. The light moved away then, and she returned to the wallpaper, but the light quickly returned, running down the side of her face again, and finally settling once more on her belly. He knew then that the light was a laser scope. There was a gun trained on her.

The Robber Baron cleared his throat, breaking the silence apologetically. "This is something called real-time streaming video, I'm told," he said. "Any delay between what you see on the screen and reality is so slight as to be meaningless." He took the device back and dropped it back into his pocket. "We can achieve this"—he broke off, searching for the right words—"sense of intimacy at any time.

District Attorney Warren Sims stared at a crack in the sidewalk. A tuft of grass was breaking through. He had stopped sweating. "All right," he said, his voice cracking as though his throat were dry. "I'll quit."

The Robber Baron chuckled. "Oh, no," he said, clapping Sims on the shoulder as though they were old friends. "That's the last thing in the world I want." He tapped his cane on the sidewalk. "Your predecessor never saw a bribe he didn't take. He was a fawning sycophant. Useful, of course. But there were no teeth there. Everyone assumed, more or less correctly, that he was a marionette and I held the strings. You, on the other hand . . ." He chuckled again. "You hate me. You made it clear when you were elected that you were gunning for me and you have the credibility of a zealot. When you do my bidding, no one will suspect it and you will be infinitely more useful to me because of it."

Sims shook his head. He looked smaller, as though he'd lost weight and grown stooped and old all in the space of a few heartbeats. "I'd rather die," he said.

"Oh, no," the Robber Baron said. "No, you won't be doing that. Because if you kill yourself to escape me, I'll kill her anyway. Horribly, of course, to make the point to anyone else who finds himself in your situation." He shook his head. "If you leave town, I'll find you and kill her. If you kill yourself, I'll kill her. If you defy me, I'll kill her. And your child, too, once it's born. The only possible option you have is to do whatever I say, when I say it." He patted Sims on the shoulder. "I'll give you small victories, Warren," he said. "You'll still triumph from time to time." A bus chugged by, black exhaust billowing out. The sun sank finally behind the horizon. "It won't all be terrible," the Robber Baron concluded.

But it was terrible, of course. Warren Sims was free to pursue anyone unaffiliated with the Robber Baron. In fact, the Robber Baron made the convictions of those who opposed him nearly a foregone conclusion. But Sims was dead inside. Even the scent of his baby daughter's hair seemed tinged with ashes. Every moment with his

new family was shrouded by his fear of what the Robber Baron could do to them. He had no more free will.

———————

Five hours ago

So when the Storm Raiders, the heroes of Vanguard City, contacted the district attorney's office to inform Warren Sims of their plan to come to Devil's Cape to arrest a long-forgotten band of carnival freaks reported to have joined the Robber Baron's employ, it took the highly respected, reputedly incorruptible Sims less than five minutes to get the details to the Robber Baron. If it was a decision that would haunt him for the rest of his life, it wasn't the first.

Police in Montevideo are still searching for clues in the gruesome deaths of an American business-man and his entourage. "It was the worst thing I ever saw," said a police source who refused to be named. "The American was bitten to death by some kind of wild animal. One of his bodyguards was burned to death, a second had a crushed skull, and his secretary was strangled." Three months have passed since . . .

— The Associated Press, Montevideo,
twenty-one years ago

THIRTEEN

Devil's Cape, Louisiana
Three hours ago

*l*odged amid a parched concrete landscape of ware-houses and industrial buildings called Gray Flats, Butler's Billiards had never been a draw for Devil's Cape's tourists. A neighborhood fixture since the late 1950s, the pool hall usually pulled in a small after-work crowd, which was quickly reduced to an anemic group of regulars by dinnertime. For the past week, though, even the regulars had been giving the place a wide berth. A new element had moved in.

"I am tiring of this place," Errando Geringer said. He idly flicked cigarette ashes onto the green velvet of Butler's newest pool table, watching as one hot orange ash faded to gray.

His companion, who was bent over his cue, preparing to sink the seven ball in a side pocket, raised his head and gave Geringer a dark look. "So leave," he said flatly, standing so that his heavy paunch pressed against the side of the table. Hector Nelson Poteete didn't look like much. He was only about five-foot-seven, his thin red hair turning to gray, his weight heavy around his stomach. But Geringer knew he could melt steel in his hands if he wanted to. He could burn Geringer into ashes without even stopping to set down the pool cue.

Geringer's nose wrinkled. "This place stinks of piss and cigarettes." He brushed a long lock of greasy brown

hair out of his face. The fact that he was smoking himself didn't seem to occur to him.

"So leave," Poteete said again. The stick slammed into the cue ball, which slammed into the seven ball, which slammed into the pocket. But the cue ball rolled off to the wrong side of the table, and Poteete's next shot would be much more difficult. He grunted and reached for the chalk.

Geringer dragged on his cigarette, exhaling through his nose. He opened his mouth, then closed it. "Hector—" he said.

Poteete walked to the other side of the table, bent to look at the layout of the balls. "Just spit it out," he said. "Whatever it is, you've been dancing around it for an hour and a half and I'm sick of goddamn waiting. Spit it out."

Geringer ground the cigarette out against the side of the pool table. The veneer smoldered and turned black. "Why'd you bring us here, Hector?"

Poteete looked around the room. The other people in the pool hall, even the bartender, shifted nervously under his gaze and looked away. The jukebox in the corner kicked into some country song, and the man standing by it jumped guiltily as Poteete's eyes cut toward him.

"I don't mean this place, Hector," Geringer said quietly. "I mean Devil's Cape."

Poteete turned back to the pool table. He lined himself up for a bank shot, grunted, hit the cue ball, and shook his head in disappointment as it careened into the eleven and nothing went anywhere close to any of the pockets. "We've been a lot of places," he said.

Geringer didn't reach for his cue. He put his hands in his pockets and just stood there looking at Poteete. Tall, slender, and masculine, Geringer would have looked like he belonged on a magazine cover except that there was something missing in his gray eyes.

"What?" Poteete said.

Geringer tilted his head. "Please don't blow me off," he said. "You know this is different."

Poteete and Geringer and the rest of the *Cirque d'Obscurité* had been a lot of places. After they were exposed in Vanguard City, they'd gone to Rio de Janeiro. Then Sao Paulo, Montevideo, and up and down South America. After that, there'd been the Caribbean. Then Africa for a time. Eastern Europe. Thailand and Malaysia. Perth for a few days before the Aussies had chased them off. They'd spent a while in Germany and Austria, where Geringer had been the only one to speak the language. He'd liked that. They'd been back to America a few times, but never for long. And here they were in Devil's Cape, just a few miles from Langdon Fork, where they'd been changed. And they were doing something that they'd never done before. They were growing roots.

Poteete sighed and blew smoke out of his mouth, although he didn't have any cigarettes. "I expect a lot of questions out of Stecker," he said. "But not out of you." He set the pool cue down on the side of the table. "I bring you along because I know you won't drag me down with a lot of unnecessary questions."

They both knew this bullshit. He brought Geringer along because they were the only ones who could pass for normal.

Geringer shrugged. He picked up his own cue and walked around the table. He barely took the time to line up, but pulled off a double bank shot, sinking the fifteen ball into a corner pocket and lining himself up just right for a shot at the eleven ball. "Everyone's wondering," he said. "We run for more than twenty years and then we stop running and you don't even talk about it with us?" He sent the eleven into one side pocket and the twelve into the other with a single shot. "Sasha's got family not ten miles from here, but she doesn't know what to do about it. Stecker's—" he shrugged again. "You know him. Things he does, only reason we haven't had more trouble over him is we move on so fast no one has a chance to take measures. And now we're even on the TV."

Poteete was looking at the table, his eyes unfocused. "I'm tired of running," he said. A black waitress in a

denim miniskirt and a low-cut, tight blue T-shirt that read COME BREAK YOUR BALLS AT BUTLER'S BILLIARDS walked by, carrying a beer to someone else, but Poteete snatched it off her tray. She started to say something but walked away quickly when she saw his expression. He watched her legs, then turned back to the pool table and sipped at the beer. "Moving around was a kind of insurance," he said. "I think I'm getting us another kind of insurance."

Geringer tapped a pocket with his cue, then tipped the eight ball toward it. The ball spun languidly, teetering at the edge, then dropped inside. "With the Robber Baron?"

Poteete smiled, swallowing more beer and then wiping froth from his beard with the back of his hand. "Opportunity knocks," he said. He nodded at the table. "Another game?"

With a frown, Geringer reached for the rack and began placing the balls inside. The waitress walked back in their direction—one of the selling points of the place was that the waitresses would set up the balls for the players, generally bending over to do so with exaggerated slowness—but he waved her off. He was sliding the rack back and forth on the top of the table, packing the balls together tight, when he saw someone walking up to the table.

"Werewolf?" the man whispered.

Geringer turned quickly and gripped the man's arm tight, his fingernails digging into the undersides of the man's wrist. "Don't say that name here, dumbass," he said.

It was Nick Kalodimos, son of Costas Kalodimos, who was one of the Robber Baron's top cronies. Geringer smelled fear on him. And curry. But despite the pain, despite the fear, Nick Kalodimos met his eyes. "I'm here on orders," he said. "A message." He was tall and thick-necked, with buzz-cut black hair and olive skin. He was wearing jeans and a tight black T-shirt that showed off his muscles. He was proud of those muscles. He looked over at Poteete. "You know who from."

Poteete took a swig of his beer. He smiled a little. Geringer realized that he was quite satisfied about something. Politics, he figured. The Robber Baron sending Costas Kalodimos's son to give them a message, that was a compliment to the *Cirque d'Obscurité,* a slap in the face to the Kalodimos family. Nick Kalodimos was feeling it, too. Despite his swagger, he was angry to be there on this errand. "Yeah," said Poteete. "So tell us what you've got."

Nick smiled then, a little of the fear dying off, replaced by satisfaction. "There are some people coming into town tonight looking for you—you and your buddies," he said. He pulled his arm away from Geringer, glancing down at the streaks of blood on his arm from Geringer's nails, trying to be nonchalant about it. "They're gunning for you," he said. "So the big man, he wants you to be prepared." He made a point of sticking his thumbs in the pockets of his jeans, ignoring the cuts. "The Storm Raiders are coming for you," he said.

An hour after dusk, our sails furled and our oars quiet in the waters, we found ourselves looking upon the fortress of the masked devil St. Diable. Some of the men were afraid and prayed to Heaven. But we pressed on, for we sorely wanted to send Diable to gaol or to Hell. And then St. Diable and his men attacked from the darkness, running their ship into ours and climbing upon us. They were more like a kennel of hounds than men. They threw stinkpots and granado shells ahead of them, then ran in screaming with axes, cutlasses, knives, and pistols. I saw the masked madman himself run Captain Crabb through with his sword. I called out to God and dived into the water . . .

— Excerpted from
The Sea Journal of Hamilton Grubbs,
Written by Himself, 1731

FOURTEEN

*T*he small cluster of buildings and the short runway that made up Fyke General Aviation Airport were poised at the far north end of Devil's Cape, not far from Worldwide Papyrus's Fyke paper mill. Built in 1955 by a club of flying enthusiasts, the airport had waxed and waned over the decades since, with the hard times nearly always shadowing the good. It still had a flurry of traffic during the daytime—mostly people taking flying lessons or the occasional Devil's Cape businessman who chose not to use the Devil's Cape Lakeside Airport or Sebastian Hebert International Airport. At night, though, it was almost always quiet.

Not this night. This night was chaos.

The Storm Raiders, the superheroes of Vanguard City, nicknamed "America's Super Team," had landed their specialized aircraft at the Fyke airport shortly after dusk amidst no fanfare. Within minutes, they'd been murdered.

Now the small airport was a cacophony of emergency workers, reporters, gawkers, and mourners. Firefighters had extinguished the tiny inferno that had been the Storm Raiders' plane, and fire trucks stood with flashing lights on either side of the blackened wreckage like bodyguards with no one to protect. Dozens of police cars had swept into the area, as had television trucks, ambulances,

and cars of "interested parties," including the mayor and his entourage. None were parked in regular parking spaces. They were spread across the parking lot, scattered here and there up and down the runway, sprawled on the grass like late night picnickers. Three helicopters, two of them from national news outlets, swept back and forth overhead, jostling for position, their spotlights streaking across the disaster below, searching for new angles, new footage to transmit to a shocked and riveted public.

The air was hot and moist, and the scent of the fire lingered in the air. To Jason Kale, formerly Jason Kalodimos, it hadn't been an unpleasant smell at first—at least until he stopped to think about what he was smelling. Then it became sickening. He was a television crime reporter and he'd covered fires before, but this was different. This was malevolent.

Jason had seen a lot since that night with David Dees nearly twenty years earlier. Jason had been the wild child then, playing at being a thug, playing at being the "bad son." But the violence of that night, the violence that Julian, the golden child, had showed so quickly and with so little remorse, had changed them both. Jason had drawn back, distanced himself from every member of the Kalodimos family except his father, started paying more attention at school and spending most of his free time hanging around his father's restaurant, silently trying to make amends for what he had done.

Julian, on the other hand, had found the violence exhilarating and unfettering. Suddenly, he was the one working for Uncle Costas, and seemingly going further with it than Jason ever had. He still hid their powers, but more than once, Jason spotted his brother with blood on his clothes, or found people turning away from him in fear. One spring day not long after their seventeenth birthday, Jason went into a Korean donut shop for some kolaches and the owner, a heavy, wrinkled man named Nah Jin, soiled himself at the sight of him. Tears of fear and shame ran down the man's cheeks and he wordlessly waved his hands like fragile birds until Jason finally

turned and left the store, a half-uttered apology on his lips, realizing that Nah Jin had mistaken him for his brother.

Their mother, Desma, had died of a heart attack when the boys were ten, and their father had always treated them equally until Jason's flirtation with the "family business" had begun. The tension between Jason and his father had grown, until the air around them seemed filled with static electricity whenever they were in the same room. Even after the transformations brought on by the murder of David Dees, it had taken years for Jason's relationship with his father to heal; Pericles seemed alternately to ignore Julian's behavior and to blame Jason for it.

Jason and Julian, who once were inseparable, sometimes even sharing the same dreams or sensations—once, Jason had suddenly felt the overwhelming taste of oranges on his tongue, only to learn later that Julian had been eating one at that very moment—grew more and more uncomfortable in each other's presence. Both attended college in Devil's Cape, Jason majoring in broadcast journalism and Julian in business law, but their circles were separate, and they took to wearing their hair differently to avoid being confused for each other. Jason had started wearing glasses he didn't need.

When Jason had begun his career as an investigative journalist for WTDC News, he'd changed his name to Kale to keep people from making the connection between him and his family. He'd even done stories on members of the Kalodimos family, although he avoided those when possible. He'd received no retribution, though most of his family avoided him now. He wondered if his father's influence had protected him, or if perhaps Julian was responsible.

"You figure we'll be here all night?"

Jason had been staring at the wreckage, watching police crews taking pictures of the carnage. Two of them were chuckling over some joke and it made him want to throttle them. He turned around to see Dexter Koo, the WTDC cameraman working with him that evening. "Probably so," he answered. He nodded at the laughing crime scene technicians. "Get a little footage of them, will you?"

Koo shrugged. "Y'okay," he said, raising the camera to his shoulder. In his late forties, Koo was of medium height and weight, with long hair that stretched halfway down his back. He usually tied it off at neck level with a rubber band. He had a wispy moustache and was a perpetual gum chewer. "You're always making me get shots like this that we'll never use," he said, smacking the gum. He didn't sound angry, just bored. One of the worst assassinations in the history of the world and Koo was blasé about it. Jason wondered sometimes just what it would take to ignite a fire in Dexter Koo.

"We might use it for B-roll," Jason said.

Koo shrugged the shoulder that didn't have a camera on it. He was adept at performing a wide range of activities without making a sound or moving the camera as much as a quarter inch from where he wanted it to be. After a few seconds, he nodded to Jason. "Got it," he said. "I'll keep an eye on them in case they high-five each other or something." He smiled, purple gum showing between his teeth.

Jason was looking at the mass of lights and the wreckage, at the bodies of the Storm Raiders strewn around. The police hadn't covered them up. He wondered if even the really good cops of Devil's Cape resented the fact that the Storm Raiders had come to the city to clean up a mess that they'd failed to take care of themselves. "It was the *Cirque d'Obscurité,*" Jason said.

"Yeah?" Koo was only mildly curious.

"Yeah," Jason said. He turned toward Koo and nodded for the cameraman to record him. Jason was tall and muscular, his skin darkly tanned, his brown hair wavy. He'd been told that the clear-lensed glasses he wore made him look distinguished and educated. The producers had tried to get him to wear contacts, but he'd put them off. The glasses made him look less like Julian, and that was what was important to him about them. This night, he'd taken off the navy blazer he'd been wearing and had thrown it in the WTDC truck. He'd rolled up the blue sleeves of his shirt, but hadn't loosened the dark brown tie he wore. He stared into the camera, not sure what to say at first. Finally, he just began to talk. "Devil's Cape is a very different city than Vanguard City," he said. "Vanguard City was named for a hero, Devil's Cape for a pirate. Vanguard City glistens with chrome and is said to be the cleanest city in the world. Devil's Cape wallows in darkness and corruption, and its streets are perpetually choked with smog." He saw Koo raise his eyebrows behind the camera, but barreled on. "Vanguard City has heroes, but Devil's Cape has criminals. And when Vanguard City sent its Storm Raiders to Devil's Cape, Devil's Cape murdered them."

Koo lowered the camera. "Well, shit," he said. "Now there's some more footage we won't be using. You realize we work for a Devil's Cape TV station, yeah?"

Jason waved it away. "It's late and I'm mad," he said. "Eighty-five percent of what I say tonight is likely to be crap."

Koo shrugged and raised the camera again. He blew a bubble, then popped it. "Do me a favor and keep it to sixty-eight percent crap like usual, okay?"

Jason looked at the wreckage again, then back to the camera. He nodded for Koo to resume filming. "The last confirmed combat death for the Storm Raiders was twenty-two years ago in Vanguard City," he said, "when the third Doctor Camelot fell in battle to the carnival troupe called the *Cirque d'Obscurité,* a group allegedly spotted in Devil's Cape several times in recent weeks. The membership of the Storm Raiders has changed little since that time. A new person reportedly assumed the mantle of the Swashbuckler six years ago, and Velociraptor retired two years later, replaced by the Winged Tornado. But until tonight, the team remained essentially unchanged for more than two decades, a consistency practically unheard of in the superhero community, well-known for its shake-ups."

Over Koo's shoulder, Jason saw a heavyset man in a tan suit approaching. He sighed. "Take five, Dexter," he said.

Koo flicked the camera off, glanced at the man walking up, and made the gum in his teeth snap. "Y'okay," he said. He set the camera in their van, made a point of locking the door, and looked with distaste at the big man who had walked up to Jason. "I'll go see if the cops left anything in the vending machines," he said to Jason, then walked away, whistling the song "Officer Krupke" from *West Side Story*.

Jason nodded resignedly at the fat man. "Sergeant Bilbray," he said.

Dustin Bilbray wiped his florid face with a thick handkerchief he pulled from a jacket pocket. "Mr. Kalodimos," he said. "Always a pleasure to be approached by the media."

Bilbray had been the one doing the approaching, but Jason let that part of the statement go. "It's Kale now, sergeant," he reminded the man.

Bilbray nodded, his jowls shaking. "Yeah, yeah," he said. "'Course. That's for the cameras, I know." He raised his eyes to Jason's, his expression cunning. "But we both know who your family is."

It wasn't worth an argument, Jason thought. He stared at the disaster area. The police had set up a perimeter with a series of uniformed officers and orange cones. It was ostensibly to protect the crime scene, but with more than a dozen cops inside the cones, plus the mayor and an aide and the district attorney, it was clear it was more for show than anything else. Everyone knew what had happened. Everyone knew who'd ordered it. Everyone knew it would be a cold day in hell before anything much was done about it.

Jason could see pretty well at night, as well as over long distances. Extraordinarily well, actually. It was one of the abilities he and Julian had. He saw a police officer nearly trip over the boot of Patriot, the leader of the Storm Raiders, the rest of her body hidden by tall grass.

The officer looked down at her, contempt and anger on his face, and kicked her leg. He looked up suddenly to see if anyone had noticed him, and Jason forced his gaze away. "Sergeant," he said, "do you suppose you could do me a favor and get me a look inside there?" He nodded at the area inside the cones.

Bilbray patted himself with the handkerchief again. He whistled softly. He was a notorious suck-up, always on the lookout for an advantage or, better yet, a bribe. Jason's Uncle Costas had joked about him one night at Zorba's. "That coonass Bilbray," he'd said, "when he was born, the first thing that came out of his mother was his hand." He'd pantomimed this, to the laughter of several of his men.

"I'd owe you a favor," Jason said.

Bilbray looked after Koo. "No camera," he said.

"No camera."

"No messing with the crime scene."

"Of course not."

"Five hundred," Bilbray said.

Jason looked at him. Devil's Cape never ceased to amaze him. The brazenness of it. He'd have trouble getting it reimbursed. With the camera, it wouldn't be a problem, but five hundred dollars just to walk through there? But he needed to go in. It pulled at him. He needed to see these people, what had been done to them. "Okay," he said.

Bilbray ran the handkerchief under his chin, then wadded it up and stuck it back in his pocket. He leaned in close to Jason, crooked his head at the crime scene, and lowered his voice to a whisper. "Come on."

Bilbray walked nonchalantly between two cones, nodding at a uniformed police officer standing there, and Jason followed him. Jason kept his eyes down, not making a deal out of it, not forcing anyone to acknowledge his presence. The roar of the helicopters overhead was giving Jason a headache.

The first body they came to was Swashbuckler's, some thirty feet from the plane. He wore the sort of blousy ruffled shirt that Errol Flynn might have worn in a pirate film, pale blue and open low in front with ties stretched across his muscular chest. He wore high, heavy red gloves and flexible knee-high pirate boots over black pants. A red mask covered his entire face except for his eyes, which stared glassily at the helicopters overhead. There was no blood, but each of his arms and legs had been broken multiple times. They were bent in jagged angles like a doll worked over with a hammer.

Jason spotted thick furrows in the grass between the plane and Swashbuckler's body. There was dirt and grass in the heels of his boots. He'd been dragged from the plane and had dug his feet in more than once trying to stop it. Like his predecessor, the hero lacked any superhuman powers that anyone was aware of. They were trained acrobats and specialists in savate, a French martial art that combined aspects of boxing with kicking maneuvers. The force that had pulled him forward was strong and fast and implacable.

"Kraken," Jason whispered.

"What's that?" Bilbray cupped one ear. "Damn helicopters," he said.

Jason shook his head. "Nothing," he said.

Jason had seen photographs of Kraken of the *Cirque d'Obscurité,* and video footage of the group's long-ago battle with the Storm Raiders in Vanguard City, when Doctor Camelot had died. Kraken was a revolting, hairless figure, his skin dry and smooth and scaly like a snake's. His body was fluid, bending and curving like a dancing cobra, unhindered by the limitations of joints or the angularity of bone. And he could stretch. In the battle on Vanguard City's Roscoe Clay Bridge, he had reached one arm across three lanes of traffic to snatch a hostage off of a motorcycle.

In his imagination, Jason could see the Swashbuckler's death. The young man had jumped gracefully out of the plane onto the runway, and Kraken had reached out from the grass, not far from where Jason now stood, grabbing him without warning. Maybe by an arm, maybe by the waist. Kraken had dragged him forward. Swashbuckler had dug his heels into the ground, trying to gain leverage and stop the motion, but he'd been dragged along regardless. He'd struggled to free himself, but with no leverage, no joints to press against. The Kraken's arms had coiled around him again and again, first around the legs, then the arms, and finally the neck, the crack of his bones breaking sounding like a row of dominoes going down.

"I bet he was a little light in the loafers, you know what I mean," Bilbray said, peering down at the broken hero.

Jason looked at him.

"You know, that shirt, that outfit."

Jason wished he could close Swashbuckler's eyes for him. The smell of the fire was beginning to die off as the normal smells of Devil's Cape pushed through. Rotting vegetation and decay from the swamp, pollution from the cars and the factories, the sulfurous odor of the paper mill, a hint of flowers blooming somewhere in the distance.

"I'll look into that," Jason said dryly. "For my report." He chewed on the inside of his cheek, almost asked Bilbray if he could quote him on that, but there wasn't any point in antagonizing the man. They weren't done here yet.

Bilbray smiled. Two of his front teeth were cracked and streaked with brown. "You got a good sense of humor," he said. "Take after your uncle."

God, I hope not, Jason thought.

The sergeant's smile widened. "Hey," he said. "You like pancakes?"

Jason raised his eyebrows, but didn't answer.

"Come here," Bilbray said. He led Jason over to the tarmac, then gestured expansively at what looked at first to be a pile of rubbish in the middle of a cracked pothole in the runway.

It was the Winged Tornado.

"Maybe waffle is a better word here," Bilbray said, chuckling to himself, "or sausage patty." But his amusement died as he saw the look on Jason's face, and he dropped his eyes to the ground and shuffled from one foot to the other.

The Winged Tornado had been the newest member of the Storm Raiders, a tall young man with white, feathered wings like an angel's growing from his back. No one knew where the wings had come from or how they worked—the hero had defied physics as he soared through the sky at breathtaking speeds. He'd worn a light gray Kevlar uniform covered with swirling cloud patterns, a stylized tornado emblazoned on his chest. A gray mask covered the top half of his face, reinforced by a lightweight metallic helmet, thin and aerodynamic like a bicyclist might wear.

He was a flattened mess now, broken and shattered and bloody, hardly recognizable as having been human.

"There's one of the wings there," Bilbray said, more subdued, pointing farther down the runway where a crime scene technician was snapping photographs. "And the other one landed near the plane." He pointed again.

Each of the wings was intact, as wide as a tablecloth and nearly as flat. The feathers near the base of each wing where it had joined his back were red with gore, but the rest were pure white like a dove's.

Jason could imagine this death, too. When the heroes were attacked, the Winged Tornado had burst out of the vehicle and straight up into the air, flying up high to position himself to help his teammates below. But Osprey had been up there waiting for him.

The first reports of the *Cirque d'Obscurité* had mentioned sightings of a young girl with wings, but she had never been identified and hadn't participated in combat. But by the time the group was identified in Eastern Europe years later, that had changed. She was older and fiercer, bristling with knives. Special curved blades that extended from her gloves like talons. Long, triangular weapons called katars or Bundi daggers that she held by horizontal hand grips so that the razor-sharp blades sat above her knuckles, designed so that she could punch an enemy and drive the blade right into him. Bandoliers of slim throwing knives. If the Winged Tornado had resembled an angel, then she had resembled a cruel hawk. They called her Osprey and she was as deadly as any of them.

Jason pictured the Winged Tornado high in the night sky, not seeing Osprey swooping down toward him. She caught him there, clinging to his back with her talons and slashing with her knives. She severed his broad wings and they pinwheeled through the air like maple seeds. And then she simply let him fall hundreds of feet to the tarmac.

Jason tried not to think of the sound of the impact, tried not to wonder whether the hero had fallen silently and stoically to his death or had screamed all the way down.

He tried not to wonder whether he could have stopped all this, had he been there.

He closed his eyes, saying a silent prayer—he didn't know to whom or what—for the Winged Tornado and the others. When he opened his eyes again, he saw District Attorney Warren Sims watching him from another part of the runway. Their eyes met, and then the D.A. turned away. Jason saw him wipe his forehead with a trembling hand. His face was slack and as he walked onto the grass, his steps were unsteady. At least someone else gave a damn, Jason thought.

"You ready, for the next one, Mr. Kalodimos?"

Jason didn't correct the name this time. He just nodded.

They moved closer to the burned-out plane. Miss Chance lay sprawled on her back, a small red hole in the center of her forehead. Blood soaked into the dirt below her head, and if Jason had stepped to one side, he probably could have seen some of the damage that the bullet had done on its way out of her skull. He didn't.

In the mid-eighties, Miss Chance had been considered a sex symbol to rival Madonna. Girls around the world donned purple and green harlequin masks in imitation of her. She'd been notorious for her low-cut uniform, curvy figure, and big hair. Jason had had a Miss Chance poster in his room.

And now he stared sadly at her corpse. She was in her mid-forties by now, but must still have been beautiful. The uniform was less revealing now, and more practical. She'd worn an armored purple jacket over a purple-and-green-striped unitard that stretched to just below her knees. Left shoe green, right shoe purple. The gloves just the opposite. Gold hoop earrings, a touch of lipstick, and that famous mottled green and purple mask. Her hair was shorter than in her youth, her skin as smooth as porcelain. Her eyes were shut, but there was no illusion that she was asleep. She was dead. She was gone.

"They killed her first," Jason said.

"You think so?" Bilbray asked. He was curious, like he hadn't given it much thought, like figuring out exactly what had happened didn't much matter.

"She was the most dangerous," Jason said.

Bilbray bit off a laugh. It came out like a wheeze. "Come on," he said. "You've got Patriot who can bounce bullets off her tits and that Chink guy who can shoot lightning out of his ass . . ."

"Raiden was Japanese American," Jason said quietly. And of course the lightning could come from anywhere and usually came from the man's hands.

Bilbray pulled out the sweat-covered handkerchief and blew his nose loudly. "Whatever," he said. "Me, I'd probably take him out first, then the black girl." Patriot was black. She was also probably close to fifty. "Then maybe the dude with the wings and the faggot in the blouse." Jason just looked at him. Bilbray gestured at Miss Chance with his handkerchief and went on. "I'd save her and the little guy for last." By little guy, he meant Sam Small.

"Sergeant," Jason said, "I owe you a favor and I owe you five hundred dollars, but if you don't either shut the hell up right now or start talking about these men and women with some degree of respect, I'm going to find some way to hurt you very badly."

Bilbray stared back at him. His nostrils flared and

he stuck out his chest. He dropped the handkerchief, which fluttered down and landed against the side of Miss Chance's head. He balled his hands into fists. "I should—" He broke off, and Jason could feel him backing down. The chest dropped. The fists unclenched. The sergeant forced a laugh that sounded as artificial as a wind-up doll's. "Yeah," he said finally. "Yeah, you're a lot more like your uncle than I thought."

No, Jason thought. I'm a lot more like my father than you think. Instead, he looked back down at Miss Chance.

Bilbray followed the look and hurriedly snatched the handkerchief back up, shoving it into the depths of a pocket.

"She was supposed to use 'luck magic,' " Jason said. "She manipulated probability. She and her powers were unpredictable. One time, she was in a warehouse and there were fifteen hired gunmen there with rifles. She ended up with her back up against a wall and they lined up like a firing squad to kill her. Their rifles jammed. All fifteen at the same time. Most of them went for their sidearms, and those jammed, too. All but one of them, and he missed his shot. The ricochet came back and hit him in the chest. The rest of them gave up after that." Jason shook his head. "She was the most dangerous," he said again.

"This rifle didn't jam," Bilbray said. His tone was spiteful.

No, Jason thought. It didn't jam because she didn't know it was there. It was that shot that had announced the ambush.

Most of the *Cirque d'Obscurité* wouldn't use rifles, Jason figured. They had other tools at their disposal. But there was one man with them—they called him Gork for some reason—who was a mass of burn scars. No real powers that Jason knew of, except that he was supposed to be either impervious to pain or in so much pain all the time from his injuries that additional pain didn't make an impression on him. Kraken had waited nearby in the grass for the chance to grab someone, maybe planning to get Swashbuckler or maybe just seizing the first opportunity that came along. But Gork had been planted farther away, with a long-range rifle, a sniper scope, and one mission: to kill Miss Chance first. To take any luck out of the equation.

"How did they know?" Jason asked himself.

"What?" Bilbray's voice was still angry.

"This was a carefully planned ambush," he said. "How did they know when and where the Storm Raiders were going to be?"

Bilbray's smile was smug and tight. "This is an ongoing investigation," he said. "I can make no comment at this time."

Jason turned his back on him and walked closer to the plane.

Patriot's body lay close to the wreckage, curled on one side. Jason had known that she was big—"Amazonian" was a word often used to describe her in the press—but was still surprised at the sight of her. She must have been about seven feet tall, her body heavily muscular. She wore a flaglike uniform—blue boots; red pants; blue belt; a shirt half blue and half white, with half of a white star intruding into the blue; a blue and white mask that exposed her eyes, her mouth, and her forehead and hair; red gloves. Her skin was smooth and dark brown. She'd worn her hair long and in tight curls; the few white hairs stood in stark contrast to the black.

Patriot had been the leader of the team since Doctor Camelot had died more than twenty years earlier. She was bulletproof and could lift several tons, but the *Cirque d'Obscurité* had killed her.

Jason could see singe marks on the back of Patriot's uniform, and pieces of debris in her hair. She'd been outside of the plane when it had exploded. The force of it must have been incredible, but it hadn't been enough to throw her forward. There were no dirt stains on her knees or gloves, no marks in the ground to indicate that type of a fall.

Her neck was broken, her head twisted forward and to the right. Someone—it had to have been the Behemoth, the brutish strongman of the *Cirque d'Obscurité*—had come up behind her, perhaps even walking through the wreckage of the plane, and managed to snap her neck.

"Time to go," Bilbray said. His voice was tense.

Looking up, Jason could see the mayor and chief of police looking in their direction. He nodded politely at them, then turned to stare at the Storm Raiders' plane. Even though the fire crews had put out the fire, the heat coming off of the wreckage was sweltering. Hector Hell, he thought. The firemaker.

"Raiden?" Jason asked.

Bilbray chuckled a little despite his new urgency. "That nice aroma you smell isn't baby back ribs," he said. "It's him. Blast blew him apart, fire cooked him. They found his head. No question, really."

Jason sighed. He remembered images of he'd seen of the hero, who'd taken his name from a Japanese word meaning "thunder and lightning." Raiden had worn a maroon karategi, or karate uniform, with a thick royal blue obi, or belt, and a sort of golden mantle on his shoulders. He was thin and muscular, with long, black hair he kept in a ponytail. His entire body seemed to crackle with electric sparks. He had never worn a mask, but it hadn't seemed necessary, as the electricity that rippled across his body obscured his features. To Jason, Raiden had always seemed noble and brave, someone to emulate.

Something on the ground caught Jason's attention.

"We gotta go," Bilbray said. He put one hand on Jason's arm at the wrist and the other at the elbow. It was a police technique. He could look like he was escorting someone politely, but all he needed to do was apply a little extra pressure at the wrist to cause pain and get the person to move along.

Jason didn't budge. It would take someone far stronger than Dustin Bilbray to make Jason move when he didn't want to. Still, he didn't want to make a point out of it,

didn't want Bilbray to get an inkling of just how strong Jason really was. He twisted his arm out of the sergeant's grip and squatted near the ground. "Just a second," he said. A rusty coffee can lay on its side in the grass. Maxwell House. Good to the last drop. "What about Sam Small?" he asked.

Sam Small had been called the "six-inch man" because he had the ability to shrink himself to the size of a doll. He was shorter than his teammates even at full size, but athletically built, with thinning brown hair, tanned skin, and a ready smile. He wore a dark green uniform with brown leather gloves and boots, and reinforced leather padding at the shoulders and chest. His mask resembled a pair of green-tinted safety goggles, and he carried an assortment of tools on his belt. He was often underestimated, but his ability to strike from surprise and to use the size-changing ability to his advantage had helped his teammates often over the years. Even when at his smallest size, he was said to be able to lift as much—and hit as hard—as a full-sized man.

"Goddamn it," Bilbray said, "the chief is going to have my ass if I don't get you out of here."

The word was that the chief was a friend of the Robber Baron's. But that didn't mean that the chief had any allegiance to Costas Kalodimos. The Robber Baron often pitted his friends against each other. And even if the chief were friendly with Uncle Costas, that didn't mean that he would cut Jason any slack. And even if he cut Jason slack, it could be ugly for Bilbray. Jason looked up at Bilbray. "What about Sam Small?" he repeated.

Bilbray was sweating heavily. "Dead in the plane, we figure," he said. "No sign of him. Probably cinders."

Jason nodded and stood up. "All right," he said. "Let's go." And with one foot, he casually and carefully ground out any evidence of the tiny footprints he'd noticed in the dirt beside the coffee can. Sam Small, the six-inch hero, hadn't been in the plane when it exploded. He might not be dead at all. But the Devil's Cape police sure as hell didn't need to know that.

At the WTDC truck, Koo was crunching sour cream and onion potato chips and listening to a Nirvana CD. He'd stuck the purple bubble gum behind one ear. "You know, if you get special access to a crime scene, a camera can be handy. I'm just saying."

"Part of the deal," Jason said shortly.

"See anything good?"

Jason shook his head.

"We done here?"

"No. We might get some more footage. The D.A.'s here. I'm going to try to interview him."

Koo popped a chip into his mouth. He pointed. "Isn't that his car driving away?"

It was. Sims's tires squealed off into the darkness like he couldn't get away fast enough.

"Got a plan B?" Koo asked.

Jason stared at the floor of the truck. He saw the Winged Tornado falling from the sky, saw the tidy red hole in Miss Chance's forehead.

The *Cirque d'Obscurité*. Under orders from the Robber Baron. In a way, he'd been relieved to see evidence pointing to the carnival troupe—the methodology of the murders, the weapons used. Just last month, Jason had heard reports of a masked superhuman working for Costas Kalodimos. The masked man, who called himself Scion, had demonstrated powers just like Jason and Julian's—incredible strength and speed as well as flight. Jason had little doubt as to who the masked man was. But at least Julian hadn't been responsible for this. Jason couldn't imagine him working with others, particularly the *Cirque d'Obscurité*. Hector Hell and his teammates might work for the Robber Baron, and Uncle Costas might work for the Robber Baron, but Jason figured that they were rivals for power, regardless, just as the members of the Kalodimos crime organization were rivals with the Ferazzolis. "He plays them against each other," he said.

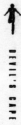

"What's that, ace?"

Jason looked at Koo. "Just figuring some things out," he said.

"Y'okay," Koo said. He stood up. "You do that." He crumpled the potato chip bag and tossed it on the floor of the truck. "I'm gonna stretch my legs and see if there's anything worth filming. You find something you want to point a camera at, you just shout, okay?" He pulled the gum from behind his ear, popped it back in his mouth, and climbed out of the truck, slamming the door behind him.

Jason took his glasses off and stared at them. The Storm Raiders had defended Vanguard City for decades. Devil's Cape had murdered them within seconds. In many ways, he thought, they had come to a city as foreign to them as any in the world. They didn't know how Devil's Cape worked.

If they'd landed in a crowd of people, if they'd let the public know that they were on their way, they might have had a chance. Instead, they'd landed in a remote airstrip usually deserted at night. And they'd told someone that they were coming. Someone who'd told the Robber Baron, who'd sent the *Cirque d'Obscurité*.

He wondered who the Storm Raiders had told. The mayor? The chief of police? The district attorney? A friend?

And what had they been doing here in the first place? That one was pretty easy.

There'd been a mysterious arson in the Silver Swan district, a heavily insured night club that had gone out of style and become a money pit, burned to the ground, with no cause identified. No accelerants used to create the blaze. Untraceable.

Residents of Crabb's Lament had spotted a huge winged figure flying overhead late at night. An angel with knives, they'd said.

Two sisters from Elizabeth Colan Junior High had reported being approached by a man wearing a long trench coat despite the heat. He'd propositioned them and they'd run away when they saw his face, which they described as hairless and covered with green scales.

Someone had broken into a storage center in Gray Flats, ripped the huge paneled door of one unit right off of its hinges and thrown it into the water of Palm Lake some two hundred yards away. The unit had contained old equipment from a bankrupt traveling carnival called Ma's Spectacular Amusements.

A news report had connected these isolated incidents into the supposition that the *Cirque d'Obscurité* had returned to the United States and were holed up somewhere in Devil's Cape.

Jason's news report.

The *Cirque d'Obscurité* had killed Doctor Camelot more than twenty years earlier, then had moved around the world, on the run most of the time. Until now. Jason's investigation had told the Storm Raiders where to go to bring their teammate's murderer to justice. But things hadn't worked out the way they wanted.

Someone should have stopped this from happening. Someone powerful enough to help them. Someone who knew Devil's Cape.

Jason should have stopped this.

The mighty Hercules, whose shoulders afterwards upheld the sky, was one of them. And there were Castor and Pollux, the twin brothers, who were never accused of being chicken-hearted, although they had been hatched out of an egg; and Theseus, who was so renowned for killing the Minotaur, and Lynceus, with his wonderfully sharp eyes, which could see through a millstone, or look right down into the depths of the earth, and discover the treasures that were there; and Orpheus, the very best of harpers, who sang and played upon his lyre so sweetly, that the brute beasts stood upon their hind legs, and capered merrily to the music.

— Excerpted from *Tanglewood Tales*,
by Nathaniel Hawthorne

FIFTEEN

*I*n his dream, Jason knelt by a rocky shore, ocean waves crashing, the sea bubbling as the rocks churned it into foam. Gulls cried out overhead. There was one thick patch of sand and he was digging in it, sand up to his elbows, shaping something.

He was shaping himself, building himself out of sand. As he raised his head up and looked at what he was doing, he saw his own body before him, not made of sand, but of skin and sinew and bone, unmoving, pulse beating in the throat, eyes closed.

"It's time for the vestments."

In the dream, Jason knew the voice, although he'd never heard anything quite like it before. A man's voice, gravelly, strained from salt and sea. Commanding and sad and impatient.

"I don't know how," Jason said.

"Palaemon was the son of Hephaestus. He knows how to forge, how to make armor and smith gold. Admetus had herds of cattle and knows how to work leather."

Argonauts. Palaemon and Admetus were Argonauts.

Jason dug his hands into the gritty sand. He began to pat handfuls of it onto the body in front of him. It molded to the form like clay, hardening into a flexible form like leather.

"Dark blue like the depths of the Aegean," the voice said. And the blue spread throughout the leathery armor as though dye were pulsing inside.

"Gold for the fleece," the voice said. Jason dug deeper, pulling strands of gold from deep in the earth. As he watched the gold run sparkling through his fingers, he felt the dream slipping from him and fell into another dream.

He was flying through the soot-tinged clouds over Devil's Cape, moonlight cutting him in stark relief, a mask on his face, a cape fluttering in the wind behind him. A name came to him, but it disappeared, a whisper in the dark night.

———————

Twelve hours after the deaths of the Storm Raiders

Since he wanted to be unrecognized and inconspicuous for the shopping expedition, Jason wore a beaten baseball cap and a cheap pair of sunglasses. He didn't shave that morning, and wore a simple white T-shirt over cut-off blue jeans and sandals. Instead of his car, he took a bus to Bogan Heights, the city's unofficial arts district, a collection of antique shops, bric-a-brac kiosks, and pink stucco coffeehouses, getting off at Emmert Street and making his way through a twisted alleyway to a leather wholesaler. One wall of the store was decorated with nothing but row upon row of cow skulls. Head down, voice a soft mumble, he bought more than he'd need, paying cash, and stuffed it into a heavy knapsack.

From Emmert Street, he caught a trolley car deeper into Bogan Heights. An unwashed man sat next to him, tapping his foot and singing along loudly with music only he could hear. At D'Agostino Court, Jason got out and walked into a huge and dilapidated art supply store, its cavernous ceiling buckling and stained brown from water damage. Though it hadn't rained for days, water dripped steadily into half a dozen buckets spread here and there inside on the floor. The air was musty and thick. Jason bought twenty bottles of dye, a swivel knife, needles, and two spools of heavy-gauged thread. His wad of cash got that much thinner, the knapsack that much fuller. He bought himself a watermelon-lime snowball while he waited for the next trolley, and had nearly finished it when it came.

There was an area near the center of Devil's Cape called Chinatown, but that was a misnomer. It was more of a jumbled hodgepodge of all of Asia. One particular apartment building called the Lo Center summed it up for Jason. An eleven-story brownstone painted white and maroon, the Lo Center dated back to 1917 and featured heavy, curved eaves reminiscent of a pagoda. Trumpet vines crept up the walls and tangled around the shingles on the eaves. Four statues stood guard at the corners of the rooftop—a Chinese dragon, Krishna, a samurai warrior, and a huge-bellied Buddha. It had become known as the "flag building" because nearly every window sported one or more flags, a proud tradition of the residents, many of whom were born and died there. There were American flags, the state flag of Louisiana, and the masked skull and crossbones adopted by the pirate St. Diable. There were flags from China, Taiwan, Japan, Pakistan, India, Tibet, North Korea, South Korea, Vietnam, Thailand, Myanmar, the Philippines, and Indonesia. There were college flags and seasonal flags and even one that Jason recognized as the flag of Liechtenstein. A narrow but lush lawn surrounded the building, and most days it was filled with children playing soccer or football.

The rest of Chinatown might not be as much of a mishmash as the Lo Center, but it was close. Head down, the visor of his cap casting shadows over his face, Jason walked past the Lo Center and made his way to a jewelry store that he knew fenced stolen goods for the Pang Hui tong, which in turn paid an "operational fee" to the Robber Baron. He dropped down a larger stack of bills of larger denominations and left five minutes later with half a bar of gold in his satchel.

He smelled frying chicken and spices and stopped at a walk-up restaurant counter for a spring roll before catching a bus to Miller Avenue. At a scientific supply shop there, he bought safety goggles with reinforced glass.

When he got back to his small apartment, only a block away from the apartment where his father now lived, he dropped the knapsack on a thick wooden dining table with a crash, then went into his bathroom, where he threw the cap and sunglasses on the floor, undressed, and showered and shaved. For some reason, it was important to him that he looked like himself for this. When he dressed again, he left his usual clear-lensed glasses sitting on the bathroom counter and walked back to materials he'd bought.

Since David Dees had died, Jason had done little with his powers except hide them. Part of that was guilt—not so much over Dees, but over what Jason's brother Julian had become. The rest? Fear, indecision, doubt—some combination of those.

The deaths of the Storm Raiders weighed on him. Julian's activities as the flying criminal Scion—one more masked villain in a city drowning in crime, but protected by no heroes—weighed on him, too. Someone needed to stand against the Robber Baron, the people who swore loyalty to him, and the other criminals on the streets of Devil's Cape. *The Cirque d'Obscurité.* The Ferazzolis. The street gangs. The Pang Hui tong. Even Jason's own family, including his twin brother. Someone needed to oppose them. The Storm Raiders had tried, but it wasn't their city. Devil's Cape had made short work of them. Devil's Cape hadn't had a hero in generations. It needed one. Desperately. But there was no one else. Only Jason.

He jerked open the knapsack and upended it, dumping the contents across the table with a crash. And then, his skin flushed, his breathing slow, his eyes wide as though overtaken by a vision or a fever, he began to work. With techniques he'd never used before in his life,

but that seemed to come naturally, he began to assemble a uniform, the vestments from his dream. One word came to his parched lips again and again as he worked.

Argonaut.

"The flags at town hall behind me stand at half mast. I stand stooped, my eyes red, my heart heavy. This is a terrible day for Devil's Cape, a terrible day for America. We grieve at the loss of these heroes and we will find those responsible and bring them to justice.

"Still, I ask for caution and compassion during this time. It's vital to understand that, no matter how noble their aspirations and history, the Storm Raiders were here without authorization, outside of any reasonable jurisdiction. This matter is in the capable hands of the fine men and women of the DCPD. The last thing we need at this trying time is for any other vigilantes to come to our fine city seeking retribution. This is an internal matter, and anyone coming here to interfere will do so against the will of the people of Devil's Cape. Anyone disrupting the police investigation will be prosecuted to the full extent that the law allows . . ."

— Excerpted from a press conference held by Devil's Cape Mayor Randy Bowers the day after the assassination of the Storm Raiders

SIXTEEN

Devil's Cape, Louisiana
Two days after the deaths
of the Storm Raiders

*K*ate Brauer, Ph.D., swore softly to herself. Navigating the knotted streets of Devil's Cape in her small Mercury, pulling the heavy trailer filled with her possessions, was a nightmare. Her air conditioning had gone out just north of Tuscaloosa, and now, fighting through traffic in Devil's Cape's Soirée Bleue Ward, she'd been forced to turn on her heater to keep the engine from overheating. Even with the windows rolled down, she was sticky with perspiration, and the interior of the car was damp with humidity. Legend had it that the streets of Devil's Cape had originally been laid out not for the convenience of the area residents, but to allow for enough twists and turns that the pirates who had founded the town could use the terrain to avoid pursuit. Glancing back and forth between her map and the crowded streets around her and the bewildering combinations of one-way streets and crooked roads, Kate had no reason to doubt the stories.

It took her an hour and a half, three stops for directions, and two cell phone calls until she finally came to the narrow, three-story Creole townhouse that was to be her new home. "Huh," she said to no one in particular as she came to a stop in the middle of her street—more of an alley, really. She flipped on her hazard lights, then climbed out of her car to move aside the trashcans her realtor had used to block off a parking space.

Once she'd parked her car and double-checked the heavy locks on the trailer, she grabbed her overnight bag from the passenger seat and headed toward her front porch. A radio nearby was playing flamenco music—something from Ramon Montoya—and she could see children down the street, shouting to each other and splashing in water from an open fire hydrant. She waved to them, but the only child who noticed stared back unsmilingly. "Welcome to Devil's Cape," Kate said softly.

Her new house faced Thibodaux Court, a small Russum Ward cul-de-sac that had changed little since the early 1800s. The house, built in 1803 for a notorious Spanish smuggler named Juan Marco Quintana, displayed wrought iron balconies on the second and third floors and a stucco façade. Her front door and the two windows that flanked it were crested with graceful arches with Victorian flourishes. All the windows were barred.

Her key worked smoothly in the lock, though the door creaked as it opened. The air was musty and tinged with lilac. She'd memorized the floor plan before leaving Vanguard City, so she made her way to the master bathroom on the second floor with few surprises. The hardwood floors of the house were smooth and worn, but sturdy. The house creaked a bit as she moved around, but that suited her. She'd be able to hear anyone moving around. The bathroom itself had old fixtures, but running water had been installed in the house in the 1940s and most of the pipes had been replaced in the early 1990s. The wiring was relatively new, too, and the house was set up for cable and broadband Internet access.

Kate threw her sweaty clothes into a corner, pulled a towel and bar of soap from her bag, and showered in a clawed bathtub with no shower curtain. She'd have to unpack soon, but the niceties of setting up her bedroom and bathroom were far from her mind. She towel-dried her short, black hair, dressed quickly, not bothering to mop the water off her tile floor, and climbed the stairs to the third floor.

The top level of the house seemed cramped—its ceiling was less than seven feet tall and to all appearances, there was room for no more than a small parlor or storage space there. That appearance was a sham. Old Juan Marco Quintana had constructed a cleverly hidden room in the top of his house, one where he could store his smuggled goods. It had remained more or less a secret through the years except to its owners, and the realtor's mention of the room had sealed the deal for Kate.

She found the secret panel without much difficulty based on the realtor's explanation, and used her key to open the room. Stale air swept from the room, but the hidden area behind the panel was everything she'd hoped for—clean, large enough for her needs, and wired for electricity. A second hidden doorway in back even gave her access to a neighbor's rooftop.

She nodded in grim satisfaction. Her lab would go in this room. In this room, she would alter her father's armor. In this room, she would become the new Doctor Camelot.

She closed the door and walked out onto her third-story balcony. The previous owners had left a tattered flag hanging there. It rippled in the humid wind. With deft fingers, she untied the knot holding the flag in place. Pulling on the flag's rope, she lowered it all the way, raised it to its highest point, and then slowly lowered it to half mast, tying the knot back. The Storm Raiders were gone. But their murderers would be brought to justice.

Patient exhibits diminished affect. Threats from other youths produce no reaction. Mother's visits produce little reaction except perhaps mild guilt. Only demonstrated interest is apparent fascination with evaluation process. Enjoys turning questions around on me. In one meeting, I ended up revealing more about myself than he did. Genius-level intellect. Insightful. Manipulative.

— Excerpted from St. Tammany Parish
Juvenile Detention Center,
psychologist's evaluation of Cain Ducett,
twenty-one years ago

SEVENTEEN

Devil's Cape, Louisiana
Three days after the deaths
of the Storm Raiders
3 a.m.

As he had for several nights now, Dr. Cain Ducett, a respected psychiatrist who specialized in working with the criminally insane at Devil's Cape's Holingbroke Psychological Institute, dreamed of blood and fire.

He pulled his bed sheets over himself, despite the heat of his room. He felt nauseated, his skin itched, and sweat soaked his pillowcase. It stank of fear.

He swore, throwing the sheets aside and sitting up. His body felt strangely light as he padded his way to the bathroom.

He turned on the light.

The rigidly controlled Dr. Cain Ducett was not given to fear. If anything, he displayed a cold calm even in the face of the most horrible revelations from his patients.

But this was different.

The reflection he faced in the mirror was not his own.

He saw a young woman's face, pale, pretty. But the eyes. He knew that face, remembered having seen it before when the eyes were nearly invisible, filled with dark blood after he'd almost killed her. Jazz.

He screamed. And then the image smiled at him and the mirror shattered.

He blinked. What was left of the mirror showed only his own reflection. He splashed cold water onto his face.

He'd eaten nothing but raw carrots and yogurt for dinner, yet he had another taste in his mouth, a spicy oyster po' boy like the one he'd been eating that hot August day. A hint of RC and Jim Beam, too, though he hadn't touched alcohol in more than twenty years. He vomited suddenly and violently, barely steering himself to the toilet in time, his hand hitting the flusher before he was even done. He had a terrified feeling that what was coming up wasn't carrots and yogurt, and he couldn't bring himself to look. He flushed again, repeatedly, eyes shut, then stumbled to the sink again, putting his face beneath the faucet.

The mirror was still cracked. He stared at each of his hands, fully expecting to see one covered with blood, but they were uninjured. He must have broken it, though. He must have broken it another way.

He'd had a hallucination once before, about a week after he'd nearly killed Jazz. He'd seen red-black fur growing on his arms, demonic ears growing from his head, tough, translucent skin growing out of his armpits and stretching up his arms and down his abdomen until, when he spread his arms, it looked like he had venous wings stretching out of his body. He'd beaten his mother and a neighbor in his panic and rage, and had nearly killed himself before he'd let a hostage negotiator, Salazar Lorca, talk him into surrendering. Of course, by that time, the episode had subsided, and he saw that he was in truth the same Cain Ducett as always, human and normal, except possibly for the empty place where his soul was supposed to be.

What had broken that damn mirror? He stretched his hand forward to touch the glass, then yanked it back. For just a moment, he thought he'd spotted a haze of fine red-black hairs on his hands, that his fingers were ever-so-slightly elongated. He closed his eyes, then carefully stared at his hand. Nothing.

What in the hell had he seen? He shook off the thought. It was a vision, a carryover of a bad dream. He prayed it wasn't a psychotic episode, reviewed the medication he'd distributed to patients that day, calculating whether

he might have exposed himself to some of it, causing his dreams, the hallucination in the mirror.

Nothing.

He looked at his watch. Just past 3 a.m. He was past sleep, though, could still imagine the drowning light, falling into it, Jazz's blood-filled eyes, the fine hairs sprouting on his body. He took a shower, first very hot, then icy cold, then dressed for work. He stared briefly at the remains of the mirror, shook his head, and headed for the asylum.

"Crime in Devil's Cape is like no place else. Well, Sicily, maybe. But way more diverse, you take my meaning? And Sicily don't like those masks the way Devil's Cape does.

"It's set up like a feudal system, you see. F-E-U-D-A-L, like medieval, not futile, though I guess it's that, too. You got your average skels on the street, they're like the peasants. They owe so much up the food chain they're never getting their heads out. Then you got your little lords, your overseers or what have you. Then you got your big lords—or earls or viscounts or dukes or whatever. Like Tony Ferazzoli or whoever's running the Pang Hui tong these days, or your Uncle Costas.

"Yeah, I know who you are. You think you walk through this door without me knowing who and what you are? You probably know more about this shit than me.

"So anyway, you got your big lords and most of the time they hate each other and play off each other. They'll slit each other's throats, you give them half the chance. But they only screw with each other within certain parameters. Certain things they can do, certain things they can't. And that all boils down to the king and what he lets them get away with. "You got some knights, too, now, running around. The ones who wear masks. And sometimes they report up to the big lords and sometimes the little lords and sometimes straight to the king.

"And of course you know that no matter how much he throws at local charities and how much he tries to pretend his shit don't stink, that king right now is the Robber Baron. And before him, there was the Hangman, whose death the Baron probably arranged. And back in the days of old Eliot Ness, there was John Dusk. And when someone kills off the Robber Baron, may that day be today, someone else will step in, sure as anything. And long live the king.

"Of course everything I just said is off the record. Probably slanderous. True, though."

—FBI agent Stan Reuler, excerpted from an interview with WTDC News's Jason Kale

EIGHTEEN

Devil's Cape, Louisiana
Three days after the deaths
of the Storm Raiders
3 a.m.

Jason Kale took another sip of bitterly strong coffee from the paper cup in his hand, resisting the temptation to look at his watch again. A warm breeze fluttered his red silk tie, and he absently pressed it back down. The street was dark and empty. Someone—maybe kids, maybe vandals, maybe one of the warring gangs that fought endlessly over this piece of turf—had smashed the streetlight. Anyone else would have been nearly blind in the dark, but Jason could see the streets as clearly as at any other time of day—the windows with their dirt and peeling paint, the trickle of oily water making its way to the sewer grate, and the misshapen rat scratching its way along the edge of a dumpster. Somewhere off in the distance, he could hear an ambulance siren.

His cameraman, Dexter Koo, was squinting off into the darkness, smacking loudly on a piece of grape bubble gum, the video camera on the ground at his feet. Every once in a while, Koo would say "shit" softly, but that had been the extent of their conversation for the past half-hour.

Jason finally looked at his watch. Another five minutes and he'd give up. They were long past making the eleven o'clock news.

His source, a pinch-faced man named Lenny Buchholz, was a leg-breaker who'd lost both his earlobes when a pimp yanked his hoop earrings out of his ears during a shakedown. Lenny had promised Jason a scoop on the Troll, a monstrous, shadowy figure who some people said weighed nearly six hundred pounds and who had once decapitated an elderly woman with a baseball bat, then fed her head to the pack of dogs he kept with him. The Troll was supposed to be the leader of a gang called the Concrete Executioners.

But Lenny wasn't here.

"You've been had, man," Koo said. "Not the first time." He looked down at the ground, at the satchel Jason had brought along with him, but not opened.

Jason shrugged. "Maybe," he said. He pushed the satchel over to one side with his foot. Koo had asked him about it earlier and he'd shrugged it off. "Change of clothes," he'd said. It was accurate, but it had been clear he didn't want to talk about it and that had gotten the cameraman's curiosity up.

A sudden noise startled them. At first Jason thought Lenny had finally arrived. But then he heard the heavy footfalls of a near-giant and the baying of dogs. He stared down the street and saw a hulking form that could only be the Troll. The man—if he were even human—was even more grotesque than Jason had heard. He had green skin and yellow eyes without irises. Huge, curving horns like a ram's sprouted from the sides of his head. He was easily eight feet tall and covered with short fur. He wore a leather coat that seemed to be several jackets stitched together, and he carried a huge club in one hand, six feet long and covered with steel and metal studs at the top. His other hand held a writhing mass of leashes, each barely holding back a fierce mongrel dog, the smallest of them weighing at least eighty pounds. They sniffed and salivated and growled and tugged hard at the leashes, even when hooked barbs in their collars drew blood on their throats. When the Troll cleared his throat, half a block away, it sounded like he was crushing rats in his chest.

"Buddha's left ball," Koo said. The gum fell out of his mouth. He ran, a mad, crazy sprint that took him out of the dead-end alley where they stood and on down the street. He stumbled once, pulling himself to his feet on a metal trash can that clattered over to one side, and then he was gone. But there was no way that the Troll hadn't heard the noise, and he was closing fast.

Jason's only blessing was that the Troll was still distant enough not to have spotted him. But he was in a dead-end alley. There was no way for a normal man to escape without running into the street after Koo, where the dogs would surely run him down. Carefully, quietly, Jason set down the cup of coffee, picked up Koo's camera and his own satchel, and flew in shadows to the rooftop.

The smart thing would be to run away. He'd been set up, and obviously the Troll was looking for him. But if he didn't interfere, the dogs would run Koo down. And Jason Kale had never liked to run.

Quickly, he huddled there on the rooftop, the snarling of the dogs coming steadily closer, though the Troll was clearly in no hurry. Jason zipped open his satchel and pulled out the uniform that had haunted his dreams.

The bodysuit was navy blue, like the deepest waters of the Aegean. The shoulders and upper chest were reinforced with leather and threaded with gold. He stripped and pulled it on, shoving his other clothes into the satchel. Then he pulled on brown leather gloves and boots and a wide belt of the same leather, studded and buckled with gold. He threw a long, flowing blue cape onto his back, fastening it in front. And then he reached for the mask. It was formed to cover his whole head, leaving only his chin and mouth visible. Tinted glass lenses shrouded his eyes, both to make it harder to recognize him and to keep the wind from obscuring his vision when he flew. He stared at the mask for the space of several breaths, thinking of the step he was about to take. The quiet moment felt like a prayer. And then he pulled it on.

Jason set Koo's camera on a ledge and carefully aimed it at the street below. His shot set, he flew high into the air, then landed in front of the Troll, his heart thundering and his cape billowing out around him.

The Troll's yellowed eyes widened, a snarl drawing up the corners of his mouth. "And what are you, exactly?" he asked.

"I'm Argonaut," Jason replied. "And I'm tired of people like you running my city."

The Troll snorted and released the leashes, letting his dogs swarm forward. He gripped his huge club in both hands, swinging it backward, and rushed forward, his footsteps shattering paving stones that had decorated the street for more than a century.

Jason rolled forward and to one side. His cape fluttered in front of the dogs, enraging and distracting them, and he snatched several of the loose leashes. One dog bit his arm, but howled in surprise as some of its teeth broke. The dogs' breath was hot and fetid. They smelled like rotten meat. Jason yanked hard on the leashes, pulling the baying dogs down and toward the street, then rapidly knotted the leashes together. The dogs snarled and yapped at him and each other, but they were pulling each other over, unable to move together to get at him. They howled, scratching and biting at each other in frustration, but all their movement only served to cinch the leashes tighter together.

But two of the dogs were still loose, and the Troll loomed closer. He kicked one of the trapped dogs to the side, stepped in toward Jason, and then swung the huge club hard toward Jason like a batter aiming to rip the cover off the ball.

Jason dropped flat to the ground, inches from the cracked mortar and cobblestones, and felt the club swing by just overhead. One of the dogs lunged in, trying to bite Jason in the face, but Jason reached up and elbowed its lower jaw. Its mouth slammed shut, blood spurting through its teeth as the tip of its tongue was severed. It whined, dropping backward, and Jason shoved it into the other loose dog with his foot, sending both spinning back down into the alley. Not even having time to figure out where the Troll was, he rolled to the side, then heard a thunderous crash as the club slammed down to the point where he'd just been.

"I'll kill you!" the Troll shouted.

"I don't think so," Jason said. He sprang to his feet. For Jason, the problem with the huge club was that it gave the long-armed Troll tremendous range. For the Troll, the problem with it was that it was next to useless in close.

Jason stepped in near the Troll, tight enough to smell the unwashed, animal stench of his body odor, tight enough to make out the uneven stitching in the coat that the Troll had sewn together for himself. He jumped upward, smashing the crown of his head in to the Troll's flat, wide nose, then punched the Troll five times in quick succession just under the breastbone. They were fast, hard punches with little momentum but lots of strength, and the Troll gasped and wheezed as the air rushed out of his lungs.

The Troll dropped the club and reached around Jason to squeeze him and crush him in his arms, but Jason was much stronger and tougher than he'd expected, and while he trying to crush Jason with his trunklike arms, Jason was grabbing him back, keeping him from taking another breath.

It only took a few seconds before the Troll began to topple, starved for oxygen. Jason let him start to fall, then punched him hard in the back of the head, forcing him to the street.

Jason pulled the Troll's jacket off and tied his arms together with it. Then he got to one knee, put his arms under the Troll's huge frame, and lifted him over his head, onto his shoulders. The gleam of a streetlamp made the gold threads on his chest shine.

As Jason flew into the air, directly in view of the video camera he'd put in place, his cape fluttered behind him and the Troll's dogs howled.

Let them stay here, then. They are as acclimated and as content as their afflicted minds will allow. Let the whole haunt be devoted to them, to preserving what sanity they retain. And keep the place lit bright. Its shadows are fierce and fearsome.

— Excerpted from a letter written by Janus Holingbroke to the caretaker of his children and nephew, 1900

NINETEEN

Devil's Cape, Louisiana
Three days after the deaths
of the Storm Raiders
4:30 a.m.

Devil's Cape was no place to drive just before dawn. The smog hung over its streets and the glitter of predawn had a way of sucking the light out of the city's streetlights, headlights, and neon, turning the world an impenetrable, smoky gray. The stragglers on the streets at that hour were drunk as often as not, driving as though alone in the world, uncaring of the darkness, unconcerned for each other. The city had more DWIs per capita than any other in the United States, and its bars were open twenty-four hours a day. A former Devil's Cape fireman had purchased a retired firetruck after he'd put in his twenty years and did a good business contracting with the city to spray blood off city streets after fatality wrecks.

Dr. Cain Ducett was usually a cautious, meticulous driver. He drove no more than ten miles over the speed limit. He signaled. He came to a full and complete stop at stop signs. But not this night. On the night of his dream, he drove toward the Holingbroke Psychological Institute like a bat out of . . . well . . .

"Like a bat out of hell," he said.

After tearing out of his apartment garage, windows down, air roaring around his head, he blew through a red light at Ayers Boulevard without even tapping the brakes of his Chrysler Crossfire. He swerved around a beer delivery truck and had driven three miles in two minutes

and ten seconds before realizing that he hadn't turned his lights on yet. He flipped on his lights in time to see a line of cars up ahead and slammed on his brakes, skidding through a patch of oil and nearly smashing into the rear end of a Harley Davidson. When the biker turned around to give him the finger, Cain saw Jazz again, her face staring at him from the reflection in the biker's helmet. The half moon he'd carved in her cheek with his switchblade glittered bright red.

"Hallucination," he muttered. "Hypnopompic. Visual. Auditory. Gustatory. Olfactory. Tactile. Stress. Sleep deprivation. Projection."

In the dim interior lights, his fingertips seemed to end in claws. Reddish fur bristled on the backs of his arms. He pulled the Crossfire into the oncoming lane, gunning it through the intersection with Lockheardt Street. The scent of burned rubber ripped through the night air.

He spotted Jazz twice more before he made it to the asylum. Once standing on a bridge overlooking Chien Jaune River, the mists and smog swirling up to her waist, a beatific smile on her face, a halo of blood around her head illuminated by the moonlight. And once staring out at him through the plate glass window of a sawdust-floored bar called Smith's Roadhouse, sipping from an open thermos, letting the liquid pour down her throat like she'd opened a vein. That time, after he'd driven past, he heard her whispering in his ear. "Cain," she said. "It's time, Cain."

When he jerked his head around, there was nothing there.

He tried to calm himself, tried to slow his hammering heart. He slipped a Debussy album into his CD player, keyed up "The Girl with the Flaxen Hair." Hypnotic music. But it was distant background noise. His mind drifted back twenty-two years to Run-D.M.C.'s "Walk This Way" blasting out of 5-D's speakers. He smelled blood and hot asphalt. He couldn't help but floor the accelerator.

When he reached Holingbroke's parking lot, he squealed into a parking space, then forced himself to

hold still for a moment. The skin under his arms itched and he remembered when he'd imagined he had wings. He could hear the buzzing of mosquitoes.

The Holingbroke Psychological Institute had begun its life in 1884 as a huge, brooding gothic structure, the home of the eccentric brothers Harvey and Janus Holingbroke, who'd made a fortune in the West claiming bounties and striking gold. By the turn of the century, the brothers had headed back to California, leaving behind three adopted children—all of them psychologically disturbed—and a provision for caretakers. Over the years, that caretaking evolved into full psychological treatment facilities and a broad base of patients. More modern wings had been added in the 1960s—they increased the number of patients the institute could treat and augmented the building's ability to treat dangerous patients safely. But the jutting white and gray arms of the new wings with their reductive, modern lines were an eyesore in the old building, alien and disquieting.

Cain forced himself to be still for thirty seconds, forced himself to breathe in through his nose and out through his mouth. His face didn't feel like his own, and he was terrified to check the mirror. Reaching into his medical bag, he cut his eyes around the parking lot, making sure it was empty. He debated between Haldol and Thorazine, between pills and injection. On the one hand, the last thing he needed was to be caught shooting up in the institute parking lot. On the other, he needed fast results, needed to make this psychotic incident stop. He rolled up his pants leg, then filled his syringe with a strong dose of Thorazine. Checking the parking lot once more for others, he carefully placed the syringe into a vein on the underside of his knee and drove the plunger home.

The pain was good. Sharp and distracting. But it didn't last long. He carefully disposed of the syringe and needle in his bag, took deep breaths, calculated the paths the drug would take through his circulatory system. He needed to get in to his office. He turned off the Debussy and raised his windows. When he looked through the

driver's window to make sure, once more, that there was no one in the parking lot to see him, he saw the monster in his reflection. His face was twisted and elongated, covered with dark scarlet fur. His irises gleamed red in the parking lot's lights. Huge fangs jutted from his lower jaw. "No!" he shouted, closing his eyes, jamming his hands against his face to block his vision. But he could still feel the fur, bristling against his face and his palms.

"Yes," said Jazz's voice—calm, amused.

Reluctantly, he opened his eyes again, saw now not his reflection, or the monster's, but Jazz's face, pale, eyes filled with blood.

"This isn't real," he said.

"No?" The corner of Jazz's mouth turned up in a sneer. And then the window exploded inward, showering Cain with chunks and shards and cubes of glass. He felt cuts on his face, arms, and throat, felt blood trickling down his chest. His first instinct was to bat the glass away with his hands, but he knew better, knew the damage he could do to himself brushing at broken glass. He sat there for a moment, listening. But Jazz—or his hallucination of her—was gone. There was only the sound of the night— the rustle of wind through the banana trees, the chatter as pieces of glass fell slowly from his body to the floor of his car, and the buzz of insects. A glance into the rearview mirror revealed his own face, not the monster's. He was bleeding, and a chunk of glass hung in one eyebrow like a decoration, but he was himself. He held himself painfully still, then slowly unlatched his door and stepped out into the parking lot, carefully shaking the glass loose from his face, his hands, his clothes.

The mosquitoes sensed his blood. They swarmed around him, digging, biting, flying into his eyes, and he couldn't do a damn thing about them without risking digging an overlooked piece of glass further into his face. He slammed the door shut. The car was open to the world, but he couldn't be bothered with that now. He reached back into the car, lifted out his medical bag, shook a few pieces of glass from it onto the pavement, and walked slowly and purposefully toward the doctors' entrance. There was no way not to be observed by the security guard at the door, but he couldn't be bothered with that, either. He just needed to avoid having the slurred voice and foggy brain that the Thorazine was going to give him, and to do that, he needed to move fast.

He wondered idly if there really even was blood on his face, glass in his skin, or if that was just another part of the hallucination. No sense going too far down that road now. If he did, he'd start to wonder if he'd left home, if he even existed.

He shook his head slowly. He was disassociating, losing it. The Thorazine and the psychosis were affecting his judgment, his thought processes. His face and neck hurt from the glass, his arm from the shot. His arm? His leg. He'd driven the needle into his leg, hadn't he? Nothing seemed quite right. He glanced around, felt the weight of prying eyes watching his progress to the door. But there was no one following his progress, was there?

"Damn it, Jazz," he muttered. He gripped his disjointed thoughts as tightly as he dared and opened the door to the asylum.

"What the hell happened to you?" asked the security guard at the door, rushing forward to help.

Cain winced, frustrated at the effects the Thorazine was already having on his system. He couldn't remember the guard's name. The two of them talked about—what was it?—hockey whenever they saw each other. Cain had had a patient with a Wayne Gretzky fixation and that had started it. They were two black men in Louisiana in the delta talking about hockey. Cain didn't know anything about it, and the guard probably didn't either, but it was the only thing the two of them could think of to talk about. They didn't know each other and had different education levels, and had formed that one simple connection and knew next to nothing about what else to say to one another. And now Cain had forgotten the man's name.

He put on his most charming smile, which hurt, because it forced a chunk of glass deeper into his lip. It probably looked maniacal besides, what with the dripping blood and all. "Like you said, man, sitting on the front row against the glass is a crapshoot. One eighty-mile-per-hour puck at the right angle and you're sucking glass chips." Knowing it wasn't selling, he turned the smile down a turn, self-deprecating. "Ah, I did something stupid." True enough. "I was out late with some friends and got back into my car afterward, realized I forgot something, and turned funny. Smashed my face right into the window. Didn't know those things could shatter this way." He was conscious of his blood dripping on the tile floor. "I was pretty close to Holingbroke, so I drove over here. It's not as bad as it looks and I can clean it up myself without dealing with an ER."

The guard—Dennis? Dwayne?—furrowed his brow. "You're the doc, doc," he said. His jaw tightened. "I'll get the janitor to mop up after you."

Cain nodded, the movement painful. His head was fuzzy with the Thorazine now. "Thanks," he said. He waved in a friendly and dismissing gesture at the other man, then turned to make his way toward his office by the least-frequented route he could.

"Dr. Ducett?" The security guard had come up behind him, laid a hand on his shoulder.

Cain stopped. He found himself pushing down an urge to punch the man. Cain Ducett was no longer a violent man. The urge disturbed him. "Yeah?" he asked, turning to face the guard—Darren. The guard's name was Darren.

"You, uh, need a hand?"

Cain shook his head. "No, I've got it," he said. He started to walk down the corridor again, but Darren didn't remove his hand.

"You're not, uh, going to be treating any patients for a while, are you?" Darren's voice was even. "I mean, till you take some time to clean up, take a shower, maybe change into different clothes? Your cuts and all, you know, might disturb some of them." Except he didn't mean that, Cain knew. What he meant was that he thought that Cain was drunk or high, and he had no business seeing patients in that condition.

"Don't worry," Cain said. "I'm fine. But I'm not seeing any patients for a few hours."

Darren released his shoulder then and patted it awkwardly. "Okay, then. Good. That's good." His Adam's apple bounced up and down and his eyes cut to the floor. More blood. "Don't you worry about this," he said. "We'll get it all cleaned up." He grinned at Cain. "We'll call in the Zamboni, you know?"

Cain nodded again and made his way down the hall toward a stairwell.

The Thorazine biting into his brain, he made it up the stairs, then down the hallway to his office, his hand reaching out often to touch the wall and support him. The bleeding had more or less stopped, or at least he was no longer dripping on the floor.

It was when he pulled the door to his office open that he heard Jazz's voice again.

"You running away, Cain?" the voice asked. "Turning your brain to sludge to get away from your debts?"

He walked into the empty room and closed the door behind him. The room reeked of Jim Beam and marijuana. There was no sign of Jazz in the room, but a yellowed newspaper tabloid was spread across his desk, open to a story about "the Devil Baby of Dubai."

"I never ran from a damn thing in my life," he said quietly to the empty room. "That's part of my problem."

The Thorazine wasn't working its magic. It was slowing his brain, his reactions, blurring his thoughts, but the hallucinations were still there. Hefting his medical bag, he walked into the small bathroom inside his office, one of his few perks, and stared into the mirror. For the moment, at least, he saw his own face. It was coated with blood, torn and bleary-eyed, but it was his. Working quickly, afraid every second that the mirror would explode, that it would be filled with Jazz's bloodied face, or the monster's, he plucked the shards of glass out of his face and neck and arms with a pair of tweezers and a hand towel. He'd need a stitch or two, he thought, but he couldn't handle that right now, not with the Thorazine, so he applied pressure with a slowly reddening towel.

"You're running now," her voice said, and he imagined he could feel her lips brushing against his ear, though he saw no one.

Ducking away from the mirror, he limped back into his office and grabbed his telephone. He would talk to Salazar. Salazar would know what to do.

It wasn't until he'd pushed the last button that he realized he hadn't dialed Salazar's number at all. He'd called Jazz's old home. Before more than a single ring could sound, he slammed down the receiver. This was all too much. He locked the door from the inside, wedged it shut tight with a doorstop, and dropped into the chair behind his desk.

"Cain?" Jazz's voice came from the bathroom. He knew that if he walked over there and looked into the mirror, he'd see her. "We need to talk, Cain. You need to stop pretending that what's happening isn't really happening."

He didn't rise. "What do you want from me, girl?" he asked the air. "I don't hurt people anymore. You saw to that. You changed me, you and that voodoo that you do."

He stopped, wondering what the hell he was talking about. Jazz hadn't done anything but be his victim. The trauma he'd felt over the incident had triggered a psychotic episode that had ultimately led to his salvation. That was the gospel according to Cain Ducett. It had nothing to do with voodoo.

The Thorazine was thickening his mind. He couldn't concentrate anymore. His face hurt. Cradling his head in his arms on the desk, ignoring the crinkling of the newspaper that couldn't be there, he tried to drift off, to let himself sleep, praying to a God he didn't believe in that his brain chemistry would right itself by the time he woke. As he closed his eyes, he imagined his body shifting, the skin flaps growing underneath his arms, the fine hair rising on his skin, his ears stretching. He imagined horns and a tail. He gnashed his teeth together, squinting his eyes shut further. Why wouldn't this end?

And finally, resting like that, he fell asleep.

Don't get so caught up in the bustle and street vendors of Little Athens that you overlook Zorba's on Sarandakos Avenue. Yes, its décor is kitschy. But the service from charming owner/operator Pericles Kalodimos and his crew is truly Old World, and the food is a delight to smell and taste. In particular, be sure to try the delicate pastitsio, which . . .

— Excerpted from
A Devil's Cape Traveler's Guide

TWENTY

Devil's Cape, Louisiana
Three days after the deaths
of the Storm Raiders
5:30 a.m.

Despite their differences and the various preoccupations that drove them, Jason and Julian made an effort to join their father for breakfast at Zorba's early every Sunday morning. They had to be there by six-thirty to have time to eat and talk and still beat the brunch crowd. The Sunday after Argonaut's televised battle with the Troll, after the deaths of the Storm Raiders, the three men found themselves gathered together earlier than normal, sipping at Pericles's strong coffee and finding conversation difficult.

Pericles had torn down the red velvet wallpaper in the 1990s, replacing it with a series of frescoes of Greek heroes and a collection of ferns. The frescoes were now chipping and peeling, and one of the innumerable Kalodimos cousins had modified the heroes' anatomies on one wall with a steak knife and fountain pen. Pericles had patched it up as best he could, and barred the cousin from the restaurant for a year, but now he was talking about putting the red velvet back up again.

Jason stirred a spoonful of sugar into his coffee and scraped at his eggs—a moist omelet with tomatoes and feta cheese—with his fork. Lenny Buchholz's body had been fished out of Bayou Garceau nearly twelve hours before Jason had fought the Troll, but the news hadn't reached Jason until just before he got to the restaurant.

Someone had chained a hunk of concrete to Bucholz's foot and perforated his belly with an icepick to let the gases escape, but they'd left him in the shallows and a water skier had slalomed into his head. The Troll was already out on bond and had sent a bouquet of lilies to Buchholz's mother.

Jason finished his coffee, then poured some more from a steaming pitcher. He leaned in too close and the steam fogged his glasses. He absently pulled them off and polished them on his napkin.

"I still don't understand why you won't get contacts," Pericles said. "Or even that Lasik surgery or whatever they call it. A man on television, he looks more trustworthy without glasses."

Jason shrugged and slipped them back over his nose. He was grateful that his father never seemed to realize that he wore clear lenses. He glanced at his brother, then looked away. "They say it makes me look more intelligent," he said.

"So what? So you need to buy into that garbage? You wear these glasses, you change your name . . ."

"Pop, that's over and done. You think anyone's going to listen to crime stories from someone named Kalodimos?"

Pericles stood up from his chair, the movements slow but angry, his arms still muscular, but wrinkled like old leather, the white hairs bursting out of his scar tissue like razor wire. "We're not all crooks, Jason."

Again, Jason found himself glancing at his brother, then quickly cutting his eyes away. He started to answer, but Julian beat him to it.

"No, Pop, we're not," Julian said. And now Jason couldn't help but look. There was a beatific smile on Julian's face, with only a hint of smugness. Julian had grown a goatee and streaked his hair with golden highlights, another way of the twins separating themselves, and he scratched the hair on his chin as he spoke. "But Jason's right, you know. In this city, he'd never get on television with our name—at least not the way he wants.

Too many bad apples." He gestured to his father. "Would you get me some more bacon, while you're up?"

Pericles lifted a plate of bacon from a nearby serving table and carried it over. Using stainless steel tongs, he set some in front of Julian then, almost as an afterthought, in front of Jason.

"Thanks," Jason said quietly.

His father nodded, then grinned at Jason, his teeth yellow, and nodded again. "So changing your name, did it spare you the old Kalodimos temper?"

Jason smiled back. "Not so much, Pop."

Pericles jabbed the air in Jason's direction from across the table with a piece of bacon. "Saw your news program a few minutes ago with that Troll thing. Who was that man fighting him again? I couldn't catch the name with the dishwasher running." Before letting Jason answer, he turned to Julian. "You see that show, Julian?"

"I saw it," Julian answered. He wiped his mouth with a napkin, his eyes intent on Jason.

"Argonaut," Jason said.

"What was that?" Pericles asked.

"Argonaut," Jason repeated. "The hero's name was Argonaut."

Pericles Kalodimos sat very still then, like a man who'd suddenly found himself alone in a room with a hungry lion. His tanned skin paled and his eyelids quivered. When he spoke, it was as if he had marbles in his mouth. "You know this Argonaut, Jason?"

"You okay, Pop?" Julian asked, but his father ignored him.

"I know him a little," Jason said. "He intends to stay in Devil's Cape, I think. Said he wants to make a difference here."

His father finally blinked then, his eyes moving back and forth from son to son. "Argonaut, then," he said. He nodded his head. "A strong name. Greek, that's good." He began to clear the table. "Argonaut," he repeated. "Yes, I hope he stays in the city," he said. He sipped at his coffee. "Pirate Town could use someone like him."

He walked off to the kitchen then, his arms loaded with dishes and silverware. With his back to his sons, he couldn't see the two of them staring intently at each other, as if trying to read secrets in each other's eyes. Despite the cosmetic differences in hair, clothing, and glasses, they looked like two sides of a mirror.

doubloon dog: An incredibly loyal and vicious person or animal. Named for Devil's Cape's famed Doubloon Ward, where, according to popular legend, the guard dogs are trained to be so completely loyal to their masters and so merciless that they have to be put down immediately if their masters die, lest they wreak havoc.

—Excerpted from *The Phrase Book: A Look at the Evolution of Modern Slang*

TWENTY-ONE

Devil's Cape, Louisiana
Three days after the deaths
of the Storm Raiders
6 a.m.

Dawn was breaking over Devil's Cape's historic Doubloon Ward. Wisps of fog snaked across streets lined with cast-iron lampposts designed to look like the gaslights that had stood there more than a century before, when horse-drawn carriages rolled along the roads instead of cars. The families in the ward were among the city's richest. They were predominantly old money, but while in other cities that might imply respectability, in Devil's Cape it often meant that their ancestors had been pirates who had plundered and pillaged alongside St. Diable himself. This carried a certain cachet, but with it a taint, as well. The families of Doubloon Ward guarded the stolen wealth they'd inherited from their ancestors with unmatched zeal and the barest jot of guilt. More often than not, the homes of Doubloon Ward had iron gates, shuttered windows, and state-of-the-art security systems.

Tony Ferazzoli's mansion stood at the heart of the ward, one of a crescent-shaped spattering of such buildings curving around Bullocq Park, tightly packed. Those old pirates had wanted the grandeur of sprawling homes, but didn't trust each other enough to build more than a couple hundred feet apart. They preferred to keep their neighbors within close sight, just as in their days at sea.

Tony had inherited the building from his father Lorenzo, who had inherited it from his brother Arturo, who had extorted it from the previous owner, a descendent of a British pirate named Jack Hicks, who had manned a cannon in one of St. Diable's fleet of ships. Under heavy fire, Hicks had fired the shot that had doomed a French galleon called *Roi des Corsaires* and had been rewarded for his nerve and aim.

The house reflected Hicks's experience with cannons. At first glance, it was in the traditional French Creole style. A wide gallery in the front, a timber frame covered with *bousillage*—a mixture of mud and Spanish moss dried, flattened, and pressed against the unfinished walls, forming a natural insulation—protected with weather boards. Thin wooden columns and French doors. Airy to fight the Louisiana heat. But further inspection showed the modifications that had been made, first by the pirate Jack Hicks himself, and later by others, probably Lorenzo Ferazzoli for the most part.

There were narrow windows between the more traditional ones, the paneling around them reinforced by extra timbers. They slid open to form murder-holes—thin spaces through which the pirate could have fired his gun from relative safety. Even more dramatically, Hicks had added four turrets to the house, one in each corner, almost like crows' nests. A rusting cannon still rested in each as testament to tradition, but years ago Lorenzo Ferazzoli had added modern armaments to the turrets—some kind of mounted machine guns he'd ordered from Eastern Europe called KGKs. He'd once threatened to turn Costas into dog meat with one of them.

There were other modern modifications, too. There were electronic sensors, of course. Bright lights to turn the lawn into high noon even on a cloudy night. And every piece of glass in windows was bulletproof now, something else Lorenzo had bragged about. As if Costas would have shot him through a window. He chuckled a little to himself. As if the bulletproof glass had saved him when Costas had decided it was finally time for old Lorenzo to die.

"The house that Jack and Lorenzo built," Costas Kalodimos muttered as he steered his Lexus onto Tony Ferazzoli's cobblestone driveway, not bothering to acknowledge the guard standing on duty in the gate building.

"What's that, Dad?" Costas's son Nick—named after a cousin who had died years before in the infamous fire at the Naked Eye that had killed dozens, including Costas's Uncle Ilias and the Hangman—sat beside him. Nick had an earpiece jammed in one ear and was nervously drumming his palms against his thighs. For whatever reason, although he hardly ever wore anything but T-shirts that showed off the muscles he was so proud of, Nick was wearing a crisp-collared long-sleeved blue shirt and hadn't even rolled his sleeves up.

Costas waved a hand. "Nothing," he said. "Just wondering who's going to live in the house now Tony's gone."

"Probably Vinnie," Nick said.

Vincent Marcus was Tony Ferazzoli's nephew and served more or less as Tony's lieutenant. It would be a good fit. A lean, dark man with spectacles and an accounting degree, Marcus was smarter than Tony had been. Hungrier.

Nick shrugged. "One goomba's the same as another," he said.

"A philosopher," Costas said, smoothly parking the Lexus behind the Robber Baron's huge crimson limousine and switching off the ignition.

Nick's hands were still patting at his jeans. Probably rap music he was listening to. Or one of those party girl divas.

"Would it kill you to wear a nice pair of pants for a change?"

Nick looked over at his father and ran his hand through his short hair. He yanked the earpiece out and turned off the music player clipped to his waist. "It just might," he said. He looked out the window. Even in the dim light, it was obvious that the lawn, usually meticulously

landscaped, was in a state of decay. Thistles and dande-
lions pushed through patches of browning grass. Nick
shook his head. "The new Ferazzoli's letting things go to
shit already," he said. "How hard is it to get some spic to
yank your weeds?"

Costas reached over and unclipped the music player
from his son's belt.

Nick glanced at his father, but didn't respond. He
tapped the glass instead, glancing back at the gatehouse,
where there was no sign of movement. "No one even
going to walk us inside? Tony was a sack of garbage on
legs, but even he knew to treat us with a little respect, you
know?"

"I know," Costas said. He opened the door and
stepped outside. The air was warm and dank. There was
an edge to it, ripe. Like a feral animal was nearby. There
was pipe smoke, too. The Robber Baron's.

Nick got out, too, and slammed his door loudly.
Making a point.

Costas gave him a withering look. "It's early Sunday
morning," he said. "You pissed at Tony's neighbors,
too? Maybe one of them should have run out of bed and
walked you to the door."

Offended, Nick stomped up to Tony's entryway.

Not for the first time, Costas wished Nick could be
a little more like his cousin Julian. Of course, that was
part of the problem. Costas trusted Julian with more
responsibility that he was willing to give his own son,
and all three of them were painfully aware of it. Nick was
younger, true, but he was old enough that that excuse
was wearing thin. Costas sighed, walked past a pair of
black-faced lawn jockeys—Tony had never been either
politically correct or blessed with a modicum of taste—
and rapped on the door.

They waited.

Nick rolled his eyes, brushing at his short hair again.
His scalp glistened with sweat.

It was oddly quiet. On the other occasions when he'd
been to the house—both in Lorenzo's day and in Tony's,

usually when the Robber Baron wanted his lieutenants to make nice—there'd been a clamor of barking dogs. Doubloon dogs. But it had been quiet the first time after Lorenzo died, with his dogs put down and Tony not having any yet. And he supposed Tony's dogs had been killed, too, though he had difficulty imagining anything being loyal enough to Tony Ferazzoli that it would mourn his death.

They waited.

"The hell," Nick muttered.

Costas held out a hand for his son to be patient.

The door swung open with a squeak. At first, Costas thought it had opened all by itself, that the foyer was deserted. At one point, in the days of Lorenzo Ferazzoli, that entry point into the mansion had been grand. White walls and white marble floors. Bronze sconces and a crystal chandelier. Now it was a cluttered, jumbled mess. Tony or his wife had hung a Degas on one wall and a Kandinsky on the other. A Persian rug lay awkwardly in the middle of the floor, and someone had clearly used it to wipe his feet. Gold sun-catchers dangled amidst the bronze. A Victorian étagère with chipped black varnish stood against one wall, a looking glass propped against it.

But then Costas saw in the reflection in the looking glass that the room wasn't deserted after all. A scaled hand held the door handle tight. The arm attached to the hand curved through the length of the foyer and around a corner toward Tony Ferazzoli's living room like a thick, quivering snake.

Kraken of the *Cirque d'Obscurité* was there.

Costas and Nick looked at each other. Nick tugged uncomfortably at his sleeves, then stepped into the foyer, Costas behind him.

Kraken stepped forward, his hand still on the door, his arm shortening as he walked, the skin wrinkling like an elephant's trunk and then slowly smoothing out. His face was completely hairless, the ears flat against the skull. When he smiled, they could see that all of his teeth

175

ended in sharp points. He let go of the door and dropped his hand to his side. "Well, look who's here," he said. He wore a sleeveless red shirt and blue denim shorts. He was barefoot, walking oddly on the sides of his feet. The smile was menacing, challenging.

A portly man with thinning, graying red hair and a matching beard walked around Kraken into the entry-way, and the temperature in the foyer climbed something like ten degrees in three seconds, going from cool to sti-fling. The looking glass against the étagère fogged over. Hector Hell. From what Costas had heard, most of the *Cirque d'Obscurité* wore normal clothing most of the time. Their otherness was enough to set them apart, to alien-ate and frighten those whom they wanted to alienate and frighten. But not Hector Hell. Even early in the morning in Tony Ferazzoli's mansion, he was wearing a costume. He looked ridiculous in the form-fitting yellow spandex with the flame patterns running up and down his body like the decals on a 1977 muscle car. Even his flowing red cape and cavalier boots didn't hide the fact that every extra ounce of body fat was on corpulent display. But the hint of flames flickered in his eyes, and the sheer heat coming off of him reminded Costas just how much danger he would be in if he crossed the man.

"Costas," Hector Hell said, affecting a more genu-ine smile than Kraken's. "Glad you could join us." He reached out his hand.

Costas steeled himself and shook hands, afraid he would be burned. The other man's palm was very warm, but not enough to scald. He could feel heat inside, though, like taking a hot pan out of an oven with a thin oven mitt. "Hector Hell," Costas said with no inflection. "I didn't realize you and your . . . people were going to be here this morning."

Kraken chuckled. "You were expecting Tony Ferazzoli?"

"Shit, no," Nick said, crossing his arms and standing up straight. "We just weren't expecting you."

Kraken's smile broadened. "Hadn't you heard?" he

asked. "This is our place now." By the tone of his voice, it might have meant the mansion. Or it might have meant Devil's Cape itself.

———————

The whole gang of *Cirque d'Obscurité* freaks was assembled in Tony Ferazzoli's living room, clustered around the Robber Baron like he was holding court. Costas supposed he was.

The living room itself was a typical Tony mishmash. Tony had picked his furniture and decorations and toys because they were expensive, not because they were beautiful or functional. Tony Ferazzoli had no problem putting a Louis XIII sitting chair in front of a Danish Modern desk on top of a Persian carpet, then using the desktop as a place to store the remote controls for all the electronic equipment he never bothered to figure out how to use.

It was a big, low-ceilinged room. The Robber Baron sat in a leather recliner, legs crossed, puffing on his meerschaum pipe, gray smoke flowing across the ceiling in gentle waves. The woman—Osprey—sat on the edge of the chair, her side just barely pressed against the puffy sleeve of the Robber Baron's arm. She wasn't dressed in the full armored leather regalia that Costas had heard she usually wore into battle, but she still was wearing a lot of black leather. A fetish, maybe? A tight leather halter top left her tanned belly exposed. Her belly button was pierced—a diamond glittered there. She wore a leather miniskirt, too, with some kind of trench knife strapped to her calf. Huge feathered wings stretched out of her back. She had them spread out wide and they cast shadows over the Robber Baron. Costas wondered if she was sleeping with him. Out of the corner of his eye, he caught Nick gaping at her, and elbowed his son gently.

The Behemoth stood at the back of the room—towering, bare-chested, arms crossed, head bent slightly to keep it from grazing the ceiling. He was grotesquely muscular, veins bulging. With the exception of his face, his entire body was covered with tattoos. Many of them were stretched and distorted, torn apart by whatever had changed him from what he had been into what he had become. But there were enough remaining to get the gist. They were animalistic and violent. A snarling tiger here, a black widow in a web there. A king cobra fanned out and preparing to strike. A twisted tree trunk with a haunting face, limbs outstretched. A red devil holding a pitchfork. Thick tusks jutted from the Behemoth's lower jaw. His nose was squashed flat like a gorilla's, the nostrils gaping. He ignored Nick and eyed Costas with wary intelligence, a smile curving slightly over those huge tusks.

The Werewolf was perched on the Louis XIII chair by the desk, feet tucked under him. He looked not too different than Costas might have imagined from a horror film—fur covering his body, an elongated snout, jutting ears like small sails. A long tail protruding from a hole cut into the back of his jeans. He growled softly as he saw Costas looking at him, and Costas's heart skipped a beat. But the old Greek refused to look away. The Werewolf wore a sleeveless white wife-beater shirt with the slogan COME BREAK YOUR BALLS AT BUTLER'S BILLIARDS on the front. Cut-off jeans and no shoes. Costas had heard that the Werewolf could look human if he wanted to. Handsome, even. But this morning he sat there covered in fur, staring at Costas with angry yellow eyes, idly digging furrows into the leg of a four-hundred-year-old chair with a clawed hand.

The mass of scar tissue they called Gork stood behind the Robber Baron. He wore a white T-shirt and jeans and had a .44 Magnum Colt Anaconda strapped in a shoulder holster across his chest. His neatly pressed clothing contrasted with his visible skin. He was covered with burn scars and some wounds that looked fresh, like nothing ever healed quite right for him. A trickle of blood ran down one side of his head, curving down the ear and soaking into the collar of his shirt. He didn't seem to notice, nor did he seem bothered by the smoke curling out of the Robber Baron's pipe and into his face. He just stood there staring hungrily at Osprey, jaw slack.

Hector Hell and Kraken followed Costas and Nick into the room, shutting the door behind them. Costas could still feel the heat coming off of Hector Hell. Sweat trickled down the back of his neck.

Costas felt frightened in that room as he never had with Lorenzo or Tony Ferazzoli, as he never had with the Hangman or the Robber Baron. There was a sense of otherness about the *Cirque d'Obscurité,* of wrongness. They made him want to run.

Instead, he forced his attention to the Robber Baron, looking into the other man's eyes through the mask. "Baron," he said. "this isn't quite what I expected when I got your call."

The Robber Baron puffed on his pipe. He leaned over slightly to one side, pressing his arm against Osprey's side. She leaned into him.

Sleeping together, then.

"You were expecting Vincent Marcus?" the Robber Baron asked. "A changing of the guard from one member of the Ferazzoli clan to another?"

"Something like that."

The Robber Baron puffed again.

Hector Hell chuckled. It was a harsh, false sound.

The Robber Baron gestured expansively with the pipe. "We went through that before," he said. "With Lorenzo's unfortunate passing." His eyes were cold as he watched Costas. He hadn't been happy when Lorenzo Ferazzoli had died. "That didn't work out very well," he said. "Tony was an incompetent. He nearly exposed me more than once. Vincent Marcus is a cut above that, but only barely. There's a place for him in my organization, but not at my side."

"Speaking of incompetent," Hector Hell said with a sneer. "What's the deal with the Troll?" He held out his palm and a small blue and orange flame surged in the center of it. He watched it flicker, mesmerized, a smug smile on his face.

Costas's stomach went tight. The Troll was the new leader of a black gang in Crabb's Lament called the Concrete Executioners, or the CEs. The CEs pushed most of the drugs in Crabb's Lament. They got the drugs from Costas's organization. Costas looked at the Robber Baron. It was bad enough if the Robber Baron blamed Costas for the Troll's arrest. But Hector Hell piping in like that and questioning Costas . . . it just wasn't the kind of thing people did in front of the Robber Baron.

But the Robber Baron didn't say anything. He didn't even look perturbed at Hector Hell. He just stared at Costas, the top of a graying eyebrow appearing above his mask.

"The Troll's already out on bail," Costas said shortly. "There's nothing there."

Kraken settled himself into a cushioned leather couch, limbs twisting together in knots. He scratched at the scales on his neck. "He was caught by some guy called Argonaut," he said.

Costas glanced at him. "So what?" He turned back to the Robber Baron.

"Argonaut's a Greek name," said the Werewolf. His voice was clear despite the lupine face, his accent Germanic. Costas turned to him. The Werewolf was still scratching at the Louis XIII chair. Tiny wood shavings fell to the carpet.

"Hey, that's a funny accent you got," Nick said, bristling and glaring. "That German or German shepherd?"

The Werewolf popped to his feet, growling deep in his throat, the hair at the back of his neck standing up.

"Errando!" Hector Hell snapped. "Not now."

The Werewolf glared at Nick, who glared right back. But then the Werewolf twisted his head just a bit to one side, his throat turned toward Hector Hell—a sign of submission. And he sat back down.

Costas felt a mix of exasperation and pride. Yeah, it was a bad time to be mouthing off, but Nick wasn't backing down to the same kind of fear that his father was feeling. He looked at the Robber Baron. "I don't know anything about this Argonaut," he said.

The Robber Baron nodded. "He's a curiosity," he said. "But not much more. Others have tried to take this city away from me, but it hasn't worked out well for them."

"Sure as hell didn't work for the Storm Raiders," Gork said. His eyes glimmered. He was remembering helping to kill them, Costas thought. He had enjoyed it.

"Frank," the Behemoth said from behind him, "zip it."

The Robber Baron waved a gloved hand. "Not to worry," he said, taking another puff on the pipe. "Costas is loyal. If we can't talk openly amongst ourselves, then we would live in fear, wouldn't we?" His eyes burned into Costas's.

Costas's heart hammered. What did the Robber Baron know? What did he suspect?

The Behemoth shook his head. He uncrossed his thick arms, and Costas saw that he was holding something in his huge, clawed hands. A gray squirrel, squirming and struggling to get free, its puffy tail shaking back and forth. It bit his finger, but he didn't let go. Instead, he stroked its back with a long, jagged claw. "How do you know he's loyal?" he asked. "A mule will labor ten years willingly and patiently for you, for the privilege of kicking you once."

"Hey!" Nick shouted. He reached for his gun.

Costas grabbed his son's arm. For a second, he had visions of Nick dying. Hector Hell burning him, Osprey stabbing him, Kraken strangling him. He felt as though he might vomit. "No," he said. "No, Nick."

The Behemoth laughed. He held the squirrel up to his lips and kissed it.

Nick relaxed in Costas's grip. He dropped his hand.

The Robber Baron raised a finger. The drama didn't seem to interest him. Instead, he turned around in his chair and looked at the Behemoth. "Twain?" he asked.

"Nah," the Behemoth said, pulling the squirrel away and staring into its eyes as though fascinated. "Faulkner."

Then he bent forward and bit off the squirrel's head. Blood gushed onto his naked chest, dripping down to the thick carpet. He tossed the squirrel's body into a wastebasket and crunched on the skull. It sounded he was chewing ice cubes.

Osprey rolled her eyes.

Kraken laughed quietly to himself.

The Werewolf sniffed the air. He leaned forward, body angled toward the wastebasket, then stopped himself and leaned back.

Gork seemed finally to notice the blood trickling down his own neck. He brushed at it with scarred fingers, then wiped them on his jeans.

Hector Hell shook his head gently and clucked his tongue.

The Robber Baron just smiled wistfully. "Faulkner," he repeated. He turned back to Costas. "Hector will be taking over Tony's organization," he said. "Perhaps you and Nick should sit down. We have a number of things to discuss."

———————

"They're like animals," Nick said, back in the car. Costas had asked him to drive.

"Yes," Costas said.

"They're goddamned freaks," Nick said.

"They were playing it up," Costas said. "They're showmen. It's what they do. They wanted us off guard and intimidated."

"Did you see that with the squirrel?"

"He used to bite the heads off chickens in the carnival. It was an act."

Nick pounded the steering wheel as he gunned the car down the streets of Doubloon Ward. "The Robber Baron was eating it up."

"Yes," Costas said. "He wanted me intimidated, too."

"Us," Nick said.

"Us," Costas agreed.

"You've been working for him since before I was

born," Nick said. "Why does he want to intimidate us now?"

Because I'm getting old, Costas thought. Because he's getting old. Because he knows Scion—Julian—is loyal to me, and he doesn't like the idea of me having access to that much power. Because he knows I arranged for Lorenzo Ferazzoli to get killed against his wishes. Because he likes to shake things up.

"I have no idea," he said to his son.

"Those freaks are the problem, Dad," Nick said. "We need to do something about those freaks."

Costas shook his head. "No," he said. "They're a symptom." The Robber Baron was the problem.

Costas reached under the passenger seat and pulled out a small blue phone. It was disposable and untraceable, only to be used once. He pushed a button. Somewhere on the other side of the city, an identical phone rang.

"Bad meeting?" Julian's voice was calm, maybe a little amused.

"Yeah," Costas said.

He couldn't send Julian against the Robber Baron, not directly. It would be too easy to trace back, too messy. The *Cirque d'Obscurité* complicated things. They were too powerful. Julian was tough, but not that tough. They needed a different angle.

"So?" Julian said.

"That plan we discussed?"

"Yeah."

"Time to pull the trigger," Costas said.

"Okay."

Yes, then. Use the money for nurses and alienists. Help our children, but bring in others, too, and help them. But do this for me: Concentrate on the ones no one else wants. The truly mad, the violent, the hopeless. There are other places for rummies and eccentrics, poets and crybabies. Let Holingbroke stand for the true rejects of this world. My brother and I know quite a bit about those.

— Excerpted from a letter written by Janus Holingbroke to the caretakers of his children and nephew, 1912

TWENTY-TWO

Devil's Cape, Louisiana
Three days after the deaths
of the Storm Raiders
11 a.m.

Cain Ducett awoke to the sound of someone knocking at his office door. Disoriented, he lifted his head from his arms and his desk, blinking at finding himself asleep there. "Hang on a second," he said, his voice hoarse. He stared down at his desk. The tabloid with "the Devil Baby of Dubai" story was still there, dotted with his blood. He traced it with his fingertips. "Not a hallucination," he whispered. What the hell did that mean?

He glanced at his watch. He'd slept for perhaps three hours. He stared back at the newspaper.

"Dr. Ducett?" It was Jin Chen, the administrative assistant for the doctors in Cain's wing. Even through his thick oak door, he smelled a hint of jasmine. Her voice had an odd timbre. She was upset about something.

"Give me just a minute, Jin," he said. He walked into the bathroom, checked himself in the mirror. He was still streaked with blood, his clothes a mess. "Jin," he called out, "can it wait a few minutes? I cut myself and I look pretty bad." No sense beating around the bush. She'd see the cuts soon enough.

Jin paused for a moment, and he could hear her breathing nervously, almost a pant.

He shouldn't have been able to hear her through the door like that, but his senses seemed particularly acute.

Unless he was hallucinating again. His eyes moved back to the newspaper on his desk.

"I don't think it can wait," Jin said after a moment.

Sighing, Cain walked to the door and opened it, saying, "Don't say I didn't warn you."

In her early thirties, Jin was just a hair over five feet, slender and no-nonsense. Born in Tianjin, raised in San Francisco. Her eyes went wide at the sight of him. "Your face," she said. "I thought you meant you'd cut yourself shaving? Are you . . . ?"

He waved it off. "It looks worse than it is. My car window broke and cut me a bit." She looked like she was about to ask more questions, so he waved those off, too. "What's the emergency, Jin?" he asked.

"It's about Rusalka."

"Her name is Olena Zhdanov," he corrected, his voice mildly reproving. "Calling her Rusalka just reinforces her dissociation." Any mention of the woman under any name was unsettling, though. Olena Zhdanov was responsible for at least seven deaths. She claimed to be responsible for even more than that, and Cain had little reason to doubt her.

Born in Irkutsk, Russia, Zhdanov had come to the United States three years earlier, ostensibly on a work visa, but actually, she had told Cain in one of their first sessions, because she hoped to marry a rich American. Zhdanov was a strikingly attractive woman, with bold Slavic features and searing intensity. Within weeks of her arrival, she was engaged to a Devil's Cape oilman named Todd Eisenberg, who made millions through offshore drilling.

But some pivotal event, one Cain had never succeeded in getting Zhdanov to reveal in more than hints, had changed her aspirations and her life. On a clear December evening, the Devil's Cape police were summoned to the Eisenberg home, where Zhdanov had taken up residence. A deliveryman had discovered Todd Eisenberg's corpse, as well as those of his maid and gardener, slumped underneath the house's fresh-cut Christmas tree, its ornaments half-hung, the lights twinkling. Their bodies were

withered, desiccated. Cain had seen photographs of the scene and the corpses reminded him of mummified remains of ancient Egyptians and Incans he'd seen in museums. Eisenberg wore a silk robe open at the chest, his skin stretched as taut as old paper across his bones.

All three of the deceased had been seen earlier that morning, healthy and hearty.

A police detective had discovered Zhdanov in Eisenberg's master bath, soaking in bubbles in the Jacuzzi, weeping. They'd spoken for a few moments and then the detective had reached out a hand to help the distraught woman from the tub. He'd collapsed to the ground, withering, his arteries and veins shriveling so rapidly that his heart burst open.

Zhdanov's tears had turned briefly to laughter then, hysterical, desperate. Another police officer died before she was subdued, and then, months later, a Holingbroke orderly and a fellow patient. However she managed it, Zhdanov was able to—to use unscientific language— "leech the life" from other creatures with a touch. And she did so with a manic pleasure.

"What about her?" Cain asked quietly.

Jin sighed. "She's escaped."

Cain stepped into Olena Zhdanov's sparsely furnished room. A double bed with a flat sealed-seam mattress sat against one wall, a pressed-wood desk and matching chair against another. A small throw rug managed to cover half of the tile floor, and a trunk sat at the end of her bed. The walls were barren. A small row of books stretched across her desktop. She spoke excellent English, but preferred to read in Russian. Her selections, though, weren't by Dostoevsky or Tolstoy, or even Chkhartishvili. Instead, she read translations of Danielle Steele and Rosamunde Pilcher. A framed picture of her dead fiancé decorated a wooden chest of drawers.

Out of necessity, she'd had a private bathroom, but it was small, too; she'd had barely enough room to shower.

The small size of her room made the corpse lying on its side in the hallway seem even more jarring.

The victim, Thomas Dickerson, had been an orderly at the Holingbroke Psychological Institute for eight months. A heavyset black Creole who played piano at his church, Dickerson had been trained on security precautions in dealing with Olena Zhdanov. He'd been informed of the death of another orderly a few months after Zhdanov had arrived. At Cain's insistence as a precaution for all employees coming into contact with Zhdanov, Dickerson had even been shown photographs of the other orderly's corpse. Yet here he lay.

Cain, who had taken ten minutes to clean himself up, change, and stuff the yellowed tabloid into a desk drawer before coming up to Zhdanov's room, squatted beside Dickerson's body, careful to touch nothing, and stared at the withered features. Dickerson had weighed perhaps two hundred and sixty pounds. He'd been in his late twenties, and his skin had been smooth and youthful. Were it not for his clothing and his distinctive oiled goatee, Dickerson's corpse would have been unrecognizable. The body was gaunt and shriveled, the skin horribly wrinkled and even torn in places. Blood vessels had popped throughout his body in tiny eruptions, but the blood, too, had dried out rapidly, leaving him with starbursts of scabs underneath the skin. His shrunken eyes hung loosely in their sockets. His lips had drawn back from the rapid desiccation until they looked almost as though they were smiling. The skin was pulled against the bones in wrinkled lumps, and Cain guessed that the body that remained weighed less than a hundred and fifty pounds.

No one knew exactly how Zhdanov's "power" worked. She touched someone and that person withered, quickly dying and becoming something like this, like a mummified corpse, if she did not let go. A visiting biologist, less of a serious scientist than Cain had been led to believe, had speculated that she drained the victim's "life force," though Cain thought that that was ridiculous. He himself had wondered if her power didn't involve somehow removing the moisture from the target's body; one of the witnesses to the last orderly's death had said he'd seen steam coming out of Zhdanov's eyes and mouth while she touched him. In addition, Zhdanov had been reported to exhibit great feats of strength and stamina after inflicting her terrible damage on another person.

The police had secured the scene and had allowed Cain, as head of the department and Zhdanov's psychiatrist, into the area in order to verify Dickerson's identity and to point out anything out of place in Zhdanov's small room. A crime scene photographer was snapping various shots of the area with a digital camera.

The detective in charge was named Cynthia Daigle. Rail-thin and acne-scarred, with straight, graying brown hair that reached her shoulders, she had shockingly blue eyes and a deep Cajun accent. "You think she just got him to open the door for her?" she asked, her hands in the pockets of a blue and white pinstriped seersucker jacket that surely had been tailored for a man fifty pounds heavier than she was. She smelled of Camel cigarettes and perfume. Intuition from Estee Lauder—he'd bought a bottle for a woman he'd dated once. She'd eyed his cuts when she'd first seen him, but hadn't commented on them.

"No," Cain answered. "He was trained not to do that. He knew how dangerous she is."

Detective Daigle shrugged, squatting down by Dickerson, twisting her head and peering at him with curiosity. "She's an attractive woman, you say?"

"Even so," he answered. He gestured at Dickerson. "He was shown pictures of the last orderly she killed. He looked like this, too."

"Even so," she echoed. "An attractive woman, a soft word . . . maybe she convinced him she really needed him to unlock her door."

"No," he said flatly. "There are protocols involved, even in an emergency if he thought that she were dying or something." He peered at Dickerson. "Besides," he

added. "I don't see her as the one who clubbed him in the back of the head. With that angle, with the difference in their heights, it had to be somebody taller, and besides, what would be the point? All she'd need to do is touch him, not club him."

She looked at him curiously. "What do you mean, 'clubbed him in the back of the head'?"

He blinked, then pointed at the spot at the top of Dickerson's head where the hair was flattened and splayed out, a dark purple at the scalp subtly different from the other markings left by Zhdanov's touch. "Here," he said.

Daigle bent over Dickerson, shining a flashlight at his head and using a magnifying glass. "I'll be damned," she said. "I wonder what he was hit with?"

Cain's eyes cast around the hallway for about half a second, then he pointed. "There," he said, indicating a fire extinguisher at the end of the hallway, neatly placed back in its designated spot. "The shape of the extinguisher's base matches the mark on Dickerson's skull and there's one of his hairs stuck to the bottom."

She turned and stared at him. "You're telling me you can spot a hair from this distance?" The fire extinguisher was about fifty feet down the hall.

Cain blinked again. She was right, of course. There should have been no way for him to spot the hair, but he could see it clearly from where he was standing, could tell even that it curved like Dickerson's hair, that a bit of skin clung to the end of the bulb of the hair, meaning that it could be DNA-matched to him if need be. He saw old fingerprints on the extinguisher, probably from whoever had manufactured it in the first place, but with newer smudges across them, as though whoever had used it to club Dickerson had been wearing gloves. Under the scent of Daigle's perfume and tobacco, he could detect a whiff of men's aftershave in the hallway. He didn't recognize the brand, but he could place some of its constituents—orange blossom, coriander, cedar. Traces of it wafted past through the air. Did the scent belong to the person who had hit Dickerson? Cain could hear the mumbling of other

inmates of Holingbroke's wing for its most violent and self-destructive patients, confined to their rooms, agitated by the police activity outside. What the hell was happening here? His senses were more acute than they'd ever been, acute beyond all reason—he was even hearing whispering from several rooms and several reinforced walls away, the phrasing distinct. Could he be hallucinating again? Could the Thorazine be having this effect on him?

No, he thought. No, it was something else.

"Dr. Ducett? You spotting more hairs with your telescopic vision?"

He turned to the detective, a pleasant smile on his face hiding his churning thoughts. "Of course not," he lied. "I walked around here a bit while you were studying the room. I apologize. I figured you'd probably already noticed those things."

Her eyes on him were wary. "We'll check into your suggestions," she said.

He could hear that her heart rate had risen. He'd made her nervous. Suspicious.

"We will, of course, offer the police any assistance we can," he said.

"You do that," she said. She appeared to turn her attention back to the corpse, but her eyes were on Cain.

As he walked back down the corridor, he could feel—literally *feel*—her head lift as she gazed after him.

Dr. Cain Ducett didn't know why his senses were behaving this way. But he did know that he'd just blundered into making himself a suspect in Olena Zhdanov's escape. He didn't doubt that he could eventually prove his innocence, but any delays that the police experienced while investigating him—and his extremely difficult-to-explain behavior over the last few hours—would give Zhdanov time to get farther away, to kill more people. Cain scratched at one of the cuts on his face. Dried blood crumbled away. When he touched his fingertips to the cut, he could tell that the wound was entirely gone.

What in the hell was happening to him? And what was he going to do about it?

Better pull on your sweaters tonight, folks. We're going to drop from our high of 96 this afternoon to a bracing 87 degrees tonight, with humidity at 80 percent. Seriously, crank up the AC if you have it, and lock your doors and windows if you can stand to. It's likely to be another wild night in Pirate Town.

— From a WTDC weather report

CHAPTER

TWENTY-THREE

Devil's Cape, Louisiana

*Four days after the deaths
of the Storm Raiders
11 p.m.*

Joe Gaines had been running with the Concrete Executioners for three years, since he was eleven years old. Even before that, he'd looked up to the CEs. They walked tall in his neighborhood. Other people, even teachers at his school, even his dad, lowered their eyes when the CEs came near. Even the younger CEs wore real gold chains. They had good shoes. They strutted. The chief of the CEs, the Troll, could kick the ass of anyone on the planet.

Joe had gotten his own start in the CEs by hanging around one of them, a fifteen-year-old named Ronzelle Davis who was sleeping with a seventeen-year-old girl from St. Bartholomew's. Ronzelle had skin the color of coffee and cream, and had carved a lightning bolt into his hair. He barely noticed Joe at first, but after Joe followed him around like a puppy dog for a few days, he'd taken to patting the boy on his head. Then he started giving him errands. First, Joe just ran back and forth between Ronzelle and the girl, who was white and blonde and used hair spray that smelled like bubble gum.

Then he started doing more. He was a lookout once, when Ronzelle and some of the other CEs broke into a liquor store owned by a Mexican with graying hair and thick glasses. Ronzelle gave him one of those air horns he'd heard at basketball games, a white can with a big red

193

DEVIL'S CAPE

nozzle that sounded out loud when you activated it. He'd stood there in front of the store, hands trembling, watching for the police or a rival gang or a good Samaritan, ready to warn Ronzelle and his friends at the first hint of trouble. But no one had come. No one came when they shattered the Mexican's window with a pair of aluminum baseball bats, sending the plate glass shards flying to the far wall of the store. No one came when they broke the case of tequila and Ronzelle shoved the Mexican's face into the pool of it on the floor, forcing the man to lick the floor and cut his tongue. No one came when Ronzelle swung his bat into the Mexican's knee, which snapped audibly and forced the stoic man into soft sobs of pain. It was Devil's Cape, after all, and no one came.

Another time he held a gun for Ronzelle, who decided that his girlfriend from St. Bartholomew's was getting too friendly with a boy from her neighborhood. Ronzelle gave him the gun early one afternoon after school, slipping it into Joe's Power Rangers backpack while no one was watching.

Joe hadn't been able to help himself. He'd gone into the stall at the men's room at McDonald's and pulled the pistol out, staring at it. Later, he'd know more about guns, and this one in particular—a Rossi .38 special double-action revolver. It carried five shots and its two-inch barrel made it easy to conceal.

But that afternoon, Joe simply knew it as a gun. It felt heavy in his hand, its stainless steel barrel glinting in the florescent lighting of the men's room, its rubber grip comfortable against his palm. He lifted the pistol toward his face, afraid to point it at himself, afraid to look down the barrel, afraid to cock it. Reverently, he stared into the steel, finding his own reflection. He sniffed it, the smell of gun oil faint compared to the scent of french fries nearby.

Ronzelle bought Joe an ice cream cone that afternoon, and a bag of fries, and Joe walked happily with him a few blocks out of their neighborhood, walking tall with the knowledge of the gun in his backpack, chattering and smiling with Ronzelle while dipping his fries into the ice cream and munching them down, the salty in the sweet.

After a few minutes, they came across the boy who'd been hanging around Ronzelle's girlfriend. The boy was about Ronzelle's age, white, with dark hair slicked back and an easy grin. He wore pine-scented aftershave and his voice cracked when he spoke.

Ronzelle asked him for a smoke, then in the space of less than twenty seconds, reached into Joe's pack, pulled out the .38 special, shoved it into the other boy's belly, pulled the trigger, wiped the pistol off on his shirt, and dropped it back into Joe's pack. The boy sat on the ground, open-mouthed, tears rising to his eyes, clutching his stomach. His white hands quickly turned red. "Run," Ronzelle had said, giving Joe a little push in one direction and then sprinting off in another. And after a few seconds of staring at the dying boy, Joe had run.

The next morning, Ronzelle had told Joe that he was a CE now, and that he had to keep what had happened a secret.

It hadn't mattered, though. The boy Ronzelle had killed had been a nephew of crime boss Tony Ferazzoli, and Ronzelle was found later that afternoon in the freezer of a butcher's shop, stabbed thirty-seven times with an ice pick.

Three years later, Joe had kids following after him as he had with Ronzelle. He was used to guns now and had several, including the one that Ronzelle had asked him to hold that afternoon long ago. That one had held a special fascination for him. It hadn't been lucky for Tony Ferazzoli's nephew, and it hadn't been lucky for Ronzelle, but perhaps, he always thought, it would be lucky for him.

And he was right. It would.

In Devil's Cape, summer heat was as much a threat to the city's citizens as its criminals were. It bathed them in sweat, stole the moisture from their bodies, incited them to violence. Devil's Cape, as befitted its pirating heritage, was a city of late nights, bars open at all hours, and general carousing. But in the summertime, people stayed out

195

especially late, the heat unrelenting even in darkness, keeping them awake, invading their dreams, driving them to the streets.

It drove Joe to the streets that night, Ronzelle's Rossi .38 special tucked into the waist of his cut-off shorts, sweat clinging to his body. Cars were scuttling their way through the city's twisted streets, horns were blaring even this late at night, and the air was stagnant with the heat. Whatever breezes the nearby lake should have been bringing in were stymied somewhere, never reaching the corner where Joe stood with his friends and flunkies. Leaning against the door of a corner bar called Vern's, he was reduced to fanning himself with a Storm Raiders comic book he'd grabbed from one of the kids who flocked around whenever the CEs came by. He smelled fried chicken and something rancid from a nearby dumpster.

On a normal night, Joe and his friends wouldn't have bothered messing with the guy in the dented blue Toyota. There was just no advantage in it. The guy—he had reddish-brown hair that needed a trim, a T-shirt for some water park in Wisconsin pulled over a heavy waist, and a red plastic watch he'd probably gotten out of a vending machine for fifty cents—didn't look worth robbing. His car wasn't worth much, and it wasn't like he did anything to provoke them.

But it was that Devil's Cape heat.

It wrapped around them, put them on edge. They reeked of the heat. They thought of little but how hot they were and how annoyed they were—with each other, with the world, with the heat. And with that stranger in the Toyota who stopped on the street in front of them, trying to decide if he wanted to go into Vern's for a beer or not, the exhaust from the car's tailpipe wafting slowly into Joe's space, his corner, the pungent scent of it making him suddenly determined to beat the man who brought it to him.

So without really giving it much thought, Joe walked forward and banged on the Toyota's hood with his fist, making the car shake. "You moving?" he asked the man

loudly. " 'Cause you in my space." He sidestepped his way around the front of the car, his eyes locked on the man inside, angry at the man's surprised face, angry that the man wasn't already moving the hell away, angry that his hand hurt from where he'd bashed the hood. "You hear me, Opie?" he asked, trying to shake the feeling back into his hand, feeling for a second the warmth of Ronzelle's .38 special tucked precariously into his pants. "I don't want to smell your car anymore."

The man in the car was realizing his predicament then, but it was already too late. Joe was leaning up against the driver's window. Dwayne—more than six feet and two hundred pounds at sixteen years old, always bored, always anxious for some action—had stepped forward and kicked one of the headlights out with the heel of his shoe. Myrell had spread all ten fingers out against the passenger window, leaning forward and pressing his broken nose against it, too. Twelve-year-old JZ, eager to join the CEs, had climbed up on the trunk. Another kid, Isaac, was pulling on one of the windshield wipers.

The man honked his horn then. He was afraid, but he was afraid to run them over, too. But that just made Joe and his friends angrier. Dwayne kicked out the other headlight, Isaac yanked the wiper off, and Joe pulled out Ronzelle's pistol and stuck it against the glass. "You're giving us your car now, Opie," he said, wondering then if Dwayne or Myrell knew how to drive. "You get out of the car and give me your keys and maybe I won't cap you." On the trunk, JZ whooped and kicked his feet. The man honked his horn again, but Joe knew that no one would come running. It was Devil's Cape, after all.

"You going to kill him?" JZ asked, excited.

Joe tapped the glass with his pistol, then stuck it back into his shorts. What would Ronzelle have done, he wondered. "I might," he said. Then he nodded at Myrell, who pulled his torn old T-shirt off, wrapped it around his elbow, and then used that elbow to hit the passenger window hard, sending deep white cracks through it with his first blow.

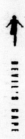

And then, as he readied himself for his second hit against the window, Myrell just suddenly disappeared from view.

"Myrell?" Joe asked.

"What the hell?" said JZ.

Myrell dropped from the sky and tumbled to the sidewalk in front of them. They all stared at him, backing away from the Toyota, no one reaching out a hand to help him. Then, in almost comical unison, they turned their heads upward.

A man floated in the air about twenty feet above their heads, hands on his hips, wearing a navy blue and gold uniform. A tight cowl covered the top of his head and his nose, the eyes hidden from view by white-tinted lenses. Joe could see his mouth and chin, his skin tan against the blue of the cowl, the chin strong and set, the mouth turned in the faintest hint of a grin. The uniform covered him tightly from his neck to his toes. He was tall and muscular, though not a body builder. More like a quarterback or a middleweight boxer. The navy blue was broken by sections of gold, as well as thick dark-brown leather. A huge blue cape hung from his back nearly to his ankles, rustling in a breeze that Joe and his friends could not feel.

"Leave the man in the car alone," the flying man said, "and go home."

JZ and Isaac hit the sidewalk running, sprinting away from the man as quickly as they could. Myrell pulled himself slowly to his feet, obviously hurt by his fall. But Dwayne and Joe were slower to move.

Dwayne glanced at Joe, ran his tongue over his lips, and crossed his arms, one foot on the Toyota's bumper. "Make me," he said simply.

The flying man shook his head. Then, in a lightning-fast motion, he swooped down toward Dwayne, flying at him head-first, and slammed a fist into Dwayne's gut.

The punch knocked Dwayne a couple of feet in the air and he fell backward into the street, moaning.

But when the flying man turned and moved toward

Joe, Joe pulled out Ronzelle's Rossi .38 special stainless steel double-action revolver with the two-inch barrel and shot him in the eye.

One of the white lenses in the flying man's mask shattered on the impact and the flying man cried out and collapsed beside the Toyota, laying there panting on his hands and knees.

Joe shot him again, in the ribs this time, then shot him three more times before the gun was empty. "Don't mess with the CEs," he said softly. Then he dry-fired the pistol once at the terrified man in the Toyota and started backing away.

The man in the uniform stood up.

Joe stared at him, his mouth dry and open, Ronzelle's gun warm in his hand. Dwayne and Myrell were already stumbling away, Dwayne clutching his gut and Myrell limping. And then he ran, too, toward home, sprinting as fast as he could.

He didn't see the masked man fly back off into the sky behind him, one hand over his injured eye, shivering despite the Devil's Cape heat.

The third Doctor Camelot never patented his weapons, never made his armor available for scientific study. But he did share some of his ancillary research—the work in subharmonics that led to his sonic blasters, the experiments in molecular bonding that led to the gluelike substance he used to detain captured criminals until the police arrived. The patents he transferred to the Storm Raiders Foundation have earned millions for the team over the years. Even these narrow glimpses into his work reveal a brilliant mind. The man hidden in the armor must have been part Edison, part Tesla, part Merlin.

— From "Whence Camelot: Five years later,"
by Leslie Flannigan, *Vanguard City Crier*

TWENTY-FOUR

Devil's Cape, Louisiana

*Five days after the deaths
of the Storm Raiders
2 p.m.*

On a sweaty afternoon, Kate Brauer walked a block over from Thibodaux Court to Chancery Street, where she'd discovered a small Chinese restaurant that served the best fried dumplings she'd ever encountered. As she walked, she admired a particularly large banana tree decorated with ribbon and a SAIL TO DEVIL'S CAPE bumper sticker.

On the surface, Kate decided, Devil's Cape wasn't all that bad. Tourists came to the city for its promise of wild parties and drinking, for dripping po'boy sandwiches and andouille sausage, for tours of abandoned pirate hideouts and haunted graveyards, for jazz and blues music that rivaled those of nearby New Orleans, for walks through cobble-stoned streets scented with bougainvillea. Lehane University was top-notch despite its reputation for heavy partying, and the city's library had an amazing collection not only of seventeenth century writings, but also other treasures, such as the memoirs of notorious gangster Marcus "Pidge" Poggioreale, who, in the 1930s, had stolen a top-secret serum from a government lab, downed it himself, and become bulletproof.

People often nodded at each other in the street. Many said "sir" or "ma'am," and the peculiar Southern drawl and Cajun twang of their speech was pleasing to Kate's ear. The heat of the city, though oppressive, also served

to slow people down a bit. Stores tended to stay open a few minutes longer than advertised, because the people in the stores never quite got around to closing them on time. For the average tourist, for the average citizen, crime was a factor only in certain neighborhoods. It was a part of the headlines, or a brief burst of noise on the news, sandwiched between the weather report—invariably hot and humid, with a chance of showers—and the latest news about the Devil's Cape Bandits' training program and chances in the fall football season.

At the Wok Inn, Kate ordered a double helping of fried dumplings and a large container of hot and sour soup from the store owner, a heavy Chinese woman named Mrs. Fong whose accent was a peculiar blend of Beijing and Old South. "Only for you!" proclaimed Mrs. Fong when she handed the order to Kate, slipping in an extra almond cookie, clearly pleased to see Kate returning already for her second meal that day.

As Kate walked back to her new home, the aroma wafted from the greasy bag, blending pleasantly with the scent of cinnamon from a fried cashew cart she passed along the way.

Her lab was coming together. The trickiest part of the move was managing to get all the lab equipment she needed into Juan Marco Quintana's secret room on the top floor without anyone—movers, in particular—knowing what she was doing.

Some of her equipment had come from her father's hidden laboratory, although much of that had become outdated in the years since his death.

But there'd been another find in his lab that had made things easier for her over the years: an old battered chest filled with gold and other treasure. She had gasped when she'd found it, tucked away with his trophies behind the remains of Deadlock's combat drone X7-J. At first, she thought he'd taken it from one of the criminals he'd fought. But then she saw the documents he'd put in an envelope on one side of the chest, under a gold and bronze astrolabe that sparkled with lapis

lazuli. They were meticulous salvage records of how he'd recovered the chest from a Spanish naval ship sunk by pirates some two hundred and fifty miles off the coast of Cape Breton Island, Nova Scotia. He'd chanced across the ship. He was deep in cold waters, testing his Doctor Camelot armor against the ocean depths, concentrating on making sure that the armor's seals remained firm and that the pressure inside the suit helped prevent him from getting the bends. He didn't notice the ship, mostly buried in marine life and silt, until he was almost upon it. But then he'd propelled himself inside and emerged with the chest held tight in his armored hands.

The chest held fine porcelain and sealed jars of spices, dozens of pearls and cut emeralds, hundreds of coins bearing the likenesses of Philip II and Philip III, and several small bars of gold and silver.

It had presented a dilemma to Kate at first. Did her mother know about it? How could she broach the subject without having conversations she wasn't ready to have? And the documents didn't mention her father's name. Instead, they clearly tied the treasure to Doctor Camelot. If she tried to sell any of the pieces, how could she avoid revealing the secrets her father had kept so carefully?

In the end, her father solved these problems for her. More notes, kept in the bottom of the chest, detailed small pieces that he had sold in the past, generally in order to pay for more equipment. He had used a contact in Vanguard City, a reformed fence whose life he had saved. The man had remained discreet in exchange for a thirty percent cut. He was still alive, and perfectly willing to resume the sales on Kate's behalf when she contacted him anonymously through encrypted telephone calls and e-mail messages. Much of the money had gone to her mother, deposited, also anonymously, in her savings account. Some had gone toward charity, including Vanguard City Children's Hospital. And the rest Kate had used herself, to purchase expensive and difficult-to-find equipment through the same fence.

Kate had been cautious in the sales, only releasing a couple of pieces at a time. But she'd practically cleaned out the chest the night the Storm Raiders had died. She took an ironic pleasure from using the treasure—sunk to the bottom of the ocean by pirates who had undoubtedly planned to plunder it instead—to finance her new plans for Pirate Town.

To keep movers from seeing anything they shouldn't, Kate had driven down to Devil's Cape with a trailer filled with scanners, processors, laboratory equipment, and enough armaments to launch a small war, leaving the bulk of her possessions for a moving truck to deliver later.

She'd loaded the equipment into large crates and used a small motorized dolly to wheel them onto the first floor of her home. Then, once the windows were covered and she had some measure of privacy, she'd broken out the exoskeleton that her father had worn within his Doctor Camelot armor. She'd retooled and resized it a few years earlier as a pet project, studying its hydraulics, replacing its body sensors with more sophisticated ones, and managing to tune up its strength enhancement to the point where she could comfortably carry more than a ton. Much more, if she wore the full armor on top of it, using its motors to augment those of the exoskeleton and to protect her from accidentally banging or pinching herself while carrying something heavy.

With the exoskeleton, she was able to set up her new lab in the hidden room, hauling her equipment up the stairs, setting up what she needed for her planned war on the *Cirque d'Obscurité:* ammunition for her various weapons, replacement parts, batteries for the armor's systems, and a high-end computer with back doors to tools she'd need, like the FBI's National Crime Information Center (NCIC) and Violent Criminal Apprehension Program (VICAP) databases, the records of the Devil's Cape Police Department, and 911 data. She'd studied more than engineering at MIT. She'd excelled at computer science and befriended an eccentric professor with a background as a hacker. He'd focused most of his hacking skills on pranks against counterparts at Caltech, but the principles applied elsewhere, as well.

And, of course, there was the Doctor Camelot armor itself. She'd modified the exoskeleton years ago—that had been an interesting challenge and a useful tool from time to time, though she'd had to keep it a secret to protect her father's identity. But the armor she'd left alone. Until her "aunts" and "uncles" had been murdered, she'd never seriously considered using the armor itself. It was a fascinating piece of workmanship, to be sure. Inspired, even. But not for her. Only now, that had changed. Now, someone had to bring the *Cirque d'Obscurité* to justice, and she couldn't entrust that job to anyone else.

Her father had been taller than she was and, of course, their bodies were considerably different. The first order of business had been resizing the armor. Or, more accurately, recreating the armor from scratch in her own dimensions. She modified it, too, along the way. She replaced heavy steel plating and the metal supports with a combination of ceramics, carbon nanotubes, and graphite and plastic polymers. In doing so, she made it exponentially more resistant to damage while cutting its weight by two-thirds. The armaments weren't her strong suit, and she left them more or less alone, only replacing pieces when technological advances made such selections obvious. The armor was armed with a high-pressure air cannon, a flamethrower, flash-bang grenades, a fast-bonding glue her father had affectionately referred to in his notes as "goop," tear gas, disruptive sonics, pepper spray, tasers, fire extinguishing foam, microwave bursts disruptive to electronics, and more.

Kate's father's specialty had been armaments, but her own specialty was information processing, and that's where she really pulled out all the stops. She'd studied digital signal processing first at MIT, and then as a design engineer at Texas Instruments, where she'd collected five patents. Her enhancements to the armor's strength and toughness would be helpful to her. But her enhancements to its sensors were real technical breakthroughs. She

added a global positioning system, of course. Her father's suit had allowed him to listen and transmit to local police and citizens' band radio. Her suit automatically scanned police radios; broadcast radio and television; and even nearby cell phone chatter, and could be programmed to flag conversations with certain key words or phrases. Her father's suit had had an AM/FM radio. Hers had satellite television and allowed her to surf the Internet and the databases she'd plugged into through her base. She gave the armor sophisticated facial recognition programs connected to government and private databases, electromagnetic scanners, a bomb and drug sniffer, microscopes, telescopes, parabolic hearing, laser-Doppler vibrometry, and an X-ray scanner. Her armor allowed her to see in infrared and ultraviolet, and its polarized faceplate protected her from sudden changes in light and allowed a variety of heads-up displays and targeting systems.

She wondered if it would be enough. Her armor was clearly superior to the armor her father had worn when he'd died, but he'd had experience. And allies.

Carrying her cooling fried dumplings and soup up the creaky stairs to her lab, she tried to plan her next actions. The armor needed tweaking, of course, and testing. But more importantly, she needed training. To a certain extent, she could do that on her own. But she needed assistance, insights, guidance. An ally. Using her key, she entered the secret door to her lab, then set up a secure, untraceable line and picked up the telephone. When the voice at the other end grunted a hoarse hello, she spoke softly, knowing that she would be aggravating wounds that hadn't even begun to heal. "Uncle Samuel," she said, "this is Kate. I have a proposition for you."

WTDC News: Covering the Cape, covering the world, covering your lives.

— From a station ad

TWENTY-FIVE

Devil's Cape, Louisiana
Five days after the deaths
of the Storm Raiders
4 p.m.

*T*he WTDC station wasn't much to look at. A '70s-era building made of chunks of concrete stuck at odd angles, it jutted out from a strip of small buildings that included three low-rent law offices, two massage parlors, and a fried chicken restaurant, all clustered along the interstate. The transmission tower was surrounded by anemic banana trees that reached little more than a third of its height. The station's large sign had been designed in fat, curvy letters and numbers considered "groovy" at the time. It was a bit of an embarrassment today, but no one ever budgeted the money to replace it.

Despite the cosmetics he'd caked onto his face, Jason Kale didn't even make it out of the parking lot before hearing the first crack about his eye. "Trying to peep through the keyhole, Kale? Get the doorknob in your eye?" He deflected that one with a wave and a smile. But it wouldn't be the last razzing he'd receive. While walking through the foyer—decorated with late-'80s photos of Devil's Cape and its citizens—he encountered the makeup artist who usually worked on him before a broadcast.

"What the hell happened to you?" she asked with customary bluntness. A lean woman with a large nose and lined face, she rarely smiled, hiding cracked, tobacco-stained teeth behind pursed lips. Her makeup, though, was of course impeccable.

Jason shrugged, smiled, and pushed his glasses slightly up his nose. "I was investigating a lead and, well, someone wasn't too happy about it." He'd decided before heading into work that afternoon that a vague answer might serve him better than a specific one.

"Uh huh," she said, voice disdainful. "You down talking to the strippers? That looks like a BRI."

He sighed, but went for the bait. "BRI?" he asked.

"Brassiere removal injury."

He forced a smile. "No, ma'am," he said. He'd found that a well-placed "ma'am" would occasionally pacify her.

It didn't work this time. She glared at him. "That'll be almost impossible to cover up," she said, unceremoniously pulling his face down toward hers and peering at the injury, pulling his glasses out of her way and scraping away some of the makeup with a sharp fingernail.

"I'm not on the air tonight," he said. "I'm just here to work on one of my stories. Tomorrow, probably. It'll have a day to heal."

She clucked her tongue scornfully. "It will be worse tomorrow," she said, releasing his face. She shook her head. "Tell you what," she said. "Don't put that junk on your face tomorrow and I won't try to break any crime stories."

He delivered what he hoped was a winning smile, though she was already walking away. "Deal," he said.

It galled him that he'd fought and captured the Troll with little consequence, but had been laid low by a kid too young to drive. He was lucky, he realized, sitting down at his unadorned desk. He'd been shot five times, once directly in the eye, and the worst he had to show for it was a shiner. He'd jumped into this Argonaut business based on a dream. He and Julian had long acted as though invulnerable, but they had no real clue as to their limitations. Or at least, if Julian had tested them, he hadn't passed on the information. That would be just like him, though. To test himself methodically, to withhold what he'd learned, to use the knowledge as a lever against Jason if the opportunity presented itself.

Devil's Cape needed someone. That much was clear.

But perhaps he'd been arrogant to decide that he was what the city needed. The Storm Raiders were experienced veterans, yet they'd been slaughtered by the *Cirque d'Obscurité*. He thought, too, of the city's last real superhero, the Gray Fog, and how terribly that man's life had been ripped asunder—his secret identity revealed to the world, his lover murdered, his own death the subject of conspiracy theories, though the only real question seemed to be whether his enemies had driven him to suicide or just outright murdered him.

And then there was Jason. He'd launched himself into a life as Argonaut, flying hero of Devil's Cape, taped himself vanquishing a monstrous foe. And now what? He'd been sent flying away with his tail between his legs by a kid with a pistol. He'd had these abilities all his life, but didn't know, really, what they were or where they came from.

Argonaut.

The name had come to him in a dream.

Why?

He'd read about the Argonauts as a child, read their stories from a battered volume he'd picked up at a flea market, its red leather tattered by age, its pages warped by water damage, thin and musty. And then one day, the book had simply disappeared from his room. He'd always suspected that Julian had taken it for some reason, though his brother denied it. And the stories gradually faded from his mind. Why was he thinking about the Argonauts now?

And what, really, was his goal here? To wipe out crime in Devil's Cape? It was impossible. He'd be like Sisyphus, condemned for eternity by the gods to roll a stone up a hill, then watch as it rolled down the other side.

And besides, powers or no, he'd just been beaten by a kid.

Staring into space, he rubbed absently at his bruised eye.

His hand was reaching out to answer the phone before it even rang. That instinct could only mean one caller. "Hello, Julian," he said before his brother even spoke. "You've never called me at work before. I don't remember giving you the number."

"What the hell were you doing last night?" his brother snapped. "I woke up weeping blood."

"Oh," said Jason, sitting straighter. "I'm a little surprised." And he was. It hadn't occurred to him that their odd connection would still be that strong.

"So was the woman in bed with me."

Jason grunted, pulling a pen from his drawer and tapping it against his desk. He caught a whiff of perfume. Musk and jasmine. He turned around, but no one was nearby. "Is she still there?"

"She just left."

"Nice perfume."

Jason could hear his brother breathing. Then Julian said, "You never answered my question."

Jason's eyes scanned the room. Again, no one was close by. "Gunshots," he whispered.

Julian clucked his tongue. "Huh," he said. "Clumsy of you."

"I know."

"What are you doing, Jason? What are you hoping to accomplish?"

"I was just wondering that myself."

"You should stop."

Jason tapped his cheek with the pen. His eye ached. His ribs ached. He had another dark bruise over his left kidney, a long scratch across one knee, a lump over one ear. Five shots. "I don't think so," he said.

He could hear Julian pacing. "You'll get yourself killed."

"What? Are you worried I'll take you with me?"

Julian released a martyred sighed. "It goes beyond that, you know. This is not a good place to be doing what you're doing. This is not a good time. Pop—"

"Don't bring him into this."

"I wouldn't bring him into this. If you screw up again, and you will screw up again, no matter how careful you are, *you* could be the one bringing him into it."

The pen snapped in Jason's hand, black ink running down his palm like blood. He threw it into the trash, wiped the ink off with a paper towel. "Do you ever wonder why we are what we are, Julian?"

His brother's laugh barked through the phone, harsh and with little humor. "What?" he said. "You mean you don't know?"

And then Jason heard the dial tone.

Patriot slugged me into a pinball machine once. Glass blew everywhere, the machine started beeping, and those little silver balls were rolling around the floor. For a second I thought she'd knocked one of my eyeballs out. Another time, Swashbuckler elbowed me in the ribs and I heard a couple of them snap just like that. But you know the hardest hit I ever took? It was from Sam Small. He jumped off a table and gave me just one pop to the jaw, and then I saw a gray light and I woke up in a prison hospital. It was those tiny fists—all that strength, so concentrated. It was like getting hit with a bullet.

— From *I Wore a Black Mask:*
Memoirs of Mr. Cyanide

TWENTY-SIX

Devil's Cape, Louisiana
Six days after the deaths
of the Storm Raiders
7 a.m.

Kate Brauer met Uncle Samuel—Samuel Cunningham—at a small news stand at the edge of the Lady Danger River. At Samuel's request, both wore running outfits, hers a sleeveless black tank top with red shorts and tennis shoes, his a gray Vanguard City Heroes T-shirt over tan shorts and some expensive kind of cross-trainer shoes. The headline "Search continues for Storm Raider killers" taunted them from the front page of the *Devil's Cape Daily Courier,* a stack of the papers squeezed between copies of *The Times-Picayune* and the *National Enquirer.*

The Lady Danger River, a thin tributary of the looming Lake Pontchartrain, was named after a masked English privateer who often crossed swords with St. Diable. One day, years into their rivalry, she simply disappeared from her ship, the *Silver Swan.* No one ever definitively proved what had happened to her, and her disappearance remained a local mystery and legend. Today, many believed that St. Diable had finally killed her, perhaps bribing one of her crewmen to poison her or slit her throat and toss her into the Gulf. Others believed that she had retired and actually married St. Diable in secret. Still others—an odd, but persistent faction—maintained that she had actually killed St. Diable then assumed his pirate identity, passing herself off as a masked man for the rest of her life.

The river itself was a thin one, once best known for its pollution due to a paper mill upstream, a failed competitor to Worldwide Papyrus's Fyke paper mill. Now, though, with the mill abandoned for the better part of a decade, the river was flanked by vegetation. Once, row after row of houses on pillars had stood on the river banks, populated largely by the families of mill workers and those who worked on Devil's Cape's docks. Now, many of them had been torn down, replaced with lively condominiums with pretentious French names and pinkish roofs.

Samuel looked older than Kate had remembered, though quite fit. A contemporary of her father's, he was probably in his late fifties. Five feet tall, he was tanned and muscular, his umber hair streaked with gray like ash. As he had walked up to her at their arranged meeting spot at the park, he'd seemed more confident than she'd remembered, his brown eyes watching her with a hint of amusement. "You're still spending too much time working on your circuits," he said, "and not enough time working on your circulatory system." He winked, taking any bite out of the comment. "You look good, though, Kate." They embraced quickly, then he nodded at a bench. "Stretch first," he said, "then run." His hands on the back of the bench, he began to stretch out one leg, then the other.

"I'd kind of been planning on talking to you over café au lait and beignets," she said, standing beside him and beginning some stretches of her own. Popular in Devil's Cape and its sister city New Orleans, beignets were French pastries dusted with powdered sugar, though the Devil's Cape bakers tended to add a little extra cinnamon, too.

He gave her a half-smile and shrugged. "Might as well start things off running," he said. "We've got a lot to cover."

She stopped her stretches for a moment, eyes seeking his. A street vendor was roasting almonds nearby and the scent of honey filled the air. "I also figured you'd try to talk me out of this," she said.

The half-smile remained on his face as he turned toward her. "Would it have worked?" he asked.

She shook her head.

"Didn't think so," he said. He pulled an antique brass watch from one pocket, glanced at it, and reset a pedometer at his waist. Then he gestured at the paved jogging trail. "Shall we?"

As answer, she began moving down the trail, already sweating in the heat and humidity.

He quickly caught up with her, his shoes nearly silent on the paved path.

They jogged together in quiet tandem for several minutes. A pair of scarlet tanagers flew by overhead.

He finally broke the silence. "You're surprised, aren't you, to see me not so broken up?"

She turned to look at him. They were moving past a flower cart, its wares bright and fragrant, many of the petals already wilting in the hot Devil's Cape sun. "I'm glad," she said.

He shrugged that off. "Look," he said finally, jogging around a puddle in the sidewalk where one of the condos was over-watering its emerald grass, "we're not going to dance around what we know, are we?"

She shook her head, squinting in the harsh sunlight, refracted through a haze of smog and thin clouds. She wasn't used to jogging, and her calves were beginning to ache. "No," she said. "Dad was Doctor Camelot. You are Sam Small. You were in the Storm Raiders together. I've known since college." She said the words like she was checking items off a list.

"Okay," he said. He had a long stride for such a short man. His tanned body glistened with sweat. "That's not everything, but it's enough for now." He glanced sideways on her, a smirk on his lips. "The cards are on the table." A jet roared by overhead as they rounded a bend in the sidewalk, turning into the entrance for the Lady Danger River Commons. Long and narrow, its edges shaded by moss-covered cypress trees, its shallow hills punctuated by banana trees and thriving with fragrant honeysuckle bushes and azaleas, the park had recently taken on a sour reputation for a series of rapes that had occurred there late at night. The park's name, of course, had inspired lurid headlines and even a few cracks from late show comedians. Although the rapist had been caught, the Lady Danger River Commons was less popular than it once had been, and city officials were pushing to change the name to something more neutral, as though the name itself were responsible for the crime.

Samuel and Kate slowed as they jogged through the park, its beauty striking to them, their voices lowered. "When your dad died," Samuel said, "it tore my heart open. I questioned myself. I questioned what we do. I questioned the world. I practically wore sackcloth for months."

They passed a trio of kids throwing a frisbee, and when the disk went wild and headed past them, Samuel pitched his body forward like an outfielder, snagging the edge of the toy, rolling into a somersault, spinning his body, and throwing the frisbee back to the kids in an easy, graceful flight. It was an Olympic-class maneuver, and the kids stared at him open-mouthed and then began to clap. He waved back at them briskly, taking a jaunty bow and resuming the jog. When he spoke again, it was as though nothing had just happened.

"I was depressed," he said. "I couldn't sleep. I cried at odd hours. It was the most terrible thing that had ever happened to me." He glanced at her.

She nodded at him to continue, out of breath from the jogging and not willing to interrupt.

"It wasn't just your dad," he clarified. He glanced at

her again. "I mean, he was a great guy and a good friend and I still miss him. But it was the reality of him dying. We weren't playing dress-up. We weren't just some club. I mean, he died, and that was it. I came to his funeral and I sat with you and you were so alone, and I thought to myself, who is going to get this little girl dressed for the prom? Who's going to make sure her date treats her right? Who's going to move her to college?"

"You did," she said.

He shrugged it off, ducking under a branch covered with pink azalea blossoms that had grown out into the path. "So the reality was there, and I couldn't get the image—I'm sorry to dwell on this, but you need to hear it—I couldn't get the image of him dying out of my head."

She winced. "Uncle Samuel, I'm not sure I want—"

His voice, usually mild, turned steely. "That doesn't much matter," he said. He increased their pace. They passed an elderly woman throwing bread to pigeons. The birds swarmed around her like a cloud. "This is the rest of it, the part we didn't mention before in your checklist of secrets." His voice went staccato. "A few nights ago you took your father's armor and emptied his secret lab. You left a note there for your mother telling her not to worry, as though that were possible. You intend to become the new Doctor Camelot and to hunt down the people who killed your father and who killed the Storm Raiders. Everyone but me."

She was struggling to keep up with him.

His feet beating rhythmically against the pavement, he stared at her. "That about sum it up?"

She nodded. "Yes," she said. She hadn't spoken her intentions out loud to anyone before. It felt good to do so, a relief. But a burden, too. A commitment. She nearly tripped on a crack in the asphalt, then righted herself.

"Then you need to listen to this, the details and all. This isn't something entered lightly." He wiped his arm against his forehead, slowing to a more normal pace, but still pressing on. "We were trying to stop the *Cirque d'Obscurité* from tearing down the Roscoe Clay Bridge." He shook his head. "They'd been hired to do it by Deadlock. You've heard of him, right? A master planner. He always planned things so that he could accomplish at least three goals at once. That time, it was—" He ticked the items off on his fingers as he ran. "Destroying the bridge so that the construction company he was invested in would get the rebuilding contract. Killing a federal

judge who always crossed that bridge at the same time of morning—the judge was about to make a ruling that would have damaged Deadlock's stock portfolio. And creating a distraction, keeping us busy so that his other hired goons could break into a bank vault across town."

He shook his head again, picking up the pace slightly. "We were tipped to it. I don't remember how, exactly. Something about the judge." He snapped his fingers. "Yeah, Deadlock had been gathering intel on the judge from people at the court, and one of them realized that the judge was in danger. Your dad figured out that Deadlock had hired some mercenaries, and pinpointed the *Cirque d'Obscurité*. He even figured out where and when based on the judge's usual schedule. So we were there at the bridge when the *Cirque d'Obscurité* attacked."

His voice pitched an octave lower. Throughout the conversation, he'd been turning to her every few seconds. But now he stared at the ground, at the path ahead, at anything but Kate. "We didn't know much of anything about the *Cirque d'Obscurité* then, and we underestimated them badly. We were holding them off pretty well. Raiden kept them dancing with his bolts of lightning. Miss Chance helped make sure that a cement truck dumped about a ton of wet concrete on Hector Hell. Velociraptor managed to pin down Kraken. I was tangling with the Werewolf, trying to grab his neck, trying to keep him from biting me in half." He stopped talking for a moment as they passed a pair of joggers heading in the opposite direction. "And then Hector Hell got off a stray shot at the bridge. His fire tore right through one of the support struts. There was an awful sound of metal rending and the road across the bridge starting to tear up." Samuel's eyes stayed forward. "Your dad flew in there, into the mess of slag and crumbling rock that Hector Hell had made, and he started to hold everything together."

Kate was panting now from the exertion, from the story, struggling to keep up with him. It had been a long time since she'd run like this.

Sensing her dropping back, Samuel eased the pace

a bit, but didn't stop running. "That armor made your father so strong," he said. "He could lift more than a ton. He got himself into the hole where the strut had been. He held everything together with one arm, using one of the tools in his armor to start to make some repairs, to patch up the hole enough that the bridge would keep standing." Samuel's own breath was getting ragged. "I could see him standing there working on the hole, his armor catching the sunlight, when the Behemoth walked up."

She felt tears in her eyes, saw them in his. "Uncle Samuel—" she started.

"Let me finish," he said. His voice was a low whisper, almost lost in his panting from the run, but she heard it. "He'd want you to hear this. He'd want you to hear this before you did what you're thinking of doing." He finally turned to her again, slowing his pace a little more. They entered the shadow of a row of oak trees. "He'd want you to hear."

She nodded.

He turned back to the path in front of them and slowed to a walk. "The Behemoth in pictures is impressive enough, but that's nothing like seeing him up close. He's about ten feet tall. Literally. Muscles on top of muscles like a huge bodybuilder. Covered with these horrific tattoos. He smells terrible, too. Like the cat house at a cheap zoo where they don't clean often enough. He smells of spoilage and death. His claws—when I'm shrunk down, those claws are as big as I am."

He shook his head. "The thing you have to know, Kate, is that your father saw the Behemoth coming. He could tell that the Behemoth was going to attack him, and he knew perfectly well how strong that man is. Just minutes before, we both saw him throw an empty school bus nearly half a mile, and he wasn't trying very hard. But your dad stayed put. I still don't know why. Maybe he hadn't quite finished fixing the strut yet. Maybe he thought his armor was stronger than it was. But he stayed there, finishing his soldering and gluing and whatever else he was doing. He stayed there and didn't flinch when the Behemoth reached out and grabbed his head in one hand."

Walking beside him, Kate started to cry. The scent of honeysuckle was fading and she was picking up the edge of something rotten in the air, something foul. She wiped an eye on her shoulder and resolutely turned her attention back to Samuel.

Samuel shrugged. "That was it, more or less. The Behemoth twisted his hand, and some joint in your father's armor broke and his neck snapped. We were all so shocked that they got away. We tried to track them down, but they went on the run, eventually leaving the country." He finally pointed to a bench and walked toward it. Instead of sitting, he began to do his stretches again, working the muscles, keeping them from cramping. He gestured for her to do the same and she did. "I nearly quit, you know," he said. "All of us did. And I was depressed for months. But then Vikki finally snapped me out of it."

Vikki was Victoria Moon, one of Kate's "aunts." She had been the superhero Miss Chance, who was supposed to be able to manipulate probabilities—luck—to her advantage.

Samuel bent far forward, massaging a calf. "The two of us were trying to capture Lionman and I had my head up my ass. I was thinking about retiring, about your dad, about how damn stupid it was for me to shrink myself down to six inches tall like a walking, talking Ken doll. So she finally turned to me and said, 'If I kick the bucket tonight, you've got to promise not to mope so damn much. I won't be responsible for you sucking that much sunshine out of the world.' And then we talked about it. She cried, I cried, and Lionman nearly got away, but then we stopped him and found out that he was planning to kill an ex-girlfriend of his—he'd been stalking her for weeks in between pulling of string of bank heists. If we'd let him get away, he probably would have killed the woman. But we caught him. He went to jail because of us. And it was better after that."

He finally sat on the bench. The bench was deep and high and his feet almost didn't make it to the ground. "All of us knew, Katie, that we could die. Every day. It's a part of what we do—of what we did. You think we went up against the blind? All of us—*all* of us—updated our wills. We were quiet on that flight down. That's part of why Winged Tornado rode in that damn plane with us—he could fly as fast as a plane, you know. Faster, really. We knew that one of us might die down here and we wanted to be together." He sighed. "We didn't figure it would go as badly as it did, but we knew that it might happen."

Kate placed a hand on his back and he leaned back into it. He patted her gently on the knee, then turned to look at her. "I promised Vikki all that time ago that I wouldn't mope if she died. I've broken that promise a bit, though I don't think she'd hold it against me, under the circumstances. But I'm not going to let the rest of my life be darkened by what happened." He smiled faintly. "And besides, that was it, you know. That day was my last time in the silly, tiny suit."

She opened her mouth to say something in reply, some protest, but he shook his head.

"I knew when you knew, you know." He smiled at the twisted words. "You were careful in your father's work-shop, but your mother could tell you'd been down there. And she called me. She wasn't sure what to do about it. I told her you were old enough, that you had to decide for yourself what to do with the knowledge, that you'd work through it. She was terrified that you'd put on the armor yourself, that you'd try to do something stupid. She wanted me to swear that, if you ever did that, I'd talk you out of it." He paused. "I didn't swear. I knew that the time might come when you wanted to do this, and that it wasn't in my nature to make you stop. So I'm not going to tell you not to do it." He pointed at her. "But start smaller. Practice. Work with me." He gestured at her. "One little run, and you're exhausted. How are you going to make out if you get into a prolonged fight?"

She shook her head. "The armor's motors make movement nearly effortless—"

He cut her off. "Yeah, and what happens if the armor cuts out? It happened to your dad once or twice. You're left carrying a hundred and fifty pounds on your back."

"It's more like sixty-five now."

He nodded. "All right, then. Next workout, you jog wearing sixty-five pounds on your back."

She looked at him and smiled. "I don't suppose you'd care to take a taxi back to our cars?"

He shook his head, a faint grin on his lips. "Nope," he said. The haze was breaking away overhead and the hot sunlight suddenly flooded the bench. He stood. "We'll keep a better pace on the way back," he said. "I won't take it so easy on you."

And she rose and began to jog after him.

I've studied sleep patterns in Chicago, London, Vanguard City, Miami, even as close by as New Orleans. Inevitably, patients in Devil's Cape spend as much as twenty-five percent more of their sleep in a state of fitful dreaming. Inside or outside of Holingbroke. It can't just be a matter of the heat. There are other patterns at play here, patterns I'm as yet unable to discern.

— Excerpted from the journal of
Dr. Dennis Marchant, Holingbroke
Psychological Institute, 1957

TWENTY-SEVEN

Devil's Cape, Louisiana

*Eight days after the deaths
of the Storm Raiders
2 a.m.*

At first, Jason's dream seemed almost pathetically obvious. Literal. He'd fallen asleep reading about the Argonauts, and in his dream, he found himself dressed in a white tunic, surrounded by faceless, muscular men, working a huge oar made from an olive tree, its surface rubbed down with sandalwood oil. The salt air filled his nostrils and the Aegean Sea was a rich blue that reflected the sunlight.

And then the woman walked down the length of the *Argo* toward him. She was beautiful. Her blonde hair was tied neatly behind her in a ponytail. Her skin was flawless. Her simple tunic clung to her.

And her eyes seemed filled with blood.

"So you're the man of the hour, huh?" she said. Her voice had a slight Southern twang to it, and she spoke English, not Greek. She glanced around at the rows of men, her red eyes apparently taking them in without difficulty. "I tell you, this wasn't the dream I planned on being part of. Nor are you the dreamer." She shrugged, her pale shoulders rising and falling, a scattering of freckles catching the sunlight. "But the one I was seeking is filled with doubts and disbelief. He's closed to me now. And yet you—you're so very open that it's like you were shining a light for me." She peered closer at him, touched his forearm as he worked the oar. "Now why is that?"

His muscles ached from the labor of working the oar. As his eyes moved out to the sea, he could tell by the movement of the foam and the spray and the seagulls in the distance that they were moving very, very fast.

"Ho!" shouted a voice to his right. Turning, he saw one of the other men at the oars come into focus. He was brown-haired, bearded, and almost impossibly muscular. His bronzed skin glistened in the sunlight. He was wrapped in a tattered lion's pelt, its huge head open in a roar. Heracles. "At last!" the man snorted in Greek. "Someone who can match my power. I've been babying poor Theseus here along." He gestured at another man, thinner and spare, whose curly black locks ran to his shoulders. Theseus's eyes, framed by long, delicate eyelashes, were a piercing slate gray that didn't reflect the light. They looked calculating and haunted. He nodded at Jason. "Ho, Argonaut," he said in a voice rough with salty air.

Jason nodded back at the two men. He looked back at the woman. A few hairs had strayed from her ponytail and they danced in the wind. He wondered how she could see with those eyes. "I don't know," he said.

"You don't seem particularly surprised," she said, gently nudging a faceless Argonaut aside and sitting beside Jason on the bench, "to be in a dream like this."

Jason watched as two men near the front of the *Argo* dropped their oars. They stood in unison, blond and handsome. The backs of their tunics were suddenly pushed open and huge, white, feathered wings sprang out, spreading against the wind. They launched themselves into the air, laughing, waving at their crewmates below. They flew effortlessly with their wings, steering themselves toward the sun in some elaborate game of tag. Calais and Zetes—the Boreads—sons of Boreas, Greek god of the north wind. Jason lifted an arm from his oar for a moment and waved at them, then quickly returned to the grueling work before Heracles' strength, unbalanced by Jason's, could steer them off course. It was very important, for some reason, to remain on course.

"I've had dreams this vivid before," he said. He thought of a dream he'd had as a child, a dream of flying. And the following day, he'd learned how to take flight and had taught Julian what he'd learned. He thought, too, of the more recent dream, the one with the beach and the vestments. "I've learned not to fear them," he said.

A gaunt man rowing in front of them released his oar and turned around. His black hair was thin and streaked with gray. *"Fear them,"* he said in Greek, his voice shaking. His eyes were the green of olives, his skin paler than the other Argonauts, the circles under the eyes dark with fatigue or worry or illness. *"You should always fear your dreams,"* the man whispered.

"Idmon?" Jason asked. Idmon the seer. He had visions. He'd known that he would die if he joined the Argonauts, yet he'd done so anyway. He'd died in Bithnyia and the city of Heraclea was built over his bones.

Idmon nodded slowly. *"And you are the other Jason,"* he said. His eyes moved languidly to the mysterious woman beside Jason and then he nodded again, in respect or sympathy.

"You were one of my heroes," Jason said quietly, grunting at the strain of the oar, barely aware that he was slipping into Greek. *"You knew you were going to— You knew what might happen to you, but you weren't afraid."*

A mocking smile crept up Idmon's lips. "You're a fool," he said, speaking in English now. "I'm terrified. I'm frightened every day as my time grows closer." He nodded at the vast, blue Aegean. "I vomit into the waters in fear."

Jason's mouth felt dry. "Then you have no choice?"

Idmon shook his head, spat upon the Argo's deck. "I choose," he said. "I am proud of my choice. That does not relieve the fear." He turned back to his oar.

Jason stared at the man's back for a moment, felt his hands gripping tight against the oar, the roughness of the wood as the sandlewood oil was slowly rubbed away.

One of the men at the front of the ship began to sing, the other Argonauts joining in. It was a coarse ditty about the labors of Heracles, clearly sung at the huge man's expense, though he joined in as enthusiastically as the others. One voice stood apart from the rest, not in volume or pitch, but in mellifluous clarity and soft beauty. It was easily the most beautiful voice Jason had ever heard. Orpheus. He strained to listen to it, to focus on that voice alone.

"You'll be waking soon," the woman said.

Still trying to focus on the words of Orpheus, he frowned at her.

"There's something I need you to do," she said.

As he listened to her, Orpheus's voice faded into the background.

A six-hour standoff in Bogan Heights between Devil's Cape police and 27-year-old Michael Orfanos ended with a crash this afternoon. Orfanos, wanted for questioning on charges of armed robbery, had entered the home of a neighbor, Nicole Cayce, 34, whom he held hostage. A police insider who preferred to remain anonymous reported that Orfanos was just on the verge of surrendering to police when a masked figure in a mustard yellow and black uniform literally flew through a skylight in Cayce's home. The figure emerged through the same skylight a minute later carrying Orfanos in his arms. Police are investigating the incident and a manhunt is on both for Orfanos and the masked figure. Cayce told reporters that Orfanos identified the masked man as 'Scion.'

— Excerpted from "Masked figure breaks police stand-off," by Dedrick Swader, *Devil's Cape Daily Courier*, local news section

TWENTY-EIGHT

Devil's Cape, Louisiana
Eight days after the deaths
of the Storm Raiders
7 p.m.

As he slowly and cautiously walked across the roof of the condemned warehouse, old tar sticking to his feet, the darkness of this mostly abandoned corner of Devil's Cape's warehouse district shrouding him, Julian Kalodimos hoped again that Uncle Costas knew what he was doing with this woman Rusalka.

She'd been stuck in the hot shack on top of the warehouse for three days now, the weak air conditioner he'd installed for her reducing the summer heat to a level that was survivable, but not at all comfortable. She ate the food he brought her, drank the water as though dying of thirst, and refrained from touching him, as he'd ordered her, but her eyes smoldered with hatred.

The shack itself, a ramshackle clapboard structure little bigger than the room that she'd spent most of the past few years in at the Holingbroke Psychological Institute, wasn't strong enough to keep her detained. What riveted her was the weakness of the warehouse. Most of its supporting structure had been ravaged first by a hurricane the prior autumn, then by the weight of an unexpected January snowstorm, until the whole building swayed in a light breeze and chunks of plaster from the upper levels routinely broke off and fell to the ground far below. Cain had watched her try to walk out of the shack, to navigate her way across the roof to a safe way down.

233

DEVIL'S CAPE

But each time she'd done so, she'd been turned back by the groaning of the roof's boards and the shifting of the roof itself. Once, her foot actually broke through the tarpaper so that she was slammed onto her face, hearing the wood splintering around her, no doubt certain that she was about to die. It had taken her close to an hour to crawl back to the shack on her belly.

Each time Julian had walked over to her shack, she'd watched him carefully, noting where he'd placed his feet, obviously planning to copy his steps and follow the safe path he appeared to be privy to.

Only, of course, there was no safe path. No place on that roof was safe at all, except for the shack itself, for which Julian had carefully constructed a series of supports running all the way to the warehouse's foundation. When he walked across that rickety roof, he was more or less flying, reducing his own weight to something in the nature of twenty pounds. She just didn't have any way of knowing that.

"I hope you like tandoori," he said, stepping softly into the shack, holding up a paper bag and another half dozen bottles of water.

Although he knew perfectly well that she'd been standing by the door watching him approach until a few seconds earlier, Julian found Olena Zhdanov stretching languidly on her cot, a diaphanous yellow nightgown that she'd brought with her stretched tight against her.

She sat up slowly, trying not very subtly to draw his attention to her body as she reached forward and took a bottle. "I am not minding it," she said. "Only I am hoping that perhaps we can eat somewhere else."

Julian smirked. Her broken English was a sham, something she'd been putting on since he'd met her to make him underestimate her. The nightgown, too, was another technique, a clumsy one. "Nice color," he said, gesturing at it. "Kind of matches mine." He was dressed, as he had been every time he had seen her, in the uniform he wore as Scion, a dark mustard yellow bodysuit with black on the sides and on his gloves. A mask covered most of his face, leaving his eyes and mouth visible. He figured that his goatee wasn't distinctive enough to make him recognizable, and besides, few people saw him dressed as Scion for long, or in good lighting.

He tossed her the bag of tandoori chicken, the scents of garlic, ginger, and kashmiri red chili powder quickly filling the small shack.

She caught the bag deftly enough, pouting at him. "You not very nice," she said.

"You not very smart," he echoed, mockingly. "I saw what you did to that orderly. I watched him shrivel up. I saw your eyes, how excited you got, the steam blowing out of your mouth like you were smoking a cigarette after a good screw." He shook his head, leaning back against the doorframe. Leaning back away from her. "You think flirting with me is really going to be very effective?"

She glared at him.

"Oh, you're pretty enough, in a Euro-trash sort of way," he went on. "But I know better than to get close to you."

She stepped forward as though getting ready to slap him.

He stood straight, stuck out a gloved hand. "No," he said firmly, watching her stop herself, considering, and readjust her nightgown. He grinned. "Beyond the fact that I won't hesitate to knock you unconscious again," he said, "you probably shouldn't try to kill me. What if you succeeded? Hell, it wouldn't take you long to run out of food and water and then where would you be?" He stretched one boot outside of the shack and slammed his foot down. Boards and metal as far as fifty feet away groaned in protest and the whole shack wobbled.

Something flickered and died in Zhdanov's eyes, and Julian felt ashamed of himself. For some reason, staring at this striking, troubled Russian woman, he couldn't help remembering the body of David Dees from years ago, lying in an alley only a few blocks away from here, the blood spreading out from him.

"Look," he said. "Eat the damn chicken. We need to talk."

"I change first," she said, gesturing to her nightgown.

He nodded. "Yeah, fine. But that's another thing. Lose the bad grammar, okay? I know your English is impeccable."

She stared at him, her hand pulling at one of the straps of her nightgown. She raised an eyebrow. "Fine," she said. "Get the hell out of my shack while I change, then. Unless you want to be a voyeur."

Her shack. He shook his head, then stepped outside, closing the door behind him. The night air was hot, as usual, and thick with smog and the diesel odor of the nearby wharf. He heard crickets chirping and rats scuttling their way through the broken building. Zhdanov called herself Rusalka after a Slavic myth about young women murdered near lakes who rose as spirits that drew men to their deaths, drowning them or killing them with the force of their hysterical, chilling laughter. And he'd seen what she could do. It wasn't drowning, exactly, but she'd laughed to herself while doing it, the light in her eyes exultant, the sweat a fine sheen on her skin. She seemed rational, for the most part, but that moment of ecstasy, while she drew the life from an orderly who was doing nothing but lying unconscious in her path through the hallway, after Julian had subdued him, was stark in his mind. It had made his next action—punching her in the back of the head to knock her senseless, an easy one. He didn't doubt that she'd been locked in that asylum for good reason.

She opened the door for him, now wearing sweatpants and an oversized Lehane University T-shirt. Backing away from him, she sat in an old wooden chair and began pulling her tandoori chicken from the bag. "So," she said, opening a container and jabbing her fork inside. "Are you finally ready to tell me why you've brought me here? Did I kill someone you care about?" Her voice had lost almost all hint of a Russian accent, and she spoke about killing without inflection, as though this were a matter of little importance.

"No," he said, though he remembered the orderly's withered corpse, wondering if the man had family, feeling responsible. "I don't particularly care about what you've done." He pulled absently at one of his gloves. He seemed to have more tolerance for heat and cold than most people, but he was still sweating inside his uniform. "Have you ever heard of Costas Kalodimos?"

She narrowed her eyes, chewing on a bite of chicken. She shook her head. "No," she said, though he wasn't sure that she was telling the truth. She looked at him. "You should bring me some cigarettes next time. I could really use a cigarette. Stolichnyes or Bogatyris. Not your American crap."

"Costas Kalodimos is an important local businessman," he said

"Maybe *he* can bring me some cigarettes," she said, taking a bite of saffron rice.

"He is very influential in the city's community."

"He is a criminal, you are saying." She shook her head, pointing at the rice with her fork. "Too much saffron. Are you wanting me to work for this Costas Kalodimos or kill him?" she asked blandly.

There were times, Julian thought, when killing Uncle Costas sounded like an excellent idea. "To work for him," he said.

She bit into another piece of her chicken. "He is an influential criminal, you say, and he has enough power to control you and to arrange this." Her hand swept the room. "But he's not influential enough that I've ever heard of him."

"He keeps a low profile," Julian said.

She snorted. "So do garbage men." She stabbed the air with her fork. "He is looking to change things. He is unhappy with his situation. He wants me to kill someone."

She was sharper than he'd suspected. "Yes," he said.

Her eyes went to his. "To reach the level you suggest he has in this city," she said, "he either opposes the Robber Baron or works for him. Yes?" She rattled off the

Robber Baron's name without hesitation, as though the man weren't one of the most powerful and feared crime figures in the history of the world.

"The latter."

She smiled, smug. "Then that is it," she said. "He wants me to kill the Robber Baron." Her smile grew. "That will be very expensive."

He was staring at her, uncertain how to respond, when he heard the cracking noise. A board on one side of the roof had snapped. He thought he heard a man's voice, probably swearing.

Someone else had made it to the top of the building.

"Wait here," he said, stepping out of the shack, slamming the door, and sprinting lightly across the roof, using his flight to make himself nearly weightless. Even without flying, he'd once clocked himself running at more than sixty-five miles per hour. He covered the space of the roof in seconds, kicking chunks of tarpaper into the air. They fluttered to the ground below like dying birds.

Julian found himself facing a tall black man in a gray suit, its fabric torn from the climb up the side of the building. The man wore a pink and blue striped tie that caught the faint glimmer of distant lights. Balancing himself on the edge of the building, standing on the balls of his feet like a trained fighter despite his conservative clothing, the man sized up Julian and his uniform. He sniffed the air. "Orange blossom, coriander, cedar," he said. "I believe that you are responsible for freeing my patient." He smiled, showing very white teeth, but the smile didn't reach his eyes. They looked as empty and dark as the smog-filled sky.

At the birth, the doctor was shocked. One nurse fainted while another ran screaming. The parents had to be sedated. An exorcist was flown directly to the scene by the Vatican. Why? Because of the baby. Baby Boy Doe was born with bright-red skin, horns and a forked tail.

— Excerpted from "Devil baby
born in city of Dubai,"
American Inquiry Weekly

TWENTY-NINE

Devil's Cape, Louisiana
Eight days after the deaths
of the Storm Raiders
6 p.m.

Jazz walked from her bathroom to her bedroom in the camelback upstairs, stairs creaking under her bare feet, shuddering once again at the thought of Gork having walked through her house. But standing in her bedroom with its black-painted walls and black satin sheets, she felt more comfortable, more confident. She was close, she thought. One way or another, something would happen tonight. The crucible was lit.

Jazz hadn't spoken to Cain—in person, at least—since the hot summer afternoon when she'd laid her curse upon him. She'd kept tabs on him, though. She'd heard about him taking his mother and neighbor hostage, heard about the things he'd been shouting. So she knew that her curse had been successful, that she'd actually managed to transform him into a beast. She'd healed, eventually, from the bash to her head, though she still suffered headaches, usually late at night, and a small scar on her cheek reminded her every day of the switch-blade he'd used on her.

She'd been surprised and somewhat disconcerted to learn that Cain had apparently reformed. He'd quit the Concrete Executioners, done his time, absorbed himself in his classes at school, studied to become a psychiatrist. She'd never really intended or wanted to "scare him straight." She'd meant to scare him to death. But she'd decided, after meditating on it many times and consulting her cards, her tea leaves, her numbers, and the soft lines on her hands, to leave well enough alone. The curse was always there, waiting, hovering over Cain, in case she needed it.

As soon as the Robber Baron walked into her home, she needed it.

She'd deceived the Robber Baron on one point. It was true that she couldn't see the future, and that she had little control over the insights she had into other people's lives. But she had her own influence. In a moment of fury and terror, she'd cursed Cain. And at other times throughout her life, focusing her concentration through certain spells and rituals, she'd been able to influence others. She could make them see or hear things that weren't there. She could talk to them in their dreams.

Not long after she'd cursed Cain, she'd been able to chase off an uncle who had been making advances on her. She'd made him dream of fire and monsters and flashing teeth, and eventually, he'd left Devil's Cape.

A customer who'd come in for a palm reading and then purchased dozens of items from her store with a bad check had been given glimpses of ghosts and rotting zombies whenever she'd looked into a mirror or seen her reflection. Within a week, Jazz had returned to her house one afternoon to find a tidy box on her gallery. It was packed with the items, three twenty-dollar bills, and a note that said merely, "Please release me."

She'd given a neighborhood crack dealer nightmares so horrible, filled with images of dying children and blood-filled streets, that he'd eventually killed himself.

And a night not long after the Robber Baron's visit, she gave Cain Ducett a nightmare of himself as a demon once again, made him see her and hear her at every turn, driven him to become the cursed monster that she'd created.

Because perhaps a monster could save her. A monster could protect her from the Robber Baron.

Only it hadn't worked. Cain should have come looking

for her, tormented, ready to do anything to free himself from her power.

Instead, nothing.

Oh, she'd disturbed him that first day. She'd even sacrificed the beloved antique full-length mirror she'd bolted to one wall of her bedroom, breaking it so that, through magical synchronicity, she could in turn shatter the window of his car to get his attention. She'd managed to sneak a copy of the old tabloid with the "Devil Baby of Dubai" story into his office.

But he hadn't come looking for her. Instead, he'd been distracted, the fear draining away from him. Her influence over others worked by initial surprise and growing dread. When she frightened others, they lowered their barriers, and she could influence them even more. But not Cain.

She had tried last night to enter his dreams again, and been shocked to find herself in someone else's. She'd seen the news reports of a new superhero in Devil's Cape, Argonaut, and it had been simple enough to deduce that she was in his dream. But she'd been unsure why—something to do with his abilities, not hers—and unsure what to do with the opportunity. Perhaps Argonaut could protect her from the Robber Baron, and she could forget about Cain. But that didn't feel right. She needed Cain. She needed to break him away from whatever was distracting him. She needed to force the curse to take hold of him again.

So that was how she had used the opportunity of Argonaut's dream. She'd fed the man a pack of lies and sent him after Dr. Cain Ducett.

Wherever he steps, whatever he touches, whatever he leaves will serve as a silent witness against him.

— Excerpted from Edmund Locard,
author of *E'enquete criminelle et
les methodes scientifique*, 1920

THIRTY

Devil's Cape, Louisiana
Eight days after the deaths
of the Storm Raiders
6 p.m.

It took Cain days of searching, avoiding increasing scrutiny from Detective Cynthia Daigle and her team, to find Olena Zhdanov. He was more and more amazed at the acuity of his own senses and wondered if they had suddenly come into focus, or if they had always been this sharp, but he had been denying that to himself. A question, he had decided, for another day, though one not too far in the future.

He began with the aftershave, following its wafting trail through the halls of Holingbroke. Strangely enough, it led to the roof and then ended. There was no easy egress from the roof, and no clear reason for someone to have gone up there. But he spotted two of Olena Zhdanov's hairs stuck against the mortar of the building's brick façade. He left the hairs in place, but decided not to mention them to the detective.

As he went through the course of his workday, treating his patients, leading group and private therapy sessions, and dealing with the inevitable fallout of an escaped patient, he found himself thinking more and more about the roof of Holingbroke, about Zhdanov and whoever had arrived to break her free.

He'd made little progress with Zhdanov during their years of treatment together. Oh, they'd developed something of a rapport. They exchanged pleasantries

through the thick glass wall that separated them, a necessity because of her abilities. She'd spoken to him about her childhood in Russia, her parents, her friends, her dreams of coming to America. She'd wept when discussing the day when her powers had manifested and when she'd "accidentally" killed Eisenberg and the others.

But almost everything she'd ever told him was a lie.

She'd told him elaborate stories about her childhood in Moscow. Her father, she said, was a police officer, her mother an administrative official with the Communist Party. She had an older brother, but she was her parents' favorite, the jewel of the house. She'd wept when she'd discussed her brother's death in Afghanistan.

Cain had checked into her background. She was from the Siberian city of Irkutsk, not Moscow. She had no brother. She was the middle of three sisters. Her father was a fisherman in Lake Baikal, the deepest lake in the world. Her mother died during an influenza outbreak. Zhdanov and her two sisters had all been involved in a boating accident during which her sisters had both drowned and Zhdanov had caught pneumonia.

He'd tried to lead her to tell him the truth, but she elaborated on her lies instead. He'd ultimately confronted her with the facts as he knew them about her family, and she'd exploded in rage, trying to break through the glass barrier between them with her fists, shouting at him in Russian, raging in anger, until she finally collapsed in tears, her fingernails torn and bleeding, three knuckles, as they'd later discover, cracked from the impact with the glass.

He taped their conversations as a matter of course, and he'd had her outburst translated. She'd been ranting and had called him a number of names, but interspersed with her tantrum were stark words where she seemed to confuse her rage against him with a deeply held resentment against her father: "I drowned Mavra and Sofiya," she'd said, speaking of her sisters. "I suffocated Mother beneath a pillow. I made myself breathe

the cold water so that I would grow sick. And you still never loved me."

Cain never really heard truth from her again. After that incident, she returned to her stories of a Moscow life, a dead brother who never lived, a father who caught criminals instead of fish and who loved her.

He pitied Zhdanov, and he wanted to help her to face the truth about herself and the terrible things she had done. But now his first priority was making sure that she was locked away where she couldn't kill anyone else.

Zhdanov had few ties to other people. Most of her family was dead, of course, and her father remained in Russia. She'd arrived in the United States a very short time before killing Todd Eisenberg, and she had been in Holingbroke for nearly three years. On the one hand, Cain could see little reason for anyone to break her out of the institute, especially this long after she'd first been admitted. On the other hand, despite the warnings all staff and even some fellow patients who came into contact with her received, she was an attractive, manipulative, seductive woman. It wouldn't have been impossible for her to convince someone that she needed to be "rescued."

He visited her room again after the police had cleared the scene. Most of her clothes were missing, as was a pillowcase that presumably had been used to carry them. But the few cosmetics she was allowed remained untouched in her bathroom. Even her winter clothes were missing from her chest of drawers, but the toiletries remained. It made him wonder. Had she been expecting to leave, would she really have packed winter clothing? He decided then that she hadn't packed her things at all. Someone else had grabbed her clothing from her drawers and thrown them into her pillowcase. Whoever it was—the man with the aftershave, presumably—hadn't thought to pack her toiletries. So this was a surprise for her. She'd been unready.

Cain had stood in her room, staring at her bookshelf, her remaining possessions, thinking about it. His eyes

had flicked to the mirror in her bathroom, and he'd remembered Jazz, the monster he'd seen in the mirror, the yellowed tabloid he'd crammed into a desk drawer. And then he forced himself to return his thoughts to Zhdanov. It was safer to pursue an escaped psychopath, he thought wryly, than it was to think too hard about the other questions facing him.

The scent of the aftershave was fading even to his vivid senses. If Zhdanov hadn't expected to leave, he thought, then that meant that concentrating on her might be a mistake. The police were undoubtedly concentrating on finding out where Zhdanov would be inclined to go. Would she flee back to Russia? Would she connect with old friends? Would she hide someplace she'd known well before she'd been locked away?

But what if she wasn't running the show? What if the man with the aftershave was in charge? Then he would be the one to follow.

As a student, inspired by conversations with Detective Salazar Lorca, Cain had written a paper about Locard's exchange principle, named for the French forensic scientist Edmund Locard. Conceptually, anytime two things came into contact, they exchanged something, leaving traces of their interaction. Dust. Hair. Threads. Tiny bits of skin.

Detective Daigle and the police technicians had searched Zhdanov's room and the hallway thoroughly. But had they missed anything? Cain had spotted the mark on Thomas Dickerson's head. He'd spotted Dickerson's hair on the fire extinguisher. He'd smelled the aftershave. Could he discover something else that they had not? Some trace of the man who had helped Zhdanov escape—or abducted her? And if he did, could he sort it out from the mess of other things present in the room—traces of Zhdanov's life there, of the cleaning crew, of the police doing their search, of Cain himself?

He doubted it.

The roof, though . . .

The police hadn't searched the roof. They'd had little reason to do so. It wasn't a reasonable escape route. Few people ever had reason to go up there. And yet he'd found Zhdanov's hairs there. The man had taken her to the roof, or else she had led him there.

He'd searched the roof again. Thinking about dust and tiny bits of evidence, he'd scoured the rooftop, looked at the gravel that covered it.

Near Zhdanov's hairs, he found tiny bits of tarpaper. The Holingbroke roof was covered with gravel in places, concrete in others—primarily the newer wings—and shingles in others. But not tarpaper.

It was summer in Devil's Cape, which meant humidity, pollution, and pollen. The trees surrounding Holingbroke were heavy with pollen; he'd often had to treat his patients for aggravated allergies. Peering carefully around, he focused his eyes and could see that nearly everything up there was dusted with pollen. But not the tarpaper. It hadn't been up there long.

Cain Ducett was a methodical man. He walked back down to Zhdanov's room. Earlier, he'd been afraid that he couldn't sort meaningful traces of evidence in the room from traces that the police themselves brought in. But now he was looking for something specific. He found it almost immediately, just inside the aluminum trim around the door. A tiny bit of tarpaper, scarcely thicker than a thread, near the doorway.

He returned once more to the roof. He could smell bougainvillea nearby, hear zydeco music and laughter from a party a few blocks away. Judging by where he'd found the tarpaper up there, by very faint smudges that he could now notice in the pollen, the man who had broken Zhdanov out of her confinement had actually been standing on the ledge on the north wall.

There was no clear reason to be on that northern ledge. The ledge overlooked a gentle hill covered with a mass of vegetation. There was no good place for a ladder there; it was just too high. There were no convenient trees to climb down, no place below where a

249

DEVIL'S CAPE

vehicle might be parked. There wasn't even a good place to tie a rope on the northern wall. It was as though the man had flown away.

Cain Ducett was a methodical man. He scoffed at the idea of the man flying. It could happen, of course—a number of superhumans had proven able to fly—but such things were rarities. So proceeding on the assumption that the man had stood on the ledge with Zhdanov, Cain proceeded to hypothesize every reason he could think of that didn't involve flight, then test those hypotheses. But nothing made sense. The man couldn't have jumped safely, and there were no impressions on the ground below. There was no evidence to suggest that he had remained on the roof and then reentered the building. Two of the other ledges were slightly more promising methods of exit than the northern one, but there was no sign that the man or Zhdanov had approached those ledges.

So he decided to test the flying hypothesis.

If the man had actually flown away carrying Zhdanov, Cain thought, he would have wanted to avoid being spotted. If flying was rare, then it was also incredibly conspicuous. That meant avoiding bright lights, avoiding crowds. The escape had happened early in the morning, shortly before dawn. If he'd flown for very long or very far, he would have found himself increasingly visible. And the man had presumably chosen that northern ledge as his takeoff point for a reason.

Half a mile north of the institution, across a river, there was a strip mall just off the Canal View Highway. If the man had parked a car there, he could have flown up to the edge of the parking lot with little risk of being seen. Much farther than that, and his risk of exposure increased astronomically.

Cain's car was at a body shop, which was replacing his shattered window, and in the meantime, he was driving a small rental car. He steered it toward the strip mall, then paced around the parking lot looking for anything to support his guess.

It took him less than five minutes to find another of Zhdanov's hairs.

From that point, it had been less difficult but more time-consuming. A convenience store had been open in the strip during the time the man would probably have approached, but the clerk who would have been on duty at the time wasn't available. Cain returned eight hours later, during the clerk's shift, and then discovered that the clerk did recall seeing a car, a red Mercedes, in the parking lot during the time in question. He even remembered the first three letters of the license plate because they happened to be his initials. A carefully worded phone call to Salazar Lorca had revealed that there was only one red Mercedes in Louisiana that had a license plate starting with those three letters. It was registered to the Devil's Delights Food Distribution Company, which was located in Devil's Cape's warehouse district. It was also, Lorca had informed him warily, a suspected front for the Kalodimos crime family. "What the hell are you into, Cain?" he'd asked.

Talking on the phone to his old friend, Cain had rested his face on the palm of his hand. The scratches from the broken glass were gone now. He could see things that he knew were beyond the realm of human vision, hear whispered conversations held two stories away. His mind cast back to the time he'd held his mother and poor Mr. Marcus hostage, the way he'd heard Salazar coming to the door before he'd even gotten there, known that he was dealing with a plain-clothes cop instead of a uniformed one by the sound he made while walking—despite the space between them, despite Mr. Marcus's panicked noises, despite his own panic. He thought of the reflection of the monster that he'd seen, the images of Jazz that had come to him. "I don't know, Salazar," he said quietly. "I just don't know."

He'd spent what free time he could watching the Devil's Delights warehouse. The car was undoubtedly a company car, probably used by someone in the

Kalodimos family or someone highly placed in the organization, but there was always the chance that the person might stop by the warehouse. And eventually he did. Even from a hundred feet away, Cain could smell the familiar aftershave. Orange blossom, coriander, cedar, and perhaps a hint of vanilla. The man was tan and muscular, his hair cropped curly and short, brown with blonde highlights. He had a moustache and goatee, also colored blonde, and was dressed casually but expensively—a designer label blue golf shirt over tan chinos and penny loafers with no socks, a Rolex watch on his wrist.

When the man left the warehouse, Cain followed.

A native of Devil's Cape, Dr. Cain Ducett joined the Holingbroke staff in 1995 and has served with distinction in a variety of capacities. He is currently director of the Behavioral Health Unit, the first African American to hold a position of this level at this institution.

— From the Holingbroke Psychological Institute web site

THIRTY-ONE

Devil's Cape, Louisiana
*Eight days after the deaths
of the Storm Raiders*
5:30 p.m.

Jason Kale didn't like being led around by the nose. "There's something I need you to do," the woman in his dream had told him. And then, the breeze of the Aegean Sea blowing over both of them, the rhythmic sounds of the Argonauts at the oars echoing in their ears, she'd told him about Dr. Cain Ducett of the Holingbroke Psychological Institute. He was a monster, she told him. She'd visited his dreams and learned his evil desires. He had superhuman powers and had to be stopped before he killed someone. She had been urgent and eloquent and persistent.

And she'd been lying.

Even in that strange, disorienting dream state, Jason had known that the woman was real. But there was a desperation about her, too. The way her red eyes had flickered when she'd spoken, the timbre of her voice. She was certainly desperate to get Jason to chase after this doctor. What wasn't clear was why she was so persistent about it.

Jason was an investigative reporter. Prophetic dreams or not, he did his research.

Dr. Cain Ducett was a respected psychiatrist specializing in treating the criminally insane. He was a director at the Holingbroke Institute and had risen to that level at a relatively young age. He had published several papers and was credited with improving the conditions and safety record of his area.

He was also, Jason learned after digging further, a former member of the Concrete Executioners. Jason thought of the boys he had fought in the street, the gunshots. He thought about the Troll. He rubbed unconsciously at his eye. Ducett's juvenile records were sealed, but he clearly had a background of violence.

The escaped psychopath Rusalka—Olena Zhdanov—had been a patient of Ducett's.

Jason had reluctantly phoned Sergeant Dustin Bilbray with a few questions, and Bilbray had been delighted to tell Jason, off the record, that Ducett was being looked at as a possible accomplice in her escape. Bilbray seemed very amused about that for some reason.

Cain Ducett was a dichotomy. Former gang member, respected psychiatrist, suspect in a murder investigation. Whether the dream woman had been lying to Jason or not, he decided to get a better look at the man.

Jason found Ducett just as he was leaving the institute one evening. Tall, muscular, and handsome, the psychiatrist was wearing an expensive gray suit and a pink and blue tie. Starting his own car, Jason followed him through the twisted streets of Devil's Cape.

Jason was more than a little surprised when Ducett pulled up to his uncle's Devil's Delights Food Distribution Company and began to stake it out.

CEs. Bring it.

— A graffiti design on a
brick tenement in Crabb's Lament

THIRTY-TWO

Devil's Cape, Louisiana
Eight days after the deaths
of the Storm Raiders
7:30 p.m.

Julian Kalodimos stared at the black man in the gray suit who had just scaled the wall of the decrepit warehouse.

"Orange blossom, coriander, cedar," the man said. "I believe that you are responsible for freeing my patient."

The orange blossom bit sounded like gibberish to Julian, but the second part was clear enough. The man was looking for Rusalka.

"How the hell did you climb that wall?" Julian asked. "This building's ready to fall down around our ears."

The man shrugged. He flashed his white teeth again. He looked exhilarated, almost high. Julian had seen the look often enough, working alongside Uncle Costas's men. The man was itching for a fight. The man brushed absently at a tear in his jacket. "I guess I have some underutilized talents," he said. "Now where is Olena Zhdanov?" His eyes flicked to the shack. He knew perfectly well where she was.

Julian stared at him. Most people, seeing him in his uniform, were intimidated. It wasn't the uniform so much—it was more utilitarian than designed to strike fear in others' hearts. It was more the concept of it. *I am faceless,* the uniform told those he encountered. *I will not hesitate to do whatever the hell I want. I am separate from you. I am more than you.* This man barely seemed to notice. Julian felt hot, all of a sudden, in the uniform. He didn't

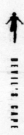

particularly like using his powers against others. He didn't particularly like fighting.

"This is how this is going to work," he said. "You're going to leave now. Or I'm going to throw you off the building." He spread his gloved hands. The mustard-yellow cloth on his arms was tight against his skin.

"You know what Zhdanov can do?" the man asked. "You saw what she did to that orderly you clunked over the head?"

Julian blinked. There had been no cameras in the hall-way; he'd made sure of that. He wondered how the man knew what he knew.

"The orderly's name was Thomas Dickerson," the man continued. "He played piano at the Tyler Lane First Baptist Church, and sometimes he played for the patients in the common room. His favorite song was 'Great Balls of Fire' and he had a weakness for sweet potato pie."

"Enough," Julian said. "I'm sorry that man died, I really am. I kind of lost control of her for a minute. She just bent down and—" He broke off. "But you—you I'll kill without hesitation if I need to." He thought about walking across the roof to the man, but instead, he took flight, hovering two feet off the ground, drifting slowly, relentlessly toward the man. "They call me Scion," he said. "If you've read the papers, you know that I'm not afraid to hurt people. It's time for you to go."

The man stepped off the ledge onto the rooftop, legs spread carefully, distributing his weight. As Julian moved closer to him, the man pulled his jacket off and rolled up his sleeves. "You know," he said, "I should really talk through this with you. Open a dialogue. Establish a rap-port. Convince you that Olena Zhdanov is no use to you and that you would be best served by turning her over to the authorities." With two deft yanks, he unknotted his tie and pulled it off, stuffing it into a pocket. "But the truth is that I'm in the mood for a fight." He spread his arms and gestured at Julian with his fingertips—the ges-ture a clear challenge to move closer.

Julian actually hesitated for a moment. He wondered if the man was secretly hiding a gun. He remembered the pain he'd felt when Jason had been shot. What in the hell was making this man so confident? And then he rushed forward.

———————

Cain was unsure of his own motivations. It was one thing to postulate that a flying man had rescued or kidnapped Olena Zhdanov, and then to find evidence supporting that hypothesis. It was quite another thing to see the man actually flying. It was one thing to realize that his senses were sharper than other people's, and another to challenge a notorious criminal with superhuman powers to a brawl. He'd found as he climbed the building that he was stronger than he'd expected; he'd been able to tell the most dependable spots on the building to place his hands and feet and, a few times, he'd simply driven his fingertips into the surface of the building like an ice climber chiseling handholds for himself. But that, too, was a long way from fighting someone with Scion's reputation.

Scion wore a full-length uniform of dark yellow and black, crisscrossed with brown leather straps across his chest. His face was covered by a mask, but below the mask, Cain could see a short beard and a set jaw. Cain smelled his aftershave and, somewhere in the distance, tandoori chicken. The night air was humid, hot, and polluted. He could hardly see the stars. He could hear his own heart pounding. Scion's, too.

When Scion finally made his move, it was with a speed that Cain could barely process. He swooped forward into a tackle, slamming into Cain's chest and driving him to the surface of the roof, which promptly fractured under the strain. Chunks of concrete, plaster, wood, and steel broke free and began to tumble down below. A jut of metal sliced through Cain's shirt and into his back, scraping against a rib. He gasped in pain and raised his arms to push Scion away, but the masked man was too fast for

him again. He jabbed Cain in the eye with his right hand, then followed it with a left to the jaw that loosened Cain's teeth. Cain tasted coppery blood.

Using the crumbling rooftop to push himself up to his knees, Cain tried again to raise his arms to protect himself from the flying man who hovered over him, punching him again and again, a strange, dissociative calm in his eyes. Cain finally managed to block one hit, grabbing hold of the other man's arm and pushing it to the side, and to deliver a punch of his own. Despite his aches, he could feel the force in his blow, and Scion rocked back, raising a hand to his jaw.

Then Scion said, "The hell with this." He flew backward, away from Cain for a second, and then pivoted his body, rushing forward again, grabbing Cain by the right arm and the left leg. He lifted Cain from the roof and then, with a grunt and a heave, hurled him over the side of the building.

The two hardest punches I ever took were in Devil's Cape. The first one was Pepe's right hook. The second one was also Pepe's right hook, about half a second later.

— Excerpted from an interview with
retired boxer Marty Blank, *Sports Illustrated*

THIRTY-THREE

Devil's Cape, Louisiana
Eight days after the deaths
of the Storm Raiders
5 p.m.

Kate Brauer had spent two exhausting days training with Samuel.

She'd protested again, the morning after their run along Lady Danger River, as he led her into Pepe's Athletic Center on Miller Avenue, that she needed to be concentrating on her armor far more than her body. The center—named for Pepe "The Diable Dodger" Matehuala, the famed welterweight—had once been a gathering place for many of the city's boxers. It still sported framed black-and-white photos of athletes from times past; old gloves hanging from pegs, their leather cracking; and a row of brightly colored speed bags along one wall. But the center's boxing ring had been yanked out, its old, nicked floors covered with mauve carpeting. And the place fairly bristled with chrome—free weights, treadmills, stationary bikes, rowing machines, and more. Now it catered to working professionals looking for exercise on their lunch hours, and Kate wondered what old Pepe might have thought.

Samuel had gestured her over to an elliptical trainer, showing her the routine he intended for her to work. "I was the Storm Raiders' athletic trainer, you know," he said, keeping his voice low.

Resigned to it, she began working the machine, feeling her already sore muscles begin to protest the new routine.

"Really?" she said. It surprised her for some reason.

"Yeah," he said. "Patriot was a natural athlete because of her powers. She could wake up and sprint all day if she wanted to, probably carrying a car on her shoulders. But that was from her powers. She never had to work at it."

He stopped her for a second, adjusted the angle of the handlebars, and nodded at her to start again. "The Swashbucklers were trained athletes, of course."

The first Swashbuckler had been her Uncle Charles. After he'd died from leukemia, a young Bosnian decathlete named Alija Spiric took over his name and uniform.

Samuel chuckled. "They were a lot alike. Full of flash, impatient, and absolutely lousy at telling anyone else how to work out." He shrugged. "So it was me. The Winged Tornado used to be a competitive bicycler—did you know he rode in the Tour de France against Lance Armstrong?—before he grew his wings. He was pretty good at coaching. But by the time he joined the team, everybody was used to going to me for lessons, so that was that."

Uncle Samuel gestured at her to pick up the pace. "One time in Vanguard City," he said softly, "we were fighting Mirrorman. We didn't realize it, but he'd rigged up some sort of shunt that allowed him to redirect electrical charges." He shrugged, moved her hands to a higher position on the handlebars, twiddled with a knob to increase the tension. "Raiden hated Mirrorman—in addition to his other unappealing traits, Mirrorman was a raving bigot, especially against Asians. And we knew from experience that he wouldn't . . . ah, crack and give us seven years' bad luck if we hit him hard." He chuckled at his joke. "He was a pretty tough guy."

Samuel leaned closer, keeping his voice pitched low. "So Raiden let loose at him with a lightning bolt. I can't remember how many volts that was."

"Probably several hundred million," Kate said, remembering that Raiden's electrical output had compared favorably with the average thunderstorm.

"Yeah, okay," he said. He tightened the tension knob a

little more. "Don't slow down," he told her. "You've got to keep your heart rate up."

She flicked him a reproving look, but kept up her pace. "Your story," she said, her voice coming out more of a pant than she liked.

"Yeah, so Raiden blasted him full in the chest. But Mirrorman used this shunt and bounced the lightning bolt right into your dad."

She blinked. The Doctor Camelot armor was insulated, of course. She'd added additional insulation to what her father had had, and she used far less metal in her armor, relying more on ceramics and carbon polymers. But an electrical charge of that magnitude could still be devastating, particularly to the less advanced version her father had used.

Samuel smiled and nodded at her reaction. "Uh huh," he said. "You see where I'm going with this. Your dad's armor was fried. He wasn't too hurt—just a little shaken up, and it singed his hair some." He chuckled. "Made it stand on end, too, just like in the cartoons." He tapped on the machine. "But there he was, stuck with a hundred and fifty pounds of dead weight. Fell on his back like a turtle and had a time of it getting back to his feet, and then he pretty much had to beat a slow retreat while the rest of us took out Mirrorman." He pointed a finger at her. "And that's why you're going to keep working out like this."

And that had settled that. He'd put her through a variety of torturous exercise regimens, dictated her diet, forced her to step away from her designs and get extra sleep at night. "This won't be forever," he'd said. "Once you get to the point where you're in really A-class shape, we'll cut back some. You'll go on maintenance exercises, just an hour or two a day, and we'll have one or two of those beignets and some café au lait, like you wanted. But we need you to do this now."

There'd been a heavy workout that day. But tonight, she thought as she headed back to her new home, was going to be something special. Tonight she was taking the new Doctor Camelot armor out for its first test flight.

The rate of gravitational acceleration on Earth is approximately 9.81 meters per second per second.

— Excerpted from a physics textbook

THIRTY-FOUR

Devil's Cape, Louisiana
Eight days after the deaths
of the Storm Raiders
7:30 p.m.

When Jason had seen his brother arrive at Uncle Costas's food distribution plant, and then had seen Ducett following him out, he'd decided to pursue the two of them a different way. He dressed as Argonaut, flying high into the Devil's Cape smog, obscuring himself in the night. It wasn't too difficult to follow the cars, even from a great height.

The night air stank of pollution typical to Devil's Cape—smoke from a nearby paper mill, diesel fumes, car exhaust, rotting fish and vegetation, a landfill—but it was still exhilarating to fly, especially to fly fast to keep up with the cars. The air rushed around him in a soft roar that drowned out the noise of the city. His cape flapped in the wind. And the broad panorama of Devil's Cape was spread before him. The neon and raucous parties of the Silver Swan district. The fishing boats moving along Lake Pontchartrain. The night traffic of the Canal View Highway.

When Julian parked at the decrepit warehouse, Jason hovered and watched with interest as he saw his brother pulling on his uniform, which Jason had never seen him in. Their uniforms weren't really all that different. Jason's was blue and gold and brown where Julian's was mustard yellow and black. And Jason had a cape and protective white lenses over his eyes—for all the good they'd done him when he'd been shot—while Julian had neither. But the cuts of the uniforms and the shapes of the masks were

very nearly the same. Just one more connection between them.

When Julian—dressed as Scion now—ascended the building, Jason flew down and landed at a slightly taller building a block away, wishing he had brought his binoculars. He'd watched in fascination as the psychiatrist, who had parked his own car not far from Jason, moved to the building and began to scale its side.

He recognized the warehouse, now that he'd given it some thought. It belonged to his Uncle Costas, but had been abandoned after it had suffered some structural damage. The Devil's Cape police department had had its eye on the place at one time, then stopped caring about it when it was obvious that the Kalodimos crime family had moved out.

He'd seen Julian and Ducett talking—they were too far away for him to make out what they were saying—and then looked on with some dismay as they began to fight. He felt the sudden pain when Julian was punched in the jaw. He was uncertain whether to intervene. He had finally decided that he needed to get over there and break up the fight when he saw, with surprised shock, that his brother had thrown the other man from the building.

"Oh, hell," he said. Jason streaked toward the condemned warehouse, arms outstretched, moving as quickly as he could.

But he could tell that he'd never make it to Ducett in time.

———————

Cain fell.

One of the negative aspects of having sharply acute senses was that he could tell with some precision the extent to which his body was accelerating as it approached the ground below. He didn't scream, but the air whipping past him sounded like a scream anyway. His shirt was ripping in the wind. His shoes fell off. His face, chest, and back were on fire from Scion's battering—not that that was likely to be a concern for long.

Cain fell.

Images rushed through his mind. Shoving Jazz back against the asphalt. Dustin Bilbray waddling away from him in terror. 5-D Binoe crying. Shouting at Mr. Marcus. The day Tyrell Smith tried to stab him with the toothbrush shiv. Salazar Lorca's sad, wise face. Jazz's eyes filled with blood. Olena Zhdanov sobbing and breaking her knuckles on the glass divider. Thomas Dickerson's shriveled body. Scion's masked face.

Cain fell.

The air roaring around him, heart pumping, eyes tearing from the wind and reaction, Cain's mind filled with his hallucination again, the devil creature. In his imagination, he felt fine scarlet and black hairs growing on every inch of his body. His fingers elongated, dark claws scratching through the night air. Long, twisted horns sprouted from his scalp. His teeth grew jagged, needle-sharp canines protruding from his lower jaw almost to his cheekbones. His irises turned as red as Jazz's eyes. Red as blood. His veins pulsed hot. His shirt tore into pieces as his muscles bulged, the fragments catching the air and fluttering away from his body like doves. His feet stretched and warped, curving around their arches like talons. Venous flaps of skin stretched out from his arms to his sides, extending down his rib cage like bats' wings.

Cain fell.

Seeing the ground approaching so close, the rigid, controlled Cain Ducett let out a low moan of terror. It came out as a growl. Blood and fire and thoughts of the monster filled his mind, and it galled him that he was about to die filled with such images. The hell with it, he thought, spreading his arms wide to meet his fate.

And then Cain Ducett flew.

His outstretched arms caught the air and he was yanked upward, his fall turning into a sudden ascent. His breath went out of him and he gasped, choked. He began to fall again and he batted his arms wildly. He found himself propelled upward once more, the motion coming more naturally now.

Cain had a keen, disciplined, analytical mind. That mind was moving full-speed now, suggesting and rejecting dozens of possible explanations for what he was experiencing, though he knew on some level that there was really only one explanation: The hallucination of turning into a devil creature wasn't a hallucination at all. It never had been.

Spreading his arms, Cain spiraled his body down, landing safely on the ground on feet that felt foreign to him—broad and long and clawed. "Oh, God, Jazz," he whispered, his voice a rasp. "What did you do to me?" He stared at his hands and arms. They were more heavily muscled than he had ever seen them, covered with fine fur, a dusky scarlet. His fingers ended in sharp black claws. He touched his face. It was warped—the lower jaw jutting out, teeth protruding from the mouth, the ears hugely elongated, horns erupting from his head.

"Oh, God," he whispered again. Fear and shock were in his voice, but there was also exultation.

◆

Jazz was dozing in her room, black satin sheets pulled over her body, when it happened. She had slept little since the Robber Baron had visited her, and the sleep she managed was shallow, troubled, and at odd hours. When she felt Cain's curse activate again, felt him shift into the form she had created for him, she sat upright in her bed, staring at the black walls. "Oh," she whispered into the darkness. "It is about damn time."

She had kept a shard of broken mirror propped on a teak end table beside her bed. She bent over it now, staring into it, watching her eyes fill with blood as they did when she worked her magics. "Come to me, Cain!" she shouted, her voice filling the small room. "It's time to come to me!"

◆

Racing hopelessly to catch Ducett before he hit the ground, racing to stop his brother from becoming a murderer again, Jason saw the psychiatrist's metamorphosis with shocked disbelief. The plummeting Ducett stretched and elongated. Black and red hairs grew from his skin. He sprouted horns and claws and wing flaps under his arms. He looked like the devil himself. And then suddenly he spread his arms, stopping his fall. He beat his arms gracelessly for a few seconds, rising and falling in the air, then slowly spread his wings and glided to a landing on the ground below.

Jason stopped his own flight in midair, hesitating.

Ducett looked surprised, but did he know what was going to happen to him? Did Julian? What were they fighting about, anyway?

Jason flew back up into the night sky, moving rapidly to avoid being seen, aiming for the low clouds.

———————

Julian Kalodimos walked slowly back toward the shack, sighing and rubbing his sore jaw. He didn't enjoy killing people. And now he was going to have to find somewhere else to put Zhdanov, which was a major complication. It had taken some serious thought and planning to come up with the trap he'd placed her in. In the shack, she knew that if she tried to touch him, if she did to him what she'd done to the orderly, then she would probably never make it out of the ramshackle building alive. Until she was a willing confederate, until he had persuaded her to help Uncle Costas, getting near her—and, especially, trying to move her—was extremely dangerous. He'd have to come up with another plan before someone came and found the doctor's body.

He was glad that he had missed hearing the man's body strike the ground. He'd heard the sound before, caused the sound before, and it haunted him.

The man hadn't screamed. "He didn't scream" wasn't much of an epitaph, but there'd been worse. He shrugged. Walking lightly across the damaged roof, he wondered if there was any chicken tandoori left.

And then he heard a rage-filled shout and felt something slam into him.

Cain swallowed. He'd grown, too, he thought. He was maybe a foot taller. His shirt and shoes and socks were gone. His pants had split along the legs. "The Devil of Dubai," he whispered, his voice pitched lower than he was used to, his baritone voice gone bass.

Jazz's voice suddenly filled his ears. "Come to me, Cain!" she shouted. "It's time to come to me!"

Cain walked to the building and stared at a window of reinforced glass installed in an exit door. His face was more or less as he'd expected it—distorted, demonic. The needle-sharp teeth he'd felt in his lower jaw glistened white. Tiny red and black hairs covered his body in a fine fur. The horns were curved, twisting like corkscrews. There was a little bit of Cain Ducett in that reflection—his cheekbones, his eyes except for the irises, which had turned blood-red, his hair. But not much. "Okay, Jazz," he muttered to himself, a twisted smile on his demonic face. "I think under the circumstances that I can squeeze you in."

But he had something else to take care of first. There was Scion, who had hurled him from the building. And there was Zhdanov, who was probably an even graver danger to the city.

Spreading his new wings and using his powerful legs to launch himself into the air, Cain took flight.

The air rushed around him again. His heightened senses seemed, if anything, even sharper in this form. He didn't just see the edges of the building as he flew past. He heard them, heard the ambient noise of Devil's Cape echoing off of them. He heard them like a bat would hear them.

He heard something else, too. The night air passing around a solitary object above. There was something floating directly above him in the low-lying clouds. A human form.

Scion, he thought.

Cain thrust himself even faster through the air, approaching the form. All the anger and fear and

confusion that had been boiling in him since that dream had shattered his controlled life a few days earlier erupted from him as he screamed and then tackled the flying form, smashing with his fists, tearing with his claws.

———————

Jason saw the demonic form of Cain Ducett flying up, but he felt confident, until it was too late, that the man couldn't possibly see him and wouldn't be focused on him if he did. And then Ducett slammed into him, knocking the breath from his lungs, stunning him as surely as the bullet to the eye had. His Argonaut uniform was made out of thick, durable fabric, reinforced with leather, but Ducett's claws tore through it, tore into his side. The pain felt hot, awful, and he could feel blood running down.

"Wait," he said, but his voice was faint in the night air. He shoved the monstrous figure away, sending Ducett spinning about forty feet to one side, but the winged man was already turning back.

Ducett grabbed him again, slammed a knee into his side, punched him in the kidney. His clawed fingers glanced off of the protective lenses Jason had sewn into his mask, and he was grateful that he'd taken time to replace the one that had been shattered by the bullet.

They skirmished like this for a few seconds, Ducett clawing at him like a wild beast, scratching, yelling, and raging, and then Jason shoving him away. And then Jason reached out for Ducett and grabbed him by the wrists. After all, he thought, he had the strength of Heracles. He pivoted their bodies, pulling Ducett's arms in back of him, maneuvering him into a painful hold. Autolycus, he thought, had been a wrestler. "I said wait," he said, his breath coming back to him, his side still burning. He twisted the man's arm again. "Wait, damn it."

———————

Julian fell to the roof with the shock of the blow he felt. It set the rooftop shaking again, pieces underneath him breaking loose. As he scrambled to his hands and knees and then literally flew a few feet into the air, he saw a ten-foot-by-ten-foot section of the roof just break free and fall to the floor below. It didn't stop there, the heavy chunks of flooring working downward with increasing mass and momentum like falling dominoes, until a huge channel was open nearly to the bottom of the building. "Hell," he said.

He felt something slice into his side, felt scratching as though from claws. "Jason," he said softly. He wasn't being attacked. Jason was.

And then, hearing the yelling again, he looked straight up. Far overhead, he could see his brother, his silly cape billowing around him, fighting some kind of winged creature. "This just gets better and better," he said.

He heard crashing sounds from the building. That little fall of his, breaking the chunk of the roof loose, was triggering something much larger, and he wasn't sure that the building would survive it.

His side was already feeling better. He looked up at Jason, wondering what he was doing there, who he was fighting. And then he decided to concentrate on the business at hand. The fight above was an opportunity, and Julian Kalodimos wasn't one to overlook an opportunity.

He sprinted to the shack and thrust the door open. Olena Zhdanov sat on her cot, eyes wide as the room swayed around her.

"We're going," he said simply. "Try anything on me, and believe me, I'll kill you before you finish me."

Her deep eyes seemed to be considering the possibility, but then she nodded. "I'm ready," she said. Her seductive smile didn't reach her eyes.

His arms—and therefore his new wings—locked painfully behind his back, Cain wondered if he'd made a mistake. He'd thought he was attacking Scion. How many other flying men would be in the area? The man had the same build. He moved the same way. His voice was the same. And he smelled the same, too. The aftershave—orange blossom, coriander, cedar, vanilla. But as they struggled, he could see that the uniform was a different color. The man didn't have a beard. He wore a cape. But still . . . the same scent? The same voice? The same way of moving?

Cain had been a street fighter, full of action and reaction, chaos under the surface. He'd spent years establishing rigid control of himself, honing his intellect, training his impulses. But now, in this demon body, the scent of blood in the air, filled with anger and frustration over his lost control, he lashed out. "Scion," he said, "I've had enough of you." His arms locked, he craned his head around and bit the other man on the arm.

"Damn it!" the other man swore, shoving Cain away again, freeing him. He grabbed at his bleeding arm.

And Cain seized the opportunity. Reaching out with both hands, moving as fast as he could, he slammed into his opponent, flew him down hard and fast onto the rooftop below.

The roof shuddered and snapped when they struck it, and an area around them about the size of Cain's Holingbroke office broke away, forcing them down into the level below, clouds of disintegrating plaster filling the air and choking them. Somewhere nearby, one of the few remaining windows exploded into splintered shards. Rivets popped out of concrete in a staccato *pop-pop-pop* like gunfire. Concrete cracked, then crumbled, chunks of it falling down in a small avalanche. Sparks danced through the air. A support girder groaned and creaked, then began to bend, ultimately folding in on itself at a weak, rusted spot with a grinding grunt. With a sudden, jarring crash, they fell again, smashing their way down through the poorly bolstered center of the building, plummeting perhaps two or three more stories. The south wall began to buckle, concrete blocks popping out until it seemed to be making a gap-toothed grin. Falling cinderblocks slammed everywhere, exploding like mortar fire.

And then the whole building collapsed around them.

Katherine Brauer—Kate joined TI in 1999 and was elected Distinguished Member of the Technical Staff in 2004. She currently works at the Vanguard City Technology Center and has made significant contributions to the company in the areas of . . .

— From "Seven technical innovators honored with promotion to TI Fellow," *Infolink*, internal news site for Texas Instruments

THIRTY-FIVE

Devil's Cape, Louisiana

*Eight days after the deaths
of the Storm Raiders
7:15 p.m.*

Kate opened the door to her secret room, letting Samuel inside as she went through the last steps of her preflight preparation. "Welcome to the Juan Marco Quintana Memorial Laboratory," she said, the hint of a smile on her lips.

Samuel was wearing jeans, sandals, and a Hawaiian shirt. A dragon cavorted with a topless dancer across his chest. "Where y'at?" he asked. "That's Louisiana for 'how's it going,' I think."

"Hey, where y'at?" she said. She had brought a bamboo Chinese paneled wall into her lab as a changing area, and her armor was currently shrouded from view inside. She gestured at the one chair in the lab not piled with data books or DVD-ROMs, then moved behind the panel.

Eschewing the chair for the moment, the short man peered around the lab. He stared for a moment at the framed picture that Kate had borrowed from her father's own lab, the picture of the Storm Raiders—her "aunts and uncles"—posing in their uniforms with their masks off. He moved on without comment, taking in the dozens of machines, the computer hookups with multiple monitors, the shelves that supported hundreds of pounds of armaments for her armor. "You've got beaucoup equipment here," he said. "You could put most universities to shame."

She chuckled. "You should stop with the lingo, uncle," she said. "You'll hurt your mouth." She stepped back out from behind the panel, a powerful Xenon flashlight in one hand. Shining the flashlight back toward the armor, her gaze pensive, she said, "Ideally, I'd like to have a clean room, but that's beyond what I can do for the moment."

"So you going to let me see it?" he asked, gesturing at the paneled wall. On the main panel, a Chinese fisherman was casting his pole back, ready to throw his hook forward into the sea. A gray heron flew over the calm waters.

She flicked off the flashlight and nodded. "Yeah," she said. "I am." Kate was wearing light sweatpants and a thin, long-sleeved cotton shirt. The armor had interior cooling, so she wasn't likely to get overheated, and it was better to have a layer of cloth between herself and the armor. She pulled her short hair back with a headband, then held a finger up to him. "Just a sec," she said.

Kate hadn't expected the claustrophobic feeling of climbing into the armor. She'd used the exoskeleton before, had tried on every single piece of the armor multiple times, including the helmet. But somehow, stepping into the ensemble was different. Her breath felt tight. She thought of Fortunato in Poe's "The Cask of Amontillado," slowly being sealed behind a brick wall. But in truth, the air inside the Doctor Camelot armor was flowing freely, filtered, slightly oxygen-rich. She whispered a voice command—she had backup controls that would allow her to activate the same protocols manually, but voice was her primary means of control—and a series of projected displays appeared inside her faceplate. She pivoted one arm, testing the range of motion. The armor moved with her without discernible lag, the digital signal processors interpreting and reacting to her motion in real time.

"Are you ready, Uncle Samuel?" she asked. The voice that emerged from her armor was pleasant and melodic. It sounded like a normal, everyday female voice with a wide range of pitch, timbre, and emphasis. It just didn't sound like Kate's voice. She'd developed an algorithm that altered her voice enough to make it unrecognizable as her own and to baffle any attempts to match her voice print, but that still sounded eminently human. As a tribute to the Doctor Camelot heritage, she'd also given the voice the hint of a British accent.

"On pins and needles," he said. "Are you waiting for me to throw doubloons or something?"

Kate stepped out from behind the paneled wall. The armor was sleek and curved, its joints nearly seamless. She'd shined it, and most of it sparkled liked burnished chrome. The Doctor Camelot coat of arms—a sword laid across a shield with a purple background behind them—had been carefully emblazoned on the upper left side of her chest as well as her left shoulder, bearing tribute to the three men who had carried the name before her. The armor was a testament to miniaturization and compressed space. Her father's armor had been bulky; not only had it weighed about 150 pounds, but it had added inches to his height and more to his circumference. Kate's armor, although stronger and more durable than his, added only a few centimeters to her, except at her forearms, which were broad in order to hold her various weapons, and her back, which contained jet propulsion systems and concentrated fuel cells. While her father's helmet had resembled a medieval knight's, with a metallic faceplate that covered his face and slightly limited his range of vision, Kate's helmet was significantly different. The front of it, surrounding her face, looked like smoked glass. Anyone looking at her could clearly tell that a woman's face was inside, but the details were obscured enough that no one could identify her. Nor could they see the dozens of projected displays and gauges that allowed Kate to monitor her armor's systems and extensive suite of sensor devices. A short amethyst cape dangled from her shoulders to just over the exhaust vents of her jet pack, another tribute to her predecessors' sense of style. The cape was more or less there just for decoration; it would break free easily if someone tried to use it to grab hold of her.

"Wow," Samuel said. "I wish your dad could see this."

Kate smiled behind the smoky faceplate. "Glad you like it," she said.

He finally sat in the chair she'd offered earlier, eyes taking in every detail. "So that's really as durable as his?"

She nodded. "More durable, actually."

"It's odd actually getting to see your face," he said, "even though I can't quite recognize you."

She tapped the faceplate. "I thought it would be useful to look more human, more approachable," she said. "And if my armor's systems kick out, then I might lose my various heads up displays, but I can still see out."

"But if it breaks, the glass in your face . . ."

She shook her head. "This plate can take a mortar shell," she said. "If something's powerful enough to break the armor, then more than likely I'll already be dead from shock waves passing through." She held up a hand. "Don't worry, though. It's tougher than Dad's in pretty much every way." Including the neck joints, she thought but didn't say, the image of the Behemoth and his huge tattooed hands invading her mind.

Samuel's eyes sparkled. "The chestplate's pretty different than your dad's too," he said. He made an exaggerated gesture with his hands, teasing without being flirtatious. "Isn't that kind of . . . un-aerodynamic?"

She smiled. "It's comfortable," she said. "And I don't want there to be any question about my gender."

"Oh, I wouldn't worry about that," he said. He contemplated her. "You ready, Katie?"

"Yes."

He nodded, then gestured at the variety of machines stretching around the room, broken only by her framed picture of his team and the plastic plant she'd placed in one corner as a half-hearted attempt at decoration. "So," he said, "I'm like your mission control?"

"If you don't mind," she said. "Just for the time being. I ultimately shouldn't need someone here monitoring things, but I'd appreciate it this time." She'd quickly run through the various monitors and machines, explaining what system each sensor was reporting on, what each machine was there to do.

Finally, he said, "You're stalling, Katie."

She nodded, clasping him gently on the shoulder, and then opened the hidden door that led to her neighbor's rooftop. Waving at him, then closing the door between them, she walked quietly across the roof, putting some distance between herself and her home before starting. "Can you hear me?" she asked softly, transmitting back to the machines in the Juan Marco Quintana Memorial Laboratory.

"Where y'at?" he said.

She grinned. Looking at the streets below, she cycled through ultraviolet and infrared displays, reassuring herself that no one was watching her. Then she ignited her jet pack, its muffled engine a mere whisper in the night air.

And she flew.

———————

Before leaving the building, Julian had tossed Zhdanov over one shoulder in a fireman's carry with casual disregard. She needed to touch his skin, he figured, in order to hurt him, and therefore, his only truly vulnerable spot was his face; the uniform covered the rest. With her rear near his head and her legs in his arm, she'd be hard-pressed to reach up and zap him, and good manners be damned.

"*Otpusti menya, ti Amerikaskoe gavno,*" she yelled at him as he stepped out of the shack. Dispensing with the ruse of walking across the roof, he flew her across the building and down one side, heading toward his red Mercedes. "*Kakova hrena?*" she shouted in his ear. "*Ti letaesh?*"

"If you're going to swear at me," he said, "at least do it in English."

Twice on the way, he reeled in sudden agony as his brother was injured in the battle above. When they reached the car, he dumped Zhdanov unceremoniously on the gravel, trying to keep his composure and catch his breath.

"You son of a bitch," Zhdanov said, pulling herself to her feet, the palms of her hands bleeding from where she had tried to catch herself, pieces of gravel and dust falling from her hair.

Wincing from another injury, he raised a fist. "Take one step toward me," he said, his breath ragged, "and I'll knock you unconscious."

She stared at him, eyes flashing, rubbing blood from her hands onto her sweatpants in scarlet streaks. She spat a piece of gravel onto the ground. "This is how you recruit me to help you?"

He shuddered in pain again. He was sweating again in his uniform. "No," he said, his voice weak. He turned and pointed at the building. "This is how I save your goddamned life."

The crashing, tearing sounds inside the building crescendoed. The warehouse began to rock back and forth. Chunks fell out of the south wall. It looked, briefly, like a grinning skull. And then the wall came down, the other walls pulled along with it, collapsing inward and outward and every which way. A stray concrete block sailed over their heads, smashing into the windshield of Julian's Mercedes.

Julian felt sudden agony in his back, his legs, his side. He collapsed to his knees, staring at the warehouse as it turned into rubble. "Jason," he whispered.

Zhdanov took a half step toward him, though he couldn't tell whether it was in concern, need, or anger. She stopped when he held up a fist again, though he had trouble closing his fingers. "What did you say?" she asked.

He stared at the ruin of the warehouse. The aches were easing a bit, and he wondered what that meant about his brother. He wondered if Jason might be dying. He took a step toward the building then stopped himself. "Nothing," he said. Uncle Costas would need a report. He yanked the cinderblock off his car and threw it a hundred feet away. The broken windshield would be conspicuous, but less so than flying through the air away from a collapsed building with a woman slung over his shoulder. "Get in the car," he said. "We're leaving."

His thoughts a whirl, he watched the building in his rearview mirror until it was out of sight.

———

"Uncle Samuel, this is amazing," Kate said, her body arcing through the night sky over Devil's Cape, the Doctor Camelot armor flickering in the lights of the city. Her jet pack nearly silent, Kate could hear the chugging of distant cars, the flickering and popping of her cape in the wind, the soft rush of air around the armor.

"Glad to hear it," Samuel replied tightly over her communicator. "This gizmo says you're doing something like eighty per. You think you might want to slow it down a little bit, just in case?"

Below her stretched the galleries, art studios, antique bookshops, and internet cafés of Jocque Boulevard. Gaudily painted murals lined the sidewalks, and street vendors hawking woven bracelets, glittering jewelry, pralines, and roof slates painted with pirates and clowns were just beginning to pull up their kiosks, folding tables, and blankets for the night. She slowed the armor to sixty-five miles per hour and ascended another two hundred feet, plowing through a cluster of startled bats. "Are you seeing this?" she asked.

"Yeah," he said, and she heard the smile in his voice now. "Yeah, I see."

Kate executed a flawless hundred and thirty-five degree turn, pivoting her body toward the tourist-filled Silver Swan district, its sky streaked with spotlights, its streets rumbling with jazz, zydeco, and laughter. "I could barely feel that turn," she said. "The kinetic bafflers are doing their job." The armor was buttressed with 26mm self-compensating shock absorbers in place not only to protect Kate from jarring shocks, but to allow her to reorient herself rapidly without injury.

Then she heard a loud rumble.

"What's that?" Samuel asked.

"You heard it, too?"

"Yeah," he said. "Over your transmitters and through the walls. It was loud, whatever it is."

"Hang on," she said.

Her faceplate allowed for a variety of small heads-up displays, positionable throughout her peripheral vision. She could queue up analysis of her internal systems, review sensor data, watch just about any television program broadcast in her considerable range, connect to the Internet, and scan through the databases she was connected to through her lab. All the screens were customizable—she could view what she wanted when she wanted.

"Hell," she said. "Echo analysis shows the point of origin as the warehouse district, probably at Pier 42. Decibel level approaching one fifty, but unsustained, something loud but quick, like an explosion or building collapse."

She was already turning in that direction, increasing her speed to ninety miles per hour. The armor flew her smoothly through the air. Her eyes flicked to another screen.

"Three 911 calls lodged in the vicinity. I'm getting automated transcriptions—" She paused. "Yeah, a building's collapsed. Not known yet if it's an explosion or not. No sign of fire." Her eyes flicked to another screen. "I've got the address now. Parish records show the building as scheduled for demolition, but not for another six weeks."

"Kate," Samuel said, his voice tight again. "This is a test flight. You were going to fly around a little bit and come back."

"My ETA's thirty-seven seconds," she answered. "Plans change."

Jason's body ached. He was wedged in somehow, concrete or a wooden beam running under his spine, which was twisted at a bad angle. His legs were trapped, too, swallowed in an immovable mass of rubble. Something—maybe a shard of metal—was jammed into his side under the ribs. He couldn't tell how deep it was, but he felt cold there, though he could feel warm blood trickling down lower. He couldn't see anything, but figured that was because the mass of the building over and around him was blocking off any ambient light. His eyes, at least, didn't seem to be injured.

He coughed once, the pain of it agonizing with his punctured side. "Ducett?" he called out. "Ducett, you alive in here?"

The building hadn't settled yet. Around him, he could hear chunks falling down, debris creaking ominously. He heard water trickling. The plumbing had surely been turned off when the building had been abandoned, but maybe there'd been some water trapped in the pipes or in a toilet somewhere.

He tried to move his legs. They hurt, but he could feel them moving a little inside the rubble. The trouble was that the wreckage of the building had him wedged in. To get free, he was going to have move the weight aside—and this probably meant hundreds of thousands of pounds—or he was going to have to pry himself out. Given the wound in his side, that didn't sound too promising. He was strong. He could lift a car over his head without difficulty. But this was different. He didn't have leverage. Any move he made could make the debris shift again, cause another collapse. And Ducett was probably in here, too.

"Ducett?" he called out again.

About fifteen feet above Jason and to his right, some rubble shifted. Small pieces of rock or concrete or plaster showered down on his face and he coughed painfully again.

"I'm here." The voice was deep and rich.

"Ducett?"

"Yes." A pause, a deep breath. "Scion?"

Jason coughed again, his mouth full of dust. He felt the weight of the building around them. It had been a while since someone had mistaken him for his brother. And never quite so dramatically. "No," he said. "I'm Argonaut."

"Oh." Some more rubble shifted. Ducett sighed. "We're both trapped here. The air's probably not going to last long—it already smells stale. You might as well do me the courtesy of telling me the truth instead of lying to me. Maybe you are Argonaut, like you said. Maybe you have two uniforms or something. But you're Scion, too."

Jason shook his head in the darkness. The Argonaut Lynceus could see underground, the books said. He wished that he could, too. "I'm too tired and too sore to be lying right now," he said. "I'm not Scion."

"Bullshit. I talked to you on that rooftop. Your voice is the same. Your goddamned aftershave is the same."

Jason blinked. Then he actually chuckled once, though that hurt almost as badly as the cough. Pop gave them the same aftershave every Christmas. He hadn't realized Julian wore it, too. "Look," he said. "I guess you've got a pretty keen sense of smell. But this is a waste of our time. I'm Argonaut, not Scion. Scion is someone else. I . . . know Scion. I'm not really prepared to tell you any more than that, but I'm not him."

Ducett seemed to digest that. "You're bleeding," he said.

"Yeah." Jason swallowed. "You can see in this?"

"No. No, it's more . . . I can just tell."

He could smell the blood, Jason thought. It hadn't bothered Ducett to tell Jason he could smell the after-shave, but the blood—animals smelled blood. He wasn't comfortable putting himself in the same category with an animal.

"I'm not sure how bad it is," Jason said. "Something's stuck in my side." His lips were dry. He listened to the trickling water again, wishing he could drink some of it. "And you slashed me up, too."

Ducett was quiet for a minute. "Sorry about that," he said. His voice was flat, but Jason thought he might be sincere. "Argonaut, huh?"

Jason tried again to shift his body. Something shifted below him, and he could hear metal and concrete groaning in protest. He stopped. "It seemed to fit," he said.

"I read about you in the paper," Ducett said. "You caught the Troll."

"He went free the next day," Jason said. "He's the leader of a street gang. The Concrete Executioners."

Ducett grunted. "That's what the paper said."

"You used to be the leader of the Concrete Executioners."

Ducett was quiet.

Jason continued to hear the sounds of the debris shifting, the water dripping. Any sounds from outside were muffled, but he thought that maybe he could hear sirens.

"He was after my time," Ducett said. "I never met him. I think he started out in New Orleans, then came over here." He paused. "Why the hell do you happen to know so much about me?"

Jason's legs were starting to go numb. His circulation was cut off. He shifted some more. "I don't really know all that much," he said. "The whole 'turns into a seven-foot-tall flying devil' thing went right under my radar."

Ducett actually laughed at that, a rumbling, crackling sound not that different from the shifting of the rubble in the collapsed building that trapped them. "Yes," he said. "That came as something of a surprise to me, too."

"But you rallied."

The amusement fell out of Ducett's voice and he sounded haunted. "No, not really," he said. "And you evaded my question. How is it that you know so much about me?"

Jason thought about it for a moment, then said. "You know any blonde women with eyes filled with blood?"

Ducett sucked air through his teeth. It sounded like a hiss.

"I had a dream," Jason said, "about a woman like that. In the dream, she told me you were evil, that you were going to kill someone, that I had to stop you. I have reason to believe my dreams sometimes." He thought of pale-skinned Idmon, the circles under the man's eyes, the gray streaks in his black hair. *Fear them,* Idmon had said in Greek, his voice shaking. *You should always fear your dreams.*

"I've come to respect my dreams, too." Ducett's words were a soft whisper. "She told you I was evil?" He sounded as though the idea hurt him.

"It was a dream," Jason said. "And she was lying, I think. She was desperate for me to pursue you for some reason. Something terrified her. She was telling me what she needed to in order to get me to look for you."

"And it worked."

"And it worked," Jason echoed. "What were you doing here? Why were you following . . . Scion?" He'd almost said "my brother."

Ducett was quiet for a moment, and Jason wondered if he'd picked up on the verbal stutter. Finally, Ducett said, "Scion abducted a patient of mine named Olena Zhdanov and brought her to this building."

"Oh," Jason said. Olena Zhdanov. Rusalka, whose touch could kill. What in the world was Julian thinking? His side, where the piece of metal—a piece of rebar?— was stabbing him, had gone from cold to hot. He felt out of breath. "Why?" he asked, panting.

"I'm looking forward to asking him," Ducett said, "once we get out of here." His voice was angry, resolute.

"Speaking of which—" Jason needed to concentrate on escape first, his brother later. He wondered what Julian was doing with Rusalka, whether Uncle Costas was behind it. Julian was nearby. He had to feel the injuries Jason had suffered. Would he be coming to help?

Ducett grunted. "I'm wedged in tight," he said. "Cinderblocks, a support beam, lots of plaster and gravel and dust. One arm's pinned down, and so is my—" he broke off. "My tail," he finished, "Never had that problem before." He cleared his throat. "I can maybe climb free, pry my way out, but I don't see how I can do it without burying you."

Jason nodded. "I'm wedged in, too," he said. "And like I said, something's jabbed in my side." He thought about it. "Your tail's pinned, so you're still in that . . . that other form?"

"Yeah." Ducett's voice was tight.

"Change back. You should be able to slip free."

Ducett sucked air through his teeth again. "I'm stronger like this," he said finally. "I'm not sure I could bear the weight otherwise. And—" he broke off, hesitated for a long moment. "I'm not sure if I *can* change back."

"Oh." Jason thought about that, thought about the intellectual man stuck in the body of the monster.

"How about you?" Ducett asked. "Can you pull yourself free?"

"Maybe," Jason answered. "I'm strong, and I can fly, if the debris under me gives way."

The strength of Heracles, he thought. The flight of the Boreads. He considered their options. Should he stall and wait for Julian to come to help them? No, he decided. He couldn't count on anything from his brother.

"When you're ready," he said finally, "do what you have to do, and I'll fend for myself."

Steer clear of the warehouses along Provost Street,
especially after dark.

— Excerpted from
A Devil's Cape Traveler's Guide

THIRTY-SIX

Devil's Cape, Louisiana
Eight days after the deaths
of the Storm Raiders
7:45 p.m.

*K*ate arrived at the broken warehouse before the emergency vehicles did. She found a man staring into the wreckage, his brow furrowed. He was wearing tattered blue jeans and a red and brown flannel shirt that must have been sweltering in the Devil's Cape heat. His hair stretched down past his shoulders in oily strings, his beard scraping his collarbone. His body and clothes were caked with dirt and grime, and it was evident that he hadn't bathed in quite some time. His shoes didn't match. Enraptured by the destruction, he didn't notice her near-silent approach. As she landed and walked over to him, she was grateful for her armor's air filtration system. "Excuse me," she said through her voice-altering speakers.

The man turned and stared at her, his mouth gaping open. He was missing a lot of teeth. "Who da hell are you?" he asked. He had a thick Cajun accent.

"I'm Doctor Camelot," she said. She felt a rush of pride at the words despite the circumstances. "Did you see what happened?" She began a hard scan of the wreckage with her sensors. Sonar, radar, X-ray, explosive detection, ultraviolet, infrared.

The man shrugged. He reached out with a tentative finger, poking her armor. It might have been an accident that he happened to poke her left breast, but she doubted it.

She gently slapped his hand away. "Stop that," she said. "Did you see what happened?"

He shrugged again, squinting at her, trying to see through her faceplate. "Building wen' down like London bridges," he said.

"Was there an explosion? An impact?" She wasn't detecting any explosive trace, but she was also still pretty far from the building. She set a program to analyze the structural data she was gathering, to plot out the weakest and strongest points based on the density of the materials.

"Nah," he said. "Don' t'ink so. Dat buildin', she shook in a good wind. Ain't no surprise she come undone." He turned away from her again, looking at the building. "She come down real good," he said. "She was what, seven, eight stories? Now she 'bout two, maybe." He glanced at her. "You a cop?" he asked.

"No," she said. "Was there anyone inside?"

"Did I stutter?" he said. He said the next bit slowly, enunciating every syllable. "That. Building. Shook. In. A. Good. Wind." He shook his head. "Have to be crazy to go in deah." He scratched at an armpit. " 'Sides, the doors was bolted up good 'n tight."

"Okay," Kate said. She began to walk closer to the building.

"Hey!" the man called out. "You t'ink there's anything good in deah?"

Kate stopped and stared at the destruction. Plaster dust floated in the air. A banana tree twenty feet from the building had been cut in half from a flying chunk of concrete. She heard sirens approaching. "I don't know," she said.

Samuel's voice came over her communicator. "Hey, Kate, you seeing this?"

"Seeing what?" she asked. Her voice only transmitted through the armor when she wanted it to. Samuel could hear her, but the man standing near her couldn't.

"This infrared display. It's on one of your monitors."

She brought the readout up as her primary display.

The infrared picked up temperature differentials. The building itself was a hodgepodge mess. It had been a hot day, and the building had been without power for months, meaning no air conditioning. So most of the building would have been very warm. And the collapse would have driven the hot against the cooler, stirring up the temperatures of the debris. Friction was another factor. But as she stared at the display, adjusting it slightly to bring variances into clearer focus, she noticed something of interest. There was a "blue spot"—something relatively cool—much cooler than the ambient temperatures. It piqued her curiosity. A block of ice? An air conditioning unit? But then she noticed something that made her forget about the blue spot altogether. In the middle of the collapsed building, in what her analysis program told her was one of the least stable areas, were two "red spots"—areas that were warmer than the surrounding temperatures. They were just over ninety-eight degrees Fahrenheit. And human-shaped.

"Oh, no," she whispered.

⸻

Cain's eyes stared around the enclosed space. At first, he hadn't been able to see anything at all, but now he was adjusting to the darkness and could make out the shadows of structures—a jutting piece of concrete here, a tangle of rebars there. He smelled decay and dust and blood.

He could dimly make out Argonaut's form, about fifteen feet away. The man's breathing was ragged and blood still trickled from the wound in his side.

Cain had decided to trust Argonaut for the time being. The man was obviously hiding something, something about Scion, but he seemed sincere. He'd been tense when Cain had accused him of being Scion, but his heart rate had actually begun to subside as he assured Cain that Scion was a different person. He wasn't lying.

Which meant that Cain had attacked an innocent man and brought a building down on top of him.

"Look," he said. He moistened his dry, dusty lips and then winced as he felt one of his needle-sharp teeth slice into his tongue. He'd have to get used to that. "I tackled you. I brought you into this."

Argonaut's voice was amused. "So give me a bouquet of flowers afterward."

"You've got a better chance if—"

"Look, Ducett," Argonaut said. "My chances aren't too different one way or the other. You concentrate on getting yourself out of this first, and I'll tough it out. I've been shot in the face with a .38 special, and it didn't kill me. I'll take my chances." His voice was one-third bravado, two-thirds bravery.

"Okay," Cain said. "On three. One, two . . . three."

There was no sense taking half measures, he thought. It was like pulling off a band-aid. Best done quickly and without hesitation. He yanked his trapped arm free, twisting his body and thrusting backward with his legs to try to free his tail.

Pieces of broken concrete shook free of him, cascaded down, tumbling into each other, heading toward Argonaut.

Argonaut was moving as well, thrusting his arms out, forcing his trapped legs out of the rubble. Cain heard him gasp once as the metal was forced deeper into his side, and then the caped man pushed himself free of it.

Cain was pressing against a collapsed wall. It leaned over them at a diagonal angle, barely holding together, probably what had protected them from most of the debris. If he could get around it, he thought, he could probably make his way to the surface. He thought he could see a little bit of light penetrating from outside now, and he caught a hint of fresh air. He heard sirens. Argonaut, below him, was shoving heavy chunks of concrete out of his way. "Up here," Cain said. "If we can make it around this wall and the rubble on top of it . . ." He set his shoulder against it, pressing hard.

Argonaut floated up to him, cape stretched out in back of him, jaw set, confident. "Then we move the wall," he said. He felt his way along it, set his own shoulder against it. "Now," he said.

The two men pushed in concert, Cain using some sort of reinforced pillar as support for his feet, Argonaut simply floating in the air, flying against the wall.

They lifted and pushed, muscles straining, their strength incredible, trying to break free.

They almost made it.

But the wall they were lifting, already damaged, was holding much more weight than it was ever meant to. The rubble over them and around them had fallen together like a house of cards. Very, very heavy cards. They'd been trapped in one pocket of air, with most of the mass of the building hanging over them, protected to some extent by a girder here, a strut there, a huge chunk of concrete flooring there. And the wall they were pushing against suddenly fractured, letting the mass of the building descend on them.

───

"Well, that could have gone better," Argonaut muttered, pinned once again, his mouth full of blood. He'd been unconscious—he wasn't sure how long. "Ducett? You . . . alive?"

He heard nothing from Ducett, just the sounds of the rubble settling.

"Ducett?"

And then he did hear something new.

"Don't move," said a woman's voice, somewhere in the darkness, distorted by the debris.

He almost laughed. "Don't worry."

"Hang on. I've almost got you."

He raised his eyebrows under his mask. He heard a soft hiss, like a hose, and then light broke through as a large chunk of concrete was pulled away over his head.

A figure advanced cautiously, leaning down over him. It was a woman enclosed in some kind of armor. Much of it was covered with dust, but the rest gleamed in the dim light. "Can you tell me the extent of your injuries?"

she asked. She had a faint British accent. Her face was covered with smoked glass, but she seemed to be peering intently at him.

"I think I can stand up now," he said.

She put up a hand. "Hold on," she said urgently. She leaned forward, pointing her arm at some of the debris, and some kind of liquid streamed out, coating part of it. The liquid smelled sharp and antiseptic. She repeated this in a few other places.

"What are you doing?" he asked.

"This is an astringent, a fast-bonding polymer." She shrugged. "Goop. It's helping to provide increased structural integrity." She looked at him. "You're Argonaut, I take it."

He nodded. "Can I move now?"

"Be my guest," she said. "You don't have any broken bones, although two of your ribs are cracked. The increased density of your skin likely helped to protect you from the worst of the damage."

He blinked behind his mask. "You just X-rayed me?"

"That's right." She reached down. "You need a hand?"

For some reason, he felt mildly indignant. "Shouldn't you have asked permission before doing that?"

Her hand remained in front of him. "Probably," she said. "You'll also be relieved to know that you're not pregnant."

He took her hand and let her pull him up from the hole he was in. His side still hurt from the wound there, but it felt good to be able to move again. "Thanks," he said. As he looked around, he saw that an incredible amount of rubble had been cleared. Perhaps a dozen emergency vehicles—ambulances, fire engines, squad cars—were stretched around the area, several of them with spotlights pointed in their direction. He spotted a WTDC truck, recognized the cameraman Dexter Koo, filming a tight shot of him and the woman in the armor. He smiled slightly, then turned so as to keep from giving the cameras too good of a look at his face. The whole area around the ruined building was cordoned off, but the emergency workers were all on the other side of the barriers. He looked at the cleared rubble. "You did all this yourself?"

"I helped a bit toward the end," said a deep, rumbling voice. It was Ducett, red fur, tail, claws, horns, and all. Jason nodded in relief. The man was cut in several places, but none of the injuries seemed particularly serious. Ducett smiled back at him, the flash of red over the sharp teeth looking unintentionally menacing. It was the first time Jason had really seen the man up close when they weren't fighting. Ducett stretched out a clawed hand, leaning in, his blood-red eyes intent. "We didn't have much of a chance to talk down there," he said, looking Jason in the eye. "You can call me Bedlam."

Bedlam. An appropriate name, Jason thought, reflecting not just chaos, but an asylum.

"And I'm Doctor Camelot," the woman said.

He nodded at her. "I always liked that name," he said. Then he looked at the crowds again.

"I asked them to stay back," Doctor Camelot said.

"And they listened?"

"I asked them very nicely," she said. "And e-mailed their bosses diagrams showing just how dangerous this entire ruin was to anyone approaching."

He stared from her to Ducett—Bedlam. "How long between the second collapse and when you freed me?"

"About a half-hour," Bedlam said.

"Scion?" he asked.

Bedlam shook his head. "No sign of him," he said. His lip turned down in frustration. "Or the other one."

Doctor Camelot's face turned from Argonaut to Bedlam and back again. "Something I should know here?"

Jason looked at her. Her armor gleamed like chrome in the bright lights. A vibrant purple cape hung from her shoulders. Judging by the piles of rubble, she'd moved several tons of debris in a very short time. Most of it by herself. He was grateful to her, but he wasn't sure how much to trust her.

People were moving past the cordons now. A police captain. A reporter Jason knew slightly. A fire marshal. He wasn't ready to be caught up in all of this. And besides, he needed to talk to his brother.

"Another time," he said. He looked at Bedlam, who nodded. "We should talk," Jason said. "Tomorrow night, nine o'clock, at the Gray Fog statue."

The others nodded. Then, as the authorities and reporters began to approach more quickly, the three of them flew away in separate directions.

"Wait, damn it!" the police captain shouted, his face florid.

But they had slipped into the night sky.

So the newest angel to protect the twisted streets of Pirate Town has horns and a forked tail? He'll fit right in.

> — Excerpted from "New capes in
> Devil's Cape," by Ed Clugston,
> *Devil's Cape Daily Courier*, editorial section,
> the morning after the warehouse collapse

THIRTY-SEVEN

Devil's Cape, Louisiana

*Eight days after the deaths
of the Storm Raiders
8:45 p.m.*

*C*ain flew.

Stretching his arms and the tight flaps of skin that spread out beneath them, Cain cut through the dark Devil's Cape sky. The dank air bristled against the short fur covering his body. Argonaut and Doctor Camelot had headed in their own directions, and he found himself alone in the air, nothing but a few bats nearby.

He flew.

Cain had flickered tonight from the cool-headed psychiatrist to the cold-hearted street fighter he'd been, then to a wild animal driven solely by impulse, then back again. But right now, there was no cold analysis, no criminal checking the angles, no beast burning to rip itself free. There was just a sense of release, of the wind fluttering around him, of weightlessness.

He flew.

He soared out of the warehouse district, arcing over the series of channels that led to Lake Pontchartrain and the scattering of homes around them. Keeping himself high in the sky and out of sight, he steered himself over the haunted streets of Crabb's Lament, the neighborhood where he'd grown up. He passed his old apartment building, then slowed and hovered over the spot where he'd shoved Jazz onto the concrete. The air seemed

thick. He smelled gunpowder and wondered if anyone had died in his old neighborhood that night. And then he flew to the shotgun house where Jazz now lived. He circled a few times, wings outstretched, ears cocked to be sure that no one was near, then landed beside an old lacebark elm.

A hand-painted sign propped against the curling metal fleurs-de-lis of her front gallery read, PALM-READING, TAROT READING, VOODOO CURSING, AND ALL THAT JAZZ. He stepped forward quickly, his clawed feet scratching at the gravel. The sound of it made him look down at himself, at his distorted body, the vicious hands, the thin, red fur. She is nothing to me, he lied to himself, the image of the thin girl flying back against the concrete filling his mind. Whatever I owe her, I don't owe her this.

And then he stepped forward. He felt too rushed to knock, but the door was locked. Feeling the knob seize up in his hand, he suddenly thought of gloves, fingerprints, evidence, and Detective Cynthia Daigle. He hadn't done anything legally or morally wrong by coming here, but there were worms crawling through his gut. Jazz was scared of something, Argonaut had said. If she was powerful enough to turn him into this, powerful enough to reach into his mind, to break glass around him, to twist his dreams away from him—not to mention Argonaut's—then what in the name of hell would leave her sounding so worried? He had a dark ride in front of him.

His fingers were different in this form, his prints obscured by their elongated shape, by the stiff, bristly hair that seemed to cover him. Even so, he reached his long fingers into his pocket, pulling out the tie he had stuffed there ages ago before his fight with Scion, and wiped the knob. Then, gripping the knob with the tie, he twisted hard and pushed on the door with his shoulder, enjoying for a brief second the strength his new form gave him. When he was inside, he turned and closed the door behind him.

"You could have knocked." Jazz stood leaning in a doorway across the room, looking at him. She wore cut-off blue jeans and an oversized black T-shirt with a sketch of Lady Danger on the front. Her long, blonde hair was tied back in a ponytail and her skin was pale. She looked little different than she had at fourteen, though her eyes were sadder. The room was decorated with the types of artifacts she might sell to her customers. Incense filled the air. The sight of her shook him, like the years were washing away. He felt guilt and grief and anger.

He gestured at himself. "I didn't feel like terrifying your neighbors."

She shook her head. "I could run naked out the front door, screaming, my entrails strung behind me like a row of sausages, and my neighbors wouldn't bat an eye."

Now close to seven feet tall, Cain filled the room. He stared at her, trying to force himself not to relive the memory of shoving her back. "What have you done to me, Jazz?"

She shook her head. "Don't ask stupid questions, Cain."

He spread his arms, the elongated fingers stretching from one wall to another, the claws flexing. "Look at me," he said.

She nodded. "And you mocked my white voodoo," she said, the hint of a smile on her lips.

He blinked. "I'm sorry for that," he said. "I'm sorry for what I did to you."

"You're paying for that doorknob."

He breathed hard, staring back at her. "That's not what I meant."

She shook her head. "What do you want from me, Cain? I know what you meant. I know that you have tortured yourself for years over what you did to me that afternoon. And I don't care. I'm glad you've suffered over it. You deserved to suffer over it." Her eyes were hard.

"I'm not denying that," he said. "But this—" He raised a hand to his head, felt the thickened jaw, the jutting teeth, the elongated ears, the horns.

"I cursed you that day," she said. "I cursed you, and that fact hasn't changed in all the years since."

"The first time this happened to me, I snapped," he said. "I nearly killed my mother and our next-door-neighbor, Mr. Marcus. A detective named Salazar Lorca talked me out if it. He told me it was a hallucination. He offered me the salvation of reality, of intellect, of reason."

Jazz said nothing, just stared back at him.

"I built my life around that," he said, "around using reason, understanding the forces that drive our minds. I built my life around the understanding that what happened to me that night was a trick of my mind."

"Surprise," she said with another mocking smile.

His fists clenched. "The hell with this," he said. He turned to open her broken door.

"Wait," she said, her voice soft. "Sit down and talk to me."

He let go of the door, but remained standing. "I'm not even sure how to sit with this," he said, gesturing helplessly at his tail.

She laughed outright then, great cascading laughter that washed over the room until even dour, angry Cain chuckled a little bit. "I imagine," she said, "that you could figure out a way around that little problem, but you could just as easily turn back into your other form."

He stared at her. "I can do that?"

She snorted. "You did it years ago when you changed for the first time. What makes you think you can't do it now?"

And it turned out to be easy. He closed his eyes, concentrating, and the monstrous form just slipped away from him. He was normal Cain Ducett once more, although still dressed in nothing but a pair of pants split at the legs, with a hole near the base of his spine where his tail had pushed through.

Jazz reached up and touched his face with a sort of wonder. "You look old."

Unconsciously, he clutched the hand that she'd touched to his face, squeezing it almost tenderly in his own. Then he let go, staring at her. "What do you need from me, Jazz?"

She told him.

If you're in Boston, you hobnob on Newbury Street. In Chicago, you don't miss Michigan Avenue. In Devil's Cape, look no further than Lockheardt Street for a taste of what the city has to offer.

— Excerpted from
A Devil's Cape Traveler's Guide

THIRTY-EIGHT

Devil's Cape, Louisiana
Eight days after the deaths
of the Storm Raiders
8:45 p.m.

*J*ulian lived in a penthouse apartment in Devil's Cape's Soirée Bleue Ward. Just north of the Silver Swan district, the Soirée Bleue had one long, crowded thoroughfare, Lockheardt Street, along which ran a series of antique streetcars that dated back to the 1910s. Lockheardt Street was also filled with foot traffic—Lehane University students going back and forth to their classes, dorms, and favorite watering holes in the area; street vendors selling Mardi Gras masks, knock-off Gambina dolls, bottles of perfume, and T-shirts; and a wide selection of tourists, amateur artists, and homeless. The other streets, though less crowded, formed a tangled maze of one-way roads, blind alleys, twists, and turns, the typical confusing mess attributed by some to the city's pirates founders, by others to the pirates' dogs, who, allowed to wander free in the area before it was well-settled, developed their own meandering paths.

His uniform torn, his side still bleeding, Jason soared over the Soirée Bleue, his cape crackling behind him like a flag in a thunderstorm. Whipping by the gargoyles atop the Lehane University clock tower, he landed heavily on Julian's veranda, which was green and purple with bougainvillea vines. Grabbing his brother's sliding glass door with both hands, he yanked it and popped it off of its hinges, storming inside.

"Julian!" he yelled.

The sliding glass door opened into his brother's living room. It was spare. An Oriental carpet stretched over bleached wood. A tan leather sofa faced bookshelves and a built-in entertainment center, in which rested a wide-screen television. A single print by a local artist hung from one wall—a trombone player standing alone in the middle of Lockheardt Street, body tilting back, back arched like a cat's, belting out a song into the empty night.

The kitchen, adjacent to the living room, sparkled with stainless steel utensils and chrome fixtures, barely touched. A wine rack against one wall held perhaps thirty bottles, and Jason guessed they'd probably be valued at more than five thousand dollars; Julian's tastes were expensive.

Nothing seemed out of place. Jason felt no hint of his brother's presence. He wasn't home. Jason had flown over in an angry rush, but it wouldn't have made sense for Julian to be there. He'd left the warehouse scarcely an hour earlier with Rusalka, wearing his mask, and would hardly have brought her to his own home.

Jason walked through the rest of the penthouse anyway, looking for signs of where his brother might have taken Rusalka, but he knew there wouldn't be any. Julian was too meticulous, too careful. And besides, his plan had apparently been to hold the woman at the warehouse for some period of time. Since the plan was disrupted, Julian would have been forced to improvise.

What did he want the woman for in the first place? Was there something Uncle Costas wanted her to do? Or was it Julian himself?

The phone rang. He picked it up off the cradle and pressed it to his ear without saying a word.

"Water my plants while you're there, won't you?" Julian asked. "I think I forgot this morning."

Jason sighed. "I like the painting in the living room," he said. "Is that a Kerageorgiu?" He knew it was. He had one in his own living room, though he hadn't realized that Julian liked the artist, too. It wasn't surprising.

"Cost me a bit," Julian admitted. "So how much damage have you done to the place? You tripped the alarm and the security company paged me. You'll be relieved to know, if not surprised, that they know better than to inform the police."

"You'll be relieved to know, if not surprised," Jason echoed, "that I wasn't killed when that little deathtrap of yours came tumbling down."

"I've been waiting for news with bated breath," Julian said. His tone was sarcastic, but there was an edge to it.

"You really were worried." Though apparently not enough to do anything about it.

"Did you catch the psychiatrist?" Julian's voice was tense.

Ducett. Julian had thrown Ducett off the building. He hadn't seen Ducett turn into the devil-thing—Bedlam.

"Yes," he said. "He's alive."

A pause. "Good," Julian said. "I felt a little bad about him." A little bad about trying to murder someone.

"What the hell are you doing, Julian? She's a psychopath."

"Cute, though."

Jason stared into space. A framed picture of their parents rested on Julian's bookshelf beside a copy of *Crime and Punishment*. In the picture, they were on a rare vacation, a long weekend in La Pesca. Pop wore a tasseled sombrero, Mama a sundress. They were smiling, lifting frozen margaritas to the camera. "You're not—" Jason said.

"No," Julian said. "No, I'm not touching her."

"Where are you, Julian? I need to talk to you."

"So talk. Turn up the thermostat a few degrees, too, will you? It might be a few days until I get back and I don't need to pay for all the AC."

Jason was tempted to turn the temperature all the way down, but it felt childish. He looked away from the picture of their parents. It felt odd to him, standing there in his brother's empty apartment, the Argonaut uniform wrapped around him. He glanced down. He was bleeding on his brother's expensive rug. "Julian, please," he whispered.

There was silence for a few seconds, then, "Uncle Costas is scared. I've never seen him like this before." He swallowed. "Tony Ferazzoli's dead, you know."

Tony Ferazzoli was the only son of Lorenzo Ferazzoli, who had led the Ferazzoli crime organization for nearly thirty years. A dynamic figure, known for the pin-striped suits and wide, brightly colored ties he wore, his thick head of white hair, and his passion for horse racing, Lorenzo had had a long and bitter rivalry with Costas Kalodimos, its roots dating back to the men's grandfathers and Prohibition. Both men had ultimately been beholden to the Robber Baron, but they sparred with each other, indulged in petty and vindictive behavior— Jason remembered a brisk winter day when he and Julian had discovered Uncle Costas's Doberman pinscher dead on the street, shot between the eyes—and tried their best to edge each other out of the Robber Baron's favor. Lorenzo had died under mysterious circumstances about six years earlier. His crushed body was found in historic Bullocq Park, not far from his home, in the middle of a cluster of rose bushes. He'd fallen from a great height, though no tall buildings were nearby. Jason had always suspected Julian, but he had never asked.

Tony Ferazzoli, who had stepped into his father's place as leader of the family business, had lacked Lorenzo's flair and drive. He had a canny but disorganized mind. He was prone to superstition and had gained more than fifty pounds in the first year after his father's death. He was perceived as weaker than his father and had had little open conflict with Uncle Costas; he was too busy defending himself from threats within his own family to worry about external enemies.

"When did that happen?" Jason asked.

"A week or so ago."

Jason hesitated. "Did you—"

Julian grunted. "Not me," he said. "And not Uncle Costas. He didn't like Tony Ferazzoli, but he liked the fact that the Ferazzolis had their wings clipped with him in charge. I bought him a bottle of ouzo when it happened. We'd shared a few glasses after Lorenzo bought the farm." He said it like Lorenzo's death was an act of nature, a natural event in the great path of the cosmos, not as though it was something he himself had caused. But he had, Jason knew. "But he shoved it away. He was pale. Sweating. 'I'm going to need some help,' he said to me."

Jason pulled a towel out of a drawer in Julian's kitchen and pressed it against the wound in his side. It quickly blossomed red with blood. "How did Tony die?"

"No one's seen a body," Julian said. "But there are rumors."

"Marcus?" Vincent Marcus was Tony Ferazzoli's oldest nephew, his second in command and also one of his main rivals for control of the family.

"No, Marcus was surprised when it happened. You should have seen his face—he looked like he won the lottery and landed a Bandits cheerleader on the same day." Jason wondered just under what circumstances Julian had seen Vincent Marcus's face when the man had learned of his uncle's death.

"Then who?"

"It was the Robber Baron," Julian said. "Or the *Cirque d'Obscurité* on his orders. The word is that they won't be finding his body because the Werewolf barbecued him in some honey and cayenne pepper and ate him."

Jason closed his eyes then looked at his side again. The bleeding had nearly stopped, but the cloth was filled with blood. He winced as he pulled it from his side, ripping part of the wound open again, and replaced it with another cloth. He threw the first one in the trash. "You believe that?"

Julian clucked his tongue. "I don't know about the specifics," he said. "But yeah, the Robber Baron gave the order, and his monster squad pulled it off."

"Why? And why is Uncle Costas scared?"

Julian was silent for a moment. "I think he did it because Tony was incompetent. He was screwing up too

much, and the Robber Baron was tired of it. And Vincent Marcus isn't getting the nice little package wrapped in a bow that he thinks he's getting. The baron's going to turn the Ferazzolis' operations over to Hector Hell."

"But the *Cirque d'Obscurité* are mercenaries," Jason said. "They're hired goons the Robber Baron brought into town. They're not the type to take over organizations like the Ferazzoli crime machine."

"And yet . . ." Julian said.

"So Uncle Costas is afraid that the Robber Baron's going to do something similar to him?"

"Yes."

"And Rusalka? He wants her as what? A bodyguard?"

"No," Julian said. "An assassin."

The sudden appearance of a new Doctor Camelot in Devil's Cape has stirred Vanguard City from its grief, giving the city of gold new hope and new focus.

— Excerpted from "Return of Camelot?"
by Leslie Flannigan, *Vanguard City Crier*,
the morning after the warehouse
collapse in Devil's Cape

THIRTY-NINE

Devil's Cape, Louisiana
Eight days after the deaths
of the Storm Raiders
8:45 p.m.

*I*mpressive," Samuel said as Kate returned to her lab.

She'd been walking inside, a smile behind her faceplate, exulting in the unexpected success of the evening, but she stopped and stared when she caught sight of him, perched on the edge of her desk. He was less than six inches tall. Instead of his Sam Small uniform, he was wearing the same blue jeans, Hawaiian shirt, and sandals he'd been wearing earlier, only smaller. "Look, Malibu Ken," he said.

She shook her head. "I knew intellectually that you were Sam Small," she said. "I knew about your powers, knew that you could shrink, but seeing it in reality—"

He smiled self-deprecatingly. "Takes your breath away, doesn't it?" He adopted a faux radio voice. "The amazing Sam Small, the ultimate in miniaturization. Just slip him into your pocket and go!" He shrugged, returned to his normal voice. "It's comfortable sometimes."

Kate carefully removed her helmet, setting it on a stand she'd put in place for that purpose. She'd have to do something to get all the dust off. And the bugs that had splattered against it. She looked sideways at him. "That's not why you shrank this time, though, is it?"

"Would it make you more comfortable if I returned to normal?"

She began to remove her armor. She wondered how

it was that his clothes shrank with him—were they specially treated in some way, or did the effect arise with him? What if he took off his shirt and left it there? Would it eventually revert to its normal size? Reports she'd read on him indicated that he could still lift as much while small as he could at normal size, despite the decreased muscle mass. Was that accurate? And why wasn't his voice higher pitched when he was small? She brushed her questions away. This wasn't the time. "That's up to you," she said. "And you didn't answer my question."

He jumped to the ground. It was a drop of perhaps thirty inches, but proportionally, that was like a drop of thirty feet for him. He landed without difficulty, bowed slightly, and then began to grow back to his normal height. "Voila," he said. The process of growing had taken him just a few seconds. "You got that under control?" He gestured at her armor.

She stepped out of the rest of it. "I'll need to clean it," she said.

He nodded and grabbed a rag, carefully lifting her helmet from its resting place and starting with it, buffing it vigorously with the cleaner she passed over to him. "Sometimes," he said, "it's easy to get caught up in the amazing aspects of the things we do and lose track of the banalities." Pressing a finger into the rag, he scraped a splattered mayfly off her faceplate.

She stepped over to her computer monitor and entered a few commands. She'd set a program to capture and record any media references to Doctor Camelot, and after her appearance at the collapsed building tonight, there were a lot of them. Setting three of her monitors on silent playback of the coverage, she grabbed a rag of her own and began to work on the armor's torso. The words DOCTOR CAMELOT IV appeared brightly on the screen across footage of her removing rubble from the site. "So you reminded me of your amazing power," she said, "as a way of helping to keep me grounded."

He smiled. "You've spent a lot of time with me the past few days," he said. "I'm short. I sweat. I stammer over

my words sometimes. My hair's growing gray. And I can't bring myself to like jambalaya no matter how many times I try it." His hand dragged the cloth briskly over the helmet. "I'm an ordinary guy with my own baggage and demons and bad habits. But when I shrink down, when you see a man the size of a G.I. Joe standing there, you forget that. Even though you know me pretty well by now."

On the monitor a video was playing footage of her pulling Bedlam from the wreckage, lifting him up. The cameras spotlighted them for a second, the female knight in shining armor sitting on a broken piece of concrete wall, the demonic-looking man spread unconscious across her lap. From the camera angle, they looked very briefly like Michelangelo's Pietà. That image, she realized, would be on the front page of the paper in the morning. She turned her attention back to Samuel. "So you're saying that these people I met, Argonaut and Bedlam, no matter how amazing they appear, they're normal, too."

He nodded. "And flawed," he said. And any hint of a smile dropped away from his face. "Remember this, too, Kate. They're from Devil's Cape, which is probably the most corrupt place in all the world." He shook his head. "In Devil's Cape, you can't trust anybody."

I understand and support my brother's intentions
in this matter. But it seems to me that our building
was meant to be a home more than a prison. I am
disturbed by the reports we have heard, and were
Janus not so ill right now, I would make haste to see
the situation for myself.

— Excerpted from a letter written by
Harvey Holingbroke to the caretakers of
his son, niece, and nephew, 1915

FORTY

Devil's Cape, Louisiana

*Nine days after the deaths
of the Storm Raiders
7 a.m.*

After a long night's sleep, Cain's first stop back at Holingbroke was a guard's station on the third floor. The guard posted there in the mornings, a hulking, moon-faced bigot named Cletus, was notorious not only for paying too much attention to the female patients, but also for leaving his spot unattended for long bathroom, coffee, and smoke breaks. He rarely bothered to secure his equipment, either. Cain had complained about the man half a dozen times, but even in today's job market, it was hard to find people willing to pull guard duty at an asylum, and the administration had hung on to the man.

Sure enough, Cletus's station was deserted. Barely breaking stride, Cain reached down and snatched the man's shotgun from where it sat on a shelf below his desk, snagging a non-regulation baseball bat at the same time. The shotgun was loaded with special "bean bag" ammo used as a last resort to subdue dangerous patients, not kill them, and Cain knew it might come in handy in the night to come. He wouldn't mind getting Cletus in trouble again, either. Maybe this would be the straw that broke the man's job security.

He had just stowed the weapons in his office when he heard a knock at the door. Without really thinking about it, he knew before letting his visitor in that it was his friend and fellow psychiatrist, Eli Rosencrantz. Tall and

lean, with wavy black hair and a soft voice, Eli had a keen mind and a gentle manner.

They talked idly for a few minutes before Eli slipped in the real meaning for his visit. "Detective Daigle went out of her way to bump into me in the hallway yesterday," he said.

"Yeah?" Cain said. "Did she come out and ask you if you think I freed my patient, or did she beat around the bush?"

Eli grinned nervously, fingering a silk tie. "I don't think she's much the beating around the bush type," he said, "though she tried. I believe the conversation went from 'How about that heat wave?' to 'I met your friend Dr. Ducett—what an interesting guy' to 'Do you think he was doing the patient?' in less than thirty seconds."

"Did you tell her that if I wanted her free, there were a lot easier ways—including pronouncing her cured of all mental irregularities?"

Eli leaned back against the doorframe of Cain's office. "She seemed to realize it would take more than that, but admitted that you would have had to be stupid to break Zhdanov out the way she was broken out, given all the other methods you could have used given your authority."

"So you think she's going to back off?"

He shook his head, running his fingers through his wavy hair. "No," he said. "She seems to think you *are* that stupid. Or were seduced into it."

"To which you said?"

"That you are the smartest man I know, that you are the most rigidly controlled man I know, and that there was no possibility that you would have acted improperly with a patient, because A, you know how stupid that would be, and B, you have never been that impulsive in your life."

Cain smiled at his friend, but images pulsed in his head. Handing an eightball to a Baptist minister and taking cash in return. Shooting a hole in 5-D Binot's belly. Shoving Jazz. Holding his mother at gunpoint. Climbing a building and attacking the superhuman

Scion. Transforming into a winged devil. Not impulsive? He shook it off. "I appreciate the support," he said.

Eli leaned forward again. "Yeah, well," he said, "I also told the detective that if she left you alone, I'd sleep with her."

"And?"

"She's considering it."

"Glad to hear it," Cain said. He wondered how much more trouble Daigle would be. With luck, he'd be able to bring Zhdanov back to Holingbroke and that would be the end of it.

But Eli's penetrating, gold-flecked eyes registered dozens of questions. He stared at Cain for a few seconds. "Darren said you came in the other day with your face cut," he said. That was Eli's way. The long pauses. The carefully chosen topic shifts that really prodded back at the issues at hand from different angles. The casual statements that were really questions. Cain tried to place the name for a moment. Darren. Then he remembered. The security guard. The "hockey fan." Eli's other questions went unspoken. Why didn't Cain's face look cut right now, he wanted to know. Why had the most rigidly controlled man he knew arrived at Holingbroke before dawn with blood dripping from his face?

Cain shrugged. "Scalp wound," he said. "You know how they bleed." He gestured at his desk. "I should be catching up with my patients who haven't escaped. I appreciate your dropping by, Eli." He smiled at his friend, but Eli was still giving him the curious stare. Despite his assurances to the detective, there was some small part of Eli that doubted, that suspected there was something wrong in Cain's life. "I'd do the same for you," he said. Cain's next statement went unspoken, too. He'd respect Eli's privacy. He expected the same.

After Eli left, Cain could feel his friend's eyes staring at his office door, deep in thought. Somewhere under Cain's skin, his wings itched.

It's just damned unfair. Carnivals aren't exactly traveling gold mines, you know. It takes back-breaking hard work to come out a little above breaking even. We were doing okay—not great, but okay—when the guys in the sideshow and my electrician ran off with a bunch of my trucks and just disappeared. That nearly crippled me, but then they showed up as some kind of hired criminals and killed a superhero, and then suddenly everyone knew that they used to work for me. The police were all over me, and the FBI, and we got this little surge of rubes—excuse me, customers—coming to see us just in hopes of getting a glimpse at the freaks, but then that dried up and suddenly every-one was staying away in droves. Like I was the one who killed your Doctor Camelot. It put my carnival right out of business. I'm just another victim here, you know?

— From an interview with Justin Ma,
former owner of Ma's Spectacular
Amusements traveling carnival,
airing on WVCTV News, Vanguard City

FORTY-ONE

Devil's Cape, Louisiana
Nine days after the deaths
of the Storm Raiders
3 p.m.

*H*ector Nelson Poteete—Hector Hell—didn't like going out without his costume, but sometimes he just had to do it in order to keep from drawing too much of the wrong kind of attention.

He needed to go talk to the Robber Baron, and the chance to drive Tony Ferazzoli's little red Lamborghini Gallardo Spyder—now *his* little red Lamborghini Gallardo Spyder—made the sacrifice of having to wear such pedestrian clothing as a white golf shirt over khaki pants worthwhile. Zero to sixty in about four seconds. The top down, air conditioning blowing, the wind rushing through his hair. On a bridge over Chien Jaune River, he topped a hundred and twenty miles per hour, weaving around a school bus on one side and a gas tanker heading in the opposite direction. He chuckled to himself when both drivers honked at him. Maybe he wanted attention after all.

Despite the stifling humidity, it felt good to be back in Louisiana, back in America. He was tired of running from country to country, looking over his shoulder. He'd spent years waking up in the middle of the night, terrified that the Storm Raiders had finally caught up with them.

The call from the Robber Baron—lord knows how he'd tracked them down to Calcutta—had been a thrilling relief. "Come to my city," he'd said. "Give me your loyalty. An alliance with me will bring your team many rewards, not

the least of them being a home. All of us will benefit as a result."

And then they'd come to the city, and the worst of his fears had come true. Some reporter had figured out they were there, and the Storm Raiders had come looking for them.

But it hadn't turned out so badly after all.

"Screw 'em," Poteete said to himself, tapping on the brakes and bringing the car down to ninety, zipping around a string of early-afternoon commuters. "They came after us and we killed them. Screw 'em."

Some other hero teams were making noises about coming after the *Cirque d'Obscurité*, but the Robber Baron had told them not to worry about it. "They won't make it far into my city," he'd said with a smile. "Didn't you hear? The mayor has asked anyone else to keep from interfering. Stay out of sight for a while and they'll back off."

The other teams weren't what scared Poteete the most, not after what had happened to the Storm Raiders. What scared him was this new woman calling herself Doctor Camelot. "She might as well have named herself Doctor Here-in-Devil's-Cape-to-Kick-Some-*Cirque-d'Obscurité*-Ass," he said. Serious revenge issues to watch out for, no doubt.

He had to slow down more now—down to seventy—as he got close to the south end of town and the business district. The Lamborghini shuddered from a gust of hot wind as he ran a red light and shot across Cap de Creus Street.

"Better keep it down," he said, slowing the car down a little more. It would be stupid to get pulled over. A complication.

He turned on a CD Osprey had made for him as a joke for his birthday. Fire songs. "Great Balls of Fire" by Jerry Lee Lewis. "Light My Fire" by the Doors. "Comin' Under Fire" by Def Leppard from the *Pyromania* album. Half a dozen others. She'd ended it with "Kumbaya" by Peter, Paul & Mary. Sasha was pretty damned funny when she put her mind to it, when she wasn't busy slicing people up with her knives.

Bruce Springsteen was singing "I'm On Fire." Poteete grinned to himself and cranked the volume up. By the time the song was over, he was approaching a set of docks on Lake Borgne and could see the Robber Baron's palatial riverboat up ahead, sitting smooth and level in choppy waters.

He swung the car into a small parking lot, where a valet in a white jacket, white shirt, and white tie nodded at him politely, waited until he climbed out, and then drove the car away to another parking lot with a quick squeal of the tires.

"No tip for you," Poteete said, walking down to the dock and the small motored skiff that would take him over to the riverboat.

The valets and skiff operators were a courtesy provided by the Robber Baron, but they were actually more for his own convenience. The small lot was too close to busy roads, too small, and too isolated from other parking for any convenient, manageable surveillance by police. And the valets quickly stashed the cars out of sight in a private garage that the police would need a warrant to observe. It didn't actually stop the police from keeping tabs on who visited the Robber Baron, but it made the whole process more difficult to accomplish, especially without him knowing about it. It seemed a little overly choreographed to Poteete, but at least the covered garage would keep seagulls from shitting on the Lamborghini.

He nodded at the skiff operator, dressed identically to the valet, and climbed aboard. The air smelled of salt and dead fish, but it wasn't too unpleasant. The skiff's motor was nearly silent; the loudest noises he heard on the brief trip were the crashing of small waves against the bow and the cries of seagulls.

The Robber Baron's riverboat, named the *Bloody Dirk* after the masked pirate St. Diable's favorite ship, was huge, decorated like the classic riverboats of the nineteenth century, including a working, retractable paddlewheel, yet equipped for high-speed travel with a hydrofoil design the baron had once seen employed on China's Yangtze River. The *Bloody Dirk* had three decks, one for the bridge and operations, one for entertainment—the Robber Baron hosted a masked ball on board every year at Mardi Gras—and a third for the Robber Baron's own use. The riverboat glistened with fresh white paint and red trim. As often as not, her trappings were plated with gold.

Poteete met the Robber Baron in a covered porch area at the front of the boat. It was netted off with fine silk mosquito netting, but again Poteete wondered if the netting weren't there less as protection against insects and more to keep the Robber Baron's meetings private.

The Robber Baron's gaucho hat hung on a peg on the wall. Gray threaded his black hair. "What can I pour you?" he asked.

Poteete shrugged. "Mint julep," he said, lowering himself into a padded wicker chair.

The Robber Baron smiled, walking over to the bar, pulling a frosted silver mug from a freezer and gently crushing mint leaves inside. "A Southern cliché," he said. He added ice and raw sugar and a splash of water, then poured in a slug of Kentucky bourbon.

Poteete smiled back. "You try getting a decent mint julep in Gdansk or Gaberone," he said. "I did without them for a long time."

The Robber Baron handed him the drink and sat. "I'm not sure I can allow you to stay in Tony Ferrazzoli's mansion for much longer."

Allow. Poteete watched as the frosty sheen on his mug began to turn translucent from the heat in his hands. He thought of the moment he'd blasted the Storm Raiders' plane, fire arcing out of his hands, coating the plane's metal skin, sinking inside and igniting the fuel. He thought of watching the plane blow up, the thud he felt in his chest from the force of the explosion. He thought of Raiden, the hero who controlled lightning, and how he'd been torn to pieces because of Poteete's flames. He looked at the Robber Baron, whose face looked narrow and lined behind his mask. *Allow.*

"We like it there," Poteete said.

Their eyes met. The Robber Baron's were blue-gray, intent. There was an edge there, as though he knew the

kinds of thoughts going through Poteete's mind. The Robber Baron was at once amused, unafraid, and scornful.

They continued to stare at each other for a few seconds, Poteete increasingly feeling the weight of the other man's gaze, the power of his presence.

Poteete looked away first, consciously trying not to flinch.

"Be that as it may," the Robber Baron said, "these new players who showed up at the building collapse add a random element. Keeping you in place in an affluent area such as Doubloon Ward would be flaunting my influence. I don't flaunt."

Poteete looked around the porch area where they sat, at the gilded fixtures, the silk brocade on the partitions, at the Robber Baron's clothing. "Uh huh," he said.

The Robber Baron chuckled. "Well, yes," he said. "I suppose I do flaunt. But only within certain parameters. Keeping you in that building might be tempting fate."

Poteete sipped the mint julep. The heat from his hands had melted the ice and ruined it. He set it down. "So we'll lay low," he said. "It's not like we've been throwing block parties."

"Your presence there is known."

"By Costas Kalodimos. Who *you* invited there."

The Robber Baron sighed. "That might have been an error. Costas has been loyal to me for many years, but he hasn't taken well to your presence here, to our alliance."

Poteete pictured the mansion, the down quilt he'd taken to using at night. "Tony Ferazzoli was a problem, too," he said. "And we fixed that problem."

The Robber Baron stared out into the waters of Lake Borgne, a lagoon, actually, that connected to the Gulf of Mexico. He sighed. "He's been a good soldier," he said. He drummed his gloved fingers on his chair. Finally, he nodded. "Stay in the mansion for now," he said. "Lay low. Be on guard. We'll give Costas a few days to come around. Or to hang himself."

Dress casually for Zorba's and wear comfortable shoes in case you have to wait to get inside. The restaurant doesn't take reservations, but usually even the longest lines mean no more than a half-hour wait.

— Excerpted from
A Devil's Cape Traveler's Guide

FORTY-TWO

Devil's Cape, Louisiana
Nine days after the deaths
of the Storm Raiders
8:45 p.m.

*P*ulling another piece of chicken and a bit of onion from the skewer and popping them in his mouth, Costas Kalodimos stared across the table at the Russian woman. Her hair was tied up in a scarf, her eyes hidden behind sunglasses, but she was still strikingly beautiful. This was the woman who sucked the life out of her enemies with a touch?

The two sat alone together at a booth at the back of Zorba's, his brother's restaurant, filled to capacity with the dinner crowd, with a dozen people standing outside waiting to get in. Costas ate there often, as did several members of his organization, but they never did business there.

Yet he couldn't meet the woman in one of the places where he usually did business, as he suspected that they were probably under observation—if not by the Robber Baron himself, then possibly by one of the law enforcement agencies that wasn't being paid to stay away. And he couldn't meet her somewhere he never visited, because his departure from routine would arouse suspicions. So he had broken his word to his brother not to bring his business to Zorba's and met her here. A small thing, he thought, breaking his word, compared to the pressures weighing upon him.

He nodded at her. "The avgolemono soup is good,"

he said. "Egg and lemon and rice and milk. My brother adds a touch of cream. You should try some."

She nodded, leaning forward and spooning some up, her eyes on his from behind the shaded lenses of her glasses.

He took another bite of his chicken souvlaki, dipping his fork down to his plate to get just a little more lemon butter sauce into his mouth. Costas was a heavy man with gray hair that he kept slicked back. His eyes were such a dark blue that they were nearly black, like a shark's. "I have read your police files," he said, "and those from the institute." He said this casually, as though he was privy to such things as a matter of course. The police records had been no problem at all. A phone call. And while he had been unable to obtain the files of Zhdanov's psychiatrist, his contacts had acquired copies of Zhdanov's records at the Holingbroke Psychological Institute for less than the cost of a tank of gasoline.

"The soup is tart," she said, turning up her mouth. But she swallowed another spoonful readily enough.

Costas tapped his fingers on the white tablecloth. He had thick hands with sparse gray hairs. He wore a thick wedding band on his left hand, a heavy gold signet ring and a pinkie ring on his right, the pinkie ring glittering with four dozen diamonds. A gold Rolex was wrapped around his left wrist, a thick gold chain around his right. Midas's hands. "These files indicate to me that you are intelligent and stable," he said. "When you want to be."

She shrugged. "It is a matter of perspective," she said. "You can trust me if you like." A stray hair had fallen free of her scarf and she brushed it back inside. She was a wanted fugitive, but when she cast her eyes around the room, it was with casual disinterest.

He watched her hands. They looked normal enough. Slender, pale, the nails cut short and unpainted. But they could turn a person into a corpse with a touch. The files he'd seen had included crime scene photos.

Costas feared little in this world, but he was glad for the table between them, the Luger he kept under his jacket. "My employee told you what I want." He leaned forward. "We don't need to speak of it directly."

Zhdanov slurped loudly at another spoonful of soup, burped softly, and covered her lips with her fingertips in an exaggerated expression of dismay. "Please excuse me," she said. She was mocking him.

Costas's expression turned cold. He squeezed at his knife handle in irritation, cutting off another bite. "Do we have an understanding?"

She took her time sipping some water before answering. "Your employee is an interesting man."

Julian was more than an employee, of course, but Zhdanov didn't need to know that. He wondered sometimes if he'd still be alive without his nephew's assistance and power. He was fortunate, he knew, to have someone with Julian's abilities by his side. The two of them had kept the boy's abilities secret from the rest of the family, the rest of the organization. When it became time, for political reasons, for Costas to make it known that he had a superhuman working for him, they had invented the Scion identity.

Costas had often wondered if his nephew Jason had similar abilities, though Julian had long denied it. But Julian had never let him pursue the matter. "I will work for you," Julian had told him once, his jaw set. "I will be your good and loyal soldier. But Jason and Pop are off limits. Forever."

He flicked his dark eyes at Zhdanov. "And you are an interesting woman," he said, though the words came with little inflection, his face empty. "You will do what I wish? I can arrange transportation, passport, papers, compensation."

"Passport, papers, transportation, yes," she said. "I wish to fly to Russia." Which probably meant that she wished to go anywhere in the world but Russia, but did not want to be traced. "And the compensation. Three million. In euros."

He stared at her.

She waved a hand. "No haggling, please. I am a psychopath, remember? Psychopaths do not haggle." She ate another spoonful of soup. "If you do not wish to pay me this, I will walk out. I will not kill you today, so it is up to you." She stared at him and smiled. "I am almost certain that I will not kill you and everyone in this restaurant." She poked her spoon at him, smile broadening. "Quite likely not."

Pericles Kalodimos limped over to his brother's table, a steaming tray of baklava in his hand. His eyes were disapproving, but then they usually were, when Costas was around. "Everything all right, Costas?" he asked, smiling, though the smile was that of a good host, not of an affectionate brother.

Zhdanov laid her hand on Pericles' tanned, scarred forearm, her eyes on Costas. "I would very much like to try a piece of the baklava," she said. Her smile was still broad, amused. Her eyes were pleased and manic and Costas saw the insanity in them then. He realized that she would not hesitate to kill his brother right there in the crowded restaurant in front of him. She'd enjoy it. Her fingers danced lightly on his brother's arm. "It smells so sweet," she said.

His heart hammering, Costas nodded at her. "I'll pay," he said. "I'll pay."

Dislodging his arm from Rusalka's light grip, giving her a genuine smile as he set a plate of baklava in front of her, Pericles looked quizzically at his brother. "I'll bring you the bill, Costas," he said. "Would you like me to pack some up for Agatha?" Agatha was Costas's wife.

Costas almost laughed in relief when Zhdanov moved her hand away from his brother and reached for the baklava. Here a monstrous creature had nearly drained the life from his body, and the oblivious, good-hearted Pericles was worried that Costas might be cheating on his wife. "Yes," he said, "thank you."

Three million euros would be hard to pay, but he

would manage it. His eyes returning to Zhdanov, Costas thought that he could almost imagine a future without the Robber Baron.

Eleven years ago, a superhero calling himself the Gray Fog began to fight crime in the streets of Devil's Cape. For several months, he brought hope to Pirate Town. The Gray Fog publicly exposed corruption in an elite police unit, captured a superhuman criminal called Eightball, and brought dozens of thieves, rapists, and murderers to justice.

But about six months after he first appeared, his real name was leaked to the media and the front page of the *Devil's Cape Daily Courier* ran the headline "Gray Fog unmasked!" in 130-point type. Before breakfast, almost everyone in the city knew that the Gray Fog was actually a Devil's Cape patrol officer named Malcolm Toussaint.

This wasn't the first time that a hero was unmasked. Certainly, "secret identities" had been revealed to reporters before. They often kept that information private, just as undercover police officers or active intelligence agents are protected. But except in the case of masked heroes who actually work for the government, there's no privacy law in place. Journalists who keep these secrets do so out of courtesy or in exchange for information or favors.

Such courtesy obviously wasn't extended to Toussaint. In addition to the Daily Courier, three local news stations, including this one, broadcast his name during their morning reports.

Toussaint went into hiding immediately after the revelation. Within thirty-six hours, a Devil's Cape police officer named Jean Blount, who was Toussaint's roommate and lover, was killed during what Captain Harold Accomando of the DCPD called "a routine raid gone bad." One police source, who wishes to remain anonymous, says that Blount was ordered into a dangerous situation and that when he called for backup, officers nearby were ordered not to respond.

Toussaint fractured under the strain. He never returned to his home or to the police force and began to patrol as the Gray Fog nearly nonstop, becoming increasingly violent. Those who encountered him said that he seemed manic and agitated. They said that his eyes were bloodshot, his face was covered with stubble, and he smelled unwashed.

Within three weeks after his identity was exposed, Toussaint was found hanging from a bald cypress tree in the middle of Bullocq Park.

Police ruled his death a suicide, but some people contend that he was captured and murdered instead . . .

— Excerpted from *The Masks of Devil's Cape*, special documentary airing on WTDC News, Jason Kale reporting

FORTY-THREE

Devil's Cape, Louisiana
Nine days after the deaths
of the Storm Raiders
9 p.m.

*T*here weren't many hills in Devil's Cape. The city's average elevation was only nine feet above sea level. But there were a few gentle slopes here and there, and in the 1850s, an entrepreneur named John Bullocq had made a fortune selling landfill to Devil's Cape's wealthiest citizens, transporting dirt into the city by the shipload so that they could have hills to build their mansions upon, from which they could look down upon the world. When the Civil War began, Bullocq's fortunes fell, and he was left with a tremendous amount of extra landfill with no good place to put it. He dumped it in one general area, creating a half-moon of soft, rolling hills that comprised what eventually became known as Bullocq Park.

His wings spread wide, his tail flickering behind him, Cain glided the last mile into Bullocq Park, searching the low hills for signs that someone else might be in position to overhear. But he saw no one he didn't expect to be there.

Nine o'clock, at the Gray Fog statue, Argonaut had said. Though he'd been hounded and vilified in his last few weeks of life, the Gray Fog had been mourned by many of the city's residents, Cain included. On the fifth anniversary of his death, a statue of him had been placed in Bullocq Park as a memorial. Cain remembered donating ten dollars to the organization responsible for putting it up.

He was the last to arrive. Argonaut was standing not far from the bronze statue, in the middle of telling a story about one of the fallen hero's successes, a battle with Eightball.

Argonaut had a strong, handsome jaw and was flashing Doctor Camelot a charming smile filled with white teeth. She, in turn was nodding, standing close. At one point, she rested a metal-encased hand on Argonaut's shoulder. Cain wasn't certain why the contact and Argonaut's easy smile bothered him, but it did.

"Good evening," Cain called out to them, his voice a carrying whisper in the night. They turned to watch his approach, and he saw Doctor Camelot take a half-step backward, either startled at being spotted so close to Argonaut, or dismayed at the sight of Cain. He was, he knew, a monstrous sight. Sighing, he landed beside them, his clawed feet digging into the grass under his weight.

"We were waiting for you," Argonaut said, "before really getting into the point of why we're here."

Cain nodded. He looked at the statue. As omens went, he wasn't sure that gathering at the memorial to a ruined, dead hero was a good one. He felt on edge. His demonic body made him feel uncomfortable, scrutinized, mocked, counterfeit, as though he had walked into a crowded room dressed in a garish costume or not dressed at all. As it was, he hadn't been able to think of any kind of shirt that might accommodate his wings, but he purchased a large pair of black pants that fit him in his "Bedlam" form, and had cut a hole for his tail. He felt ridiculous, but not as ridiculous as he had with his suit pants splitting from his transformation. He'd slung a satchel over his shoulder. It held the security guard Cletus's shotgun and baseball bat.

Cain felt anxious to start this conversation, anxious to finish it. He felt the weight of Zhdanov's freedom, the danger that hung over Jazz like a cloud. He wanted to take action, not strike up a conversation, even with potential allies. He decided to jump right into things.

"I haven't always been like this," he said, spreading his clawed fingers. "This is new to me and, I hope, temporary." He looked from Argonaut to Doctor Camelot. They were watching him patiently, respectfully. Their demeanor showed curiosity, but any hint of discomfort at his form was gone or hidden. He wondered if, beneath their apparent calm, they were as uncomfortable as he was. "I gather from your uniforms," he said, "that you both intend to become superheroes." The word felt odd in his mouth. "I don't," he said. "I have just two goals. One is to capture Olena Zhdanov, also known as Rusalka." His eyes flicked to Argonaut. Argonaut knew Cain's reasons for wanting to capture Zhdanov, but he was keeping his mouth shut. "The second," he said, "is somewhat more complicated." He swallowed. His tongue felt odd in his transformed mouth. "Basically, I need to secure someone's safety. And doing that is going to mean taking down the *Cirque d'Obscurité,* the Robber Baron, or both." He might as well vow to catch the moon, he thought.

Argonaut smiled ironically. "As long as you're starting small."

Cain could see that he'd repaired or replaced his damaged uniform. His wound was healing, but it hadn't set yet. Cain could still smell a hint of blood. And, Cain noted with grim amusement, he'd changed his aftershave.

Doctor Camelot's armor was bright even in the thick, dark evening air. "I'm sure it won't surprise you to learn that I also intend to stop the *Cirque d'Obscurité,*" she said. Her voice held a touch of a British accent, but there was something slightly off about it, the cadences not quite right. Had his hearing not been so sharp, he probably wouldn't have been able to detect the distortion. She was using some mechanical means to alter her voice, he realized. "They murdered my predecessor," she said. "And they murdered the Storm Raiders. They're the reason I'm here in this city." She nodded at Cain. "I've read a number of reports about Rusalka and her abilities.

I'll be happy to help you capture her, as well."

Argonaut nodded. "And on that note," he said, "I think I might have an idea who can tell us where to find her."

"You won't have to look far for him," said a voice behind Cain.

All three of them turned suddenly. It was Scion. He stood, arms crossed, leaning against the bald cypress from which the Gray Fog had hung himself. Or been lynched. Scion was smiling smugly, pleased with himself.

Beside him, Doctor Camelot raised one of her arms. A soft electric whir came from inside her armor—she was preparing one of her weapons. "This is Scion," she said. "I have visual ID on him. He's wanted for aggravated assault, homicide . . . a string of others."

"You weren't there a moment ago," Cain said to Scion, spreading his arms again, preparing to tackle him.

Scion shook his head. "Nope," he said, still leaning against the tree, unconcerned. "The speed of Aethalides, the stealth of Autolycus."

Cain didn't recognize the names.

After a pause, Doctor Camelot said, "Argonauts. They were Argonauts."

Even through the distortion of her voice alteration, her words crackled with tension and doubt. Her arm still pointing at Scion, she turned her head to look at Argonaut. Behind her faceplate, her eyes were wide and agitated.

Argonaut held up a hand. "Let's just hold it for a second," he said. "We don't want to escalate this. Scion can provide us with the information we need."

Scion raised an eyebrow, his grin mischievous. "Ah, the tactics of Theseus," he said.

"Stop it," said Argonaut.

Cain looked from Scion to Argonaut and back. No wonder he'd mistaken one for the other, he thought. They were brothers. They were twins. "Castor and Pollux," he said.

"Aha!" said Scion. "A classicist! Though I think 'Polydeuces' is in favor more than 'Pollux' these days."

"I said stop!" Argonaut shouted. He stepped toward Scion, fist raised.

"Oh, like that's going to do a lot of good," Scion said. "You might as well punch yourself."

Argonaut lowered his arm slowly, though his gloved fingers were still clenched. "Tell me what you're doing here," he said. "And what you want. It's not like you to volunteer information."

Scion stood straight, pulling away from the tree and uncrossing his arms.

Cain stepped slowly to one side. He wasn't prepared to rush Scion yet. The man apparently had information to share and Cain was willing to let him say his piece. But he wasn't going to give him an opening to get away, either. Off to the side, he could feel Doctor Camelot circling in the other direction, the same thought on her mind, though she kept looking back at Argonaut, her distrust obvious. Cain could hear her rapid heartbeat through her armor.

Scion had to notice them circling around him, but he didn't react. "My, um, avuncular employer," he said, the words drawing some further reaction from Argonaut, "has managed to hack me off. He and I have a few rules in place, and he's broken one of them."

"What do you mean?" Argonaut asked. He was growing tenser.

Scion hesitated. Despite his nonchalance, he was tense, too, reluctant to reveal whatever he was about to reveal. When he got to it, the words flowed out of him quickly, in a rush. "I put him in a position where he could contact Rusalka and make a proposition to her. I have no problem with the proposition itself. I encourage it. I think it's a grand idea." He was being flippant, working himself up to the gist. "But he decided to meet her someplace that displeases me. I can't really do anything about it directly. It would be far too complicated. But you fine fellows—you could intervene. You could do something about it. And I could wash my hands of the damn thing." He shook his head. "It's where he's meeting her, you see, that bothers me."

Argonaut's voice was ice-cold. "Where is he meeting her?"

Scion wetted his lips with his tongue. "A restaurant called Zorba's," he said. "Maybe you've heard of it."

Cain knew that Argonaut was fast. He'd seen him move quickly over the building that had collapsed. But he had no real concept of the scale of the man's speed. Argonaut simply erupted into the air. He flew unseeing through the branches of the cypress tree, shattering one of its limbs, which fell heavily to the ground. Before it landed, Argonaut was out of sight.

"Yep," said Scion. "I thought that that might do it." He looked at Cain and Doctor Camelot. "Well, come on, heroes," he said. "What are you waiting for? You want directions?"

"No," Doctor Camelot said. "I can find the way." Her arm was still pointed at Scion's chest. She looked at Cain. "I clocked at him more than three hundred miles per hour," she said. "He's in a big hurry to get to her."

Cain nodded at the spot where Argonaut had been standing. "I trust him," he said. He gestured at Scion. "We could try to capture this one," he said. "But it would take us a while."

Scion smiled. "Cocky," he said.

Cain looked after Argonaut again. "No matter how powerful he is," he said, "if she touches him, he could die." He thought of Thomas Dickerson's withered corpse.

Doctor Camelot nodded. "So we go."

And they flew into the air after Argonaut, the flap of his wings and the jets from her armor faint whispers in the air.

Little progress again today. Even when she's at her most engaged, it's clear to me that the bulk of her attention is elsewhere. Her fantasy worlds hold more substance for her than reality does.

— From Dr. Cain Ducett's session notes on Olena Zhdanov, six months earlier

FORTY-FOUR

Devil's Cape, Louisiana
Nine days after the deaths
of the Storm Raiders
9:02 p.m.

Olena Zhdanov's mind was not like other minds. She could effortlessly juxtapose numerous conflicting impulses and plans, switching without hesitation or even awareness from one absolute resolve to another. Stepping past the late dinner crowd on her way out of the restaurant, Olena was exultant. Her mind cascaded with images of the things that three million euros might bring to her. She saw fur coats, diamonds, a lushly decorated condominium overlooking the Black Sea.

At the same time, she was drawn to the people she was walking by, their hunger and anticipation for their meal, their vibrant chatter, the sweat of their bodies, their smiles. Just one, she wondered. Couldn't she take just one of them without someone noticing, without bringing about her own capture or death and any hopes of experiencing the three million euros that Costas Kalodimos had promised her? Without thinking about it, she scanned the line of people waiting, selecting as though from a smorgasbord. What about that fat one, she thought, with the panama shorts and the green T-shirt and the patch of sunburn on his balding head? Or the black child with the videogame clutched in his hands, thumbs working the buttons in a flurry, eyes intent? Or the athletic blonde woman in the short black dress, her tanned thighs flashed to all around her every

345

time a gust of air blew down the street?

And even while deciding on floor plans for her Black Sea condo, even while picking out a potential victim from the line, she was playing through an imaginary conversation with her father in her mind. *Oh, Papa,* she would say, *I have missed you. You look tired from your days on Lake Baikal, Papa. Let me rub your feet.*

She was wondering, too, about Costas Kalodimos and his brother, the one with the tray of sweet baklava. Wouldn't it be fun, she thought, to kill two brothers at once? She began to turn back into the restaurant.

And then she saw the rush of dark blue and gold in the air.

———

Flying as fast as he could to his father's restaurant, Jason was furious. Furious with Uncle Costas for endangering his father. Furious with the murderous Rusalka for daring to intrude in his life this way. Furious with his brother for lots of things—for becoming involved with Uncle Costas's criminal organization, for freeing Rusalka, for being so damned coy about revealing the information that their father was in danger. And lying under that, Jason was furious with himself. If he had never fallen in with Uncle Costas himself years ago, if he had never allowed himself to be blackmailed by Detective David Dees, if he had never gone to his brother for help, then perhaps Julian wouldn't be where he was today and their father wouldn't be in the danger he was in now.

The city rushed past him below. He flew over taxicabs and buses, streets and canals, pedestrians and vagrants, homes and offices, all in a blur. He didn't slow or reduce his altitude until he was over Sarandakos Avenue, and then he plummeted to the crowded sidewalk in front of Zorba's, his cape billowing out behind him.

He'd never seen Zhdanov in person, only seen photos of her in the news room. But he spotted her right away turning into the doorway, the scarf around her head and the sunglasses at this time of night both conspicuous. The

people near her probably thought she was a celebrity trying to avoid the limelight, or one of Devil's Cape's many eccentrics. It didn't occur to them that she was an escaped homicidal maniac on the run.

She saw him coming. She turned toward him, a deer in the headlights look registering on her face for a second, then, strangely, a sort of delight.

With her in the doorway, his options were limited. He couldn't tackle her—that would pull both of them into the restaurant and endanger any number of other people, including Pop. And she was close to the line of people waiting to get inside.

He landed right next to her, grabbing her by the shoulder and the waist, ready to pull her someplace more isolated. Despite the heat of it, he was glad of his uniform, the way it covered most of his body. She killed with a touch, and the only really exposed parts of him were his chin and his mouth.

But it wasn't him she reached for.

As soon as he had his hands on her, Zhdanov's arm shot out, grabbing another woman by the wrist.

The woman, her blonde, short hair carefully coiffed, her tailored black dress glistening with a row of sequins near the neckline, turned and began to protest. But then her mouth opened wide. She gasped, her eyes rolling back in her head, her tan skin growing pale and wrinkling, shriveling in front of Jason's eyes.

Horrified, Jason reacted quickly, pulling Zhdanov toward him, breaking her grip on the other woman's arm.

The blonde woman collapsed on her back on the sidewalk, muscles convulsing, her skin hanging loose on her bones, eyes sunken into their sockets, mouth opening and closing silently.

Zhdanov sighed in a kind of ecstasy, steam snaking out of her lips. And then she punched Jason in the chest.

The blow felt harder than the gunshots, harder than any of the hits he'd received in the fight with Ducett. It was like a wrecking ball smashing into his sternum. He flew backward across the street, smashing into a flower cart. It collapsed under his weight, roses and carnations scattering in the air.

By the time he'd righted himself, she'd gone back into the restaurant.

———————

Kate could have flown faster, but she held back a little to allow Bedlam to keep up with her. Argonaut had flown off alone, but they'd be more effective working in concert. Besides, the extra seconds gave her time to prepare.

Accessing her databases, she determined that while a blueprint of the restaurant, Zorba's on Sarandakos Avenue, was on file with the parish, it had never been rendered electronically. She was able, though, to pull up a satellite photo of the block it was on, part of the area called Little Athens, zooming in to get an idea of where she was going.

"Things are accelerating kind of fast here, Katie," Samuel said over her communicator. He was again sitting in her lab, talking her through what she was doing. She didn't really need his assistance in pulling up information from databases—that she could do herself. But she'd wanted his advice.

"I know," she said tightly. "Argonaut seemed trustworthy at first blush, but I don't understand his connection to Scion. And I wasn't expecting to be flying into combat tonight."

She and Bedlam flew over Ayers Boulevard, then zipped under the Vollenweider River Bridge, sending hundreds of sleeping pigeons flying.

"You could bail," Samuel said. "Head back here, let things sort themselves out."

He didn't sound like he thought that likely, so she didn't bother to reply to it. "What's your read on Bedlam?" she asked. She looked over at the man. He was cutting tirelessly through the air with broad strokes of his winged arms like an Olympic-class swimmer doing laps. A satchel was strapped to his back. She briefly flipped on the X-rays, identifying a shotgun and an aluminum baseball bat. She hoped he knew what he was doing with the gun. Her eyes flickered over his skeleton on her display, the goatlike horned skull, the elongated bones of his hands and feet, the tail extending from his spine. And then she turned off the display, embarrassed at the intimacy of it.

"It's a shock," Samuel said, "getting any kind of super-human abilities. And his?" She could feel the shrug. "It's got to be blowing his mind. The fact that he says this is something temporary tells me he's either got a way of switching back or expects to, but even so, it's weighing on him. Velociraptor—Jose—went through all sorts of discomfort about his powers, and he could go back and forth from dinosaur to normal guy."

"Bottom-line me here, Uncle Samuel," she said. "We're almost there."

He chuckled. "What do you think? Trust him for now—trust both of them for now—but not too much. Leave yourself an exit."

"Hell," she said.

"What?"

"Argonaut's down." She saw him pulling himself out of the flower cart, preparing to head back inside. She took in the sight of the mummified woman moaning softly on the sidewalk outside the restaurant, a crowd of people milling around, some trying to assist her, others recoiling. She'd read that Rusalka was rumored to have increased strength after draining one of her victims. Judging by Argonaut's position, that was true. She pointed at Bedlam. "Take the back," she said. "There's an alley half a block around, but you're better off flying over the roof."

He gave her a startled nod, quickly gaining altitude and arcing over the building.

"You seeing this?" she asked Samuel.

"Yeah," he said. "I'm calling 911. Corrupt or not, the cops are going to have to show up and help. Ambulance, too, of course. That woman—she looks bad."

Argonaut rushed over to the woman's body, torn between it and the interior of the restaurant.

"BP's down," Kate said, "breathing shallow." She landed between Argonaut and the crowd. She held up a finger to Argonaut. "One second," she said. "We go in together." Then she turned to the crowd. "You and you"—she pointed to two men—"carry her away from the scene. An ambulance is coming. Find a blanket or something to wrap her in to keep her warm. Get her some water." She gestured at the rest of the crowd, letting her armor amplify her voice like a megaphone. "Everyone else, move away from the area immediately. There is a dangerous felon inside this building. Move-move-move!"

The crowd scattered, the men she'd selected carefully carrying the woman down the street.

"That was nice," Samuel said over the communicator as Kate and Argonaut walked toward the door to the restaurant. "And by the way, she's probably not the only dangerous felon in that restaurant."

"What?" she asked.

"I was pulling up information on Zorba's from one of these computers of yours, and it tells me that the restaurant is owned by a Pericles Kalodimos. His brother, Costas Kalodimos, is head of the Greek mafia here in Devil's Cape—although he's never been convicted of anything, of course."

"Great," she said. She turned toward Argonaut. "Let's go."

———

In the midst of pouring a cup of coffee for a customer, Pericles Kalodimos heard the yelling and screaming coming from outside. Setting the thermos down next to the half-filled cup, he hobbled toward the door to see what was happening.

The woman in the scarf, the one who'd been eating with Costas, was walking back inside, her sunglasses slipping off her face. People on either side of her were recoiling.

He turned around, looking for his brother. Costas, leaning over a plate of galaktobouriko—an egg custard baked in filo—fork halfway toward his mouth, swore at the sight of her, hopping up from the table and moving for the back door.

Pericles heard a megaphone outside, the words muffled except for the last ones, "Move-move-move!" The police, he thought. The police were finally here to arrest Costas. Though he wondered what the woman in the scarf had to do with all this. She brushed past Pericles' waitress Charmaine, who seemed startled, swaying in place at the woman's touch. And then she was making a beeline for Costas, tossing her sunglasses on the ground, her eyes alight, a wide, frightening smile on her face.

Pericles knew, then, that there was something seriously wrong about this woman, and that she meant Costas harm. Whatever his faults, whatever his crimes, Costas was Pericles' brother. He stepped in front of the woman. "Miss," he said, "I'm going to have to ask you to leave my restaurant."

The wild, wide smile never left her face as she reached for him, fingers on both hands spread wide.

And then suddenly, in a rush of air, a man stood between them. He wore a dark blue and gold uniform, and a cape that hung almost to the floor. "No," the man said, reaching out and pushing the woman back. "No."

Pericles stared at the man. He'd seen him in the news. Argonaut. He'd wondered, when he'd heard the name, but now, standing next to him, he knew. "Jason?" he whispered.

Jason turned toward him, exasperated but smiling, "Hush, Pop," he whispered back. "Run. You've heard about Rusalka on TV? This is her. *Run.*"

Pericles stared at the woman. She'd staggered back a few feet when Jason had pushed her, but now she was pressing in again. "But she had dinner with Costas," he said, not quite understanding what was going on. Jason looked very impressive in the uniform.

"Go!" Jason shouted.

The woman stepped forward, and behind her, Pericles saw another woman entering his restaurant. She was wearing some kind of polished armor. Seeing Jason glance back at him again, Costas nodded. "All right, all right."

And then the woman—Rusalka—reached out to Jason. Distracted by Pericles, his son didn't avoid her hand in time. She reached up and caressed his cheek.

Jason screamed. His skin seemed to wrinkle and bulge under her touch. He gripped her hand in his, trying to pull it away, but he seemed unable to do it. Pericles thought he could see his son's bones under the woman's fingers.

And Rusalka seemed entranced. Her eyes quivered in their sockets. Her tongue ran along her upper lip. There was something frank and sexual about the expression on her face. Her scarf fluttered to the ground. Smoke curled around her and Jason. "There's so much," she said softly, her voice a moan. "Oh, God," she said. "Oh, Papa."

Pericles cast his eyes around the restaurant, looking for something to get this woman away from his son.

And his eyes lit on the thermos of hot coffee he'd been holding, now twenty feet away.

———

Cain had flown to the back alley as Doctor Camelot suggested, lifting his body over the rooftop and landing lightly on the cobblestone "old city" pavement of the alley. A dumpster nearby smelled of spoiled food. The neatly tied garbage bags that had been tossed inside had been ripped open by a homeless man searching for scraps or recyclables. The man stood there still, hunched over the bags, muttering to himself, barely registering the fact that a winged demon had landed less than fifteen feet from him. Cain saw with grim amusement that a CEs tag—graffiti from one of the Concrete Executioners—dominated one brick wall, an elaborate kaleidoscope of spray-painted color.

It had made sense to cover the back door in case Zhdanov attempted to escape that way. What they hadn't counted on, though, was that she wasn't the only one looking to escape. Just as he landed, people began running out of the crowded restaurant into the alley, making their way to the street beyond. A woman screamed at the sight of Cain. He pointed her toward the street. She blinked and ran, high heels clicking on the cobblestones.

A heavyset, gray-haired man glittering with gold— rings, a bracelet, a watch, a necklace—seemed stuck in the crowd. Pushed out the door, he turned to go back inside, ready to fight his way back in. He reached inside his jacket, where Cain saw the bulge of a gun.

Cain grabbed the man's heavy wrist just above his sparkling bracelet, pulling him away from the crowd, back into the alley. Snarling, Cain leaned forward, putting his own face mere inches from the man's. "No guns," he said.

The man was obviously shocked at the sight of him, but he stood his ground. "I am going back through that door," he said.

"No," Cain said, his voice crackling like fire. "You're not."

Cain shoved the man toward the street. The man took a few unbalanced steps, turned and looked at Cain again, and then quickly headed out of the alley and into the crowds.

Once he was gone, Cain stepped back away from the door again, away from the exiting crowd into the scant shadow of the dumpster, trying his best to become inconspicuous, afraid of sending panicked people back into the restaurant.

Careful to watch the crowd, careful to make sure that Zhdanov wasn't attempting to slip out with the others, Cain stood in the alley, heart hammering, wanting nothing more than to push his way through the shoving crowds and make his way to Zhdanov inside. But there were too many people, too much fear and confusion. He had to wait until they cleared out.

And then he heard a woman screaming.

Kate saw Rusalka grab Argonaut's face, saw her ecstatic reaction. "Oh, hell," Kate said.

Argonaut had grabbed at Rusalka's hand, but he seemed unable to pull away.

Kate stepped closer, pointed at the Russian woman, and blasted her with her air cannon—releasing air compressed to three hundred and fifty pounds per square inch in a small burst.

Rusalka was thrown away from Argonaut and across the restaurant, smashing into a table. She lay there for a moment, and Kate wondered if she'd badly injured the woman, but then she saw the Russian quickly pulling herself to her feet.

"You okay?" Kate asked Argonaut.

He had fallen to his knees when Rusalka had been knocked away from him, but was rallying. "I feel weak," he said, "but I'll be okay." He started to pull himself to his feet, but collapsed backward again. He was going to be out of it for a few seconds. It was up to her.

"That was not very nice," Rusalka said. She grabbed a metal chair and hurled it at Kate. It slammed into her with incredible force, staggering Kate backward. She had Argonaut's strength, Kate realized.

And then Rusalka leaped across the room like a pouncing cougar, grabbing Kate, rending at her armor with her hands.

"What the hell?" Samuel shouted over her communicator. "I'm getting all sorts of warning lights."

Kate struggled to push the woman away. "She's incredibly strong," she said. "And she's twisting at the armor's joints. She's trying to break me open." She tried to get in position to shoot the air cannon again, but the Russian was ready for it, holding her arms, preventing her from getting in position to shoot.

"Don't you have some kind of electric current in that thing you can shock her with? Your dad once—"

"No," she interrupted him, not ready to listen to

another story of battles past at this moment. "My armor's less conductive than his. I've been developing something, but it's not ready yet."

She butted Rusalka with her head. Blood flowed into the Russian woman's eyes, but she kept smiling maniacally. Kate looked over at Argonaut. He was still shaken, still trying to pull himself to his feet. Zhdanov began to concentrate on Kate's left arm, twisting at the elbow, and Kate realized that it was only a matter of time before the joints there broke under the pressure. Given the insane woman's strength, Kate's arm would probably be ripped off. She amped up her speakers to maximum yield. "Get the hell off me!" she shouted. The words echoed through the restaurant, and Zhdanov winced in pain as the sound blasted her eardrums. But she didn't let go.

Where the hell was Bedlam?

The reinforced carbon and plastic polymers at the left elbow joint reached their critical stress tolerance and cracked.

And then an elderly man with tanned, wiry arms and a shock of white hair stepped forward and threw a pot of steaming coffee into Rusalka's face.

———

Rusalka was screaming, clutching at her burned face, but Jason saw that she was far too close to Pop. One grab and Pericles Kalodimos would be joining Desma at the cemetery at Devil's Cape's Greek Orthodox Cathedral of the Ascension. Jason was nauseated, dizzy, weak. His face felt shriveled where she'd touched him. But that didn't matter. He rushed forward, unceremoniously punched Zhdanov in the jaw with all of his waning strength, and then grabbed his father and flew him out the front door to the safety of the street beyond.

"You're a feisty one, Pop," he said.

The old man blinked at finding himself in the street, then placed a tanned, scarred hand on his son's shoulder. "And you are a hero, my Argonaut," he said.

Jason leaned forward, kissed his father on the forehead, and rushed back into Zorba's.

———————

Cain reacted to the scream, brushing by the last of the escaping patrons, one of whom screamed and bashed him on the head with a cell phone as he burst into the restaurant.

It was Zhdanov, he saw with some relief. Zhdanov had screamed. Coffee dripped from her burned face and she was looking around for a new target. Cain saw Argonaut flying out the front of the restaurant with an elderly man in his arms. It looked like the rest of the bystanders were gone.

Doctor Camelot rose awkwardly from the ground, one arm pointed at Zhdanov. "Be careful," she said. "She touched Argonaut for a few seconds. She has some of his strength."

Hell. Cain nodded. Every instinct was telling him to tear into Zhdanov, to hit her while she was distracted, to pull the shotgun from his back and shoot her. The wild demon was free in him and he was itching to fight. Zhdanov was a remorseless killer, a monster who literally stole the lives of the people she touched.

But she was also his patient.

Doctor Camelot had steadied herself now. "On three," she said.

Cain shook his head. "Give me a minute," he said. He thought of Detective Salazar Lorca, who had kicked down his door and saved his life, in his own unorthodox manner, all those years ago.

"Olena," he said, stepping forward, arms at his sides, "it's time to surrender."

Zhdanov looked at him, eyes wild, taking in his appearance. "What monster are you?" she spat.

He nodded. "They call me Bedlam," he said. "And yes, I look pretty awful. But I'm not looking to hurt you, Olena. I want to help get you to people who can give you the assistance you need."

She looked frantically around the room, eyes cutting back and forth between the front door and the back, considering the plate-glass window.

"You're not going to be able to escape this room, Olena," he said.

She narrowed her eyes at that, pulling a glass of ice water from a table, dipping a napkin into it, and dabbing at her face.

"Doctor Camelot and I don't want to use force against you," he said.

Even through her armor, he could hear Doctor Camelot snorting at that. She was agitated, angry, ready to strike.

He focused his red eyes on Zhdanov. "But we will use force, Olena," he said, "if we need to in order to keep you from leaving here and hurting more people."

"Stop saying my name!" she shouted. "Stop trying to handle me!" But she wasn't moving.

Argonaut stepped into the doorway, but Cain stopped him with another slight shake of his head. Looking from Cain to Zhdanov and back, Argonaut nodded, setting his feet and spreading his shoulders, filling the door. He wouldn't move unless he had to, but he was prepared. Cain saw a web of wrinkles in the shape of a hand on the man's cheek. He'd been too tough for Zhdanov to kill during the time she'd had, but she'd hurt him, nonetheless.

Police sirens were approaching. Ambulances, too.

"Why don't you sit down?" Cain said to Zhdanov, gesturing to a chair with a clawed finger.

She stared at him and suddenly looked tired and sad. Then she sat down, and it was over.

357

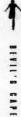

**Incident In The 2900 Block Of Sarandakos Avenue.
Devil's Cape, LA** — This evening, members of the
Devil's Cape Police Department are investigating
a paranormal assault at a local restaurant. The
offense occurred at approximately . . .

— From the DCPD police log

FORTY-FIVE

Devil's Cape, Louisiana
Nine days after the deaths
of the Storm Raiders
9:45 p.m.

*T*he night of the building collapse, they'd avoided the press as much as possible. Before she'd pulled Cain and Argonaut from the wreckage, Doctor Camelot had briefly introduced herself to the authorities on the scene in order to convince them to let her lead the rescue effort, and the news media had recorded her doing that. Other than that, everything had been from a distance.

But tonight, they made brief statements, identifying themselves, explaining about the fight at the restaurant, and then answering "no comment" to anything else, including persistent questions about whether they were going to form a "super team" in Devil's Cape and what they intended to do next.

Argonaut was the most comfortable in front of the camera, Cain the least. He felt the reporters' fear, the discomfort of people looking at him, the fascination with his demonic form. When one reporter asked him if he was a Satanist, he waved a clawed hand, said "That's enough questions," and stomped away in anger.

But then he spotted Detective Cynthia Daigle, directing officers on the scene, making plans to transport Zhdanov away.

He walked over to her, clawed feet scratching at the sidewalk, red-black fur dotted with sweat. "Thought you should know," he said, "we found out that she had help

breaking out of the asylum." He never used the word "asylum" aloud at work, but used it purposely now to distance Bedlam from Cain Ducett.

He'd startled her, and a cigarette dangling from her lips fell to the sidewalk, smoke rising between the two of them. Daigle swallowed, then narrowed her eyes, trying not to look intimidated by the demonic man standing in front of her. "Yeah?" she said.

He nodded, his horns cutting through the smoke of her cigarette. "It was another superhuman," he said. "The one called Scion. They had some kind of falling out." He ground out her cigarette with his bare foot.

"Huh," she said. She seemed disappointed, a little deflated. She'd wanted it to be him, he knew.

"He took her to that building that collapsed," he offered. "Maybe you can find something there."

She shrugged, trying to hide the disappointment, trying to act nonchalant standing in his shadow. "Maybe so," she said.

He walked away then, feeling her eyes on him, but he knew that he had accomplished what he needed. She wouldn't be pursuing Cain Ducett anymore.

———

Jason was helping two SWAT team members and Doctor Camelot secure Zhdanov in a police van when he noticed his father mopping coffee off the restaurant floor, his hands quivering.

Jason turned to Doctor Camelot. "You got this?"

She nodded, holding Zhdanov rigidly in place with an armored hand while the police officers added additional restraints.

He walked into Zorba's, closing the door behind him. He and his father were alone.

"You okay, Pop?"

Pericles leaned on the mop and wiped sweat off his forehead with the back of his hand. He nodded. "And you? How's your cheek?"

"I'll be fine."

Pericles nodded again. "There's ice," he said. "You know where it is."

"Yeah," Jason said. "I'm okay." His father's hands were still shaking. His hands on the mop looked like those of a World War I flier fighting the throttle. "You should maybe sit down, Pop," he said, resting his hand gently on his father's shoulder.

Pericles carefully rested the mop against the edge of a table and lowered himself into one of the booths. "Costas brought her here," he said.

Pushing his cape out of the way, Jason sat across from his father in the booth. A half-eaten gyro and plate of fries sat in front of him and he shoved them over to one side. "I know," he said.

"I was afraid she would kill you," Pericles said.

"I was afraid she would kill *you.*"

His father guffawed, a single eruption of noise. He sat up straighter. "You make me proud," he said.

Jason smiled. "You, too, Pop."

Pericles sat there, the shaking in his hands subsiding. "So," he said. "It's Argonaut, huh?"

"Yeah."

"And Julian? He's the other one I've read about? Scion? Who rescued Mikey Orfanos from the police?"

Jason lowered his eyes. "I'm sorry," he said.

"Me, too." Pericles picked up a napkin and brushed some crumbs off of the tablecloth.

"He's the one who let me know," Jason said. "That Uncle Costas was bringing that woman here."

Pericles shook his head. "He sent you, but he didn't come."

Jason didn't know what to say to that.

"Those golden threads were real," Pericles said softly.

"What?"

His father stared at a sculpture on the wall, a recreation of a piece of one of the friezes on the Parthenon. Two riders on galloping horses, one of the horses actually flying, all four of its feet in the air. "Not too long before you were born," he said, "actually, a little more than nine months before you were born"—he smiled devilishly at Jason—"your mother and I went home on holiday."

Home meant Greece.

"We visited family. We visited beaches. We drank wine and ouzo and danced a lot." His eyes went back to the frieze. "It was good for us," he said. "Time away from Costas and our uncle Ilias."

Jason nodded.

"And one day, a peddler approached me with two small urns. They looked very old. They were painted with Greek warriors." He gestured at a picture hung on the wall. "Like that," he said. "He told me that they were very, very ancient, that they held threads from the Golden Fleece."

Outside the restaurant, the police van holding Zhdanov pulled away.

"He said to me, 'You will think I am trying to trick you, but that's all right.' He smiled at me. 'I will sell you these urns for fifty American dollars each.' "

Pericles shrugged. "It was not a fortune, and they looked very nice—I could hang them in the restaurant. I haggled with him, told him I only wanted one urn. 'You need both,' he says to me. 'You will have twins and then you will believe me. You need both. They will become like the Argonauts.' "

Jason sat up straighter. "This is before we were born."

Pericles nodded. "He was very insistent, a little crazy, maybe. So I bought the urns, thinking I'd hang them in the restaurant."

"But you didn't."

"Oh, I did," Pericles said. "Until you were born. And then, the night before your baptism, I had a dream about those urns and the threads the man said were inside."

A dream.

"And you opened them up?"

Pericles nodded. He told Jason about the peculiar baptism he'd dreamed about, the one he'd performed on Jason and Julian. "There were golden threads inside, one in each urn."

"Not exactly Greek Orthodox, Pop."

Pericles smiled sadly. "It is a lot of responsibility, what I've done to you and your brother."

Jason wondered about the peddler. He wondered where Julian was, what he knew. "It's okay," he said. He reached across the table and rested his hand on his father's shoulder.

Pericles stiffened. Jason pulled back his hand, but then realized that his father wasn't reacting to him. He was reacting to something outside.

Costas Kalodimos was standing at the window, staring at the two of them, glowering.

———

When Jason walked outside, his Uncle Costas was standing across the street by the ruined flower cart, hands in his pockets, staring at him. Never one to waste anything, Costas had pinned a fallen yellow rose to his lapel.

The smart thing to do would be to keep his distance from his uncle, but there was an urgency in the old man's eyes. Taking his time with it, Jason walked across the street to him. "Something you need, sir?" he asked.

Costas glowered. "Cut the crap, Jason," he whispered.

"I don't know what—"

Costas held up a finger. "Don't insult my intelligence," he said. "I don't see you so often anymore, but I see Julian every day. He works for me. You two try so hard to be different, but you can never get away from each other—you're the same underneath. And I saw you with your father."

Jason stared back at him.

Costas shook his head. "I know Julian's secret and now I know yours, but that's not the point here. The point is that you might not have meant to do it, but you screwed me over here. This"—he gestured at air, but it was clear he meant Rusalka—"was my chance at surviving the next few weeks, and you took it away."

"I don't owe you anything," Jason said.

Costas jabbed a thick finger at him. "You tell that to your aunt when you're putting flowers on my grave," he said.

Getting angry now, Jason pushed the pointing hand down. "I don't know what you're talking about," he said. He lowered his voice. "And besides," he said, "who says I would bring flowers?"

Costas's eyes grew flinty. "These freaks," he said, "this *Cirque d'Obscurité*. They're going to kill me."

His uncle's breath smelled of onions. Jason was getting tired of standing there with him. He pulled back. "We'll take care of them, too, in due time," he said.

"Jason!" Costas hissed, moving close. "You want those bastards? You want to take them down? You take them down, and I'll make it worth your while, you understand me?"

"I don't need your bribes," Jason said. "And I intend to take you down, too. We'll track them down, and then we'll turn our attention to you."

Costas ignored the threat. "Track them down?" he said. "Track them down? Is that what you need?" He mopped at his sweating forehead with a handkerchief, then leaned forward. "Jason," he whispered, "I can tell you where they are tonight. I can tell you where they are right now."

The beautiful illuminated clock tower of Lehane University is one of the most popular symbols of Devil's Cape. It also offers ones of the best possible views of the city. Alas, that's a view denied the typical Devil's Cape traveler.

In the late sixties and early seventies, the tower was a notorious gathering place for small groups of college students. They'd go up there to make out, to get high, to plan protests against the war or against police corruption. But in 1975—on Mardi Gras night, of course—a handful of students went a bit overboard in their carousing and pranks. They painted the clock face to resemble the masked skull and crossbones symbol the pirate St. Diable.

They dressed the antique gargoyles that decorate the tower's rooftop in lingerie and painted their horns in nail polish. And they accidentally sent one gargoyle tumbling to the sidewalk far, far below. It took the university thousands of dollars to restore the tower to its usual appearance, and it invested in a sturdy security door that keeps visitors and students out of the upper levels to this day.

— Excerpted from
A Devil's Cape Traveler's Guide

FORTY-SIX

Devil's Cape, Louisiana
Nine days after the deaths
of the Storm Raiders
10 p.m.

As she soared through the Devil's Cape sky between Argonaut and Bedlam, Kate sighed at the anger in Samuel's voice.

"This is nuts!" he shouted at her over the communicator. "You're going to die, Katie! You understand me? The Storm Raiders fought together for years, we were experienced and tough, and they murdered us in the space of a minute."

"They caught you by surprise," she said.

"The hell they did! We expected them. We'd spent the flight down from Vanguard City planning for the fight. And they killed us anyway."

News helicopters were approaching, alerted to their battle with Rusalka, trying to catch aerial footage. When the pilots spotted the three heroes, they began to detour around to follow. Seeing them turn, Argonaut caught the others' attention and pointed. The others nodded and the three of them veered off, flying low through a stand of trees in Lady Danger River Park.

"The three of you couldn't take down Rusalka by yourselves," Samuel said. "She was handing you your asses and you had to be rescued by a seventy-year-old man with a cup of hot coffee."

It would have sounded ridiculous to correct him by saying that it had been a thermos, not a cup, so she let

it go. Turning away from the park at a ninety-degree angle, the three of them headed over a residential neighborhood, buzzing over shingled roofs and satellite dishes, then ducking even lower until they were just a few feet above the gently curving streets of the area, turning this way and that until the helicopters lost sight of them.

"I'm not going to sit here and watch you die on these monitors, Katie," Samuel said. "I'm just not going to do it. Call in the Southern Sentinels or the Guardians. Let an experienced team handle this."

"The mayor has told other teams to stay away," Kate said. "They'll either do what he says or else at least alert the city that they're coming. That's what happened to you. At best, there will be a delay. At worst, they'd wind up with another ambush or time for the *Cirque d'Obscurité* to hide. We could lose them. It has to be tonight."

The roar of the helicopters now far in the distance, Argonaut gave the others the thumbs up, and they regained altitude, pointing themselves once again at the location that Argonaut had learned from Costas Kalodimos, a mansion in Doubloon Ward.

"You could find them again, Kate. You could find them and bring a whole army of superheroes on top of them. I could call some people I know—"

"I am not going to let them get away again!" she shouted. Beside her, Bedlam turned his head, looking at her curiously. The sound dampeners in her armor should have prevented her from being overheard, even at a shout, but Bedlam had heard her anyway. She hadn't realized his senses were so sharp.

There was silence from her communicator.

"Uncle Samuel?"

Silence.

"I shouldn't have yelled like that," she said. "Are you there?"

Silence.

"Damn," she muttered to herself. She had cameras mounted in the Juan Marco Quintana Memorial

Laboratory, of course. Pressure sensors. She pulled them up on one of her screens.

He was gone.

"Damn," she swore again.

⸻

They were all silent at the beginning of the flight, lost in their own thoughts. Jason was relieved at his father's safety, glad they had captured Rusalka. But his face still ached from the woman's touch, and his side still hurt from the injury the night before. He still felt weaker than normal, though most of his strength had returned. And he wondered what they were doing. He'd wanted to help take down the *Cirque d'Obscurité,* but were they ready to do it *tonight?*

Spotting two news helicopters, including one from his own station, he pantomimed some suggestions for them to evade the pursuit, steering them through places where it would be more difficult for the helicopters to keep track of them.

He worried, too, about what Uncle Costas might do with the information he had.

He was still pondering that, and what to do about Julian, when Doctor Camelot spoke.

"Before we get there," she said, "we need to stop someplace for a few minutes so that I can tell you what I know about the *Cirque d'Obscurité* and what we might be able to do to catch them."

"I know a spot," Jason said.

⸻

A locked door on the bottom level of the Lehane University clock tower prevented anyone but authorized personnel—typically, whoever maintained the clock itself—from accessing the stairs to the upper levels. But Jason and Julian had discovered years ago that no one ever bothered to lock the windows on the top floor.

From behind the face of the huge illuminated clock, Jason, Doctor Camelot, and Bedlam could see the wide

panorama of Devil's Cape. The twisted, curving roads. The strange hodgepodge buildings thrown together with whatever building materials the pirates could plunder. The rooftop of the Devil's Cape Public Library, with its mix of angels and gargoyles. The Castelo Branco City Courthouse and its stained glass window of the Great Flood. And, far in the distance, boats passing each other on Lake Pontchartrain.

The tower also gave Jason a good view of his brother's penthouse apartment, where the lights were currently off.

"No one's likely to interrupt us?" Doctor Camelot asked.

Jason shook his head.

Ducett was staring out the window, fingers against the glass. Looking at Holingbroke? Jason wondered. Looking for something else?

Doctor Camelot more or less ignored the view of the city. Instead, she was focused on a blank wall. Then a bright light came out of her right shoulder and a life-sized image of Hector Hell appeared on the wall. He was standing on a mound of sand, the ocean behind him. Short and pudgy, with thinning ginger hair and a beard, he wore yellow spandex decorated in orange and red flames, accented by a red cape and boots. His hands were shrouded in flames.

"That's an attention-getter," Jason said, leaving it up to the others to decide if he was talking about the costume or Doctor Camelot's projector. He wasn't sure himself.

Ducett came and stood beside him, staring with curiosity at the figure on the wall, his arms crossed, the wing flaps dangling down. Jason wondered how much personality he could read from a photo, how much of a profile he could build based on what the man wore and how he held himself.

"Hector Hell," Doctor Camelot said, "is the leader of the team and probably the most dangerous of them. His real name's Hector Nelson Poteete. Like most of the team, he was a sideshow attraction before they got their powers, but he was a fire-eater, not a freak. Now he's a pyrokinetic, which means that he can create and manipulate fire. He can yield incredibly high temperatures and can take the heat, too; he is extremely resistant to it."

"He's got a lot invested in the *Cirque d'Obscurité* succeeding," Jason said. "The Robber Baron has given him and the team control over most of the operations of the Ferazzoli crime family. He's looking to grow roots here."

Doctor Camelot looked at him sideways, obviously wondering what his sources of information were.

He looked back at her the same way.

After a minute, she switched images. They saw a tall, twisted figure standing on the sides of his feet in front of a brick wall sprayed with graffiti, most of the words in Spanish. His greenish skin was hairless and scaly. He was barefoot, wearing nothing but a pair of red shorts. His legs and left arm looked awkwardly long, but his right arm was longer, extending far beyond the edge of the projection. "Kraken's real name is Clayton Xavier Stecker," she said. "He was the Indian rubber man in the sideshow, billed as the Karnivorous Kraken of Kiribati. Back then he was double-jointed and could dislocate his limbs without flinching. Now he takes that natural elasticity to the next level. He can now stretch his entire body to something approaching fifty feet, has above-average strength and body control, and can squash himself flat enough to slip under a door with a two-inch gap. Because of his elasticity, he's likely very resistant to blunt trauma." She looked at them. "He's a suspected rapist, too."

"I think he's the one who strangled Swashbuckler," Jason said, remembering the sight of the young man's broken body. "I saw the crime scene."

Doctor Camelot stared at him and he wished that he could see more of her face behind her mask.

The image of Kraken disappeared, followed quickly by the furry, feral body of the Werewolf. He sat hunched on all fours on the stump of a cypress tree, his elongated snout lifted upward. Foam flecked the edges of his mouth, and his long teeth were coated with blood. "This was the photographer's last picture," Doctor Camelot said. "The Werewolf is an Austrian named Errando Geringer. At a young age, he suffered from hypertrichosis, or abnormal hair growth, with long hair all over his face. He was billed as Errando the Wolf-Boy then, but whatever event gave the *Cirque d'Obscurité* team members their powers gave him the ability to change his shape. He can be a normal man, a wolf, or anywhere in between, although this hybrid stage"—she gestured at the image—"seems to be his preferred form for combat. Watch out for his claws and fangs. He's also got superhuman strength, speed, and resilience." She turned to Ducett. "Probably on a par with yours, judging by the size of the concrete blocks I saw you lifting at the warehouse."

Ducett's smile showed those needle-sharp teeth, like a bat's. "Maybe I should get a silver bullet," he said.

If she smiled back behind her mask, they couldn't see it. "He's not especially vulnerable to silver," she said. "Nor are his changes tied to lunar cycles. He is just a very powerful, animalistic man prone to homicidal rages."

No-nonsense, Jason thought. Abrupt and to the point. She was scared, he realized. They all were. The steamroller briefing was just her way of dealing with it.

Out the window, he saw the lights in Julian's apartment flick on. Was he there alone, Jason wondered? With Uncle Costas?

The quality of the next picture was poorer, the edges pixilated, the color faded. But they could make out the hauntingly damaged features regardless. Gork was turning away from the camera, some type of rifle in his hands, jogging toward a grove of bamboo. He wore a black T-shirt over jeans. Every inch of exposed skin was puckered with scars.

"Gork takes his name from a medical slang term," Doctor Camelot said. "It means—"

"Brain dead," Bedlam said. "Or so far gone it's hopeless. Stands for 'God only really knows.' It's the kind of word residents use when they're trying to act like they've seen it all."

Doctor Camelot tilted her head. "That's right," she said. "His identity's never been confirmed, but the general assumption is that he's Frank Horodenski, the carnival electrician. He's like a walking wound, his entire body covered with burns. He can't feel pain anymore, and he's very strong. You hear those reports of mothers lifting cars off of their children with a burst of hysterical strength? Well, he's got the equivalent twenty-four/seven."

"He's good with the rifle," Jason said. He remembered Miss Chance's body, the red hole in the center of her forehead. "A sniper." He looked at Julian's apartment again. He recognized his uncle's silhouette.

"He's been seen wearing a belt with a large belt buckle engraved with a skull," Ducett said. "The description I heard made me think the buckle might be a hidden knife."

Doctor Camelot nodded. "He's not really as powerful as the rest of them, but he's one of the most ruthless. We shouldn't underestimate him."

Gork's picture was replaced by Osprey's. She was flying, of course, arms at her sides, diving forward, a cruel, joyous smile on her face, a knife clutched in each hand. "Osprey," Doctor Camelot said, "is from here in Louisiana, a Creole named Sasha Crozier. She was part of a family of aerialists, but abandoned them when the *Cirque* group split off from the carnival. She was about twelve."

She shook her head. "She's got something of a knife fetish. She's got bladed claws on her gloves and boots, and it's been documented that she carries a brace of throwing knives, too." She pointed at the knives in Osprey's hands. "Those blades are called katars or Bundi daggers. You don't thrust or slash with them. You punch. It's an extension of your fist." She nodded at Osprey's image. "She was trained to be a trapeze artist from age three. She can spin and corner with those wings like you wouldn't believe. You know, the fastest animal in the world isn't the cheetah. It's the peregrine falcon. Osprey's been

clocked at over two hundred miles an hour in a dive. You don't want her diving into you with those knives."

Ducett shook his head. "You're right about that," he said.

Doctor Camelot looked at him. "She hates other people with wings," she said.

Jason remembered the crushed form of the Winged Tornado, his wings carved right off his body.

"She'll target you first," Doctor Camelot said to Ducett.

He nodded. "And that leaves the Behemoth," he said. "He killed the last Doctor Camelot." He looked at her. "He'll target *you*. And you'll target him."

She was quiet for a moment, then silently switched the image. She probably could have chosen from any of a dozen images of the Behemoth, but the one she selected was Vanguard City, taken a few seconds before the previous Doctor Camelot's death. The hero stood in his shining armor in a damaged section of the Roscoe Clay Bridge, the Behemoth's hands grasping his head. The Behemoth towered over him—he was about ten feet tall, covered with tattoos, huge tusks jutting from his mouth.

"Zechariah Woods, AKA the Behemoth," Doctor Camelot said, her voice shaking. "The Behemoth is perhaps the most powerful of them all. His strength has never been effectively measured. He is incredibly resistant to any kind of damage." She seemed about to say something more, to give more detail, but she stopped, staring at the image for a long while before shutting off the projector. "Don't face him alone," she said, her voice breaking again.

As they flew out of the tower, Jason could see his brother and his uncle, deep in conversation.

"You did what?" Julian said to his Uncle Costas, feeling the anger rise in his voice. He never spoke back to his uncle, but today seemed to be a day filled with exceptions.

"I sent them after the *Cirque d'Obscurité,*" Costas said, ignoring the implied rebuke.

The two men sat in Julian's penthouse apartment, glasses of red wine untouched on the table between them.

"There are only three of them," Julian said. "They'll be slaughtered."

"Jason is very resourceful," Costas said, the hint of a smile on his lips.

So he knew. It wasn't that great of a surprise, actually, but it was another complication.

"Our agreement," Julian said, rubbing at a sore spot on his jaw, "was that you would keep Pop and Jason out of your affairs. You haven't done a very good job of sticking to your agreement today, uncle."

Costas let his eyelids droop. "Odd coincidence, them coming across the Russian and me this evening."

"You should never have been there with her," Julian said, standing up. He sighed. The argument wasn't accomplishing anything. "You were trying to get her to kill the Robber Baron," he said, "not the circus freaks. So why not send Argonaut and the others after him instead?"

Costas shook his head and reached for his wine, taking a sip. It turned his lips red. "For what?" he said. "They're not killers like her. They wouldn't just murder him for me. They are trying to imprison criminals, and the Robber Baron is not wanted for any crimes. The *Cirque d'Obscurité,* at least, can be arrested. The police superintendent has turned a blind eye to them so far, but even he couldn't be so blatant as to let them go if they're brought into custody by a group of new superheroes in the middle of a media circus." He sipped the wine again. "I can live with the Robber Baron, if I can only get his hired goons out of the way. No," he said. "They're a different tool than she is. I needed to use them in a different way."

"They're not much of a tool if they get themselves killed," Julian said quietly.

Costas shrugged. "I didn't have any choice, Julian," he said. "They were all I had."

Julian breathed. He stared at the Kerageorgiu painting that Jason had liked, the trombone player in the middle of Lockheardt Street, putting everything he had into a song that no one was listening to. "They're not all you have," he said softly.

Costas stood up. "No," he said, his face turning pale. "Absolutely not. Anything you do is tied back to me. You cannot get involved in this."

Julian watched his uncle's face for a moment, then sighed. "I guess you're right," he said. Turning his back on his uncle, he walked to his bedroom. "I need some sleep, Uncle Costas," he said. "You can let yourself out. Don't forget to finish your wine before you go."

He closed the door behind him.

Maybe it's the air of menace that draws us to Devil's
Cape. Or maybe it's the idea that in Devil's Cape,
we can be a little wicked, too.

— Excerpted from
A Devil's Cape Traveler's Guide

FORTY-SEVEN

Devil's Cape, Louisiana
Nine days after the deaths
of the Storm Raiders
11 p.m.

*U*ncle Samuel?" Kate asked again. There was still no answer. He hadn't returned to her lab.

The impromptu briefing in the Lehane University clock tower had both encouraged Kate and shaken her. She was impressed with Bedlam and Argonaut, with their intelligence and perception. But running through the names and faces of the *Cirque d'Obscurité* had just served to remind her how outnumbered the three of them were. The *Cirque* members were absolutely ruthless and had been working together for more than twenty years. It was an incredible advantage.

The mansion where they were holed up was a problem, too. State-of-the-art sensors. Machine guns. And neighbors way too close for Kate's liking. Anyone walking a dog or returning home late from a movie became a potential hostage.

Their best hope, the three of them agreed, was to hit as fast as possible. If they could isolate one or more of the *Cirque* team and incapacitate them before they could warn the others, maybe they had a chance.

Clay Stecker—Kraken—had taken an immediate liking to Tony Ferazzoli's spacious home when he and the rest of the *Cirque d'Obscurité* had arrived there to murder

the man. Decorated according to Ferazzoli's expensive tastes, the house had a well-stocked bar, dozens of electronic gizmos, and even a small movie theater in the back. Its landscaped backyard included a huge in-ground swimming pool, a hot tub, and a high-end barbecue grill, all shaded by oak and maple trees and magnolias. The air was filled with the scent of flowers and the soft croaks of frogs. The nearest neighbors were closer than Stecker might have preferred; despite their size, the homes in Doubloon Ward were packed close together. But the neighbors seemed to keep to themselves. No one had come to investigate even when Ferazzoli had screamed his loudest.

It had been Kraken's idea to ask the Robber Baron if they could take the place over. Ferazzoli's Mrs. had left town before the blood had even dried. "Hell," Stecker had said, running an arm across the silk sheets on one of the the Ferazzolis' guest beds, "I could learn to like it here."

He was taking a dip in the pool—it helped keep his scales from drying out if he took a swim now and then, chlorine or not—when he saw three figures streaking through the sky overhead. "Oh, crap," he said.

But Kraken was a wily fighter with years of experience. Half a second after spotting the approaching figures, he stretched one arm up to Ferazzoli's house, punching through a window and setting off the loud whoop of the burglar alarm to let the rest of his team know to expect trouble. "Boys and girls," he muttered to no one in particular as he rose to meet the flying figures headed toward him, "the shit has hit the fan."

Cain spotted Kraken in the pool first and pointed him out to the others.

Hoping to keep him from alerting his teammates, all three heroes flew toward him. Cain pulled himself into a dive, feeling the wind playing against his fur.

But Kraken spotted them and reacted fast. He stretched an arm out of the pool, across the patio, and up to the second floor of the house, unflinchingly driving his fist through an upstairs window. A loud alarm cut through the night air.

Pulling the arm back and stretching his legs so that his torso hovered some twenty feet off the ground, Kraken smiled at them like the Cheshire Cat, beckoning them closer with his arms. "Y'all are in so much trouble," he said. "This won't be pretty, I promise you that."

Cain started to swoop closer, thinking that he might grab one of the man's arms and haul him into the air, when Doctor Camelot said, "Hang on."

She dove low, heading just to one side of Kraken, her armor glistening in the light coming from the water. As Kraken reached toward her, she pointed at him and a small projectile with tiny trailing wires flew out of her arm, lodging in his scaly belly. His entire, elongated body shook and danced as an electrical charge ran through him, exacerbated by the water of the pool. One arm swept spasmodically across the lawn, uprooting a rose bush and sending a chaise lounge careening end over end into the side of the house. Then he collapsed in on himself like a rubber band and fell convulsing into the water.

"Nine hundred kilovolts," Doctor Camelot said, grabbing him and tossing him to the side of the pool, where he splayed out along a series of expensive ceramic tiles. She sprayed him from head to foot in the same kind of gluelike polymer she'd used at the collapsed building to secure the chunks of rubble together. The air smelled like ozone. "That should hold him for a while," she said. "Let's go."

Cain stared at the man propped beside the pool like so much cordwood. The shrieking alarm hurt his ears. He heard a dog—or maybe it was the Werewolf—howling nearby. "One down," he said. "Five to go."

The Behemoth and Errando sat at the kitchen table, a smorgasbord of raw sausages, beef ribs, and a pork shoulder laid out in front of them, a thin trail of blood running toward the corner of the table and slowly dripping on the hardwood floor. The two of them frequently ate alone together, as their taste for raw meat repulsed the others. They'd experimented with fancier stuff from time to time—steak tartare or even sushi—but more often than not, they just got down to essentials.

The Behemoth sat awkwardly on a huge leather recliner he'd dragged into the kitchen, the only chair in the house that could bear his weight. Errando hunched over the table, gnawing at a raw sausage. He was in the form he was born in, human, but with long brown hair growing over most of his body. The sausage casing popped and squished as he chewed.

When they heard breaking glass followed by the shrill house alarm, they stared at each for a few seconds. The Behemoth pulled himself to his feet and Errando dropped the half-eaten sausage to the floor. His body began to shift, the nose elongating into a snout, his fingernails hardening into long, black claws.

"Stay with me," the Behemoth said. "They'll want to split us up. We should find the others."

Errando was in his Werewolf form now, and the loud alarm was causing him obvious pain. He howled in agony. But he stepped to the Behemoth's side as they headed toward the stairs.

___

Jason cast his eyes all around him, wishing that he could find some way to turn off the alarm, if only so that he could concentrate better. The plan, such as it was, had been to attack from the rear of the house quickly, taking as much advantage as possible of the element of surprise. They'd hoped to encounter at least one member of the *Cirque d'Obscurité* outside, but the goal had been to neutralize that person without alerting the others. Kraken was out of the fight, but now everyone knew they were there. It felt like they were already behind the eight ball.

He hovered over the house, waiting for signs that some-one was coming outside or manning one of the machine guns. He heard dogs barking in other houses nearby.

Another one of their advantages was altitude. All three of them could fly, giving them an edge over all of their opponents except Osprey.

On the other hand, flying made them targets. Jason was focusing so much of his attention on the machine gun turrets that he nearly missed an attack from another direction.

Out of the corner of his eye, he saw a bright light from behind one of the upstairs windows and instinctively dove to one side. A blast of fire, its heat incredible, seared through the air where he'd been a moment before. Below, he could see that the window where the shot had come from had been shattered, only a few pieces of molten glass still clinging to the window frame.

Hector Hell.

Jason swooped down to the house, flying through the window frame, the shattered bulletproof glass still hiss-ing and sputtering from heat. The room, a small study, was empty, Hector Hell gone.

The alarm stopped.

In the sudden silence, Jason looked around the study. An antique desk sat against one wall, a framed black and white photo of Lorenzo Ferazzoli hanging above it. Ferazzoli stood next to one of the race horses he owned, the white of his hair standing stark against the black of its mane. He didn't smile in the picture. He just stared out from the wall in utter disdain. Jason remembered how much the man had always scared him.

Jason looked outside, past the charred, smoldering wood of the window frame. Ducett and Doctor Camelot were hovering nearby. Ducett's red-black wings were fanned out and he was moving in a gentle circle, eyes wary. Doctor Camelot's jet pack hummed, but she was motionless in the air. Her motions were so carefully calibrated that he doubted she moved a single centimeter unless she wanted to.

"Hell's moved on," Jason called out to them. "Are we ready to head on inside, or do you want to wait a while longer to see if we can draw them out?"

Ducett opened his mouth to answer him, but then a noise like thunderclap shook the house and he reeled back, plummeting down, a plume of blood spraying from his chest.

———

"Hell's moved on," Argonaut said from inside the mansion. "Are we ready to head on inside, or do you want to wait a while longer to see if we can draw them out?"

Hovering in the air, monitoring the machine gun turrets with radar, Kate debated it. She'd measured Hector Hell's flames at 2,530 degrees Fahrenheit, hot enough to melt steel. She could withstand a blast like that, but she didn't want to lead the others to their deaths. Maybe she should enter the house on her own.

Then a shot cut the air and Bedlam was falling.

"Oh, God," she said, swooping down and catching him. She stared at the wound. A small hole the size of a nickel was bubbling with red blood on his chest.

The shooter—it was almost certainly Gork, and with a sniper rifle from a window or murder hole somewhere, since those machine gun turrets were still empty—had punctured a lung. Cradling Bedlam in her arms, she flew around the edge of the vine-covered pool house, hoping for some cover where she could stow him until the fight was over. Lifting him above her head, she checked for an exit wound. She found it, a ragged hole as wide across as a racquetball.

"Bullet go through?" Bedlam grunted, startling her. His voice sounded ragged from the lung wound, but she was surprised even to hear him conscious.

"Yes," she said. "We'll get you through this." She sent an automatic message to 911. Someone highly placed in the police force was working hard at looking the other way where the *Cirque d'Obscurité* was concerned, but at least she might get an ambulance here on time.

"Set me down," he said, and she was surprised to realize she was still carrying him. She bent her knees and lowered him gingerly to the ground.

"You can't leave Argonaut alone with them," he said. "Go ahead. I'll be along in a minute."

She shook her head, rested a hand on his shoulder. "I don't think you understand," she said. "You've got a pierced lung. You're not going to be able to—"

"Go," he said, his voice urgent. "I'm a fast healer. Don't waste any more time on me."

And then she could see that the small entrance wound was already closing. She stared at it.

"Go!" he said.

She nodded, patting him once more on the shoulder, then flew around the pool house, heading toward the house. Argonaut was still inside—either he had decided to pursue someone in there, or something had happened to him. Either way, she thought, she needed to get inside that house.

———

Poteete jogged heavily down the hallway, panting with the effort. "Goddamn it," he said. Standing at the window in the study, looking outside in response to the alarm, he'd spotted the caped form of Argonaut flying outside. If he'd been a little quicker, he would have torched the son of a bitch. But Argonaut had seen him flame up and dodged to one side, and the blast had missed. A wasted opportunity. And now he had to run for cover before Argonaut followed him through the obvious hole in the window.

Stay in the mansion for now, the Robber Baron had said that afternoon. *Lay low. Be on guard. We'll give Costas a few days to come around or to hang himself.* Crap.

He wished he hadn't become so attached to the house. If they'd left, as the Robber Baron had suggested, they wouldn't be facing down this attack.

He heard a noise behind him and whirled to see the Behemoth at the other end of the hallway, waving to him to follow him into one of the bedrooms. He heard a gunshot echoing from behind the big man. Gork must have already been in that room. Good. Maybe he'd hit something.

Poteete waved the Behemoth off. The last thing they needed to do was cluster together and form one big target.

"Poteete!" the Behemoth bellowed.

Poteete ignored him. He ran into the music room, which featured an out-of-tune baby grand piano and lots of dust. Tony Ferazzoli hadn't been much for the arts. But the room also had another big window, and beside it, one of the narrow murder holes that the old pirate who'd built the house had included. The murder hole had good cover, but not a lot of visibility. Poteete turned sideways to minimize his profile and cupped his hand to the window, looking outside. At the side of the pool, he spotted Stecker, stretched out and motionless, unconscious or dead, and covered in some sort of goop. Not far away, though, he saw the shining chrome figure of Doctor Camelot, flying with the demonic Bedlam cradled in her arms. Good, he thought. Maybe Bedlam was dead. It looked like Gork's aim was better than his.

He waited, trying to catch his breath, the dust from the room making him wheeze. Slowly and carefully, he stepped back and opened the murder hole. No sense blasting through the glass if he didn't need to.

Doctor Camelot flew away from the pool area, heading back to the house, her armor glittering in the moonlight. This time, Poteete took the time to aim. His next blast of fire slammed into her, engulfing her in flames. She dropped out of the air to the ground, quickly setting the lawn ablaze.

He was smiling to himself when he heard someone moving around in Tony Ferazzoli's bedroom, the room where he'd been sleeping. He closed the window, then moved down the hallway to check it out.

When Jason had seen Bedlam—Dr. Ducett—get shot, his first impulse, after a moment of sick horror, was to catch the man. But Doctor Camelot was already moving to catch him. And somewhere, nearby, there was a sniper. The best thing he could do for Ducett was to make sure that there wasn't a second shot.

The sniper wasn't in the turrets, because Ducett and Doctor Camelot had been watching the turrets. He was inside the house and close by.

Guessing at the angle, Jason smashed right through the wall to the next room, sending plaster, wood, and scraps of floral wallpaper flying, sending the photo of Lorenzo Ferazzoli crashing to the floor.

He'd guessed right. The scarred, grotesque Gork was leaning against a table by the narrow murder hole in the room beyond, a high-powered rifle in his hands. He wore an ironed black T-shirt, blue jeans, and a belt with the large, shiny buckle Ducett had warned them about. His skin was moist with oil or some kind of excretion. He turned toward Argonaut in mild surprise, but not fear.

Because he wasn't alone.

Next to Gork in the small room he'd smashed into, Jason saw Osprey, Werewolf, and the Behemoth. All three turned toward him, the Behemoth grinning monstrously.

He knew enough about them to know that he couldn't possibly take on four of them alone.

Hating the necessity of it, he ran away, sprinting as fast he could for another part of the house.

───────

Julian stood in Tony Ferazzoli's bedroom, lights off, his body in shadows.

Julian had never really liked Tony's house.

Part of that, of course, was association. Tony made him uncomfortable. He was fat and coarse and superstitious, and had been sort of a rival of Uncle Costas. And of course there was the minor detail that Julian had murdered Tony's father. Tony hadn't known that—he barely

knew who Julian was at all. He had probably even been relieved when the old bastard had died. But it kind of cast a pall over Julian's associations with Tony and his house.

On top of his feelings about Tony, though, Julian just thought the place was tacky. Tony didn't decorate his mansion. He used it to stash his loot. The bedroom was an example. Big brass bed, black satin sheets, an armoire that clashed with the rug, which clashed with the wallpaper in the master bathroom. Tacky.

He wasn't sure whether it was his disdain for the house or sheer tactical sense that gave him the idea, but he liked it for its drama and simplicity. Jason and his new friends Bedlam and Doctor Camelot had been hovering around the building, waiting in vain for the members of the *Cirque d'Obscurité* to come out. Meanwhile, the freaks were taking potshots at them. It wasn't exactly a winning proposition.

They needed to flush the *Cirque d'Obscurité* out of the house.

And what better way than setting it on fire?

"What the hell are you doing here?"

Hector Hell entered the room not ten feet from Julian. He was wearing that garish costume. Julian wondered if he'd been walking around in it all evening or if he'd taken the time to put it on when the alarm sounded. He wasn't sure which possibility was more pathetic.

"Hector!" Julian said, smiling in mock surprise. "It's good to see you." Inside, he was calculating just what to do next. Hector Hell could make fire appear wherever he wanted, could manipulate it, make it dance. He was immune to the heat, too—he could make flames crawl up and down his arms or plume from his thin lips. He could stick his hand into molten lead without raising a welt on his skin. Julian was tough, but he knew that the ridiculous-looking man in front of him could easily burn him to death.

Hector held out an arm wrapped in flames. The heat in the room rose as though someone had lit a bonfire in

the middle of Tony Ferazzoli's bed. "I recognize you, Scion," he said. He nodded toward the window outside. "Is all this your doing? Has Kalodimos gone rogue?"

His smile never dropping, Julian spread his hands. "What we have here, Hector, are a problem and an opportunity." He clucked his tongue. "The problem is that no one was supposed to realize that I was here." He held up a finger. "The opportunity, though, is that you are like manna from heaven. I was just looking for something to use as a tinder box."

If Hector Hell had been just a little faster, a little braver, he could have engulfed Julian in an inferno of flames and heat. But when Julian rushed forward, he flinched instead.

And that was all the time Julian needed.

———

Cain rested on all fours, watching his blood spread out on the tiles and trickle into the pool, the red billowing out into the water like new-forming clouds. *Go!* he'd said to Doctor Camelot. But even though he could feel his body healing, could feel his lung start to fill with air again, the pain and shock were numbing. He was badly hurt.

"I'll just sit here for another second or two," he panted to himself.

Cain? Jazz's voice in his mind.

"I'm a little busy right now, Jazz," he said. Raising himself up to his knees, he clutched at the entrance wound.

I like the name Bedlam, she said.

"I'm so happy," he said. He could feel air hissing in and out of the hole in his back with every word he spoke. "We're dealing with the *Cirque d'Obscurité* now. If we catch them, I think you should be safe."

Thank you, Cain, she said. Her voice was soft, relieved, wistful.

"And then we'll be even," he said flatly.

No, Cain, she said, her voice in his head now a harsh whisper. *We'll never be even.*

He heard a blast like an explosion then. "Hell," he said,

"that can't be good." He struggled to his feet. The wound was healing, but not healed. He could feel blood oozing down his back. "Jazz?" he said. But she was gone.

Flying would be an impossible agony right now, so Cain stumbled forward as best he could, reaching over his shoulder awkwardly to pull out the shotgun he still had stashed in his satchel.

Doctor Camelot stood motionless on the back lawn, engulfed in flames. Even as far away as he was, Cain could feel the awful heat of them.

She's dead in there, he thought. She's been cooked inside of her armor.

Nevertheless, he limped forward to her, trying to think of anything he could do to help.

———

When Argonaut dashed away, the others turned to the Behemoth to see whether to follow. Everyone acknowledged Hector Hell as the leader of the group. He was the expedient choice, since he was best equipped to negotiate with outsiders. But when it came down to a fight, the Behemoth took over.

Outside on the lawn, the Behemoth saw Doctor Camelot erupt into flames. He smiled. Poteete was an idiot for ignoring him and going off on his own, but he couldn't argue with the results.

Argonaut was running. Bedlam was shot, maybe dead. Doctor Camelot was on fire. It had made sense before for the freaks to stay together, to make sure that they weren't isolated like Stecker had been. But now they had the white hats on the run.

"Sasha and Horodenski," he said, "follow Argonaut."

They dashed out of the room.

He turned to Errando. "Let's see what we can do about cracking open that tin can," he said. The Werewolf smiled, drool dripping from his mouth, then dashed ahead of the Behemoth with murderous speed.

———

Kate's armor had measured Hector Hell's blast at Argonaut at 2,530 degrees Fahrenheit, but the flames blazing around her now were even hotter.

Her armor was struggling to compensate, to protect her. One of the readouts on her screen flickered and died as her IR sensors burned out. She activated the fire extinguisher vents included with the armory on her wrists. Nothing—the nozzles had been fused shut. She could smell the acrid smoke of melting parts. The weakest, least insulated parts of her armor were smoldering. She could feel a hot, burning spot against her ribs on one side. She told the armor to move forward, but, reacting to the heat, all of the energy in her systems was being redirected to cooling the armor and maintaining a sealed environment.

Yeah, and what happens if the armor cuts out? Samuel had asked her. *It happened to your dad once or twice. You're left carrying a hundred and fifty pounds on your back.*

It's more like sixty-five now, she had protested.

He had nodded. *All right, then. Next workout, you jog wearing sixty-five pounds on your back.*

And here she was with sixty-five pounds of dead weight around her, joints stiffening as the sealants worked to keep her alive.

She took one step forward and the armor seized up on her. She fell to the ground, setting more of the manicured grass ablaze. And then she saw the Werewolf running toward her.

"This is not going to happen!" she shouted inside her helmet. She pulled herself to her knees. Surely the Werewolf wouldn't try to bite the searing armor.

But the Werewolf's pace didn't slow. He ran across the lawn toward her, preparing to leap.

Her armor, she thought, would burn him. But the increased stress of a sudden impact by a superhuman with the Werewolf's strength? It would quite likely shatter the armor around her, and even if she survived the attack, she'd be maimed or killed by the sudden heat she'd be exposed to.

The Werewolf leaped. She threw herself to one side, praying she'd avoid him.

But then the Werewolf was knocked out of the air in mid-jump. Something slammed into him and knocked him aside.

Something small.

Staring, she saw her Uncle Samuel, six inches tall and dressed in cut-off shorts and a Hawaiian shirt, clinging to the Werewolf's neck.

───

Osprey was following right behind Jason, those shining Bundi daggers in her hands. He didn't know how she could maneuver through the tight space of the house with those wings, but she was an acrobat, after all.

She'll target you first, Doctor Camelot had said to Ducett. Well, Jason thought, she'd been wrong about that at least.

He was moving through the house as quickly as he could, trying to get away from her and keep from getting cornered by any of the others, but he was running out of room.

Enough was enough, he decided. He would head into a narrow hallway, remove the advantage of her maneuverability, and try to take her out. That was what he was here for.

He dove into a hallway on the first floor, spun around, preparing to fight her, and then noticed two things. First, Gork was standing right behind Osprey, his rifle pointed at Jason, a smile growing on his lips. And second, the walls on either side of him were on fire.

The flames had no real fuel other than the air, Kate thought. They were damaging her armor, but not igniting it. Something about Hector Hell's power, she realized, made the flames persist, like napalm. She pulled herself to her feet.

Samuel clutched the back of the Werewolf's neck with

one arm and was punching him with the other. "Get in the damn pool!" he shouted at her.

She nodded, turning back around.

Bedlam was there, moving toward her. She staggered past him, feet catching the grass aflame with every step. And then she fell in.

The sudden burst of steam was an explosion, the force sending water and vapor high into the air. For a few seconds, she could see nothing at all through her faceplate. Everywhere around her was steam and heat.

But it was a big pool.

Within a few seconds, whatever Hector Hell had done to her was over. The heat had dissipated into the mass of the swimming pool. One by one, her armor's functions began to resume.

She flew out of the pool, water and steam spraying behind her. Seventy-three percent operational, one readout informed her. She smiled. "That'll be plenty," she said.

———————

Seeing Doctor Camelot moving toward the presumed safety of the pool, Cain turned his attention to the Werewolf, who was locked in an odd battle with a tiny man.

Sam Small, he realized. The missing Storm Raider who had been presumed dead.

Hefting the shotgun with the beanbag ammo, Cain tried to get a clear shot at the slavering Werewolf.

But then he saw Argonaut fly through a window, Gork clutched in his arms, a burst of flame trailing behind them.

The house was on fire. He'd been so distracted by the flames on Doctor Camelot, by his own wound, that he hadn't realized it, but now he could see that flames were coming from nearly every part of the building.

A figure erupted from the house behind Argonaut— the winged Osprey.

Argonaut was flying high in the air with Gork, but the scarred man was struggling with him, showering him with punches that echoed through the air. And Osprey was closing in, her knives flashing in her hands. Argonaut was tough, but could she cut him with those knives? Cain had seen the damage the man had suffered in the building.

He glanced at Werewolf, but still couldn't get a clear shot. Sam Small was a veteran superhero, and he seemed to have things more or less under control.

She hates other people with wings, Doctor Camelot had said about Osprey, looking at Cain. *She'll target you first.*

Pain still running through him from the rifle shot, Cain launched himself into the air. "Hey, Osprey!" he shouted. "I'm down here!"

———

Kate took it all in. Argonaut was flying with Gork. Osprey was trailing them, but the injured Bedlam was taunting her. The mansion was ablaze. Nearby, Uncle Samuel was fighting the Werewolf. Hector Hell and the Behemoth were unaccounted for.

She jetted toward the Werewolf. Samuel clung to his ears, pounding the other man on the skull. But then the Werewolf raked at him with his claws, and he was thrown free.

Samuel rolled to his feet. When he glanced up and saw Kate flying his way, he smiled and gave her a tiny thumbs up.

He was still smiling when the Werewolf lunged forward, teeth flashing, and ate him.

———

Jason had thought that once he had Gork in his hands, the rifle far behind them, he could more or less neutralize his opponent. But Gork was raining blows on Jason's head and shoulders. The punches were rhythmic, like a man working a hammer.

Flying higher, Jason squeezed Gork, punched him back, and tried to drop him, but the man clung on to him, legs wrapped around, working in his damage.

Then Gork reached down to his waist, pulling off part of the belt buckle. Just as Ducett had warned, it was a knife. "You son of a bitch," Gork said. "I'm going to butcher you." He raised the knife, preparing to stab Jason in the face.

"I don't think so," Jason said. And pushing with all his strength, the strength of Heracles, he shoved Gork free. A startled look on his face, the man tumbled loose, falling, falling, falling . . .

The sound he made when he hit the ground was nauseating. Given what he'd heard about Gork's resilience, Jason thought the man would probably live. But he wouldn't be getting up anytime soon.

Some motion coming from the edge of the burning house caught Jason's attention. He turned and saw Julian flying out a window, low to the ground, his mustard and black uniform dark with soot.

Julian wasn't facing Jason, but he seemed to sense Jason's attention anyway. He turned and looked up at his brother. They stared at each other for a few seconds, and then Julian waved.

Jason hesitated a second, then waved back, watching his brother disappear into the night.

———

Kate stared at the Werewolf, who was licking his lips with a long canine tongue. There was nothing human in his expression.

First her father. Then the rest of the Storm Raiders, all but Uncle Samuel. And now him, too.

"I'm going to kill you for that," she said.

The Werewolf laughed then, the sound like a hyena. "He went down smooth," he said, his accent part Austrian, part animal. "You I might need a can opener for." He swaggered toward her, opening his jaws, preparing to pounce.

And then he exploded.

Fur and flesh and bone and blood splattered in every direction. The grass was littered with it.

And in the center of the mess, Samuel stood looking at her, at his full size, blood coating his face, gore dripping from him, a hint of a smile on his lips. "I should feel bad about doing that," he said. "But he should have known better than to swallow me whole."

She wiped at her faceplate with her metal glove and smiled at him. "I thought you said you'd retired for good."

"Yeah, well," he said. "Like I said, in Devil's Cape, you can't trust anybody."

Then the Behemoth came crashing onto one of the turrets, flames and smoke billowing behind him. The body of Hector Hell was cradled in his arms, his neck clearly broken. "Who did this?" the Behemoth shouted. He bent and tore the door to the turret off of its hinges with one hand, hurling it like a discus. It flew into the trees surrounding the yard, cutting half a dozen trunks off at their bases, sending the trees crashing down. *"Who did this?"*

———————

Osprey turned and dove at Cain as he rose toward her in the sky. He tried to shoot her with the shotgun as she came closer, but the motion was awkward since he had to use his arms not only to aim, but to fly. He missed.

She buzzed by him, knife flashing, slicing into his left shoulder.

Trying not to cry out against the new pain, he ducked to one side, weaved, and tried to shoot her again. The thick beanbag—actually a small bag of buckshot—sailed past her head.

"You're fast," she said, her voice soft and musical, "but I've been doing this most of my life. I'm going to bleed you."

He dropped the shotgun.

The smart thing to do, he realized, would be to try to force her to fight him near the ground. Or even to avoid the fight altogether. He was a psychiatrist. He was a man of reason. He could use logic and persuasion.

But he was Bedlam. The demonic form might seem an odd contrast to the rigid, controlled man he'd become. But he had once been a creature of emotion and rage, a child of chaos. He'd been a street fighter and a criminal, diabolic and wild.

He bellowed at her, charging, claws slashing, teeth biting, horns gouging. Letting his instincts run wild, he attacked her like the creature from hell he resembled.

And Osprey fell.

He caught her before she landed, held her unconscious body almost tenderly while he unstrapped the sheathes holding her knives and her claws. Staring at her, reveling in the fury he'd allowed himself, he realized that what he'd told Argonaut and Doctor Camelot about only acting as Bedlam to catch Zhdanov and protect someone—Jazz—had been a lie, if not to them, then to himself.

He wouldn't be giving up this feeling anytime soon.

He'd never give it up.

———

The Behemoth is perhaps the most powerful of them all, Kate had told them.

And he was angry. He bent down and set Hector Hell's corpse on the floor of the turret. Then, his huge muscles bulging, he began to tear pieces off of the mansion and throw them. A cinder block smashed into the pool house like a cannonball. A burning timber flew by Argonaut's head and lodged itself in the mansion next door.

Kate had studied the Behemoth to the extent that she could. She knew what to expect. But his sheer size and strength surpassed anything that she imagined.

Don't face him alone, she had told the others, her father's face in her mind, her voice breaking again.

But they weren't facing him alone. They were facing him together.

The Behemoth pulled the trigger and Kate flew right into the bullets, one arm crooked over her head. Better they should hit her, she figured. Her armor could take it. It was designed to absorb and disperse the kinetic energy of the impact, reducing the chance of ricochets. Flying into the bullets made sense. But the reality of the torrent of bullets thundering into her with a rattling sound like hail was almost enough to break her nerve. The Behemoth glared at her, mouth curling. The KGK should have had a hell of a kick, but his arm never wavered.

She saw Argonaut and Bedlam flanking her, one to each side. A few stray bullets zinged past them, but they twisted in the air, darting and weaving. They were facing him together. She pressed on.

Kate hit him first, sending a wave of sonic energy—a directed blast of about a hundred and fifty decibels—directly at his head. Then Argonaut was floating next to him, fists raised like a boxer, jabbing at the Behemoth's massive body, punching under the armpit, in the side, flying up and cuffing him in the ear. And then Bedlam was there, too, jumping on the Behemoth's back, smashing him with a baseball bat and scratching at him with his claws.

The Behemoth sprayed the air with bullets once more, then tossed the gun to the side. He grabbed Argonaut and slammed him into Bedlam. Both heroes spiraled over the edge of the turret.

Kate blasted him with the sonics again. He winced, and blood trickled from one ear, but his huge clawed hand darted forward and caught her throat.

He smiled. One tusk scratched against his cheek. He put his other hand on her throat, too. "This is pretty much how I killed the last one," he said. "Just like a chicken. You think I get some special prize if I make it a twofer?"

She saw her father's face, leaning down toward her, smiling while leading her away from the entrance to his secret workroom. "Don't count on it," she said. Her arms came up between his, working to force them apart.

He didn't budge at first, but his eyes widened at her strength. He began to squeeze in earnest, thumbs digging in. She made a conscious decision not to look at the instruments that would be measuring the pressure of his grip.

Then Argonaut was there, pulling on one of the Behemoth's arms. Bedlam grabbed the other, claws digging in. Blood started to trickle out of a screaming eagle tattoo on the Behemoth's arm. His grip loosened infinitesimally, but the force was still incredible.

"Enough of this," she said. "Time for you to go down." There were dozens of weapons at her disposal. She ignored them. Instead, she ignited her jet pack with full force, slamming into his chest with every bit of strength the armor gave her.

As Argonaut and Bedlam let go of the strong man's arms, Kate and the Behemoth smashed through the edge of the turret, then arced downward, finally crashing to the ground. Kate's armor and the man's body beneath her helped absorb the brunt of the impact. But nothing absorbed the impact for the Behemoth. He shuddered in pain as several of his steel-hard ribs cracked. He gasped for air. His arms dropped from her neck to his sides. He tried to curl himself into a ball to try to get his wind back, to try to pull himself back to his feet.

She didn't let him. She grabbed his neck in both hands. Her suit examined him with X-rays, measured his density. She calculated the amount of force it would take to crush his windpipe, the amount of torque she would need to break his neck.

"I can kill you," she said. "Without a problem. Like a chicken."

He stared at her. His eyes were empty of inflection. He was still gasping for air, but his gaze was unflinching.

She sensed Argonaut and Bedlam landing just behind her, Uncle Samuel walking up close. None of them moved or spoke.

She stared at the Behemoth. She wanted him to flinch.

He didn't.

She saw her father's face again. She saw the faces of her dead "uncles" and "aunts."

The Behemoth was still struggling to try to get air. Blood vessels were popping in his eyes. It would be so easy to kill him.

She sighed. She let go of his throat. As he gasped, she sprayed the air around his face with massive amounts of tranquilizers, a gray-green cloud billowing around his head. He sucked them in. He couldn't help it. He shuddered, sitting halfway up, then fell backward to the grass.

She turned to the others. "He's asleep," she said. "Just asleep."

To her surprise, it was Bedlam who put a hand on her shoulder. "We know," he said. "We didn't doubt it."

She smiled. She heard helicopters and sirens in the distance. Uncle Samuel winked at her then shrank down to doll size, jogging away toward a thicket of tall grass. As one, she, Argonaut, and Bedlam turned to face the approaching media and police.

She was starting to like Devil's Cape.

The media gathered at the Ferazzoli estate tonight had hundreds of questions for the three heroes, but one persisted above the others: "Will you be staying?"

Doctor Camelot and Argonaut looked at each other, then at Bedlam, but it was the monstrous Bedlam who leaned forward and spoke into a microphone lifted up for him. "Yes," he said. "We're staying."

— From a WTDC News special bulletin,
Jason Kale reporting

EPILOGUE

Devil's Cape, Louisiana
Two weeks after the deaths
of the Storm Raiders

*T*he study on the Robber Baron's riverboat was like a miniature museum of the history of Devil's Cape. He had electricity running through the boat, of course, but the study showed no sign of it except for the vents that allowed the air conditioning to flow inside. The room, blocked off from sunlight by a thick, pearl-brocaded curtain, was lit by dozens of candles: candles hanging in a chandelier, candles mounted on the walls, candles on the desk and the bookshelf and beside the door.

A series of maps hung on one wall, all of them of the city. The first, an aging piece of parchment said to be sketched by the pirate St. Diable himself, was drawn in thick, black lines. At the bottom, though, a message was scratched in a different color ink—it might even have been dried blood. HERE I MAKE MY MARK, it read. There was a map from the War of 1812, showing troop movements. There was a map from the 1920s, an aerial photo from the 1970s, a more recent map on which the Robber Baron had made very tiny notations in his precise handwriting.

Throughout the room were small artifacts of the city's past. A daguerreotype of John Bullocq, the dirt magnate. A Confederate officer's pistol. A flier from the city's bicentennial celebration. An antique grandfather clock. A pair of gloves worn by Charles Lindbergh when

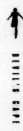

he'd visited the city. The mask worn by the Gray Fog, the city's last superhero.

But two prizes dominated the room.

The first was the cutlass said to be used by the pirate St. Diable in boarding more than a hundred plundered ships. The short blade of the weapon was just under two feet long, its steel edge still sharp. The hilt was burnished leather, the pommel a carved golden skull inlaid with ruby eyes.

The second prize was a painted portrait of Lady Danger, said to be commissioned just months before her disappearance. The painter's name was lost to history, but he had the eye for human emotion of a Caravaggio or Rembrandt. Her masked face was beautiful, the skin showing the hint of the tan she developed on the open seas, the reddish-brown hair pulled back to accommodate the narrow turquoise and black harlequin mask that hid her identity, her eyes flashing with anger or mischief.

Costas Kalodimos had always liked the portrait, and his eyes found it briefly as he followed the Robber Baron into his sanctum.

He had worried when the Robber Baron had called that the other man knew just what Costas had been doing to try to dislodge the *Cirque d'Obscurité* from the city and what actions Costas had taken against him. But their conversation had been peaceful, free of rancor. The Robber Baron had inquired about his family, about his brother's near encounter with Rusalka. He had expressed regret about the loss of the *Cirque d'Obscurité*, but had been optimistic about their future, indicating that Costas and his family would play a large role in that. And he had invited Costas back to his study for a drink.

"Wine?" the Robber Baron asked, holding up a bottle of an expensive French vintage nearly as old as Costas himself. He was dressed in his full regalia—the black gaucho hat, the scarlet mask, the black topcoat, the red shirt, the gloves and boots.

Costas nodded, taking the crystal glass gingerly as he

sat across the desk from the crime lord. He drank some, closing his eyes in appreciation of its robust flavor.

The Robber Baron sat, too, and they were quiet for a time, enjoying the wine.

Costas looked back at the portrait of the Lady Danger. "She was beautiful," he said, "if that portrait is any indication. I mean, the mask covers some of her features, but the rest—she was breathtaking. Such fire in the eyes, such spirit." He looked at the Robber Baron, the wine making him expansive. "They say that he loved her. And yet they also say that he murdered her." He nodded at the sword mounted on the wall near the portrait. "With that very sword." He shook his head. "Did she betray him, do you think? Did their conflict finally reach the point where it had to be one or the other?" He wondered what had possessed him to mention betrayal.

"No," the Robber Baron said. "Their conflict, though real, was a game to them. It was part of their give and take. It was foreplay." He ran his fingertips along his beard. "And no, she didn't betray him." His eyes, staring at the portrait, looked melancholy. "She would never do that. She loved him, too."

"Then why?" Costas asked. He set down his wine and stood, then walked over to the portrait of Lady Danger, leaning close and gazing at her masked face as though the oils in the painting could reveal secrets to him. "Why kill her?"

"You are married," the Robber Baron said obliquely. "I've dined with you and your Agatha. You are vicious and merciless and brass-balled with your enemies, yet you're devoted to her. Am I right?" There was an edge to his voice.

Costas turned toward him. The Robber Baron had stood, too. "Yes," he said.

"But what if someone told you," the Robber Baron asked, crossing to the pirate's ancient sword and carefully removing it from the wall, "that if you killed her, if you murdered Agatha, you could live forever?" He held the sword up toward the chandelier, staring at it as the metal caught the light of the candles in the room. He ran his gloved thumb along its edge. "Would you do it?" His eyes flicked to Costas's from behind his mask. "You love her. I know that. But tell me, Costas. You and I know each other well enough. We're cut from the same kind of pattern. We've toasted our successes, mourned our failures, buried our enemies. Imagine that you loved her even more than you do, that she was in your thoughts almost every moment. But you were given this—" his voice broke off as he searched for the word. His hat tilted forward, casting shadows over his eyes. "Opportunity." He nodded. The wide, thick blade of the cutlass, balanced in the air in the Robber Baron's hand, never wavered. "Would you take it, Costas? Would you take the opportunity?"

Costas was struck by the sudden change in the Robber Baron's voice. He'd known the Robber Baron for most of his life. He'd watched him kill before. Not long ago, he'd been standing next to the baron on the deck of the riverboat when he had given the order for Tony Ferazzoli to be murdered. But he'd never seen this kind of intensity, this kind of emotion from him. The man's lips were drawn and pale, the rest of his skin flushed. He was at once wistful, anguished, and angry, and the anger radiated in the air between them. Candles flickered on the Robber Baron's desk. The pendulum on his grandfather clock swung back and forth.

"No," Costas said finally, Agatha's face in his mind. He didn't see her as he remembered her from their youth. Instead, he imagined her as he'd seen her that morning, face drawn and wrinkled, eyes lined. The face she'd grown into, the result of the decades they'd spent together. "No," he said. "I don't think that I could do that."

Costas Kalodimos was resigned, rather than surprised, when the Robber Baron lowered his sword, moved forward, and plunged it into his belly. He saw the cutlass come out, covered in his blood, and clutched himself where he felt the wound. His body was on fire, the

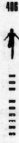

pain searing through him. His hands couldn't contain all the blood. It rushed over his gold rings, pulsed onto his Rolex watch, his gold bracelet. He stumbled to his knees and then fell to his side, legs curling up beneath him, blood soaking into the Robber Baron's hardwood floor.

"That's where we differ, Costas," the Robber Baron said. "I could do that."

He gazed away from the fallen man to the portrait of Lady Danger. As he tilted his face upward, the shadows fell from his eyes, and Costas could see that they were filled with tears, running down his mask. "I did do that," the Robber Baron—the ancient pirate St. Diable—said. He looked back at Costas, brushed at the tears unashamedly with his gloved hand. "And so you must realize that killing an old and trusted friend, one who has betrayed me, is really no great thing."

He pulled a large handkerchief from a pocket and began to clean Costas's blood from his sword.

Costas opened his mouth, but couldn't speak. He thought of the old gun in his pocket, but realized he'd never find the strength to pull it out, to use it. He was going to die here in this room, surrounded by remembrances of the city's past.

"A gut wound like that," the old pirate said, "is quite painful. It will take you a while to die." He leaned forward, almost solicitous. "I would offer you your glass of wine again, Costas, but it would pour right through you." He leaned forward, patting Costas on the shoulder. "I'll take care of Agatha," he said. "You needn't worry about that. My grudge is with you, not her."

It was a further agony, but Costas summoned the resolve to nod in gratitude. The pain was incredible.

"Well," the old pirate said. "That is, my grudge is with you and these people who are trying to take my city away from me." He shook his head. "Argonaut. Bedlam. Doctor Camelot." He said the names with a mocking distaste. He wiped one last time at the sword, then threw the handkerchief in the trash. "I made this city. I own this city. I have sacrificed more for it than anyone could ever hope to understand." He swept a hand around at the various artifacts in the room then returned the sword to its place on the wall.

As he continued to bleed, Costas began to shiver with shock and the chill of blood loss. Staring up at the Robber Baron, his mind drifted. He thought not of his son Nick, but of Julian. He wondered what Julian would do when he learned. Would he rage? Would he avenge him? Or would he bring the Robber Baron a bottle of ouzo with a wink and a smile?

Costas stared up at the old pirate, the edges of his vision going black. Before the Robber Baron, there'd been the Hangman. Before him, a masked gangster called John Dusk. Before them, there had been perhaps half a dozen others, and before them, there had been St. Diable the pirate, who had founded the city through plundered gold and the blood of his enemies. And, too, the blood of his only love. A legacy of power and corruption, it had always seemed, this succession of criminals and tyrants.

But he realized now that it was a different kind of succession.

It's time for the Hangman to die, the Robber Baron had said to him the day that his Uncle Ilias and the Hangman had died. But no one had ever found the Hangman's body in the burnt shell of the strip club. Because it wasn't really a death, just a transition from one masked identity to another. Uncle Ilias and those bodyguards had died because they were too close to the Hangman not to realize that despite differences in clothing and persona, the Robber Baron and the Hangman were the same man. But they had been, he realized now. All of them were the same man, reinventing himself.

The Robber Baron peered down at him again and sighed. "I don't enjoy watching this, you know," he said. "Is the pain bad?"

Costas was able to nod his head again. He tried to speak, but his mouth was full of blood.

"You were my friend for a long time," the masked man said. He blew air out of his mouth. It made his moustache curl. His eyes looked sad, tinged with regret. "Would you like me to help you, Costas?"

The agony was unbearable, but Costas could do nothing. He couldn't even bring himself to nod again. He pleaded with his eyes.

"For an old friend," the Robber Baron said, reaching up and pulling the sword from the wall once more, "I suppose that I can always clean the blade again."

The last sight Costas Kalodimos ever saw was the cutlass arcing down, its blade gleaming in the flickering candlelight.